THE LOST

Also by Roberta Kray

The Debt
The Pact

THE LOST

ROBERTA KRAY

Constable • London

Constable & Robinson Ltd
3 The Lanchesters
162 Fulham Palace Road
London W6 9ER
www.constablerobinson.com

First published in the UK by Constable,
an imprint of Constable & Robinson, 2008

First US edition published by SohoConstable,
an imprint of Soho Press, 2008

Soho Press, Inc.
853 Broadway
New York, NY 10003
www.sohopress.com

A copy of the British Library Cataloguing in Publication
Data is available from the British Library

UK ISBN: 978-1-84529-689-6

US ISBN: 978-1-56947-506-5
US Library of Congress number: 2007039986

Printed and bound in the EU

1 3 5 7 9 10 8 6 4 2

Chapter One

Len Curzon had a nose for a good story but this one wasn't worth a sniff. Frustrated, he dumped his elbows squarely on the table and scowled at the giant in front of him. Why had he even bothered? There were more useful things he could be doing with a Friday afternoon than sitting in a prison visiting room pandering to a minor villain's ego.

'For God's sake, BJ, are you saying you've dragged me all the way down here just to try and flog me your life history?'

'But you write them books. I've seen 'em. You did that one on Alfie Noakes.'

Len shook his head. 'I'm a reporter, son. You said you had something *important* to tell me.'

It took a while for the implication to sink in – the route through to BJ's brain was a slow one – but as it did his mouth slowly turned down at the corners. 'I thought—'

'I don't care what you thought. Remind me of how old you are, exactly.'

'Twenty-four.'

'Don't you think you're a little young to be considering the definitive biography?'

'Huh?'

Len peered down into the polystyrene cup. He blew on the surface of the thick dark brew before taking a sip and screwing up his face. Lord, even the tea stank. He was tempted to get up and walk. Sometimes he wished he'd never written those books. Now every jumped-up low-life, every hoodlum, every toerag in the land wanted to see his name in print.

'I mean, maybe you should wait a while, get a few more . . . experiences.'

But BJ refused to be discouraged. 'I've been around, Mr C. I've seen stuff.'

'Yeah, course you have.'

The problem with 'Big Jay' Barrington was that you got exactly what it said on the tin – six foot six of solid muscle, a great guy to have beside you in a brawl but with sod all in the brain department. If an original thought had ever entered his head it had exited again at the first opportunity. This accounted for why he'd already spent more than half his adult life in jail.

'I've worked with Billy Todd, Ray Stagg, all the faces. I've been there, man. People are gonna be well into it.'

Len dug deep into his reserves of patience. Through the years he had learned to cultivate the small-timers, to buy them drinks, to sit and listen to their endless cock-and-bull stories in the hope of receiving the odd snippet of interesting information. BJ might still be useful one day in the future – it was best, perhaps, not to close any doors too firmly.

'Look, I can't promise anything, okay? Things are pretty busy at the moment but go on, go ahead and tell me what you've got in mind.'

As BJ began his pitch, Len gazed down at his watch. For courtesy's sake, he'd give it five more minutes and then make his excuses. If he legged it down to the station he might still be able to catch the two thirty-four back to London. In the meantime, for want of anything better to do, he glanced discreetly round the room.

Inevitably, he recognized some of the other inmates; after three decades on the *Hackney Herald* his knowledge of London criminals and their families was bordering on the encyclopedic. That HMP Maidstone was currently housing a few familiar faces, ageing villains who had never learned from their mistakes, came as no surprise. What was more depressing was that he also recognized a handful of the younger cons. These were the no-hoper sons and even grandsons of men he had seen sent down over and over again. They were the next generations staunchly carrying on the family tradition. He sighed into his tea. It wasn't the legacy of criminality that disturbed him so much as the reminder it provided of his own advancing years. At sixty-three, retirement was snapping at his heels.

Before that thought could start to fester he made another quick sweep. This time his gaze alighted on someone more interesting. Len's eyes widened a fraction.

'Isn't that Paul Deacon?'

BJ frowned, stopped his monologue and glanced over his shoulder. 'Who?'

'Deacon, Paul Deacon. Over by the window. With the woman in the red coat.'

'Dunno, mate.'

BJ obviously hadn't heard of him, never mind made his acquaintance. Still, it was years since Len had sat through those two long and sensational weeks at the Old Bailey. Sex, politics and murder, the perfect combination, always guaranteed an excellent turnout and the courtroom had been packed to the rafters. A good show was what the public had been after and the trial hadn't disappointed.

Len continued to stare. Deacon was older, greyer, in his late fifties now but he still maintained an air of distinction. The prison regime may have stripped a little weight from his body but it had done nothing to wipe that impenetrable expression from his face. Why he had killed Tony Keppell remained a mystery. How he had even known him was another matter altogether. Deacon had been a successful politician, a socialite, a rich and successful man. The Keppells were pure gangster stock.

At the trial, Deacon had claimed self-defence, a drunken row that had got out of hand, but his evidence had been vague and evasive. When cross-examined he could not – or perhaps more accurately *would* not – explain the nature of their relationship. In fact, he had appeared curiously indifferent to the proceedings. Impeccably dressed, he had stood in the dock with a look suspiciously like boredom on his face. Arrogant was how other reporters had described him but Len hadn't been convinced. Resigned was more the word that had sprung to mind as if, despite all the efforts of his expensive legal team, Deacon had already decided that the outcome was inevitable. And as it turned out he'd been right. The jury, with little other option, had pronounced their unanimous guilty verdict in less than an hour.

Len switched his attention to the woman. He could only see her in profile, a young slim girl with shortish dark hair. She looked about twenty-five. Not his daughter, that was for sure. Deacon hadn't got any kids. So who was she? A friend, per-haps, or a *girlfriend*. There was something about their body language that suggested a particular kind of intimacy. His antennae were starting to twitch. Maybe this trip hadn't been such a waste of time after all. There might just be a story here: *Shamed politician finds sexy new love behind bars.*

'So what do you think, Mr C?'

'What?'

'About the book, man. It's the business, right?'

Len glanced back at him and nodded. 'Yeah. I don't know. Maybe.'

BJ smiled, his upper row of large creamy teeth showing three black spaces. 'See. I told you. This is gonna be big. This is gonna be mega.'

Len was only half listening. Deacon and the girl were lean-ing in towards each other, talking soft and fast. They were only inches apart. Deacon's shoulders had become tight and hunched. A row? It could be. Some kind of disagreement any-way. Deacon's left hand, curled up on the table, clenched into a fist. He didn't look pleased. She didn't look too happy either. Len saw her shake her head and sit back.

He rapidly revised his headline: *Shamed politician splits with sexy young girlfriend.* Now that could be an exclusive, a story that could be sold on to the tabloids. All he had to do was to find out who she was.

'You ever see that girl before, BJ? The one with Deacon.'

8

'Nah, man, I've told you. I don't know him. I don't know her.' Impatiently, he looked over his shoulder again and sighed. 'What's the big deal? He famous or somethin'?'

Len thought about telling him but then changed his mind. 'No, no one special. It doesn't matter.'

He continued to watch them out of the corner of his eye. Suddenly, the girl stood up. She was buttoning her red coat and preparing to leave. It was less than thirty minutes into the visit. Deacon got to his feet too. For a second the two of them stood gazing at each other before she stretched out her hand and touched him lightly on the arm. Then, without a word, she turned and walked quickly towards the door.

It was the first time Len had seen her properly. He couldn't describe her as beautiful. He wasn't even sure if she was pretty. Her face, with its small sharp chin, high cheekbones and deep-set eyes, was more striking than attractive. Then he suddenly realized – there was a hint of familiarity about her. He'd seen her before. But where and when?

Len made a decision. He scraped back his chair. If he was fast enough he might be able to follow her.

BJ peered up at him. 'Mr C?'

'Sorry.' Len looked at his watch. 'I've got a meeting. Got to go.'

'But—'

'Yeah, the book. Sounds good.' A screw was already heading towards the door, a set of keys jangling in his hand. If he didn't leave now he might lose her – along with any chance of a scoop. 'Make some notes. Send them on. I'll get back to you. Good to see you again.' He leaned forward, grabbed BJ's hand, shook it, and hurried towards the exit.

She didn't even glance at him as they were escorted back. The three of them walked in silent single file. Len was careful not to stare too hard. The last thing he wanted was to draw attention to himself.

In the foyer he retrieved his phone and newspaper from the locker and returned the key to the screw on duty. He quickly left the building, crossed over the road and waited. If she'd driven here, he'd be jiggered. Still, he could always get the registration of the car and try to track her down later.

A bitter winter wind whistled round his ears. Len turned up the collar of his coat, stamped his feet on the ground and rubbed his hands together. A minute passed and then another. What was she doing in there? If he had to hang around much longer, he'd be frozen to the pavement. He stared longingly towards the soft golden light escaping from the windows of the pub. What he wouldn't give for a warming shot of brandy. For a moment he was tempted – this business with the girl might come to nothing – but he knew better than to let a God-sent opportunity slip through his fingers. It might only be a hunch but his hunches had served him well in the past.

Who was she? He racked his brains but still couldn't place her. He'd always been good with faces – once seen, never forgotten – but names were forever evading him now. It was one of the penalties of growing old.

It was almost ten minutes before she finally emerged from the gate, glanced briefly to the left and the right, and then set off in the direction of the station.

'Thank you, Lord,' he murmured.

Len looked up at the board as he followed her on to the platform for London Victoria. There was a train due in ten minutes. He offered up another small prayer of gratitude. Not too long to wait and with a bit of luck she'd be going all the way to the city. If this did turn out to be a wild-goose chase then at least he wouldn't be too far from home.

He watched as she sat down on an empty bench, took her mobile from her bag and checked through the messages. The corners of her mouth turned down. For a while she sat drumming her fingers against her knee and then took a deep breath, pressed a couple of buttons and raised the phone to her ear.

Len decided to risk a spot of eavesdropping. He strolled casually past and halted just a few feet away. Opening the paper, he stared down at it and pretended to read.

'Hi,' she said into the phone. 'It's me.'

10

There was a short pause.

'Yes, I know. Sorry. I meant to call but I got stuck in a meeting and it just went on and on.' She sighed. 'You know what Colin's like. I couldn't get away. Once he starts talking there's just no stopping him.'

Another pause.

'Are you? That's okay, that's fine. I'm still at work too. I've got a few things to finish off. I'll be a while yet.'

Len gave her a furtive glance. She was nervously playing with a button on her coat. He noticed the gold band on her finger and grinned. A nice warm sensation was spreading through his groin. He was on to something. He was sure he was. Paul Deacon's lady friend was lying through her teeth – and now all he had to do was to find out why.

'I'll see you later.' She nodded, her dark eyes focused on the damp grey concrete of the platform. 'Yeah, love you too. Okay. Bye then.'

As she hung up, Len smartly returned his attention to the paper. It was about time he got a break. The last few years had been lean ones. Only small stuff. No big stories. He'd been starting to wonder if he'd lost his touch. But no, Len Curzon wasn't finished yet. Still, he'd have to act quickly; he hadn't been the only person in that room today. All it would take was some other savvy visitor to tip off the tabloids and he could wave goodbye to any hope of an exclusive.

When the train pulled in, he waited until she'd got on before moving towards the other end of the carriage. It wasn't busy and there was plenty of space. As she settled into her seat he sat down, two rows back and across the aisle. From here he had a clear view in case she got off before London.

He stared at the back of her head, at the dark silky hair that only just touched her collar. Who was she? It was right on the tip of his tongue. It was driving him mad. An actress, perhaps, someone he'd seen on TV? No, she wasn't the showbiz type. He wasn't really sure what type she was. Although there was a certain confidence in how she dressed – that bright red coat suggested she didn't mind attracting attention – there was also

11

a defensiveness about her body language, a barrier that defied anyone to get too close. *Look but don't touch* was the message drifting out from her.

Len glanced down at his paper. He needed a distraction. The more he dwelled on it, the less likely he was to come up with a name. While he flicked through the pages he pondered again on the Paul Deacon trial. What had happened to the wife? She'd got a divorce, he thought, shortly after Deacon had been sent down. No doubt in *her* mind then as to just how guilty he was. Or maybe it was the other stuff, all those nasty rumours, that had sent her scuttling to the nearest good solicitor.

Had Deacon been shagging Tony Keppell? There was no real evidence but that hadn't stopped the talk. Jimmy Keppell's youngest son, the runt of the litter, had been a small blond pretty boy. And only fifteen. Had the kid been blackmailing Deacon, putting the squeeze on him? The truth hadn't come out. Perhaps it never would. Some secrets stayed forever. Still, there was one fact that had never been in dispute: on a warm summer's evening, over a decade ago, Paul Deacon had picked up a gun and fired a bullet through Tony Keppell's pale and skinny chest.

Chapter Two

It was just after four when the train arrived at Victoria. The station was heaving and Len had to take care not to lose her in the crowd. She was only small, about five foot two, and he wasn't more than a few inches taller. The red coat helped to keep her in his sights. As she made her way towards the underground, he rummaged for his travel pass. Bugger, he hated the tube and especially at this time of day. It would be hot, stinking, sweaty . . . and there wouldn't be a chance of getting a seat.

He took out his phone, hoping he wouldn't lose the signal before he descended into the bowels of the earth. He punched in the number. It rang five times before she finally picked up. 'Jess?'

'Oh, it's you. Where are you? In the pub?'

'No, I'm not in the bloody pub.'

'Toby's doing his nut. You were supposed to have the Butler copy with him by noon.'

Len pulled a face. Toby Marsh was always stressing over one minor detail or another. 'Was I? Well, it's on my desk, er . . . somewhere. Be a love and dig it out for me. And look, there's one other thing. If you get the time could you—'

'No,' she snapped. 'I'm busy.'

'Go on. It won't take a minute.'

'And how many times have I heard that before? The answer's still no.' She spelled it out. 'N-O. I'm up to my ears in it. You'll have to do it yourself.'

'Please,' he wheedled. 'You know what I'm like on that computer. You could do it in half the time. I could be on to something here.'

She paused, her curiosity piqued. 'On to what?'

Len grinned as he stepped on to the escalator. 'I'll tell you later. Just dig out everything you can on the Paul Deacon trial. About ten, twelve years ago. He's the MP who—'

'Yeah, I remember him.'

'Okay. Great. Ta. I'll give you a ring in an hour or so.'

'Hey, I didn't say—'

But Len was already hanging up. He knew she'd come through. Jessica Vaughan might only be a junior reporter but she was smarter than most of her more experienced colleagues. Come to think of it, she was better looking too. He liked a woman with a bit of shape. And Jess certainly had that. For a moment, pondering on those soft seductive curves, he almost lost track of what he was supposed to be doing.

He glanced down the escalator. Deacon's girl, a few yards ahead, had stepped out to the left and was jogging down the last few steps. He followed behind, tailing her along a corridor to the Victoria line and on to the northbound platform.

No sooner had they arrived than a train roared noisily out of the darkness. The doors slid open to reveal a solid crush of bodies. No chance, he thought, but she had other ideas. Like a seasoned commuter she forced her way in and he had no choice but to squeeze in straight behind. As the doors closed he found himself jammed tight. She was only inches away. He breathed in, trying not to touch her.

As they hurtled through the tunnel, Len averted his face and gazed along the length of the carriage. Although he wasn't looking at her, he remained overtly aware of her presence, of her dark hair, the curve of her neck, of her red coat brushing against his thigh. He willed her not to turn, worried that she might recognize him.

It was four long and stifling stops before she finally got off at Euston. He stumbled gratefully out behind her. But the journey wasn't over yet. From here she crossed over to the

Northern line. By the time Len smelled fresh air again, he was in Camden Town.

It was dark outside and the temperature had plummeted. He felt the first few spots of an icy rain. Great, so now he was going to get soaked for his troubles too. He prayed she wasn't going far. Once he'd found out her address he could retire to a nice cosy pub and have that drink he so richly deserved.

Len watched as she hesitated on the kerb. For a moment she seemed undecided, glancing over towards the High Street and its shops. God, he hoped she didn't feel the urge for some last-minute retail therapy. But then she looked up at the sky, opened her umbrella, hurried over the zebra crossing and began to walk down Camden Road.

He pushed his way through the crowd and followed her. The bustling street made his job easier; there was no reason for her to notice him. For the next ten minutes he strode briskly along behind. It was only when she veered down a quiet, dimly lit side street that he began to worry. Len slowed his pace, putting a few more yards between them. He didn't want to spook her, not at this late stage. But even if she heard his footsteps, she seemed unconcerned, the click of her heels maintaining the same calm and steady rhythm.

She took the next left into the plusher surroundings of Berry Square and began rooting in her bag. Len hung back, taking the opportunity to grab a cigarette. Then, as he watched her turn through a gateway and climb a flight of steps, he hurried forward again. The three-storey house was in darkness. She unlocked the door and a second later a light went on in the hallway. Len glanced up as he strolled casually past.

He was just in time to catch another glimpse of her face as she turned to close the door. It was the eyes, those wide dark eyes . . . Like a cog falling smartly into place, it suddenly registered. He knew the name he had been searching for – *Sharon Harper!*

He smiled, elated at finally putting a name to the face, but then his smile slowly faded. It was ridiculous, impossible. What

15

was he thinking? Sharon must be in her forties by now; there was no way this young woman could be her.

Bewildered, Len stopped and gazed up at the building. After a while, another light appeared on the top floor. Still rooted to the ground, he pulled hard on his cigarette. *Unless . . .* The breath caught in his throat. His heart was starting to hammer. No, it couldn't be. Or could it? The likeness was too much to ignore. Twenty years ago Sharon's little daughter, Grace, had been on the front page of every newspaper, eight years old and missing . . .

Chapter Three

It was twenty to eight when Harry Lind limped into The Whistle, shook the rain from his hair and ordered a pint of Guinness. By rights he should be getting home but he needed a drink first. Whether his mood – or perhaps more to the point Valerie's mood – would be substantially enhanced by his detour to the pub was questionable but he pushed that thought to the back of his mind.

The row, which had started over breakfast, had been simmering all day. She had sent five texts, none of which he had replied to. He could imagine how pleased that had made her. But what more was there to say? No, he still didn't want to go to her parents' place for Christmas. No, he still didn't want to have to listen to their well-intentioned but thoroughly unwanted sympathy. Yes, he did realize he was just being bloody awkward.

Harry picked up his pint and sighed. Was he feeling sorry for himself? Yes. But he was feeling angry too. It was over ten months since it happened and he was still trying to come to terms. Nothing had been the same since he'd walked into that building, since the blast had blown him off his feet, since he'd lain buried alive beneath the rubble and listened to . . .

A thin film of sweat broke out on his forehead. He shouldn't be thinking about it. He mustn't. At least he was still breathing and that was more than could be said for the two poor sods who had walked in before him.

'Inspector Lind!'

Harry started. He turned to see a small sallow man sitting just behind. A pair of brown unfocused eyes were staring up at him. It was that annoying little reporter from the *Herald*. Len something. Carter, Cunningham? No, Curzon, that was it. There were five dirty glasses and a pile of crumpled crisp packets strewn across the table.

Harry forced a smile and nodded. 'Evening,' he said politely. Pissed again, he thought. How the guy ever managed to get up in the morning, never mind string a coherent sentence together, was a mystery.

Curzon slapped his palm against the empty chair beside him. 'Come on. Come and join me.'

Harry hesitated. All he'd been after was a quiet pint. Still, in his present frame of mind even a drunken old hack seemed like better company than his own. He took his drink over and sat down.

'So how's it going, Inspector?'

'It's Harry,' he said grimly. 'Or Mr Lind if you want to be formal. I'm not on the Force any more.'

'Oh yeah, it slipped my mind.' Curzon's over-bright tone shifted down a notch. He glanced towards Harry's leg and gave a grimace. 'Sorry.'

'Don't worry about it.'

'How are you doing? Bad business that.'

Harry didn't need reminding of what a bad business it was. 'I'm fine.'

'I should have remembered. You're working for David Mackenzie now, right?'

Which was something else Harry didn't need reminding of. 'Yes.' Of course he was grateful to Mac, grateful for a reason to get up in the morning, but investigating insurance claims, serving writs and sneaking around after cheating husbands and wives was hardly his idea of a meaningful existence.

'You deal with missing persons then?'

'Occasionally. Why, have you lost someone?'

Curzon shot him a suspicious glance. 'Maybe.'

'Anyone I know?'

18

But the reporter wouldn't be drawn. He stared down at the table, his pink-rimmed eyes narrowing into slits. 'You still sound like a cop, Harry.'

Harry flinched. He still *felt* like a cop. That was the problem. Sometimes, when he woke up, before it all came flooding back, he still imagined he was a bloke with a future instead of . . . He smartly pushed the thought away; self-pity was snapping at his heels again. 'Just showing an interest, that's all.'

Curzon grunted into his beer.

And then there was silence.

Harry wished he hadn't bothered. This was a conversation going nowhere. He'd just finish his pint and get off. He couldn't postpone it forever; it was time to face the music with Valerie.

Then the little man looked up at him again. 'Can I ask you something?'

'If you like.'

Curzon appeared to think about it some more. He lifted the glass to his lips and took a drink. His hand was trembling. 'You ever . . .' He paused again to clear his throat. 'You ever see a ghost, Harry?'

He laughed, amused by the question. 'I'm sorry?'

But Len Curzon's face was pale and serious. 'You know, someone who . . . someone who you thought was dead but . . .' He stumbled to a halt, the words apparently escaping him. His nicotine-stained fingers rose to hover round his mouth.

'What do you mean?'

Curzon hesitated and then shook his head. 'Forget it. It doesn't matter.'

'No, go on,' Harry urged. 'Tell me.' Suddenly this bizarre apparition, even if it was the result of one too many drinks, seemed infinitely more fascinating than what awaited him at home.

'I don't know.' Curzon peered at Harry as if trying to decide if he could trust him or not. 'I could be wrong.'

Harry didn't press him. If there was one thing he'd learnt through his years on the Force, it was patience. If Curzon wanted to talk – and he quite obviously did – then all he had to do was wait. He sat back and sipped on his Guinness.

Curzon shifted in his chair. He looked uneasily over his shoulder. He picked at his fingernails. Eventually, he looked back at Harry. He kept his voice low, almost a whisper. 'I saw her this afternoon. I'm sure it was her.'

'Her?'

'I never forget a face.'

'So who are we talking about here?'

Curzon frowned and immediately clammed up again.

Harry wondered if it was worth the effort. The guy was clearly three sheets to the wind. Weren't there more important things he could be doing than attempting to prise out the details of a supernatural fantasy from some drunken journo's addled brain? But then again, those 'more important things' were precisely what Harry was trying to avoid. He smiled reassuringly. 'Well, maybe you were right. Maybe it *was* her.'

Curzon groaned. 'But it couldn't be, could it? That's just the point. That's what I'm telling you. Not if she . . .' He raised his hands in a gesture of frustration. 'I mean, we're talking over twenty years. A child can't just—'

Whatever he'd been about to say was interrupted by the strident tones of a less-than-happy female. 'God, Len, what are you playing at? I've been everywhere. I've been looking all over for you. Why didn't you call me? I'm not bloody psychic!'

Harry lifted his gaze to see a very wet young woman standing over him. Soaked to the skin, she was clutching a plastic carrier bag to her chest. A fringe of pale brown hair crowned a pair of grey expressive eyes. They were currently flashing with exasperation.

'Oh, sorry, love,' Curzon said. He pushed his knuckles into his forehead. 'Shit, I knew there was something . . .'

'I've just done a tour of every flaming pub in the district. I thought it was urgent. I thought you wanted this stuff tonight.'

'I did. I mean, I *do*.'

'Well, here it is then.' She stepped forward and dropped the dripping carrier bag into his lap. 'And don't bother to thank me. You know how much I love doing unpaid overtime.'

'Ugh!' He quickly shifted the bag on to the floor and made a few ineffective swipes at the wet patch near his groin. 'Jesus, you didn't have to . . . it looks like . . .'

'It's no more than you deserve.'

Harry, who was glad of the distraction, smiled up at her. 'Hi. I don't believe we've been introduced.'

Before she had a chance to reply, Curzon said, 'Oh, this is Jess. She . . . er . . .'

The woman arched her eyebrows. 'She's the one who does all the hard work while her so-called mentor sits in the pub getting rat-arsed.' She stretched out a damp hand. 'How do you do. Jessica Vaughan. Call me Jess.'

'Harry Lind.'

She slipped out of her coat and flung it over the back of a chair. 'I suppose you two want another drink?'

'Let me,' Harry said, getting to his feet.

Jess waved him back down. 'It's okay, I've got it. Same again?'

Harry nodded. 'Thanks.' He was already late home; one more pint wouldn't make much difference. And anyway, the quality of the company had just taken a decidedly upward turn.

She looked over at Curzon. Her grey eyes narrowed as she noticed the collection of empty glasses. 'You on the bitter, Len?'

'Better make it a short,' he said. 'A whisky. Ta.'

The two men watched as she leaned against the bar. She was wearing black jeans, boots and a soft pale green sweater. Their eyes simultaneously slid down the length of her body, scanning its distinctive planes and curves.

A sigh slipped from Curzon's lips. 'Very nice.'

Harry looked at him and grinned. 'Don't you think you're a bit old for her?'

'Don't you think you're a bit married for her?'

'I'm not married,' Harry said. He felt instantly guilty for the denial. He'd been living with Valerie for the past five years. They were as good as married or at least they had been until . . . But no, even that wasn't strictly true; they'd been bickering for months before that fateful day had turned everything upside down. Would they still be together if it hadn't been for that?

Jess came back with the drinks and put them on the table. She took a seat between the two of them and raised her glass of red wine in a toast. 'Okay, gents, here's to . . . what?'

Curzon, with his nose stuck in his glass, didn't reply.

'Better days?' Harry suggested.

Jess chinked her glass against his. 'Well, they couldn't get much worse.'

'That bad?'

'Bad enough.' She looked over at Len. 'So, are you going to tell me exactly *why* I've been slaving over a hot computer for the best part of the evening? What's with this sudden interest in Paul—'

'Nothing,' Curzon said too quickly.

Harry, hearing the warning note in his voice, pricked up his ears.

'Nothing *important*,' Curzon stressed. 'I'll fill you in on the details tomorrow.'

Jess stared at him for a moment, frowned and then nodded. 'Okay.'

There was one of those uncomfortable silences. Harry looked from one to the other. That something had passed between them, a glance, an understanding, was beyond doubt. He might have been more curious if Curzon hadn't been so drunk. After all, he *was* a man who not so long ago had been claiming to see ghosts . . .

Jess turned and smiled at him. She had a nice mouth, a pleasant smile. 'Sorry,' she said. 'Work stuff. Boring. You know what it's like.'

'Sure,' he said.

'So what do *you* do for a living?'

'He used to be a cop,' Curzon said.

Harry heard that warning note again.

'Really?' Jess said.

'Now I'm with Mackenzie's.' Harry still couldn't bring himself to use the words 'private investigator' or 'private detective'. Somehow, they had a sad seedy ring about them, conjuring up an image of a little grey man in a grubby raincoat.

'I know Mackenzie's,' she said. 'Off the Strand, right?'

'That's it.'

Curzon struggled to his feet, stumbled and grabbed hold of the table for some temporary support. He swayed for a couple of seconds, his legs unsteady. 'I need a slash.'

Jess watched as he staggered across the room. 'What's wrong with him?'

'He's pissed.'

She snorted. 'He's always pissed. I mean, what *else* is wrong with him?'

Realizing that he was staring rather too intently at her breasts, Harry shifted his gaze to her face and shrugged. 'I've no idea.'

'You're his mate, aren't you?'

'God, no,' he said, 'I barely know him.'

'Oh,' she said. 'I thought—'

'Our paths have crossed a few times, that's all. I came in for a quick drink and here he was.' He paused. 'Why should there be anything wrong?'

Jess wrinkled her nose. 'I don't know. He just seems on edge.'

'On edge?'

'Don't you think?'

If Harry was thinking about anything, it certainly wasn't the state of Len Curzon's mind. He had to stop his eyes from drifting south again. The sweater she was wearing was clinging just a little too tightly to her curves and . . . He frowned down into his Guinness. *What was he doing?* He shook his head. 'Maybe it's got something to do with that ghost.'

'What?'

'It doesn't matter.' He smiled. 'So I take it you work for the *Herald* too?'

It was approaching midnight when Harry slid his key into the lock and stepped softly into the flat in Kentish Town. He had nothing to feel guilty about – well, nothing more than a mild flirtation with a curvy journalist and getting home five hours later than he should have done.

He tiptoed across the hall and into the bedroom. Valerie stirred but didn't wake. He stared down at her, at her long fair hair spread across the pillow. A year ago, he'd have stripped off his clothes and jumped straight in beside her but tonight he only sighed and wandered back into the kitchen.

A cold winter moon was shining through the window. He switched on the kettle, put his hands in his pockets and gazed out across the city. He had the feeling he was in for another sleepless night.

Chapter Four

Len pulled his coat around him and hunched down in the seat. It was early Monday morning, cold and still dark. A flurry of snow swirled around the windscreen. Shivering, he rubbed his hands together. He had parked the car across the other side of the square and was keeping an eye on the door to number twelve. It was over a week since he'd followed her back from Maidstone and he hadn't stopped thinking about her since.

He had read the file on little Grace Harper, checked out the dates and stared long and hard at the faded photographs. Could he put his hand on his heart and swear it was the same girl? Not with any degree of conviction. An eight-year-old could change a lot in twenty years. It was only her similarity to her mother, the shape of the mouth, the intensity of those wide dark eyes that continued to haunt him. And it wasn't as if he could ever forget Sharon Harper. He had worked on that story for months; her face was imprinted on his memory forever.

There were four flats in the building opposite. It was a smart converted Victorian terrace with its trim freshly painted. Beside the bell for the top floor was a label saying *Shaw*. He knew this because he'd climbed the steps on the very first evening he'd followed her. Thanks to that, and then to the Electoral Register, he had been able to find out her full name, Ellen Marie Shaw, and that of her husband, Adam. From there he had traced her birth and marriage certificates. He'd discovered that her maiden name, apparently, was Corby, that she'd been born in Cork, was twenty when she got married and was now twenty-seven. The latter fact had sent his pulse racing. *Almost the same age as Grace Harper would have been if . . .*

But not quite the same. Grace would have been twenty-eight by now. A year was still a year. And there was no other obvious connection to the Harpers. He had considered the possibility that she might be a relative, a cousin perhaps – something that might account for the similarity in appearance – but had found nothing yet to back up the theory. Sharon was an only child and the family tree, or at least as much of it as he'd been able to trace, had not revealed any Corbys.

Perhaps he was looking in the wrong place. He would have to do more digging, maybe try to track down Ellen's parents.

And then there was the mystery of her visit to Paul Deacon. What was going on between the two of them? Something she was hiding from her husband, that was for certain.

Adam Shaw was fifty-one, a grey staid-looking man who wore pinstripe suits, left the flat bang on seven twenty every weekday morning, walked to Camden Road station and travelled by British Rail to his office in Gospel Oak. They were an odd couple – and not just because of the age difference. She had a definite charisma and he had . . . well, Len wasn't an expert on what drew women to men but other than a moderate level of financial stability he couldn't spot any of the more obvious attractions.

Len yawned. He was having trouble sleeping. When he closed his eyes he only ever saw that face, the face of the child who was missing, who had disappeared all those years ago. Three times now he had got up in the middle of night and driven over here. What had he expected to see? He couldn't say. It was just a need he had, a compulsion to be near her.

He knew Jess was getting worried. He was spending too much time, every spare minute he could, on the story. If it wasn't for her he would probably have been fired by now. She had covered his arse on more than one occasion. To keep her happy, he had promised her a share in his exclusive. 'Trust me, we're on to something big.'

26

'On to what?' Jess had said. 'You still haven't told me anything. Well, only that it's connected to Paul Deacon but—'

'Bear with me for a few more days, okay? It's a hunch. You know, just one of those feelings.'

Len sensed that she thought it was one of his less sober feelings but she had let it pass, nodding gently. Jess's faith in him was starting to falter.

Maybe it was time to move things along. He hadn't learned much from his daylight surveillance, other than that Adam Shaw worked for a firm of accountants (he had followed him the previous Tuesday) and she worked, part-time, for an insurance company near King's Cross. He had followed her on two other mornings to the small, slightly shabby offices of Goodridge, Cobb & Masters where she had stayed put from nine to five apart from a short sandwich break for lunch.

His evening sessions had been even less productive. The two of them hadn't been out nor had anyone come to visit in all the hours he'd been watching. Either he had stumbled on a temporary lull in their social calendar or they permanently shied away from outside company. If the latter was true, they led an unusually insular existence. This, in turn, begged the question of whether it was from choice or necessity.

Len couldn't decide whether he should try and speak to her. If he took her by surprise, asking about her connection to Paul Deacon, he might shock a useful response out of her. On the other hand, he could spook her completely. What if she did a midnight flit and disappeared? He couldn't be here 24/7.

In fact just being here at all was growing riskier. Only yesterday some nosy old crone had banged on his window demanding to know why he was parked outside her house. He had made up a tale about being a cabbie on his break but she hadn't looked convinced. He'd had to shift double-fast before she called the cops. So now he was stuck on the other side of the square, having to squint through the bushes that covered the small central patch of snow-covered green.

This couldn't go on. He had to make a decision soon.

Chapter Five

Harry Lind wasn't having the best of mornings. It had started with another row with Valerie – no change there – continued with a self-inflicted dent to his bumper while he was trying to park his Audi in the tiny allocated space at the back of the office building, and now there was this. He read through the papers and scowled. 'You're kidding me. Ray Stagg?'

Mac placed his large mottled hands palm down on the desk. His heavy brows shifted up an inch. 'You got a problem with that?'

'Since when did we start working for crooks?'

'As I recall, he's never actually been convicted of anything.'

'Come on, Mac, you know he's an out-and-out villain.'

'Just go and see him,' he said roughly. 'Talk to him, okay? Get some details. How hard is that?'

Harry groaned. It was about as hard as having to talk to any piece of scum who you've arrested three times and never managed to make the charges stick. 'Isn't there anyone else you can send?'

Mac glanced around his office. 'Do you *see* anyone else?' He abruptly picked up the phone, indicating that the discussion – if there ever had been one – was over.

Harry went back into reception. Lorna looked up from the computer. As if his limp automatically entitled him to an extra-large dose of secretarial compassion, she gave him a soft and sympathetic smile. He frowned at her and then regretted it. Perhaps he was just being over-sensitive.

'He's not in a good mood,' she said.

'Tell me about it.' He got a coffee from the machine and slumped down in one of the brown mock-leather chairs. 'Ever wish you hadn't bothered to get up?'

Lorna smiled again, lowered her head and carried on typing. Harry sipped his coffee. His appointment wasn't for another half-hour. Even allowing for the traffic and the snow it shouldn't take him longer than fifteen minutes to get there. With nothing else to look at – the room with its bland magnolia walls was about as stark as it could be – his gaze eventually wound its way back to Lorna. She was a woman in her early forties, slightly plump, with a round friendly face and shoulder-length blonde frizzy hair. With her red apple cheeks, maternal was the description that sprang most instantly to mind. She had been with Mac since he'd first started the business and although they were clearly friends the exact nature of their relationship still remained vague. A single mother, she had two rowdy daughters who occasionally livened up reception whenever she couldn't find a sitter.

Harry flapped the papers in her direction. 'Have you seen this? Ray Stagg, for God's sake. It's a joke.'

Lorna gave a tiny shrug. 'It's money,' she said.

'Not the kind of money Mac needs to be associated with.'

'I doubt if he's feeling that fussy at the moment.'

Harry stared at her. 'What do you mean?'

She threw a quick sideways glance towards the office. Visible behind the glass, Mac was talking with some animation, and possibly a fair amount of cursing, into the phone. She lowered her voice. 'Cash-flow problems.'

A brief jolt of alarm coursed through Harry. What if *this* job was going to be pulled from under his feet as well? What would he do then? Despite his years of experience, damaged detectives weren't exactly in demand.

'How bad?' he asked.

'He had to lay off a couple of the guys last week.'

'What?' It was the first Harry had heard of it.

'I'm sure it'll be okay,' she said softly. 'It's only temporary until . . . well, until things get back on track.'

29

Harry frowned at her again. She was using that tone of voice, that kindly *I don't want to worry you* tone, which only had the effect of increasing his anxiety. No wonder Mac had been acting so antsy. And it was true that things had been pretty quiet recently. Although there was still the usual flow of writs to be served, of insurance claims to be investigated, a lot of the other work had dried up.

'I don't get it,' he said. The firm had been going strong for over ten years. Although Mac had faced problems in the past, including a bad gambling habit and an over-fondness for the bottle, he had got his act together since he'd started his own company. He'd got contacts, a good reputation, and what seemed – at least on the surface – a thoroughly thriving business.

Lorna, as if she might have already said too much, gazed over at him pleadingly. 'Oh, I shouldn't have mentioned it. You won't tell him I said anything, will you?'

'No, of course not.'

Harry swallowed the last of his coffee, stood up and threw the empty plastic cup towards the bin. It hit the rim, faltered for a few seconds and then fell on to the floor. He sighed. It wasn't as if he believed in omens but with everything else that had happened this morning he was beginning to wonder. He bent down, picked it up and dropped it in the bin. Then he headed for the door.

'See you later,' he said.

Harry deliberately didn't look at the dent before he got back in his car. He already had more than enough to stress about. While he drove along the Strand he mulled over the bad news, hoping things weren't as bleak as he was starting to imagine. Perhaps he should take Mac for a drink, try and find out what was going on. Or perhaps he should just leave well alone. He didn't want to get Lorna into trouble.

As he drove, he tried to keep his gaze focused straight ahead. Even the slightest glance sideways brought him into contact

30

with the festive decorations. All the garish lights and tinsel in the shops, the grinning Santas, the whole jolly twinkly thing, filled him with a sense of dread. How was he going to get through Christmas? This time last year everything had been different – he'd had a place, a position in life, something he was proud of. Now he wasn't even sure if he'd still have a job by the time January came around.

He took the third exit off the Holborn Circus roundabout into Charterhouse Street and then turned left on to Farringdon Road. Although it went against the grain, he decided he'd better be civil to Ray Stagg. If the assignment was kosher (although how likely was that?) he quite literally couldn't afford to antagonize him. A missing persons case, it said on the papers. Harry growled and slapped his palms against the wheel. He suspected that Stagg had made plenty of people disappear in his time.

The nightclub, Vista, was situated off Shoreditch High Street. He found the gateway, swung the Audi between two ostentatious pillars and parked on the concrete forecourt next to a bright yellow Lotus. No guessing who that belonged to. Stagg had always been a flash bastard.

In the rear-view mirror, Harry checked that his tie was straight. He ran a hand through his hair and wiped the frown from his forehead. *Professional* was what he needed to be. For the next twenty minutes, no matter what the provocation, he had to keep his cool.

He got out of the car and stared at the building. There had been a murder here once, years ago, when he was starting out in the Force. The place had been called The Palace then. He couldn't recall the name of the owner – Johnny something? – but remembered that the body had been found in the boot of his car. He grinned. That wasn't a trick Stagg could pull off too easily with that low-slung fancy motor of his.

Since the killing, the club had changed hands a number of times, been refurbished and had an extension built on to the side. Now the paintwork was immaculate and at night the bright neon sign flashed a cool icy blue. Very smart. Only

31

the ankle-deep heap of litter, evidence of last night's carousing, marred the effect.

Harry headed for the entrance, pushed through the glass doors and passed into the reception area. An anorexic-looking blonde, her dark roots showing, was sitting behind the desk. She was a sophisticated kind of a girl, the sort who had the manners to shove the gum she was chewing into the side of her mouth before speaking.

'Yeah?' she said.

'Harry Lind. I've an appointment with Mr Stagg.'

'You a cop?' she said, staring up at him.

'Do I look like a cop?' he replied.

She pulled a face and shrugged. 'Suit yourself.' Picking up the phone, she punched at a number with a scarlet talon. 'Bloke to see you, Ray. Says he's got an appointment. Harry somethin'?' She raised her eyes.

'Lind,' he reminded her.

'Yeah, Lind,' she repeated. She listened intently for a few seconds, giggled at some comment that was made, and then put down the phone. She waved a hand. 'Park yourself. He'll be free in a sec.'

Harry looked at the long leather couch but didn't sit down. His appointment was for ten o'clock and it was ten o'clock now. Instead he paced the length of the foyer, studying the walls with their array of black and white celebrity photographs. He didn't recognize many of the faces – he must be getting old.

The minutes ticked by and Harry felt his aggravation growing. It was typical of Stagg to keep him waiting. He was probably doing it deliberately, just trying to wind him up. If it hadn't been for what Lorna had told him, he'd be tempted to turn on his heel and abandon the meeting.

The foyer was quiet, the only sounds the distant drone of a hoover and a soft rustle as the girl flicked through the pages of her glossy magazine. Harry ran his fingers through his hair, released a weary sigh and with nothing else to do finally slumped down on the sofa.

It was twenty past ten before the phone rang. The blonde picked it up, grunted and then replaced the receiver.

She glanced over at him. 'Go through if you want,' she said casually, as if he might just prefer to loiter in the foyer for the rest of the morning. 'Second door on the left.'

'Thank you,' he said, standing up. 'I hope I haven't put you to too much trouble.'

If she caught the sarcasm she didn't respond to it. She simply shrugged her skinny shoulders again and returned her attention to the magazine.

Harry didn't bother to knock – there was a limit to the level of courtesy he was prepared to show a villain – but pushed open the door and walked straight in.

The office was about twenty foot square, plush, with a deep pile red carpet. More black and white photographs were spread across the walls, all of them of women and all bordering on the pornographic. Stagg was sitting in a dark leather swivel chair behind a desk that was wide enough to sleep on. He was a slim fair man, impeccably dressed in a grey designer suit, white shirt and pale pink tie. At forty-three he was four years older than Harry but at five foot eight a good six inches shorter.

'Ah, Mr Lind,' he said. 'How nice to see you again.' He smiled, showing a perfect set of teeth. 'Apologies if I kept you waiting. You know how it is – the pressures of business and all that.'

He didn't get to his feet or offer his hand for which Harry was faintly grateful. The protocol of greetings between ex-cops and active crooks was understandably vague.

'Grab a pew,' Stagg said, gesturing towards a chair. 'Coffee?'

As he sat down, Harry glanced at his watch. 'No thanks. I'm running a little late. Other appointments, I'm afraid.' He smiled back, a smile as false as the one that had been presented to him. 'You know how it is.'

Stagg lifted his chin and stared at him. 'So how have you been? I was sorry to hear about your . . . er . . . spot of bother.'

Harry tried, although it was already too late, not to flinch. He could feel his whole body stiffen but fought to keep his face impassive. Stagg was about as sorry as any villain would be to hear about a cop being permanently scarred. He took a slow breath and attempted to keep his voice steady. 'Perhaps if we could just get on with the business in hand?'

'Of course,' Stagg said smugly. He leaned forward and put his elbows on the desk. 'I presume Mac's filled you in on the basics?'

Harry frowned. Since when had David Mackenzie become 'Mac' to this hoodlum? 'It's a missing persons case, right?'

'Yeah, the brother-in-law. Al, Alan Webster. He's been gone for over a week.'

'And you haven't informed the police?'

Stagg lifted his pale brows and laughed. 'Course we have. Denise reported it. She's my sister,' he explained, 'Al's wife.'

'And?'

'And what?' Stagg said. 'They're hardly going to send out a search party, are they? They're not remotely interested in a middle-aged loser who's most likely shacked up with some slag of a blonde in the back of God knows where.'

'So you want us to try and find him,' Harry said.

'Got it in one.'

'And if we do, what happens then?'

'Is that any of your concern?'

'It is if—'

'What do you think?' Stagg interrupted, smirking. 'That if you track him down, I'll be straight round to persuade him of the error of his ways?' He shook his head. 'Forget it. Denise is old enough to sort out her own marital problems.'

'So why bother with a private investigator?'

'Because she's my sister and she's pissed off. And do you know what she does when she's pissed off? She calls me up thirty times a day to find out what I'm doing about it. Now I love my sister, Mr Lind, but she's driving me crazy. So I'd like to employ you, at whatever extortionate rates you bastards might charge, to get her off my back and take those calls for

34

me. Then maybe, just maybe, I can get some bloody peace and quiet.'

Harry sat back and folded his arms. He wasn't sure how much he believed, if any, of Ray Stagg's explanation. There could be a multitude of reasons as to why he really wanted Webster found. 'Well, I can take the details but I can't promise anything. We're pretty busy at the moment.'

Stagg's cold blue eyes slowly narrowed. 'I'm not sure Mac would agree with you.'

'I'm sorry?'

'I mean, the impression he gave me was that he was more than happy to help. He told me you'd be able to start straight away. In fact, he's even taken a deposit.'

Has he indeed, Harry thought, all his earlier fears instantly resurfacing. If Mac was crawling to the local gangsters then he must be in serious trouble.

'So,' Stagg said, pushing a buff-coloured folder across the desk with the tips of his manicured fingers. 'Here are the basics. The rest you can find out from Denise.'

Harry glared down at it. He didn't care for being dictated to, least of all by the likes of Stagg. The man was a drug baron, a thug, a pimp. He was tempted, for the second time that morning, to just walk away but he didn't. Instead, reluctantly, he flipped open the folder and glanced inside. There was a single sheet of paper with Denise's address and telephone number on it, the date her husband had disappeared and a small snapshot of Al. Harry glanced at the picture. Alan Webster was in his mid-forties, an amiable-looking guy with a pleasant smile, brown eyes and receding mousy brown hair.

'What does he do?'

'Works on the Romford market,' Stagg said.

'Selling what?'

Stagg shrugged. 'Whatever. This and that: music, CDs, DVDs.'

'Could he have been in financial trouble?'

'How?'

35

'The usual way,' Harry said, 'more money going out than coming in. Any bad habits – gambling, women, booze, drugs?'

'Not that I've heard of, but who knows. That's why I'm employing you, isn't it?'

'It's just that you mentioned earlier about how he was probably with someone else.'

Ray Stagg lifted his hands off the desk. 'Well, what do *you* think? There aren't that many options to choose from: a guy's been married for over twenty years, packs a bag and suddenly does a bunk – he's either with some tart or . . .'

'Or?'

'Or he's won the bleeding lottery or he's lying in a ditch somewhere. I dunno.'

Harry got the impression he didn't much care either. He stared at him. 'Do you get on well with Mr Webster?'

Stagg stared back across the desk. 'And that matters because . . .?'

'I was only asking.'

'He's Al. He's the brother-in-law. I can't say we've ever been the best of mates but if you want to know if I've got any grievance against him, then no – well, not until now.'

'So when can I see Denise?'

'She's waiting for you.'

Harry nodded, snapped the file shut and stood up. 'Okay. I'll be in touch.'

Ray Stagg smirked again. 'Yeah, I'm sure you will.'

Chapter Six

It was ten forty-five when the phone rang. Len checked who it was before answering, saw that it was Jess, sighed and then picked up.

'What do you think you're doing?' she asked before he had time to say anything. 'You missed the morning meeting, *again*. Toby's got a real cob on. I had to tell him you'd had an urgent call.'

'Oh, Jesus. Sorry. Thanks, love.'

'I can't keep doing this, Len. Toby's patience, such as it is, isn't going to hold out much longer. He thinks you're just sitting in a pub getting rat-arsed.' She paused and then said quietly: 'You're not, are you?'

'Of course I'm not. I've told you. I'm on to something. I just need a few more days.'

'You're not going to have a job in a few more days.'

There was a short silence. Len continued to stare out of the car window and across the square.

'Okay,' he said. 'I'll sort it. I'll talk to Toby.'

'And me?'

'Yeah, you too. I promise. I'll call you later.'

Len put the phone down and lit a cigarette. It was too soon to approach Ellen Shaw – he needed more facts, something to back up his suspicions – but time was running out. Jess couldn't cover forever and Toby would be glad of an excuse to get rid of him. Small-minded editors like Toby Marsh didn't understand the meaning of the good old-fashioned hunch; they

37

thought reporters like him were obsolete, men who should be put out to grass.

Len opened the window and angrily flicked out his ash. The snow had stopped falling and now a fine drizzly rain was turning everything to slush. He took another pull on his fag. His lungs, as he breathed out, emitted a thin unhappy wheezing sound.

What to do next? At the moment, other than his gut instinct, he had little to offer Toby. He could tell him about Deacon and Ellen Shaw, about their assignation at the jail, but that would be a disaster. He knew how Toby's mind worked: the moron would have a photographer round double quick, snapping her picture, and then he'd be running with the story in the next edition. And if Len wanted to prevent that, he'd have to tell him about what he really thought, about who he suspected she really was – which, as he didn't have any proof, would be reason enough for Toby to get out his leaflets on early retirement and send for the men in white coats.

No, he had to talk to her *before* he talked to Toby. There was no other choice. This could be his last chance for one final incredible exclusive – and no over-ambitious prat of an editor was going to foul it up for him.

Quickly, before he could change his mind, he got out of the car, crushed his cigarette under his heel and walked around the square. He turned up his collar as the rain slid down his neck. Carefully, he climbed the icy steps at number twelve, hesitated and then put his finger on the bell for Shaw.

He waited. Nothing. He pressed again, a couple of longer rings. No answer.

Len knew she was there – and there alone. He'd been watching the flat all morning and her husband had left hours ago. He tried the bell again. This time he heard a distinctive click over the intercom.

'Yes?' a small voice inquired.

'Parcel for Shaw,' he said briskly, leaning towards the grille in the doorway. 'I need a signature.'

'Er . . . oh right, okay.'

The intercom clicked off and Len took a step back. He still wasn't sure what he was going to say or how far he was prepared to go. He stamped the snow off his feet and anxiously flexed his fingers. Lord, he couldn't afford to mess this up now. It was another few minutes before Ellen Shaw finally opened the door. She was wearing a pair of blue jeans and a cream sweater. Her large dark eyes gazed up at him. They widened as she glanced down towards his empty hands.

Len's heart missed a beat. He hadn't been this near since he'd stood behind her on the tube. Close up, he was even more certain that he was right. She was the very image of the young Sharon Harper. He could still remember that poor mother, white-faced, terrified, the same deep brown eyes staring wildly into the camera.

He cleared his throat. 'My name's Len Curzon. I was hoping I could have a word with you.'

She frowned as if suspecting an imminent sales pitch, life insurance perhaps or the opportunity for a close encounter with God. 'I'm sorry. I'm rather busy at the moment.'

'I'm a reporter,' he said. 'I work on the *Hackney Herald*. I wanted to ask you about Paul Deacon.'

She visibly started but then quickly shook her head. 'I don't know who you're talking about.'

'Are you saying you haven't been visiting Deacon at Maidstone jail?'

'Please leave me alone. I've got nothing to say to you.'

Len watched her move back, preparing to slam the door in his face. 'Fine,' he said. 'Perhaps your husband will be more forthcoming.'

She stopped dead and glared at him. A bright spot of red appeared on both her cheeks. 'Leave Adam out of this. It doesn't concern him.'

'Well, if *you're* not prepared to talk to me . . .'

She hesitated, her pale lips tightening into a thin straight line. 'All right,' she said, 'but not here. There's a café on the High Street – Morgan's. Do you know it?'

'I'll find it.'

'I'll meet you there later. About four?'

Len looked down at his watch. It was barely eleven. 'How can I be sure you'll turn up?'

Her mouth opened, releasing a small strained laugh. 'Well, you know where I live. It shouldn't be that hard to find me.'

He thought about it and then nodded. 'Okay. Morgan's at four. I'll see you then.'

Chapter Seven

After a brief tour of Loughton, Harry found where he was looking for and pulled the car into the drive of a whitewashed semi with a neat front garden. Number seventeen Verity Drive wasn't a palace but it was big enough and smart enough to be worth a few bob. Harry smiled. Either there was more money in DVDs than he'd ever dreamed of or Al had a lucrative sideline.

The woman who answered the door was ash blonde, slim and in her late thirties. She bore a resemblance to her brother although it was minus his smug self-satisfied expression. Instead her face was etched with worry.

'Mrs Webster?'

She nodded. 'Are you the guy Ray called me about?'

'Harry Lind,' he said. He put out his hand.

She shook it and stood aside to let him in. 'Thanks for coming.'

Harry politely wiped his feet and walked into the hall.

'This way,' she said. She led him through into a spacious living room, professionally decorated in pale tones of beige and cream. There were two three-seater sofas and a couple of easy chairs, all so pristine that they might have been newly delivered. It was the kind of room that made him feel faintly nervous. He glanced over his shoulder to check that he wasn't leaving a trail of muddy footprints.

'Take a seat,' she said, gesturing towards one of the sofas.

Harry gently lowered himself down.

'Coffee?' she said. 'I've just put the kettle on.'

'Thanks. That would be good.'

As she disappeared into the kitchen, Harry took the opportunity to have a good look round. There was a widescreen TV in the corner, a complex music system to its right, a glass-topped coffee table with stone carved legs and a scattering of potted palms. Three large modern pictures on the walls, Mondrian-type prints in bright primary shades, provided a splash of colour.

It was hot in the room, the temperature virtually tropical. Harry wiped his forehead with the back of his hand.

'Nice house,' he said as she returned with two steaming mugs of coffee.

'Thanks. Ray helped us out,' she said. 'We'd never have been able to afford it otherwise.'

Harry instantly revised his opinion of Al's earning capacity. He took the mug from her hand and placed it carefully on the coaster on the table. 'So, Mrs Webster,' he began.

'Oh, call me Denise,' she insisted. 'Please.' She sat down in one of the large cream armchairs and crossed her legs. She was wearing white trousers, a pair of high-heeled white shoes and a pale pink shirt that reminded him of the colour of Ray Stagg's tie.

'So . . . Denise,' he began again. 'It was about a week ago that Al disappeared?'

She nodded. 'Just over.'

'And he packed a bag before he left?'

'A small overnight bag, that's all – enough for a change of shirt, a razor, a toothbrush. It's missing from the bottom of the wardrobe. It was the one he used when he had to go away to meet suppliers, contacts . . . you know the type of thing. But he always told me about it. He never just took off and disappeared.'

'But this time he did?'

Her fingers flexed, spreading out across her knee. 'It doesn't make any sense. He always rang me, *always*, when he had to go away. He'd never leave without a word.'

'Does he have a passport?'

'Yes,' she said. 'And no, he didn't take it with him. It's still here, in the drawer.'

'Did he seem worried, concerned about anything?'

'No more than usual.'

'And the usual is . . .?'

She frowned. 'The same as for everyone, I suppose: the kids, the bills, Christmas coming up, but nothing that serious. Al works hard. We get by okay.'

'So he didn't seem down or preoccupied by anything?'

'No.'

'And he hadn't been spending more time than usual away from home? I mean, in the evenings or at weekends?'

Her blue eyes narrowed a little and her voice rose in shaky irritation. 'You've been listening to Ray, haven't you? I know what he thinks – that Al's taken off with some cheap little tart. But he hasn't. He isn't like that. Al's a family man. Me and the kids – we've got two, Jake and Natalie – we're his world.' She glanced towards the mantelpiece where a set of gilt-framed photographs were lined up in a row. Along with Al and Denise, a teenage boy and a slightly younger girl smiled down.

Harry nodded and smiled. In his experience the wife was usually the last to know but best not to jump to any conclusions. 'I'm sorry,' he said, 'but I have to ask.'

She chewed on her lip for a second, her eyes becoming moist. 'Something's happened to him, hasn't it? I mean it must have. He must be—'

'Let's not jump to any conclusions,' Harry said briskly. He could see she was on the verge of tears and quickly tried to distract her. Getting out his notepad and pen, he attempted to focus her mind on something more positive. 'So talk me through the day he disappeared. It was a Saturday, right? Not the one just gone but the one before.'

Denise gave a few sniffles and wiped her nose on a pastel blue tissue. 'Yeah. There's not much to tell.'

'You had breakfast together and . . .?'

'He left at the usual time, about half-seven. The market opens at half-eight. He was fine. There was nothing wrong, I'm

43

sure there wasn't. He kissed me goodbye and . . . and that was the last time I saw him.'

'And he went to work?'

'Yes. I've been there. I've talked to the others. He opened up the stall and stayed until the market closed. It's a busy time of year. He does good trade around Christmas.'

'But he didn't come home?'

Her lower lip trembled again. 'No.'

'What time did you expect him?'

'About seven,' she said. 'Eight at the very latest. On Saturdays he sometimes went for a pint with the lads but he wasn't a big drinker. And anyway, he didn't even go that night. He just packed up the stall and left.'

'Okay,' Harry said. 'And you've talked to all his friends?'

'Everyone I can think of. None of them have heard from him.'

'Perhaps if you could give me their names and contact numbers. It could be useful.'

'They don't know anything,' she insisted. 'I've asked them all.' But still she got up, took a sheet of paper from beside the phone and passed it over to him. 'I made a list for the cops. Not that they've bothered with it. They don't give a damn. They're just like Ray; they think he's taken up with—'

Before they started going over old ground, Harry promptly said: 'Does he have a mobile phone?'

'It's been switched off since he went. I've tried it. I've tried it over and over.'

'And there's been no news on the van?'

She lifted a hand and let it drop down on her knee. 'Nothing. I gave the registration to the cops but—'

'And there's been no money removed from his bank account?'

'No. It's a joint account. He hasn't taken out a penny.'

Harry made a note of the fact although it didn't really mean a lot. A trader like Al would do most of his deals in cash. If he had planned on taking off, he'd have made sure he had a

44

hefty wad of readies on him. 'What about a computer? Does Al use one for his business?'

Denise shook her head. 'We've got one but only for the kids. He barely knows how to turn it on.'

'Are you sure?'

'Of course I'm sure,' she said, her cheeks flushing red. 'And I know exactly what you're getting at. The cops were just the same. You think he was looking for women on the net, right, going into those chat rooms and . . . You think he was chasing after some cheap bit of skirt.'

'I don't think anything,' Harry said gently. 'I promise. These are just questions that I need to ask.'

'He never used the computer. I told the cops all this.'

'I'm sorry to make you go through it all again. I know how difficult it must be. Only I'm not the cops and I need to have the details too. But believe me, I'm not making any presumptions or passing any judgements. I'm only here to help.'

Denise, staring him straight in the eye, took a moment to consider what he'd said. Then, as if she'd reached the decision that she might be able to trust him, she forced her mouth into a quivering smile. 'So do you think you'll be able to find him?'

In situations like these, Harry found that honesty was usually the best policy. He looked directly back at her. 'I can't make any promises but I'll try my best.'

Chapter Eight

Len ordered another coffee and stared dolefully out of the window. She was already twenty minutes late. She wasn't coming. Damn! Why had he ever believed her? She could be a hundred miles away by now.

He should have stayed and watched the house.

Why hadn't he?

Because he'd thought it might be smart to put in a brief appearance at the office. Because he'd been sure that she wouldn't just take off: she had a husband, a home, a life here. Because he'd thought she wouldn't *dare*. From the expression on her face, he'd been convinced that she'd keep their appointment.

How wrong could he be?

He looked down at his watch. He'd give her another ten minutes. It was possible that she'd got held up somewhere. After that, he'd go back to the flat and see if there was any sign. If nothing else the husband should be back by six.

Since talking to her last, Len had acquired a new piece of information. A useful but somewhat expensive contact in the Prison Service had informed him that Ellen Shaw had been visiting Deacon for the past six months. That was interesting. At the very least it suggested an ongoing relationship of one sort or another.

His coffee arrived. Len added two sugars, took a sip and wondered where Sharon Harper was living now. He hadn't seen her around for a while. She had moved away, perhaps, gone to start a new life where there weren't so many reminders of the child who'd disappeared. Michael Harper had died over eighteen years ago, drinking himself into an early grave. Len couldn't claim to feel much pity for him; the man had been violent, a brute. Despite an alibi for the day in question, Harper had always remained under suspicion. Quick with his fists and obsessively jealous, there was no saying what he'd been capable of.

But then again, what if everyone had got it wrong? Len thought of those dark eyes and the woman who called herself Ellen Shaw. What if Grace *was* still alive and . . .

He scanned the street, searching for that scarlet coat. Every time he saw a flash of red his heart leapt, but each time he was disappointed. She wasn't coming. There was no point waiting any longer.

Before he left, he made a quick call to Jess. 'Can you meet tonight? We need to talk.'

'I've got a class,' she said.

'What sort of class?'

'Computer studies. You know, that subject I need to keep up with if I'm going to be constantly doing your research for you.'

Len made a disparaging noise down the phone. 'Huh? Look, what's more important – the chance of an "in" on one mighty exclusive or a couple of hours banging away on some bloody keyboard?'

'Except your mighty exclusive doesn't seem to be making much progress.' She paused, sighed and then said: 'Okay, I'll meet you but only if you promise to tell me what's going on – and I mean everything, not just part of it.'

'Everything,' he said emphatically. 'I swear. I'll see you in The Whistle at half-seven.'

'If you let me down, I'll never speak to you again.'

Len put the phone in his pocket, drank the dregs of his coffee and gave one last lingering look through the window. It was twenty to five, too early for Adam Shaw to be home, but it was worth checking to see if there were any lights on. Maybe Ellen was holed up in the flat. What were the chances? Pretty slim, he had to admit, but he was willing to try anything.

He walked along Camden Road, trudging heavily through the slush. A long line of rush-hour traffic moved sluggishly along beside him. He gazed enviously at the warm interiors as his ears and nose turned a glistening shade of pink. Unwilling to lose his parking space he had left his own car in Berry Square and taken a cab to the office and back.

It was another five minutes before he turned into the dim side street that led to Berry Square. Len pulled on his cigarette, exhaling the smoke in short nervy bursts. If Ellen had done a runner, would he ever be able to find her again? She could disappear as easily as little Grace Harper.

He was about ten yards in when he heard the footsteps behind him. Casually, he glanced over his shoulder and then his brown eyes slowly widened. 'What . . .?'

There was no glint, no light strong enough for the blade to reflect off. He had only seconds to absorb what was happening. By the time he had acknowledged the existence of the knife, the gloved hand was moving too swiftly for him to avoid it.

Chapter Nine

Harry arrived back at the office just before six and parked the car with more care than he had in the morning. He had spent the afternoon on a long, tedious and, as it had turned out, utterly futile surveillance job. Karl Westwood was wise to the ways of insurance companies. After three large claims, all to do with 'debilitating injuries', he knew how to keep his head down when some interfering snoop was likely to be loitering outside.

Walking round to the front of the building, Harry strolled into the empty foyer, crossed the threadbare carpet and stepped into the lift. Pressing the button for the third floor, he waited for the doors to close. They didn't. Harry jabbed at the button again. A red light flickered but the doors remained obstinately open. 'Come on,' he murmured impatiently. When it became clear that no amount of encouragement was going to make them shift, he raised his eyes to the heavens and headed for the stairs.

After limping up three floors, he was out of breath by the time he reached the office. One of Lorna's kids, the older girl, was lounging in the corner with her face stuck in a magazine. She looked up as he stumbled inside. 'Hey,' she said.

'Hi, Maddie. How are you?'

She crossed her long skinny legs and yawned. 'Bored.'

'Poor you,' he said. 'You should try working for a living.'

'Oh yeah. And you should try going to school.'

He grinned at her. 'I've done my time, thank you.' Dropping his briefcase by the drinks machine, he took a deep breath and quickly organized a hit of instant caffeine. 'What are you doing here, anyway?'

'Waiting for Mum. The sitter's pulled a sickie again.'

He glanced towards the inner office. Lorna was sitting opposite Mac, busily taking down notes. 'How long have you been waiting?'

As if time was a concept that only elderly people considered, she wrinkled her nose and shrugged.

'Where's your sister?'

'At a mate's.' She stared at the cup of coffee he was raising to his lips. 'Don't I get one of those?'

'What's the matter – you lost the use of your legs?' But he poured one for her just the same and handed it over.

'Ta,' she said. 'I'm gasping.'

'Thirsty work, doing nothing.' How old was she now? Twelve, thirteen? He couldn't remember and knew better than to ask. Every time he saw her, she seemed to have sprung up another inch or two. At the moment, for all her adult airs, she still retained a residue of childlike charm but in a year or so she would probably be a holy terror. 'You not got any mates then?' he said to wind her up.

'Not like Kim's. They're all boring little kids.'

He took the chair beside her and sat down. 'And you're mixing with the more sophisticated types, right?'

Her dove grey eyes gave him a long assessing look. She took a moment as if deciding on whether to share a secret or not. 'Zane's my best mate. His grandpa's a villain.'

'That's nice for him.'

'I don't suppose you approve,' she said smugly.

Harry shrugged. 'None of my business who you hang out with, is it? So long as your mum's okay with it.'

Maddie widened her eyes as if her mother's opinion was the last she'd take any notice of. 'Zane says his grandpa's been to jail.'

'Well, that's where most villains end up.' Except for the likes of Ray Stagg, he thought resentfully. Some bastards just kept

50

on getting away with it. 'I take it this Zane doesn't spend his weekends robbing banks?'

She giggled. 'Course not. Zane's not like that. Zane's cool.'

'So what's his surname, this . . . er, friend of yours?'

'Why?' she asked suspiciously.

'Just taking an interest, making conversation.' He put his half-drunk coffee down on the table, folded his arms, leaned back and yawned. 'But if you don't want to talk about it . . .'

'Keppell,' she said.

'Ah,' he said. Harry knew the Keppells all right; every copper in London knew them. They were an old East End family, now living out Chingford way. He wondered which of Jimmy's sons had fathered the incredible Zane. 'So who's his dad then?'

'He hasn't got a dad. He lives with his mum.'

Harry nodded. He'd forgotten about Angela, the only girl in Jimmy's tribe of lawless offspring. Still, it could be worse. Angie, as far as he was aware, had managed to keep out of trouble for the past few years.

'Do you know her?' she said.

'Not really. What's she like?'

'Oh, pretty cool. She bought Zane a set of drums for his birthday. He's good. He's gonna be in a band.'

'Rich and famous then.'

'Zane says it's the music that matters,' she said, 'not the money.'

'Quite. Although he'll find the money helps when he needs to pay the phone bill.'

As if the concept of artistic integrity was just too deep for him to grasp, Maddie gave a sigh, slowly shook her head and gazed back down at her magazine.

A minute later Lorna came out of the office. She had a pinched expression on her face. As Harry got to his feet, she said softly: 'I wouldn't bother. Not if it's anything he doesn't want to hear.'

Harry smiled. 'Don't worry. He won't mind this.'

Mac looked up and frowned as he knocked on the door. He beckoned him inside with a cursory wave of his hand. Harry had barely stepped across the threshold when he barked:

'What is it? If you're going to have another go about the Stagg case then—'

'Not at all,' Harry said. 'Sorry about earlier. I was out of order. You were right; we can't afford to go turning down good clients. I just wanted to let you know that I've sorted all the paperwork.'

As if unsure that he had heard correctly, Mac's frown lines deepened for a second but then gradually cleared. 'Good. I'm glad to hear it. But what's with the sudden change of heart? This morning you'd have rather slit your own throat than spend five minutes in Ray Stagg's company.'

Harry tried to keep his voice neutral. 'Yeah, well, that hasn't changed – you know how I feel about him – but I went to see Denise Webster and we had a long chat. I'd like to help her. She seems genuinely worried and it's not her fault that she's related to that scumball. So, as far as I'm concerned, from now on *she's* the client I'm working for.'

Mac nodded. 'Fair enough.'

'Although there is one small problem.'

Mac sighed, a dull weary sound that floated round the office. 'Go on.'

'It's just that . . . well, with this ongoing surveillance on Westwood, I'm not sure if I'll be able to give it my full attention. I don't suppose—'

'Forget Westwood. I'll get one of the other boys on to it.'

Harry stared at him, surprised. He'd been expecting to meet some resistance, a brief lecture at least on effective time management or current staff shortages. 'Are you sure?'

'Look,' he said. 'I don't like this connection to Stagg any more than you do. So the faster it's sorted, the sooner we can all be rid of him.'

'Okay. That's great. I'll get on to it first thing.'

'And keep me updated.'

'I will.' Harry had his hand on the door handle when he

52

stopped and glanced back over his shoulder. He hesitated, uncertain as to whether to ask or not.

'What now?'

'Is everything all right, Mac?'

That frown hit the older man's forehead again. 'Why shouldn't it be?'

'I don't know. I heard a couple of the guys had been laid off.'

'And?'

'And seeing as I was the last one to join the firm, I was wondering why . . .'

'Why I'd chosen to keep you on?'

Harry shrugged.

'And you're thinking what?' Mac said gruffly. 'That maybe it's out of a misguided sense of loyalty, or sympathy, or pity for the poor old git who walks with a limp?'

Now it was Harry's turn to scowl. Instinctively, he glanced down at his leg. 'It crossed my mind.'

Mac flapped his hand again in a short dismissive gesture. 'Well, push off and occupy your mind with more useful things. You might not be the finest physical specimen in the world but at least you've got a brain. I can get muscle from anywhere.'

'I'm not a bloody cripple,' Harry snapped.

'So stop acting like one.'

Harry glared at him, his blue eyes blazing. He might still be slow on his feet but he was working out, going regularly to the gym and getting himself as fit as he could. When it came to muscle, he was as strong as the next man. At over six foot there was no reason why he couldn't . . .

It was only as Mac's mouth started to twitch that Harry realized what was going on.

He looked away and groaned. 'And if you think you can use that pathetic reverse psychology on me—'

'Go home,' Mac said, laughing. 'I'll see you tomorrow.'

It was after seven by the time Harry had ploughed through the evening traffic and got back to Kentish Town. What he needed

53

was a stiff drink, a good hot meal and some mindless rest and relaxation. A Chinese takeaway and a few hours in front of the TV should do the trick.

He had only just closed the door when Valerie came flying out of the bedroom. 'Where have you been? We're going to be late.'

'Late?'

She was all dressed up in a low-cut, revealing, slinky black dress. 'It's Scott Hall's retirement do. You didn't forget, did you?'

'Of course not,' he lied.

She hurried back into the bedroom. 'So where have you been?'

'Sorry, I got tied up.' He dropped his keys on the hall table and followed her through. 'I've been stuck on surveillance all day and then I had to talk to Mac about a missing persons case – Ray Stagg's brother-in-law as it happens.'

She was standing in front of the mirror twisting her long fair hair into a complicated knot at the back of her head. 'My, you are moving in exclusive circles.'

'I always have,' he said, stepping forward and wrapping his arms gently around her waist. This unspoken feud, with all its distance, had gone on long enough; he missed being close to her. 'And how was your day? You look gorgeous by the way, really beautiful.' He bent his head to kiss the cool smooth skin at the base of her neck. He looked in the mirror and smiled.

Her crimson lips smiled tentatively back.

'Why don't you leave your hair down?' His hands roamed up, sliding slowly around her breasts. 'In fact, why don't we just—'

'We're late,' she said again. 'We were supposed to be there at seven. Are you ready to go?'

'Come on,' he murmured. 'Another half-hour won't make much difference.'

'I can't,' she said, abruptly pulling away from him.

He stood back, confused. 'Can't what?'

She sat down on the bed, sliding her feet into a pair of black stilettos. She gave a cursory glance towards his groin before gazing up at him with a sigh. 'I mean I can't just turn it on and off whenever you feel like it. I don't know where I stand with you, Harry. It's been months since we've . . . and now you're suddenly all over me. I don't understand. I don't know what's going on.'

'Nothing's going on. I just thought—'

'I'm perfectly aware of what you thought,' she said. 'But it doesn't work like that. You can't just come home one day and act as if everything's fine. It isn't. And you know it isn't.'

'So why can't we sit down and talk?'

Valerie slowly raised her hazel eyes to him. 'Oh, is that what you were doing? Wanting to *talk*?'

'You know what I mean.' Harry held her gaze for a second, hesitated and then turned his face away. He loved her but no matter how much he wanted to repair their relationship he just couldn't have *that* conversation this evening. 'I'll catch you up,' he said. 'I need to take a shower.'

She grabbed her bag and flounced angrily out of the room. 'Fine. I'll see you later.'

He'd had every intention of going – or so he thought. It was only as he dried himself and got dressed again that his resolve began to falter. It was bad enough not being a cop any more without having to mix with them, to listen to them, to be reminded of the life he was missing out on. And that was only the half of it. If he went, he'd also have to spend the whole evening pretending that everything was fine between him and Val.

Did that make him an emotional coward? Probably. He poured himself a generous glass of vodka, slouched down on the sofa and turned on the TV.

A few minutes later he turned it off again.

He couldn't relax. He couldn't think straight. Standing up, he went over to the window and looked out. The street was empty. In the house across the way, the lights on a Christmas tree merged from gold into blue into red. He leaned his head against the cool pane of glass. What was he doing? It was time to start facing up to things, to stop running away. But could he actually do that? Running away, he thought wryly, was ingrained in the Lind family genes, a tradition that was none too easy to let go of.

Harry wanted to drink but didn't want to drink alone. Taking his glass through to the kitchen he slung the vodka down the sink. He'd go to The Whistle instead and get himself a pint. Then perhaps, after a spot of Dutch courage, he might just summon up the nerve to join his former colleagues.

Chapter Ten

Ray Stagg collected a Scotch from the bar before making his way through to the guest lounge. The club was quiet this evening, a typical Monday, the usual punters either too tired or too broke after the excesses of the weekend.

He paused by the door to study the ageing thickset man who was waiting for him. From a distance he looked benign enough, his cheeks slightly ruddy, his bushy beard and long white hair more suggestive of Santa Claus than of the brutal murdering gangster he actually was. Ray was no angel but this guy was in a different league.

He took a swig of the Scotch and swallowed hard. It had been a mistake to get involved with Jimmy Keppell; he should have politely declined the invitation. But the truth was he'd been flattered, impressed, seduced even by the prospect of working with someone of his reputation, a villain who had once mixed with so many notorious figures from the past. Who could refuse? Well, *he* should have, he should have known better, but it was too late now for idle regrets.

Ray strolled forward, forcing a smile as he approached the table. 'Good to see you again.'

Keppell raised his cold blank eyes and nodded.

'Do you want to go somewhere more private?'

'Sit down,' Keppell ordered.

Ray, although never deferential, was always careful. On this occasion, he did as he was told. 'Would you like another drink?'

His visitor glared at him. 'What I'd like,' he said softly, 'is for you to tell me what the fuck is going on.'

'No worries. I'm sorting it.'

'Have you found him yet?'

Ray tried to sound confident. 'I will have – soon.'

Keppell didn't seem impressed. 'How soon is soon? Hours, days, weeks? I've made an investment, a big investment, and if there's one thing you need to understand, son, it's that I *never* get screwed over.'

'I appreciate that.'

'Do you?' he said.

Ray nodded. 'A few days, a week at the most. I'll find him. I've got people out there. I've got people looking. He won't stay hidden for long.' He knocked back the rest of his Scotch. 'I've even got Mackenzie on board.'

Keppell's scarred burly fingers curled into a fist. 'What? You've got a fucking ex-copper on the job?'

'Believe me,' Ray said, with more conviction than he felt, 'I know what I'm doing. He owes me, owes me big-time and he won't let me down.' He decided, on balance, that it was better not to mention Harry Lind. That particular bet was a very private gamble. Knowing that Lind bore a personal grudge, that he'd do anything to put the knife in, he was counting on him to find Al Webster double-fast.

'You'd better be sure,' Keppell said.

Ray recognized the threat but kept his own response casual. 'I am.' He snapped his fingers at a passing waitress, some foreign blonde called Agnes.

'Same again?' she asked, swinging her hips as she drew up beside him.

'Just bring the bottle over.'

Ray waited until she'd strutted off before turning towards Keppell again. 'I need someone to help flush Al out and Mackenzie can do that. I know he can.'

'Are you sure?'

'I'm absolutely sure.'

58

Keppell leaned forward and placed his large hand over Ray's. 'You'd better be, son.' His fingers squeezed down hard, the pressure so intense that the bones came close to being crushed. 'Because if you're not . . .'

Chapter Eleven

Jess looked at her watch. It was ten past eight already; she'd been waiting for over forty minutes for Len to arrive. Where was he? It was hardly a question that needed answering – in some other pub, knocking back the booze, drowning his sorrows with no regard for the arrangements he had made several hours ago.

She tried his mobile again but it was turned off. It was pointless leaving any further messages. She wasn't about to embark on a tour of all his other haunts either; it was too cold outside and there was no guarantee that she would ever find him. Why did she bother? Toby was right: Len *was* a waste of space. But then Toby with his smart suits, crass opinions and creeping hands was hardly the ideal role model either.

Jess finished her beer and was preparing to leave, gathering her coat and bag, when the door swung open and Harry Lind walked in. It was over a week since they'd first met, that Friday night when they'd all had too much to drink. What had they talked about? She couldn't remember; it was all a bit blurred around the edges. She suspected, however, that they'd indulged in a fair amount of flirting. Still, that was nothing to be ashamed of.

She looked across the bar at him. He was a good-looking man, tall, his sleek black hair greying slightly at the temples. He had one of those angular, almost gaunt faces, the cheekbones sharp, the nose aquiline, the lips wide and thin. As if he were in a perpetual state of worry, there were two deep vertical lines engraved between his eyebrows. There was something about that intense, anxious look that appealed to her.

He hadn't noticed her yet. Perhaps it would be better if he didn't. He would only be embarrassed to bump into her again. Men who were attached – and she was certain that he was – had a tendency to regret their drunken flirtations. She would just put her head down, slip out behind him and . . .

But she had barely taken a few steps when she heard his voice. 'Jess!'

She looked up and smiled, pretending to be surprised. 'Oh, hello.'

'You're not going, are you?'

'Er . . . yes, actually I am. I was due to meet Len here at half-seven but . . .' She lifted her hands in a gesture of resignation.

'It's not that late. He might still turn up.' Harry reached into his pocket and took out his wallet. 'Let me get you a drink.'

'No thanks,' she said. 'I've wasted enough time this evening.'

Harry raised his eyebrows.

She winced and then laughed. 'Sorry, I didn't mean that to come out like it did.'

He grinned back at her. 'Don't worry about it. I suppose I might be able to salvage what little remains of my male pride if you agree to stay for a drink.'

Jess gazed into his intense blue eyes and had a change of heart. Where was the harm? It wasn't as if she had anything better to do. She'd already missed her class and would only be going home to an empty flat. 'Go on, then. I'll have a quick half.'

They took the drinks over to an empty table. Jess sat down and watched as he took off his overcoat and laid it over the back of the chair. Underneath, he was impeccably dressed in a dark grey suit, white shirt and tie.

'My,' she said, 'do you always make such an effort when you slip round to your local?'

He glanced down at his clothes and smiled. 'I think it's important to maintain standards.'

'And the real reason?'

Harry settled into his chair and took a sip of his pint. 'I'm on my way to a retirement dinner for a former colleague.'

'And you need a few bevvies before you can face the experience?'

'Something like that.'

Jess looked at her watch. 'Unless it's a late start, I reckon you've already missed the first course.'

'You could be right.'

'Any particular reason – I mean as to why you find the prospect of a free dinner so thoroughly resistible?'

He hesitated, the truth on the tip of his tongue before he changed his mind. 'It's been a long day.'

Sensing that on this particular subject she wasn't going to get much more out of him, Jess asked instead: 'So how is the world of private investigation?'

'Not bad. We've just taken on a missing persons case; it could be interesting.'

'Oh, anyone I might know?' She sensed his hesitation and smiled. 'It's okay, I'm not digging. I'm off duty. And anyway, I work for the local rag not the *News of the World.*'

'Sorry.'

'Don't be. You've every reason to be cautious. Never trust a reporter, right?'

'Did I say that?'

'No, but you were thinking it.'

He smiled at her over the rim of his pint. 'I reserve the right to silence. But talking of reporters, what is it with you and Len Curzon? You should think about getting yourself a more reliable drinking partner.'

'A more reliable boss would be nearer the mark. Not that he is my boss, not exactly, but he's the person I've worked most closely with at the *Herald.* And the thing is, he's good, better than good, only recently he's . . .'

'Been spending more time in the pub than on the job?'

Jess sighed. 'Yeah, I guess so. I mean, he's always been a drinker but never this bad. I'm worried about him. He's been disappearing for days on end, says he's working on something big but . . .' She slowly shook her head. 'I suppose it's an occupational hazard when you spend so much of your life sitting in back-street boozers, trying to draw the local villains into your confidence.'

'Which is not the kind of bad habit *you'll* ever be in danger of falling into.'

She glanced around at the dingy surroundings of The Whistle, looked back at Harry and laughed. 'God forbid.'

Harry was the first to look away. 'I wouldn't worry about it. He'll surface when he's good and ready.'

'I know.'

'Although it probably doesn't pay to rely on him too much.'

'No,' she agreed. 'You don't like him much, do you?'

Harry didn't but was loath to admit it. The beer and the company were gradually making him relax. So rarely at his ease, he didn't want to say anything to encourage her to leave. 'To be honest, I can't really claim to know him that well. Last week was the first time I'd seen him in a while. I'm sure he has his good points.'

'You just haven't stumbled across any of them yet.'

'I wasn't—' he began, but was interrupted by his mobile ringing. 'Sorry.'

Reaching into his pocket, he drew the phone out and stared at the screen. It was Valerie. In his head he heard the monologue that was about to follow. *Where are you? What are you doing? Why aren't you here?* Frowning, he turned it off.

'Nothing important?'

'It'll wait.'

Jess gave him a probing kind of look. 'I hope you weren't supposed to be giving the after-dinner speech.'

'It's still early,' he said. 'How about one for the road?'

Chapter Twelve

Harry woke to the recognizable sounds of an angry female. From the spare room, he lay in bed, his head throbbing, while he listened to Valerie clattering noisily around the kitchen. *Bang!* A mug went down on the table. *Slam!* The fridge door was shut. Then the radio went on nice and loud. She wasn't leaving anything to chance. She was going to have her say and she was going to have it before she left the flat this morning.

Stretching his hand out towards the bedside table he fumbled for his watch and peered through half-closed eyes at the face. It was ten to seven. He couldn't remember exactly when he'd got home. It had been late though; after two he suspected. After leaving The Whistle, they had gone on to a club off the Tottenham Court Road, a crowded, dimly lit place where they had eaten spicy tacos and drunk too much wine.

They? At the thought of Jess Vaughan, his forehead crumpled into a frown. He had a vague but disturbing memory of being in the back of a taxi, of having his arm round her, of leaning forward to . . . A small moan escaped from his lips. God, what had he been thinking? As if his life wasn't complicated enough.

Harry dragged himself out of bed and stumbled to the shower. For the next ten minutes he stood, barely moving, while the hot water thrashed down around him. Then as his limbs, if not his brain, gradually rose from their stupor, he washed his hair and scrubbed his body clean.

After pulling on a pair of jeans and a clean shirt, he took a moment to examine his reflection in the mirror. Not good.

What he needed was another eight hours' sleep but he was going to have to wait until tonight before he got it.

There was another loud bang from the kitchen. He started. Quickly, he ran a comb through his hair. He couldn't put off the confrontation forever. Better to get it over and done with. Taking a deep breath, Harry warily advanced into the kitchen.

Valerie turned, her eyes blazing.

He raised his hands in a gesture of surrender. 'I know, I know. I'm sorry,' he said sheepishly. 'And if it's any consolation, I feel like hell.'

'It isn't,' she said, 'and I'm glad.'

He poured himself a coffee and dropped a couple of slices of bread into the toaster. He was feeling faintly nauseous but knew he had to eat.

Valerie folded her arms across her chest and leaned back against the table. 'So are you going to tell me why?'

'I meant to come. Honestly, I did. I put on my suit, went out and . . .'

'And then decided that you'd rather get smashed instead.'

'Not exactly.'

Valerie's glare grew harder. 'So how was it *exactly*?'

'I bumped into . . .' He paused, realizing it might be circumspect to leave Jess's name out of this. He was in enough trouble already. 'Just some guy that I haven't seen for a while and we got talking and . . .'

'And you decided that was way more important than attending a retirement dinner for a guy you worked with for over ten years.'

'No,' he said. His head was banging, a harsh persistent throb that set his teeth on edge. 'I didn't mean that. It was wrong. *I* was wrong.' He rubbed at his temples. 'The truth is that I just couldn't face it – seeing them all again, having to make that endless small talk, having to act like everything's just fine.'

Her voice softened a little, sliding from anger into exasperation. 'But these are your friends, Harry, your mates, people who care about you.'

'Well, perhaps that's what makes it even harder.'

There was a short silence.

Harry sighed into his coffee. 'So how did it go?'

Turning her back on him, she walked over to the sink and started rinsing a cup. 'What do you care?'

'I'll call him,' he promised. 'I'll call Scott and apologize.'

'Sure. Whatever.'

The toast sprang out of the machine with a sound that to Harry's fragile brain sounded like a minor explosion. He flinched, picked it up and put it on a plate. Still talking to her back, he sat down at the table and said: 'I've told you, I'll call him. I'll sort it out.'

She glanced over her shoulder, her eyes heavy with reproach. 'This isn't just about a missed dinner. You know it isn't. You're always doing this stuff. Things have happened, terrible things, but you can't let them screw you up forever. When are you going to sort *yourself* out?'

'And since when did you become my counsellor?' he snapped and then instantly regretted it. Dropping his gaze he stared guiltily down at his toast. 'Sorry.'

Slowly drying her hands, she came over to stand beside him. 'Maybe that's the problem,' she said. 'Maybe I'm not helping you at all.'

'What?'

'Sometimes I feel like I'm only making things worse.'

Harry lifted his red-rimmed eyes and looked up at her. 'And how do you figure that one out?'

She shrugged, glancing away. 'I don't suppose it helps seeing me go out to work every morning or hearing me talk about what I've been doing. I can understand that. All we ever seem to do these days is row. And all *I* ever seem to do is nag and complain. I don't want it to be like this, Harry. I don't want *us* to be like this.'

'No,' he agreed. For all his thoughts about them splitting up, that was all they had been – just idle careless thoughts. Now he had a nasty sinking sensation in the pit of his stomach. What if she was actually going to leave him? A wave of panic swept through his body. 'I don't want it either.'

'Are you sure?'

'Of course,' he said. 'I may be bitter about a lot of things but you doing your job isn't one of them. I don't begrudge you that. How could I?'

'But it's not just—'

'I know,' he interrupted. 'I've not been thinking straight. I haven't been for months. I've been behaving like a shit.'

She laid a hand on his shoulder. 'You're not a shit,' she said. 'Well, not all the time.'

He smiled and placed his hand over hers. 'Look, why don't we have a quiet night in, just the two of us? I'll buy some food and cook. How does that sound?'

'Do you mean it?'

'Yeah. About seven thirty? It'll be good to spend some time together.'

'Okay. But you'll definitely be here, won't you? I don't want to be stood up two nights in a row.'

Harry nodded, the motion making his head ache even harder. 'I promise.'

It was the fourth time she had rung that morning and it wasn't even nine o'clock. Harry glared down at the phone. Why couldn't the woman leave him alone? It had only been a few drinks, for God's sake, a quick fumble in the back of a cab, and now he couldn't get rid of her.

'Aren't you going to answer that?' Lorna said.

'It's not important.' He turned it off. If Jess didn't give up, he'd have to call her back, but it wasn't a prospect he could face right now. Despite three black coffees and a couple of aspirins, he still felt too fragile to go through the process of letting her down gently. Perhaps, if he kept on avoiding her, she'd eventually take the hint.

He dug into his briefcase and handed a sheaf of papers over to Lorna. 'The insurance job, the Westwood case,' he said. 'Mac's going to replace me with somebody else.'

'Yes, I heard. That must be a blow.'

'Pure heartbreak.'

Lorna grimaced. 'Unfortunately there's been a slight change of plan. Mac can't get anyone else on to it until this afternoon so if you could just cover for the morning . . .'

Harry shrugged back into his overcoat. 'No can do, I'm afraid.'

'Why? Where are you off to?'

'Romford market. I need to track down some of Al Webster's pals.'

'It's Tuesday,' she said.

Harry frowned, struggling to grasp the connection. 'Yeah?'

She grinned, her blue eyes dancing with amusement. 'My, you must have had a good time last night. You don't have a clue what I'm talking about, do you?'

'Am I missing something here?'

'Only one useful little fact. The market isn't open on Tuesdays.'

'You're kidding?'

'I'm afraid not. Only Wednesday, Friday and Saturday. Well, apart from the two weeks before Christmas and we're not quite there yet.'

Harry rubbed at his temples and thought about it. That was his plan for the morning straight out the window. It also begged the question of what Al did when he wasn't flogging DVDs on his stall. Perhaps he was a gentleman of leisure. But somehow he doubted it; the upkeep of that house in Loughton, not to mention a well-dressed wife and two demanding kids, wasn't likely to come cheap.

He'd better call Denise and check it out. However, that meant switching his phone back on. Did he dare? Tentatively, he pressed the button, hoping it wasn't about to start ringing again. When it didn't, he gave a sigh of relief and smartly looked up the number.

As if she was sitting next to the phone, Denise answered promptly. 'Hello.'

'It's Harry Lind.'

'Have you found him?'

He winced at the desperation in her voice. 'Sorry. There are just a few details that I need to go over.'

'Oh.'

'It's about what Al does when he isn't working on the market. I mean, it's only open three days a week, isn't it?'

There was a short pause. 'Er . . .'

'I was wondering if he had another job.'

Again, that hesitation. 'Nothing steady,' she said cagily.

Harry gazed up at the ceiling. How did people expect you to help when they only told you half the story? 'Look, I need to know *everything*, Denise. So, if there's anything you're keeping from me, however unimportant you think it may be . . .'

'There isn't.' She cleared her throat, a slight nervous kind of sound. 'He sometimes does a bit of work for Ray, that's all, helping with deliveries and stuff at the club.'

A smile crept on to Harry's face. The morning may have started under a cloud but the sun was slowly coming out. Funny how Stagg hadn't mentioned that Al worked for him; the odds of his being involved had just shortened considerably. 'You should have told me. How often is "sometimes"?'

'A couple of days a week, an evening or two. But this has nothing to do with Ray or Vista. Al wasn't even there last Saturday.'

'I know,' he said casually. 'I'm sure you're right. It just helps if I have *all* the facts.'

'Okay,' she murmured. 'Is there anything else?'

You tell me, he was tempted to respond – there was probably a good deal more Denise wasn't sharing – but he didn't want to push her. 'No, that's it for now. Thanks. I'll stay in touch.'

Harry switched off the phone – better safe than sorry – and grinned down at Lorna.

'Good news?' she asked.

'Could be. I think it may be time to pay Ray Stagg another visit.'

'Well, seeing as I just saved you a wasted journey to Romford, can it wait until this afternoon?'

Harry thought about it. He didn't relish another shift staring at Karl Westwood's curtains but it could be more productive to go to Vista later when other members of staff would be around. He smiled at her. 'Go on then,' he said. 'Seeing as it's you.'

Chapter Thirteen

BJ stood shiftily by the door and peered into the cell. It wasn't the first time he'd wandered past but it was the first real chance he'd had to stop and stare. Deacon was distracted, his head in his hands, gazing at the letter he'd received. From the bleak expression on his face, it was clear that he didn't like what he was reading. A *Dear John*, perhaps? No, his wife had left him years ago, although there was still that dark-haired little cutie who had come to visit . . .

Over the past week, ever since Curzon had been down, BJ had been taking an interest in Paul Deacon. He had seen the way Len had watched him, how he'd pretended not to be interested. And that, in BJ's eyes, was enough to warrant a few inquiries of his own. He'd asked around and discovered, much to his amazement, that the solemn, dull, silver-haired man – the guy he had never noticed before – had once hit the headlines. The geezer had been a celebrity. Not just a successful Tory politician (politics didn't interest BJ much) but also, incredibly, the man who had murdered Jimmy Keppell's son over twelve years ago.

Everyone who was anyone had heard of Jimmy K and from all accounts he wasn't slow to exact revenge. That Deacon was still breathing was a miracle. How come he wasn't six foot under already? It was a question that no one seemed willing or able to answer.

BJ was beginning to understand Curzon's fascination.

Still unnoticed, he grabbed the opportunity to look around. As a lifer, Deacon had a cell to himself. The room was sparse, unadorned with the usual pictures and posters. There were no pictures, no bare flesh, no glossy centrefold bums or tits. Still, that was hardly surprising if the rumours were true about him and the Keppell kid. He probably preferred the boys to the girls. However, there wasn't any evidence of that either. There wasn't even a respectable display of family photographs. The entire space was as blank and anonymous as the four walls of a motel.

'You okay, man?'

Deacon looked up, startled. 'What?'

BJ nodded towards the letter. 'Bad news, huh?'

As if to hide what he was reading, Deacon quickly lowered his hand and laid it over the sheet of paper. 'Did you want something?'

BJ leaned against the door. 'Only asking.'

Deacon stared back at him. 'I'm not interested,' he said.

'In what?'

'In whatever you're selling.'

BJ looked hurt. 'Hey, I'm just trying to be friendly, man. I'm not selling nothing.'

'Good,' Deacon said. 'Because there's nothing that I want from you.'

'It don't hurt to be polite,' BJ said, rolling his massive shoulders. He turned and walked away down the passage. From now on he'd be keeping a close eye on Paul Deacon; the guy wouldn't be able to take a shit without him knowing about it.

BJ understood how the world worked, how to trade, how to barter. If he had something important he could offer Len, then Len would have no choice but to give him something back. And what he wanted – and it didn't seem too much to ask – was to see his name in print. He already saw that book in his dreams, its spine a glittering band of gold, its title a glowing homage to the glory that was BJ Barrington.

Chapter Fourteen

It was late afternoon before Lorna managed to organize a replacement. Harry, parked along the road from Westwood's house, had nothing to report to the young black guy who arrived to take over. Warren James was one of Mac's techno geeks, a specialist who normally spent his days hunched over a computer retrieving wiped data and sniffing out frauds.

'What are *you* doing here?' Harry asked.

Warren climbed into the passenger seat and grinned. 'It's good to see you too, pal. But hey, if you'd rather hang around here for another four hours . . .'

'Sorry. I'm just surprised, that's all. I mean, you don't usually do this kind of stuff.'

'Lorna twisted my arm. I don't mind though. It makes a change to get out of the office. So what's the deal with our invisible friend? Any sign?'

They both looked towards the large modern semi. There was a BMW and a 4×4 sitting in the drive, the spoils no doubt of Westwood's numerous insurance claims.

'Quiet as the grave,' Harry said. 'No one in, no one out.'

Warren nodded. 'It's been over a week. He'll make a move soon; he must be going stir crazy.'

'Let's hope so.'

'Maybe when it gets dark . . .'

Already the light was fading, the dusk settling over the street like a thin grey blanket. Soon the street lamps would come on and then, one by one, the houses would be illuminated too.

'Anyway, you go,' Warren said, opening the door. 'I'll move the car and grab your space.'

'Thanks. Are you on for the evening?'

'Only until eight, then Mac's taking over.'

'Mac?' Harry said, frowning. Things must be tight. He couldn't remember the last time he'd been out on surveillance.

Warren shrugged. 'That's what Lorna told me.'

Harry glanced at the clock on the dashboard as he manoeuvred the Audi through the entrance to Vista. After the extended shift at Finsbury Park, he was running late, the shopping still no more than a scribbled list in the back of his notebook. A quick dash round the supermarket was next on the agenda. He had the feeling that a takeaway wouldn't quite cut it with Valerie; this evening was all about *making an effort*.

The car park was busier than the last time he'd been here; some of the night staff must be working already. He found a space between a blue van and a Metro and squeezed in. The flashy yellow Lotus was parked up at the far end. Good, at least Stagg was on the premises.

Walking in, Harry found the desk at reception unattended. The gum-chewing blonde was nowhere in sight and nor was anyone else. He stood for a moment, undecided, and then strolled over to the office door and knocked. There was no response. Cautiously, he reached out and tried the handle – unsurprisingly, the door was locked.

Harry gazed around the foyer and then, hearing the distant sound of music, pushed open the set of heavy fire doors, went along a short corridor and entered the main space. All freshly cleaned and polished, it looked almost respectable. Except he knew otherwise; Vista was renowned for its hookers and its drugs. Although Stagg was careful to keep the business at least superficially on the right side of the law, it was common knowledge as to what really went on.

Without its usual crowd of sleazy customers, the club seemed larger than he remembered. As Harry surveyed his

74

surroundings, his expression gradually grew darker. Five times they'd raided this place and every time Stagg had been ready for them: no obvious drug-dealing, prostitution or even a hint of anything illegal. Some bent shit of a copper was clearly tipping him off.

There was a restaurant area over to the right and a wide stairway leading up to a balconied second floor. The only sign of life, however, was coming from the bar, a wide chrome monstrosity stretching almost the entire length of a wall. Behind the counter, three young men in matching red vests were busy bottling up while a slim pretty blonde sat on a stool smoking a cigarette. Harry instantly felt his mood lighten. The girl was wearing a tiny white dress, so short and flimsy that an idle breeze could have blown it away. His gaze was slowly roaming the length of her long brown legs when one of the men looked up and noticed him.

'We're closed,' he said sharply. He was a thin-faced kid, about twenty, with gelled-up spiky hair. A barbed-wire tattoo encircled his upper arm. The name *Troy* was emblazoned across the top left corner of his vest.

'The door was open,' Harry said.

'And? It's a nightclub, mate. The clue's in the name.'

Harry noticed him glance towards the girl as if hoping that his smart response might have made a favourable impact. But she was staring impassively down at her pale pink nails. 'Very witty,' Harry said. 'Did you learn that in school today?'

Troy's cheeks flushed red, his fingers tightening round the bottle he was holding. 'We're closed,' he repeated. 'You want to leave voluntarily or do I need to show you the door?'

'Fine. Go ahead. And then you can explain to Mr Stagg why you *tried* to throw me out. I'm sure, if nothing else, he'll appreciate your good intentions.'

There was one of those prolonged confrontational silences. The other two men, unwilling to get involved, sidled down towards the far end of the bar. The blonde, sensing a drama, stayed put. She looked up, took a drag on her cigarette and exhaled the smoke in a long fine stream.

'So?' Harry said.

Troy hesitated, the confidence slowly draining from his face. His tongue nervously licked his lower lip. 'So what do you want?'

'I want to see Mr Stagg.'

'He's not here.'

'Then I'll wait.' Harry pulled up a bar stool and sat down. He turned and smiled at the pretty blonde beside him. 'Hi.'

She gazed cautiously back.

'I'm Harry,' he said.

She nodded. 'Agnes.'

'It's nice to meet you, Agnes.'

'We can't serve you,' Troy interrupted. 'We're not open yet.'

Harry lifted his brows. 'Did I ask for a drink? Although if you want to do something useful, you could track down that boss of yours and tell him that I'm waiting.'

Troy glared at him, his pride battling with his reason. He hovered for a moment and then reluctantly moved away.

Harry watched as he picked up the phone at the far end of the bar. While he had the chance, he turned to talk to the girl again. 'Have you worked here long?'

'Some,' she agreed. 'A little.' She had a distinct accent, Russian or East European perhaps. Her pink lips curled into a smile.

Harry took the photograph out of his pocket. 'So you must know Al, Al Webster?'

The smile quickly faded. 'Who?'

'He works here. You must have seen him around.'

She looked down at the photograph and frowned. 'I am not sure.'

'Not sure of what? Whether you've seen him or whether you should talk to me?'

She slid off the stool, her green cat's eyes wary and suspicious. 'Sorry. My English . . . is not so good.'

'Good enough for you to be working here,' Harry said.

'Well . . .' As if to imply that the vocabulary required for working in Vista was hardly of the kind to be described as demanding, she gave a small dismissive shrug.

Harry pushed the photo towards her again. 'When was the last time you saw him?'

He might have made more progress if Ray Stagg hadn't suddenly crept up behind.

'What's going on here?'

'I'm doing what you employed me to do,' Harry said. 'Searching for Al Webster.'

'And you think you'll find him here?'

Harry glanced towards Agnes and grinned. '*Cherchez la femme*. Wasn't that what you suggested?'

'Not in the club,' Stagg said, 'and certainly not during working hours.'

'Oh, sorry.' Harry lifted his brows and gazed around the empty room. 'I didn't realize how busy you were.'

Stagg waved Agnes away with a curt movement of his hand. She scurried towards an exit at the side of the bar, her slender hips wriggling. Harry took a moment to admire the view.

'Well?' Stagg growled at him.

'I've got a few questions if you can spare the time.'

'Fine, we'll talk in the office.'

They walked back through the corridor. 'Most people call before they just drop by,' Stagg said.

'Do they? I guess they must be the polite type.'

Stagg unlocked the door and glared at him. 'Does Mac know you're here?

Harry ignored the question. He stepped past him into the room and took a seat without waiting to be asked. 'I'm just wondering why you didn't mention that Al worked for you.'

Ray Stagg sat down behind his oversized desk. He swept a few sheets of paper from its surface, slipping them quickly into a drawer, before answering. 'Worked?' he said derisively. 'I'd hardly call it that. He helped out occasionally, that's all: the odd delivery, shifting the heavy stuff in the cellar. I was doing him a favour – or rather doing Denise a favour.'

'So why keep quiet about it?'

'Why do you think?' Stagg said. 'Cash in hand, isn't it? What he tells the tax man or not is up to him but it doesn't do to go shouting about these things.'

'I'm not the tax inspector.'

'It's a matter of trust.'

'But you trust me enough to look for your brother-in-law?'

'Degrees of trust, then,' he said. A sly smile crept on to his face. 'I know what you people are like.'

By 'you people', Harry presumed he meant former coppers. 'But there could be someone here who knows something, someone who was friendly with Al.'

Stagg gave a snigger. 'One of the girls, you mean? I don't think so. Al wasn't here much and when he was . . . well, he hardly made an impact.'

'So when was the last time?'

Ray Stagg stroked his chin with his fingers and stared pensively at the wall. 'Let's see. It must have been a few days before he went missing. Yeah, the Thursday afternoon. We had a coachload due in from Croydon. He helped to get the bar stocked up.'

'And he seemed fine to you then?'

'Whatever. We didn't have a heart-to-heart.'

'And he wasn't here again at the weekend? You didn't see him on the Saturday?'

'No.'

Harry got to his feet. 'Okay. That's all I need for now. But you won't mind if I ask around, talk to the staff?'

'Don't waste your time,' Stagg said. 'I'll have a word. If I find out anything, I'll call you.'

'Sure,' Harry said. He wasn't about to hold his breath.

Rushing along the aisle, Harry grabbed parsnips and potatoes and tried to remember what else he needed for the evening meal. He wasn't the greatest cook in the world but could just about manage the basic stuff. A roast was what he'd been planning – even he couldn't go far wrong with that – but with the clock ticking he had a sudden crisis of confidence: would he be able to get everything prepared by half past seven?

He dithered by the poultry, gazing down at the rows of chickens: big ones, little ones, free range, corn fed. His head was starting to spin. Maybe fish would be a better bet. Yes, then all he'd have to do was shove it under the grill. He found the fish counter, picked out a couple of Dover soles and then reversed towards the fruit and veg near the entrance. Dumping the parsnips, he collected two lemons, parsley, mushrooms and a pack of green beans. Now for the alcohol . . .

He was examining an overpriced bottle of Chablis when his phone started ringing. Harry took it out of his pocket, his face falling as he saw who it was. Should he just turn it off? No, if he did that she might keep trying all night. He had to get this over with.

'Hello?'

Jess's tone was a mixture of frustration and relief. 'Harry? God, where have you been? I've been trying to call you all day.'

'Sorry, I've been busy.'

'I need to see you,' she said. 'We have to talk.'

Talk? Oh no, that was all he needed. 'Er . . . actually now's not a great time, it's not really convenient.'

There was a short uneasy silence.

'You have heard, haven't you?'

'Heard what?'

'Len's dead,' she said. Her voice faltered. 'Murdered. He was stabbed to death last night.'

The bottle slipped from between Harry's fingers and smashed on to the floor.

Chapter Fifteen

It took him a while to find the flats, a bland three-storey purpose-built block near Victoria Park in Hackney. Twice he got caught in the one-way system, in a long slow snarl of evening traffic, before eventually working out where she lived.

Harry climbed the shallow flight of steps, pressed on the buzzer for Vaughan and waited.

A few seconds later Jess opened the door and smiled wanly at him. 'Thanks for coming.' She looked pale and strained, two dark smudges of mascara shadowing her eyes.

'I'm sorry,' he said. 'If I'd known . . .' But of course if he'd answered his phone, or even checked his messages, he *would* have known. 'Sorry,' he murmured again.

'You're here now,' she said. 'Don't worry about it.'

He followed her into the communal hallway, along a corridor and then through another door to the right. Her main living space was small and economically furnished. There was only a dark blue futon-type sofa, a cane chair, a couple of lamps and a table completely covered in a heap of paper. In fact the paper, as if making a bid for freedom, had migrated into every available corner of the room.

'Welcome to the mansion.' Jess flapped a hand. 'I'd apologize for the mess but to be honest that would suggest it doesn't normally look like this.'

There was a slight slur to her voice. Harry noticed a bottle of vodka, already a third empty, sitting on the table. It was a stupid question but he still felt obliged to ask it. 'Are you okay?'

'Sure,' she said. 'I'm coping – I think. Sit down. Do you want a drink?'

Harry shook his head. 'I'm fine, thanks.' It was a combination of shock, guilt and possibly misplaced obligation that had brought him here. He still wasn't entirely sure what was expected of him.

Jess picked an empty glass up off the floor and poured herself another stiff shot from the bottle. She forced a smile. 'Well, I need one even if you don't.' After lighting a cigarette, she slumped down on the sofa.

Deliberately keeping his distance, he sat down in the chair. 'So when did you hear?'

'Early this morning. Toby rang. They didn't find him until dawn.' She took a deep drag on her cigarette. 'He was out there all night. Can you believe that? After he was stabbed he slid between two cars and . . .'

'Shit,' Harry mumbled.

'That's why I've been calling. I thought you'd want to know. I mean, you weren't the best of friends or anything but . . .' She tilted her chin, raised her glass and drank down half the contents. Her mouth formed a tremulous smile. 'I was starting to think you were trying to avoid me.'

Harry quickly glanced away. It was that evasion, along with his hesitation, that ultimately betrayed him.

Her grey eyes widened. 'Oh my God,' she said. 'You *were*, weren't you?'

'No, of course not. It's just—'

'You *were*.' She leaned forward, a short brittle laugh escaping from her lips. 'You thought, because we had a few drinks last night, had a dance, had a snog in the back of a cab, that I was after something more. You thought I was one of those sad women who latch on like a limpet and never let go.'

Harry stared down at his feet. 'No, of course not.' He could have continued to lie, to protest his innocence, but after what had happened to Len Curzon the pretence felt shallow and pointless. He lifted his eyes and frowned. 'I didn't know what to think.'

Jess glared at him. 'Jeez,' she said. 'Get over yourself. I hate to burst your bubble but you're not that wonderful.'

Harry couldn't argue with that.

She knocked back her drink and stood up to pour another. 'You don't have to worry; as it happens I'm not after your body *or* your soul. I didn't even ask you round for a shoulder to cry on. I may be drunk but I'm not that drunk. This is purely professional.'

'Professional?'

'You're a private investigator, aren't you?'

Before he could reply, Jess picked up a heavy pile of files and dropped them on his knees. 'So help me to investigate. The police suspect this was just a robbery that went wrong but they're way off the mark. I found these in Len's desk.'

Harry stared down at the files. 'What are they?'

'Evidence,' she said.

'Evidence of what?'

'That this wasn't some random mugging.'

Harry nodded obligingly. 'Okay.' He opened the first file, a thick solid folder containing extensive press reports and court summaries on the trial of Paul Deacon twelve years ago. He flipped through the pages, the headlines reviving a few distant memories: *MP shoots gangster's son*; *Slaying of schoolboy*; *Deacon gets life*.

'I don't get it,' he said.

'Read the next one,' she said, still standing over him.

Harry opened the second folder. It was equally thick. He flinched as he stared at the pictures. Missing kids always made his blood run cold. This file, although it contained a number of reports, mainly concentrated on an eight-year-old, a girl who had disappeared over twenty years ago. Grace Harper was small and skinny, her hair a mousy blonde, her eyes wide and dark. He quickly flicked through the pages, scanning the story of the search, the interviews with her parents, all the newspaper coverage.

He laid the folder down and shook his head. 'And?'

'You haven't finished,' she said.

Underneath was a much slimmer dossier. The name *Ellen Shaw* was scrawled in capitals across the front. Clipped to the inside were a few blurry photos of a young dark-haired woman, some equally bad snaps of an older man, and copies of a birth and marriage certificate. Lying loose were three sheets of paper. On the first was a handwritten account of Len Curzon's surveillance at an address in Berry Square, detailing the movements of the occupants, mainly routine journeys to and from work. The second page contained a short version of the Harper family tree and the third a list of dates over the past six months, the last of which – eleven days ago – was marked with an asterisk.

Harry closed the folder and frowned. 'What's the connection between these cases?'

'Don't you see?' She sighed as if he were being deliberately obtuse. 'The girl who disappeared, Grace Harper, and this other woman Ellen Shaw. Len thought they were the same person.'

He looked up at her, astounded. 'Are you kidding?'

'Didn't he mention to you about having seen a ghost?'

'Well, yeah, but he wasn't entirely sober at the time. I didn't take him seriously.' Harry went back to the file on the missing child and examined the pictures, comparing them to the ones of Ellen Shaw. 'What do *you* think?'

'It's hard to tell. The photos of Ellen are too indistinct to make out her features properly. I'd need to see her close up. And over the years people can drastically change their appearance – especially if they want to. I mean, everyone *presumed* that Grace was dead but what if Len was right and—'

Harry wasn't convinced. 'These could be completely separate stories he was working on.'

'So why is the Harper family tree in Ellen Shaw's file? And why were all the files tied together and locked up in his drawer?'

'Locked up?'

Jess shrugged, looking momentarily defensive. 'It wasn't a very strong lock. I knew he'd been working on a story, something big. I didn't want Toby getting hold of it.' She paused. 'He's—'

'I know who he is. Your boss. The editor of the *Herald*.'

'Yeah.' She sat down again, twisting the glass between her fingers. 'And before you start presuming that I'm just after some exclusive, some great headline to grab for myself, that isn't why I took the files.'

Harry shook his head. 'I wasn't thinking that.'

'I wouldn't blame you if you were. But Toby's so superficial, so damn ambitious, he'd have found a way to turn Len's death to his own advantage.' She stared down at the long grey tip of the cigarette and then flicked it towards an over-flowing ashtray on the floor. 'I need to find out what really happened.'

'You think it was down to Deacon or Ellen Shaw?'

'Not Deacon. At least I doubt it. He's still in jail. And he was hardly a master criminal at the height of his career. I can't see him organizing anything like this at short notice.'

'So you're thinking Ellen Shaw?'

She shrugged. 'Well, he *was* killed near to where she lives.'

'But that doesn't prove—'

'It could just be a coincidence – is that what you're saying?'

'It could be,' he said. 'Why not? I mean, he was robbed, wasn't he?'

Her eyes flashed bright with anger and frustration. 'Sure, they took his wallet and phone but so what? If you wanted it to look like a mugging, you'd go through all the motions; you'd at least try and make it look convincing.'

'Have you talked to the police?'

Her grey eyes gazed almost mockingly into his. 'Of course I have. I'm not completely stupid. I spent half the afternoon there. But guess what? Ellen Shaw beat me to it. She was down the station the minute his death hit the news in the morning, admitting that she saw Len yesterday, that she talked to him briefly, even that she agreed to meet him in the afternoon. She also confessed to knowing Paul Deacon and visiting him in Maidstone jail – although she says he's just an old friend of her father's. She claims Len was trying to stir up trouble, that he was scandal-mongering, threatening to run a story about her and Deacon if she didn't agree to talk to him.'

From what he'd known of Curzon, Harry could well believe the accusation. He'd hardly been renowned for his sensitivity. 'And you think she's lying?'

'I don't think it's that simple. And of course she has the perfect alibi – at the time Len was killed she was in Gospel Oak, in full view of twenty members of staff at her husband's workplace. Don't you think that's just a touch convenient?'

Harry laid his head against the back of the sofa and sighed. 'Just out of interest, how did you find all this out?'

'I've got a few contacts down at the station, guys who owe me a favour. It was strictly off the record, naturally.'

'Naturally,' Harry murmured. 'And did you tell the police about your suspicions? About who you thought Ellen Shaw might actually be?'

Jess laughed. 'Don't be ridiculous! They'd have referred me to the nearest psychiatric unit. Much as it may surprise you, I do know when to keep my big mouth shut. For now, this is purely between us.'

Harry didn't much like the sound of this 'us' business. 'I understand how upset you are but maybe, er . . . maybe you shouldn't do anything too rash.'

'Oh please, don't patronize me. I'm not some demented, drunken, grieving female.' She paused, staring down into her glass. 'Well, I may be some of those things but I'm not completely off my head. Len was sure that this was important.'

'Len's been permanently pissed for the past ten years.'

'True,' she said. 'But that doesn't mean he couldn't spot a good story when he saw one.'

'Yeah, exactly,' Harry said. 'A *story*.'

'You don't get it,' she said. 'If this was straightforward, simple, he'd have run with it immediately. The fact that he didn't, that he waited, means that he was on to something bigger.'

Harry glanced down at his watch.

'Sorry,' she said. 'Do you need to be somewhere?'

Harry thought about Val, about the shopping in the boot of the car, about the meal he had promised to prepare. He ought to go. But then he looked at Jess and couldn't quite bring himself to leave her on her own. 'No, I'm okay for a while. Although if that drink's still on offer . . .'

She walked unsteadily to the kitchen, brought back a glass and poured him a large one. 'I'm going to take some leave,' she said.

'Good. It'll help to get away for a while.'

Jess sat down, curled her feet underneath her and softly shook her head. 'Oh, I'm not going anywhere. I've made up my mind – I'm going to finish whatever it is that Len started. And I'm going to find out who killed him.' She shot Harry a smile. 'Which, as it happens, is where you come in.'

'Me?'

'I want you to go round and talk to Ellen Shaw.'

'I can't interfere with a police investigation.'

Jess made a growling noise in the back of her throat. 'What investigation? They've let her go. She's in the clear. They don't believe she has anything to do with it.'

'Okay,' he said. 'Then let me put it another way. Why don't *you* go round and talk to her?'

'Because I'm a journalist. She isn't going to trust me.'

'And she will trust me?'

'Sure,' Jess said. 'You've got an honest face. With a bit of effort, you can probably win her confidence.'

'I hate to mention this but I've already got a full-time job.'

'Look, how long is it going to take? Half an hour at the most. And anyway, you owe me.'

Harry frowned. 'How do you figure that one out?'

'For refusing to take my calls, for mentally slandering my good name, for labelling me as a neurotic, man-stalking, weirdo female.'

'Isn't that what's referred to as emotional blackmail?'

'Call it what you like,' she said. 'I made you a copy of the files. They're on the table.'

It was almost ten o'clock by the time Harry left. She was asleep by then, stretched out on the sofa. He took what remained of the bottle of vodka into the kitchen, poured a pint of water into a glass and placed it on the floor beside her. Then he went into the bedroom, collected the duvet and covered her over. She was going to have a stinking hangover tomorrow. Still, that was more than Len Curzon was going to experience.

Harry put on his jacket and opened the front door. Then he hesitated, walked back into the room and picked up the files. Hopefully, by the morning, she'd have forgotten all about his promise to talk to Ellen Shaw but just in case . . .

He'd only had one drink, and hadn't even finished that, so it was safe enough for him to drive. Before he switched on the engine, he tried to ring Valerie. It went directly to voicemail. 'It's me,' he said. 'Hey, I'm really sorry about tonight. I got caught up with something and . . .' Perhaps it would be better to save the explanation, along with the more abject apologies, for later. 'Okay, well, I'm on my way back now. I'll see you soon.'

He put the phone down, sighed and gazed out through the windscreen. He should have called hours ago. Why hadn't he? Sometimes he was amazed by his seemingly limitless talent for bringing down grief on himself. Now she'd be mad as hell and he'd have to work twice as hard to put things right.

When he got home, the flat was in darkness. Val must have had a call-out or perhaps she was in bed already. Either way he felt a wave of relief that their next row would be postponed until daylight. He took the files and the shopping through to the kitchen and put them on the table. Turning on the kettle, he spooned some instant coffee into a mug. It was only then that he noticed the note propped up against the pepper mill. Gingerly, he reached out and picked up the scrap of paper.

Have gone to stay with Jane for a few days. I need some time alone. Please don't call. V.

Harry scowled down at the words. He found himself thinking that she wasn't going to be alone if she was staying with Jane Anderson. Why couldn't women just say what they meant? Then his heart began to sink. What she really meant was that she wanted time away from *him*. And what that really meant was . . .

Slowly, he emptied the shopping out on to the counter. The two fish gazed accusingly up at him. 'Yeah,' he said, 'I messed up. You don't need to rub it in.' When they continued to stare, he scooped them up and dumped them in the bin.

Chapter Sixteen

Tommy Lake – known to all his mates as Tommo – was of a naturally cheerful disposition, a glass half-full type of man. The approach to Christmas usually improved his mood even more, it being the time of year when people liked to splash the cash and him being the sort of guy who could always provide something for them to spend it on. Today, however, he wasn't feeling quite so optimistic.

'Come on,' he murmured. He glanced down at his watch. His customer was late. Ten thirty, he'd said, and it was already ten to eleven. Tommo stared at the rows of boxes as he paced back and forth. He kept all kinds of stuff in his warehouse. He liked to refer to it as a warehouse although really it was only an oversized lock-up with a tiny office attached. Still, it did the job all right, providing temporary storage for the illegal booze that came in from France, the hooky electronic goods, the cheap toys, the pirate DVDs and anything else he could lay his hands on.

He checked his watch again. Maybe he shouldn't hang about. Ray had warned him to keep his head down for a while, to stay out of the way. Wise words, he was sure, but he still had a living to make. This stock wasn't going to shift itself and the bloke who'd rung was talking bulk, talking cash and talking *today*. There were some opportunities too good to pass over.

Hearing a car pull up outside, he hurried over to the entrance. *At last.* He watched as a tall, fair, middle-aged man emerged from a dark green Mercedes.

'Mr Lake?'

Tommo nodded.

The man approached, smiled and put out his hand. 'We talked last night. How nice to meet. It will be a pleasure – I hope so – for us to do business.'

Tommo nodded again. His buyer had an accent, something he couldn't quite identify but which was definitely foreign. Russian perhaps? He still hadn't provided a name but that wasn't unusual. Anyway, the bloke seemed polite enough and he was happy to trade with anyone who had a willing soul and a wallet full of notes.

It was only as they stepped inside that he felt a stirring in his guts. His nerves began to jangle. There was something wrong. He could sense it. His heart missed a beat. What if . . .? With a shudder of apprehension he glanced over his shoulder to find his worst fears confirmed.

Jimmy Keppell was standing right behind him.

'Hello, Tommo,' he said.

Tommo's face turned white and his jaw fell open. He had to fight to prevent his bowels from moving in the same direction. He might have tried to leg it, to make a sprint for freedom, if three of Keppell's henchmen hadn't already blocked his path. Where they'd come from was anybody's guess. They must have arrived in another car and parked round the corner. He watched, his eyes widening with fear, as they quickly pulled the wide steel shutters down and shot the bolts across.

'Well, what have we got here?' Keppell said. He looked around. 'A real Santa's grotto.'

Raising his hands, Tommo backed away. 'I don't want no trouble, Mr Keppell.'

The bearded man turned to his associates. 'Did you hear that, boys? Little Tommo here doesn't want any trouble.'

'Of course he don't,' one of them said. 'Who wants that?'

Keppell's mouth crept into a cruel predatory kind of smile. Advancing, he slowly raised a hand, splayed his fingers and placed them around Tommo's skinny throat. He pushed his head back against the wall. 'I don't want trouble either. All I want to know is where my fucking gear is.'

Tommo swallowed hard. He should have listened to Ray. He should never have come here. 'I dunno.'

Keppell tightened his hold. 'Last chance,' he said. 'Where's that bastard Al?'

'I dunno. I swear I don't.'

Jimmy Keppell turned and gave a nod. His three goons immediately set about trashing the place, pulling the boxes down and smashing them open. As they tore the lock-up apart, destroying everything they found, the sickly stench of alcohol began to drift through the air.

'*Please*,' Tommo croaked. 'It weren't me.'

For a second, as if he might almost believe him, Keppell released his hold. But then he casually reached into his pocket and held up an item for everyone to see. Tommo stared, his heart hammering, as the bright shiny blade slid smoothly apart from its ivory handle.

Keppell leaned forward again and placed the razor against his cheek. 'Start talking, you little ginger shit.'

'I swear,' Tommo said, trembling. 'I wouldn't steal from you, Mr Keppell. I *wouldn't*. *Never*. I helped Al load the booze into the van. There were twenty cases. The charlie was hidden inside. It didn't take long. He was out of here by six thirty.'

Tommo was aware of the movement, the swift easy slice, before he fully realized what had happened. He felt the pain a second later, sharp and fierce and then suddenly liquid as the blood poured down his face. Instinctively, he opened his mouth to cry out but Keppell's huge sweaty palm crushed hard against his lips.

'Tell me more,' Keppell urged. He lifted his hand just enough for Tommo to be able to speak.

'Al couldn't have guessed,' Tommo mumbled. 'Someone must have told him. All the cases felt the same. I made sure of that.' And he had been careful, comparing the boxes, lifting them and putting them down, removing and adding bottles until he was certain that there was no discernible difference in weight. 'Someone must have tipped him off.'

'And who could that of been?'

Tommo shook his head. His teeth were making a weird chattering sound. 'I was only storing the s-stuff for the night. I didn't say nothing, not a word, not to no one. I don't go looking for grief, Mr Keppell.'

Jimmy Keppell smiled. 'You know, if it was only me I might just give you the benefit of the doubt – but it's not just me, is it?' He looked across at the tall fair man who was standing, quietly watching, with his arms folded across his chest. 'What do you think I should do?'

'I think you should cut off his cock,' the blond man said.

Tommo's eyes widened with horror. 'No,' he begged. 'What about Ray? Have you talked to Ray?'

'Are you saying Stagg double-crossed me?'

'He's Al's brother-in-law, ain't he?' Tommo had known Ray for most of his life but had reached that level of fear where loyalty no longer existed.

Keppell lowered the blade, took a step back and calmly lit a cigarette. 'The thing is, Tommo, it's a question of respect. You know how it is. I've been ripped off and . . . well, someone's got to be seen to have paid. You do understand that, don't you?'

Tommo sincerely hoped that he didn't. But this wasn't the time for misplaced optimism. As he stared into Keppell's evil eyes, he knew exactly what was coming. He wanted to run but his legs were paralysed. He wanted to scream but no one was listening. A warm flow of piss began to run down his thigh.

Chapter Seventeen

It was almost three o'clock when DS Valerie Middleton arrived at the bland, sprawling industrial estate. It was a maze but she had no difficulty in finding the place she was looking for; already a set of spotlights had been erected, illuminating the inside and outside of the building. She parked the Citroën, got out and forged a path through the milling crowd of white coats. Holding her breath, she let her gaze roam slowly around the lock-up before reluctantly bringing her eyes back to rest on the gruesome remains of Tommy Lake.

Dean Chapman, the pathologist, placed his hand on her arm. 'You're not going to hurl, are you? Only we don't want the site contaminated.'

Frowning, she threw him a sideways glance. 'Do I *look* like I'm about to hurl?'

'Do you want an honest answer to that?'

Val turned her face away, grateful that she hadn't eaten breakfast or lunch. At least that was something she could thank Harry for. She had an instinctive urge to make a dash for the door but refused to give her colleagues the satisfaction. Even in these times of alleged equality, she still felt a constant obligation to disprove any lingering suspicions of women being the 'weaker sex'.

As though he could read her mind, Chapman squeezed her elbow and laughed. 'If it's any consolation, Mr Holt's still recovering outside.'

It *was* a consolation, if a small one. DI Frankie Holt was a sharp-faced, middle-aged, abrasive man who called himself 'old-school', a term which apparently precluded the use of manners, patience or any form of tolerance.

'So what have we got?' she said.

'He's been dead a few hours, no more.'

'Right.' Valerie took a deep breath and regretted it. It was the smell that made it worse, the repulsive combination of spilled booze, urine and that weird almost metallic odour of blood.

'Death from a thousand cuts,' Chapman said. 'Very dramatic – but not the tidiest way to go.'

There was no disputing that. The evidence of Tommy's slow and painful demise was splattered all over the floor and walls. Valerie stared at the damage, at the multiple slashes to his face, arms and legs, but the very worst was something she could barely bring herself to look at – his left foot, hanging by a thread, had been almost completely severed from his ankle.

'My God,' she said, half-closing her eyes and sinking her chin into her scarf. She didn't understand it. Tommy Lake had been a villain but only ever small-time; he'd dealt in stolen goods, smuggled booze, a bit of puff but nothing more. Why should anyone want to do this to him? He had been one of those strangely likeable guys, never aggressive, always polite, even when they'd pulled him in, as they so often had, on one minor charge or another. Avoiding his bloodied contorted face, Val made another rapid survey of his body. His T-shirt that had once been white was stained a bright disgusting shade of scarlet.

'Some kind of cut-throat razor,' Chapman said. 'From what I can see, he died from—'

'Yes,' Val said. 'I don't think you need to spell it out.'

'I'll have a full report by tomorrow.'

It was a relief when she could step outside again. Valerie gratefully drank in the air. It was hardly fresh but even the traffic fumes were better than what she'd recently been breathing. DI Holt was giving out instructions to a group of uniformed PCs. A small crowd of onlookers had grown since she'd arrived, the news of a killing having spread rapidly around the neighbourhood. It never ceased to amaze her how people liked to come and gawp; as if murder was a spectator sport, there was always a dubious minority who wanted to share in the experience.

'You okay?' Holt said as she joined him.

She nodded. 'Just about. It's not the prettiest sight in the world. And it's odd too, don't you think?'

'What do you mean?'

'Why anyone should do this to Tommo.' She found herself automatically using his nickname. 'I mean, this is more like a gangland killing, isn't it? And he was never in that league.'

Holt shrugged. 'Maybe he got over-ambitious.'

'No,' she said. 'He wasn't the type.'

'The place is full of illicit booze.'

'Of *smashed* illicit booze,' she corrected him. The lock-up had been trashed but this was no robbery. 'And it wasn't worth that much when it was all in one piece. Do you think this could be connected to Ray Stagg?'

'What makes you say that?'

'Just that they were mates, always have been since they were kids. Tommo had plenty of opportunities to go the same way, to move up into the seriously big money, but he didn't. That's why this is so odd. Maybe someone's using poor Tommo to send a message to Stagg.'

Holt didn't look impressed. 'He probably just got greedy.'

'Yes, but—'

'And idle speculation isn't going to get us anywhere. So start asking around, see if anyone saw anything. Let's do some proper police work before we go jumping to any conclusions.'

'Yes, guv,' she said obediently.

Chapter Eighteen

Jess had woken up as the early morning light spilled through the window. Feeling like an axe had been embedded in her skull she had drunk some of the water from the glass she had found on the floor, pulled the duvet over her head, curled up and gone back to sleep again. It was after noon before she'd finally surfaced, dragging herself off the sofa and stumbling into the bathroom.

Now, three hours later, she was hunched over her fifth cup of strong black coffee trying to make sense of the day before. The atmosphere in the office was heavy and subdued. No one could quite believe what had happened. Jess had only come in to clear her desk, to make sure everything was in order before starting her leave, but she hadn't yet been able to drag herself away. It was at times like these that you needed company and she couldn't bear the thought of going home to an empty flat.

She missed having someone around, someone to talk to. What was her ex, Callum, doing now? Probably lounging on a beach in Goa, his long brown legs entwined around some sun-bronzed hippy chick. Perhaps she *should* have gone with him to India. The problem was she hadn't wanted to. It was his big adventure not hers. She hadn't wanted to see the world, to live out of the meagre resources of a rucksack, and she especially hadn't wanted to 'find herself'. She had decided, seven days before their departure date, that she had a different dream – she was going to train as a journalist instead. That decision had made her one of the oldest junior reporters in town but she didn't care. It was a job that she loved and she knew she'd made the right decision. From the moment she'd got here, Len had taken her under his wing and . . .

Jess sank her face into the cup of coffee. Len Curzon had become her mentor, her friend, her drinking companion. There were no words to express how much she would miss him. And yes, he had driven her crazy at times but at this precise moment she'd have done anything to have those times back again. Feeling the tears pricking her eyes, she quickly shuffled the papers in front of her and tried to concentrate on something else.

Her thoughts drifted back to the empty flat. She was almost thirty and her love life was on the rocks. The nearest she'd got to any kind of relationship over the past twelve months was a quick fumble in the back of a taxi with a man who'd felt so guilty he wouldn't even take her calls. Thinking of Harry, she wondered if he'd been round to see Ellen Shaw yet. At least he'd taken the files off the table; that had to be a good sign.

It was twenty to four when the direct line on Len's desk started ringing. A silence fell over the room. Everyone looked at everyone else. Jess hoped it would stop but it didn't. It just kept ringing and ringing. Eventually, as she was closest, she stood up, lifted the receiver to her ear and murmured softly, 'Hello?'

'I want to speak to Len,' a male voice said.

Jess flinched, her fingers tightening round the phone. 'I'm afraid he's not . . . available.'

'When's he back then?'

'Er . . .'

'I need to talk. It's well urgent, man. Do you have his mobile number?'

'I'm sorry but . . . Can I ask who's calling?'

'It's BJ, ain't it.'

The name rang a bell somewhere in the back of her head. 'BJ?' she repeated.

'Yeah,' he said. 'Len came to see me the other week. Said he'd get back and all but I ain't heard nothing. I need to know what's going on.'

'Could I ask what this is about?'

A hint of suspicion crept into his voice. 'It's Len I want. I ain't talking to no one else.'

'Okay,' she said, 'but I'm afraid that won't be possible. There was . . . erm, there was an . . . *incident* yesterday and he . . .' She turned her back on the rest of the room but still couldn't quite bring herself to say it. The cold bleak fact choked in her throat and refused to come out.

'He hurt or something?'

'Worse,' she murmured. 'He's . . .'

There was a brief silence.

'Fuck, man,' he said. 'You mean . . .'

'Yes,' she said softly.

'Fuck,' he said again. 'What happened?'

That wasn't something she either wanted or was fully able to explain. 'I'm sorry but it's still a bit confused. It's been a shock for all of us.' She stared down at Len's desk, swept clean of its usual heap of paper. It was the unusual lack of mess that brought the reality crashing down on her with a renewed and terrible force. 'So, unless there's some way *I* can help?'

'Nah, I don't reckon.'

Jess was about to put down the phone when his name suddenly fell into place. BJ – Jay Barrington – was one of Len's contacts, a small-time villain always in and out of jail. She remembered him now, a massive guy, six foot five or more, with a wide gappy smile. 'Hold on,' she said. 'I think we've met before, haven't we? At The Bell, in Shoreditch. This is Jess, Jessica Vaughan. I work . . . I used to work closely with Len. Perhaps there's something you can do to help *me*.'

'Huh?'

'Do you have a minute?' she said. It was a long shot but she was thinking that if Len had been to see him recently, BJ might know something useful. 'I can call you back.'

A hollow laugh floated down the line. 'Not here, babe. No incoming calls to this joint.'

So BJ was back in the slammer again. 'Where are you?' she said.

'Maidstone,' he replied.

'Right,' she said, her heart leaping in her chest. *That was where Paul Deacon was currently residing too.* She'd seen a press cutting on the transfer when she'd been researching all his history for Len. She tried to keep her voice casual. 'Okay, I'll make it quick. Look, how about if I come and see you? I'm trying to sort everything out, you know, after . . .'

He hesitated. 'Nah, it don't matter.'

'It matters to *me*,' she insisted. Then, building on that initial hesitation, she swiftly added an incentive: 'Whatever Len promised. Same terms, right? You can trust me.'

His tone brightened a fraction. 'Same terms?'

'Absolutely,' she said, without having a clue as to what she was actually promising.

There was another short pause while he mulled the proposition over.

'So?' she said. 'Do we have a deal?'

'Okay,' he agreed. 'But not over the phone, man.'

'Then I'll come to you. Send the visiting order to the office, to me, Jess Vaughan.' She carefully spelled out her surname. 'I'll see you soon.'

Returning to her own desk, Jess slowly gathered her things together. This BJ lead could be just the break she needed. And even it wasn't, even if it all came to nothing, well, it still had to be better than sitting around feeling sorry for herself. It was time to get motivated. There was work to be done, files to be studied, a past to be raked over. If the cops weren't going to find Len's killer then she'd damn well do it herself.

Chapter Nineteen

Five times Harry had tried to call but Val still wasn't picking up. Not that he was surprised. He'd let her down, yet again, and it was going to take more than a few mumbled apologies to sort it out. Having the solicitor from hell, the ball-breaking Jane Anderson, whispering in her ear wasn't going to help matters either. He could imagine the kind of support that was coming from her direction: *He's not good enough for you; He doesn't treat you with respect; He isn't ever going to change.* That woman had always hated his guts.

Just to add to his frustration he wasn't making much progress down Romford market. As he went from stall to stall, working through Denise's list, he received the same repetitive replies: yes, on the Saturday Al had been his normal self; yes, he'd packed up at the usual time; no, they hadn't noticed anything odd.

It was a chilly afternoon and Harry shifted from foot to foot as he waited for Ben Taylor to finish serving. The air was filled with the smell of roasting chestnuts, hot dogs and fried onions. Breath rose from the mouths of the jostling crowd in small white clouds of steam. A waterfall of tinsel descended from Taylor's stall, yet another reminder – should one be needed – of the rapid approach of Christmas.

Eventually the customer left, weighed down with decorations of various shapes and sizes, with stars and angels and little plastic reindeer. Taylor turned to nod at him. 'How can I help you, guv?'

Harry went through his well-worn explanation of what he was doing there, how he'd been hired by Denise Webster, how he was searching for Al.

Ben Taylor was a short stocky man, middle-aged, with a mop of brown curly hair. His cheeks were ruddy from the cold. 'Still not shown up then?'

'No,' Harry said. 'Do you know where he is?'

It was perhaps the unexpected directness of the question that caught Taylor off guard. Something stirred in his eyes. Lifting a hand to his face, he quickly looked away. 'Sorry, I've not seen him since that Saturday.'

Harry sensed there was more. 'If you remember *anything*,' he persisted, 'however small. Denise is worried sick. It's been over a week. Al could be in trouble or, even if he isn't, well, she deserves to know the truth – whatever it is.'

Taylor hesitated, his forehead creasing with indecision. 'It could be nothing.'

'You could be right but—'

'How much are these?' a woman asked. She stretched out a finger to point at a selection of glittering baubles.

'Three for a pound, love.'

'Go on then. I'll take half a dozen.'

Harry watched while he dropped the sale into a carrier bag, took the money and gave her the change. After she had gone, Taylor kept his eyes averted. As if in two minds as to whether he should talk, he made a few unnecessary adjustments to his stock, shifting the holly wreaths slightly to the left, to the right, and then back to the left again.

'Have you seen him?' Harry said.

Taylor lifted his head again. 'Not since . . .' He pushed his hands deep into his pockets, hunched his shoulders and glanced uneasily around the market.

'Since?' Harry prompted.

'You won't go telling Denise, will you?'

'I can't promise that, not if—'

Taylor frowned. 'I mean, you won't mention it was *me* who

101

told you. Only she won't be best pleased. She rang when he didn't turn up and . . .'

'And you didn't tell her that you'd seen him.'

'I *didn't* see him, not after he left here.' He hesitated again before finally deciding to spill. 'But we *did* talk – on the phone, on the Saturday night, about quarter to seven. Could have been a bit earlier now I come to think of it. I'm not sure. I was in the pub with the lads and we'd had a few by then. We were heading off for a curry. I rang Al to see if he fancied it.'

'And did he?'

'No, he said he was busy, that he had things to do.'

Harry waited but he didn't elaborate. 'And that was it?'

'He was in the van. He was driving. I could hear the engine running and the sound of the traffic. But the thing is . . . er, I think he had someone with him.'

'Someone?'

Taylor puckered up his mouth as if his imminent betrayal was leaving a bad taste. 'A woman,' he said shortly.

'Are you sure?'

'Pretty much. She was talking, laughing in the background. Al put his hand over the phone for a few seconds. I didn't catch what he said to her. That's why I didn't mention it to Denise. I thought, you know, that . . .'

'Yeah,' Harry said. 'I understand.' He felt a stab of disappointment. It was beginning to look like Ray Stagg was right after all. 'And you've got no idea of who she might have been?'

'Sorry,' Taylor said.

'But Al didn't usually . . . I mean, he wasn't in the habit of—'

'How should I know?' Taylor snapped, perhaps already regretting that he had said as much as he had. 'I'm not his bloody keeper.'

Harry pressed the button and felt relief when, for once, the doors actually closed and the aged lift juddered into action. He wasn't in any fit state to climb three flights to the office. His

102

leg, for no reason he could fathom, had embarked on another of its dull persistent aches.

As he walked into the office, Maddie was sitting there again, swinging her legs and gazing determinedly down at a slim, state-of-the-art, metallic blue phone.

'Expecting a call?' he said.

She looked up, her pale face flushing. 'What?'

Harry grinned back at her. He might be pushing forty but he hadn't forgotten what it felt like to wait for that one special call. First love was always a killer. It turned you inside out and made your guts churn over. His first major crush had been on a blonde angel-faced girl called Charlotte Parr; she had smashed his heart into a thousand pieces. How old had he been? About fourteen, he thought, a little older than Maddie but with no more experience and a lot less sense.

'You want a coffee?'

'Yeah,' she said. 'Ta.' As if it was as precious as a piece of bone china, she laid the phone carefully on the chair beside her.

'Is the sitter still sick?'

She shrugged, took the coffee from him and then picked up the phone again. 'You know, I'm not even sure if this is working. Could you give me a ring from yours so I can test it?'

'I'm sure it's okay.'

'Please,' she said. 'Come on, it's not as though it's going to cost you anything. I'm not going to answer it. I just want to see if it rings.'

'It looks fine. I'm sure—'

'Just lend it to me for a sec.' She held out her hand, her eyes flashing with a solemn combination of despair and expectation.

Reluctantly, he passed it over. She tapped in the number and waited. As her phone sprang into life, Harry flinched. He saw her face fall and felt an instant rush of sympathy. He wished he could tell her about how fleeting the pain was, about how it would pass, but he knew she wouldn't listen. At her age he wouldn't have listened either.

'He said he'd call me at five,' she said.

Harry glanced at his watch. It was getting on for six. Retrieving his phone, he tried to sound casual. 'He's probably just been held up somewhere – or maybe his battery's run down.'

'Yeah, right,' she mumbled.

He might have said more but there was no point in raising her hopes. And although he never liked to make superficial judgements, if Zane Keppell *was* anything like his grandfather then she was better off without him.

Harry had come back intending to have a talk to Mac, to run over the day's events, but now he was wishing that he'd gone straight home. From what he could observe through the slatted blinds of the inner office, Mac was no more in the mood for a cosy little chat than Maddie was; deep in conversation with Lorna, he looked like the burdens of the world were on his shoulders.

And it occurred to Harry, if rather late, that he had problems of his own that needed sorting. He went out into the hallway and rang Valerie again. He paced the floor, expecting to hear her voicemail, but surprisingly she picked up. 'Hey, it's me,' he said.

'I know.'

'I'm really sorry about last night.'

A long slow sigh was the only response.

'Val?'

He heard her draw breath again. 'Why do you keep calling? I left a note. I presume you've read it. I'm just wondering what part of "don't ring me" you don't understand.'

'We need to talk,' he said.

'That would be a first.'

'There was a reason for last night,' he said. 'A good one.'

'There always is.'

'I'm serious. I should have let you know but—'

'Look,' she interrupted. 'I haven't got time for this. I've got Holt breathing down my neck. I'm trying to deal with a possible gangland murder, two outstanding assaults, a hit-and-run and a post office robbery.'

'A gangland murder?'

'At the Kepton Industrial Estate.'

Harry paused. The estate was in Hackney, not that far from Stagg's club. 'Christ, it's not Al Webster, is it?'

She made a hissing sound through her teeth. 'Oh right, so that's the real reason you rang, to check up on your missing person?'

'No, of course it's not. I was just—'

But she'd already hung up.

Chapter Twenty

After another restless night, Harry's head was filled with the odd floating remnants of dreams. The artificial light of the café made his eyes feel tired and scratchy. Although it was almost ten o'clock, it was more like dusk outside; the sky was low, grey and threatening. He glanced through the window at the gathering clouds.

The murder of Tommy Lake was front page in the local paper. The detail was scarce but, reading between the lines, Harry could imagine the brutality of his death. He sipped on his espresso and stared down at the article. Val was right – this had to be a gangland killing – but what on earth had a small-timer like Tommo done to bring down such a punishment?

Now there was a missing man and a vicious murder and both were connected to Ray Stagg. *He* wouldn't be feeling too cheerful today.

Harry read through the first few paragraphs of the report again and wondered how the inquiry was going. Of course Val would know the answer to that but he couldn't ask. At the moment, apparently, he wasn't even allowed to speak to her. He had tried to call again last night but Jane had answered her phone instead. Ms Anderson had been her usual charming self.

'For God's sake, Harry, she's told you she wants time alone. Just give her some space, can't you? She'll call you when she's good and ready.'

Which, if Anderson got her way, would probably be never. In a former age, that harridan would have been burned as a witch. It was an age Harry couldn't help feeling a certain misty fondness for.

He was still quietly seething when Jess appeared at the table. 'You're late,' he said, taking out his irritation on her.

'Barely,' she said. 'Do you ever use public transport? I had to wait half an hour for a bus.' She was dressed for the weather in a long grey trench coat, boots, scarf, gloves and a woollen hat stretched down over her ears. Pulling out a chair, she sat down opposite him. 'So what's eating you – got a hangover?'

'No.'

She grinned. 'Must be woman trouble then.'

Harry glared at her. 'I've got a busy morning, that's all.'

Jess caught the eye of the waitress and ordered a coffee. Then she turned to Harry and said, 'Does that mean what I think it does? Please don't tell me you're backing out. You *promised* you'd talk to her.'

'I'm here, aren't I? All I'm saying is that I haven't got much time.' In truth, he had been wondering if there was some way he could wriggle out of it – an awkward conversation with Ellen Shaw was the last thing he needed today – but faced with Jess's beseeching expression he didn't have the heart to let her down. 'I'll do this but then that's it, okay? I've got a case of my own to work on.'

'There's no need to make it sound like such a favour. If you really don't want to do it—'

'I will. I've already said I would.'

Her coffee came. She picked it up and took a sip. Then she reached out, took hold of the newspaper and flipped it around to study the headline. 'You think Jimmy Keppell was responsible for this?'

'He's not the only gangster in town.'

'His style though; he's a nasty bastard.' She paused. 'You know Paul Deacon killed Keppell's son?'

'And?'

'And so Len was looking into the case again. Maybe he was on to something, something that Keppell didn't want him finding out about.'

Harry's brows shot up. He sympathized with her need for answers but this latest theory was stretching it a bit. 'I thought Ellen Shaw was your number one suspect. What are you suggesting now – that it was Jimmy Keppell?'

'There's no need to sound so sceptical.' She stared at him accusingly. 'I'm simply keeping an open mind. Isn't that what all good detectives are supposed to do?'

Harry sat in the car and stared up at the top-floor windows of number twelve Berry Square. He still thought this was a bad idea. Jess was clutching at straws and if Ellen Shaw wasn't prepared to talk then he wasn't going to push her. He didn't intend to end up on a harassment charge.

According to Curzon's notes, she didn't usually work on Thursdays. Harry had tried the bell but got no reply. Rain was starting to spatter against the windscreen, the heavy drops heralding the onset of a storm. In the distance he heard a faint rumble of thunder. Well, he wasn't going to wait around forever. He had things to do, people to see – and Ray Stagg was top of the list. It could be useful to catch him today, off-balance and still reeling from Tommo's brutal death. Not the nicest of considerations perhaps but then Stagg, with his history of inflicting misery on others, was hardly deserving of an excess of compassion.

He'd give her fifteen more minutes, he decided, and if she hadn't shown up he'd head over to Shoreditch. Or maybe it wasn't even worth waiting that long. She could be gone for hours. He leaned forward to put the key in the ignition but then glanced up into the rear-view mirror and saw a small female figure hurrying down the street.

Was that her? The woman was wearing a red coat but her face was disguised by a large black umbrella. Even if her features hadn't been covered, he wasn't sure he could have recognized her from Curzon's blurry set of snaps. He waited until she'd walked through the gateway before jumping briskly out of the car.

'Excuse me. Ellen Shaw?'

She turned, cautious enough not to say yes or no, but her response was as good as any affirmation. He quickly joined her at the foot of the steps. Then, as she lifted her umbrella, he saw those wide dark eyes for the very first time. There was something about their intensity that caught him off guard. In fact, her entire face was amazing, not beautiful perhaps but so thoroughly striking as to be quite unforgettable. He found himself stumbling over his words. 'Er . . . my name's . . . er . . . Harry Lind. Could you possibly spare a minute?'

She stared silently up at him.

'It's about Len Curzon.'

'I've already told you everything I know.'

He stared back at her, bemused. 'I'm sorry?'

'I came down the station on Tuesday. I gave a statement.'

Harry wondered if he had 'cop' indelibly engraved across his forehead. 'No,' he explained, 'I'm not from the police.'

He noticed her mouth tighten, suspicion flying instantly into her eyes. 'Who are you then?'

'My name's Harry Lind,' he said again, feeling slightly foolish as he realized he was repeating himself. 'I knew Len. I just wanted to—'

She shook her head, at the same time pulling out her keys from a small leather bag. 'I've got nothing to say to you.'

'I'm not a journalist,' he said. 'I promise. I'm not after any story, any lurid Sunday exclusive.' He rummaged in his pocket, found a business card and passed it over to her. 'Actually I'm a private investigator. A friend of mine was close to Len and this has all been very hard for her.'

She looked at the card, looked at Harry and then abruptly shook her head again. She passed him back the card. 'I don't see how I can help. I wish I could but, as I told you, I've already given a statement.'

'I know,' he said, 'and I appreciate the awkward position this has put you in. I really wouldn't ask but it's been such a shock for her. I think it would help if she could just tie up a few loose ends and draw a line under it all. She knows that you had nothing to do with Len's death but because you were the last person to see him—'

'Not *exactly* the last,' she said.

'No, I'm sorry. I didn't mean—'

Suddenly a flash of lightning split open the sky. A few seconds later a loud clap of thunder made them both jump. Then the heavens opened. As the rain hammered against the pavement, Harry conceded defeat. If she wasn't prepared to cooperate he couldn't make her, and standing here doing an impersonation of a drowned rat was hardly likely to improve his chances.

But then, unexpectedly, she raised those wide dark eyes and smiled. 'You're getting soaked. You'd better come inside.'

'Thank you,' he said. He had no idea what had made her change her mind but he wasn't complaining. He followed her up the steps and then, on the doorstep, took a moment to wipe his feet and shake off the rain.

'It's the top floor.'

'Right,' he said, hoping that his leg could endure a mountaineering expedition. But his spirits sank as she started up the stairs, taking them two at a time and at the kind of pace he couldn't possibly keep up with. Gripping the rail of the banisters, he watched as her slim shapely ankles disappeared round a bend in the stairwell.

She must have realized he was lagging because on the first-floor landing she stopped and glanced over her shoulder. 'Are you okay?'

'Fine,' he said.

'You've hurt your leg.'

'It's nothing,' he said, halting for a moment to catch his breath. 'You go on ahead. I may be slow but I usually make it in the end.'

She nodded. 'We're almost there.'

By the time Harry reached the flat she had switched on a couple of lamps. The living room, with its tall panelled windows and front-facing view over the central square of green, was spacious and pleasantly warm. He shrugged off his dripping overcoat.

'Here,' she said, 'let me put that over a radiator.'

'Thank you.'

She gestured towards a wide red velvet sofa. 'Please, take a seat. Would you like a coffee?'

'Tea,' he said, 'if it's not too much trouble. I've been on the caffeine all morning. It doesn't do much for the stress levels.'

As Ellen went into the kitchen, Harry settled gratefully into the soft plump cushions and examined his surroundings. He wasn't sure what he'd expected but certainly nothing as unusual as this. Although the walls were painted a pale shade of cream, that was the only nod towards neutrality; the rest was a riot of colour, brilliant splashes of ruby, emerald and gold. At his feet a slightly tattered Persian rug lay across the bare polished boards. There wasn't anything that looked especially new or expensive but that was part of its charm. It was dramatic, even exotic, but also comfortable and inviting, the kind of place you could relax in. He thought of his own bland flat and was suddenly aware of how little effort he had put in to making it a home.

Ellen came back with two mugs of tea and passed one over to him. She sat down at the other end of the sofa, crossed her legs and gave a sympathetic smile. 'I'm sorry about your friend,' she said. 'And I wish I could help but apart from what I told the police . . .'

'Even that would be useful,' Harry said.

'I take it they haven't found anyone?'

'It's early yet but no, it seems there hasn't been much progress.'

She sighed into her mug. 'That's a shame.'

Harry couldn't take his eyes off her. She was wearing a simple round-necked sea-blue jumper, a black skirt and a pair of black high-heeled shoes with tiny bows on the front. He couldn't say what it was that attracted him. The odd thing was that she wasn't his type at all. Tall leggy blondes had always been the ones to press his buttons and Ellen Shaw was the complete antithesis: small and dark, she was almost doll-like with her smooth porcelain skin and silky black hair.

'I understand Len talked to you on the morning before—'

'We had a brief conversation.' She looked down into her tea before slowly lifting her gaze again. 'To be honest, it wasn't an entirely pleasant one.'

'No,' Harry said. From his own encounters with Len Curzon, he could well believe it. 'I'm afraid journalists aren't exactly renowned for their tact and diplomacy. I'm sorry if he upset you.'

As if to convey that it was all water under the bridge, Curzon's suffering being ultimately much greater than her own, she gave a small dismissive shrug. 'I suppose you know that he was asking about Paul Deacon?'

Harry nodded. 'From what I can gather, he was researching the original trial and somehow his inquiries led him to you.'

Ellen frowned. 'The trial? Wasn't that over twelve years ago? I didn't even know Paul then. I can't claim to know him that well *now*. We only met for the first time six months ago. He was a friend of my father's.' She paused and her dark eyes, welling with tears, took on a liquid quality. 'My father died last year and I wrote to let Paul know and . . . well, he asked me to visit.'

'I'm sorry,' Harry said. He seemed to be doing nothing *but* apologize and felt a sharp pang of guilt at inflicting even more distress on a woman who had clearly been through enough already. Why on earth had he ever let Jess talk him into this?

'It's all right,' she said, as if reading his mind. 'Don't feel bad about it. I understand what it means to want answers. I'd feel exactly the same if I was in your friend's position.'

Her voice, with its hint of an Irish lilt, was extraordinarily seductive. Harry smiled back at her. 'That's very kind of you.'

'The trouble is that I'm not sure how much I can really help. When it comes to Mr Curzon, all I can presume is that he must have seen us at Maidstone prison, seen me with Paul, and jumped to some rather fanciful conclusions. In fact, he may even have followed me back here.' A visible shiver rippled through her body. 'Oh, that's a weird thought, isn't it? Do you think he did?'

'It's a possibility,' Harry said.

'And so he could have . . . I mean, he could have been *watching* me for months.'

Harry, recalling Curzon's sketchy surveillance notes, quickly shook his head. 'I don't think so. I got the impression it was something rather more recent.'

Her red lips slipped into the semblance of a smile. 'Am I being paranoid? This has all been so . . . I'm not even sure how to explain it.' She stared down at the floor. 'But do you know what I can't help thinking? If I *had* gone to meet him that day, if I hadn't left him sitting in that café, then he might not have—'

'Christ,' Harry said. 'You can't think like that. Whatever happened to Len wasn't your fault.'

'I should have told him the truth there and then, when he asked me. Why didn't I?' She slid her hands down her thighs in a flat-palmed gesture of frustration. 'I panicked. I imagined the kind of story he was intending to write, realized how upset my husband would be and just wanted to shake the guy off. That's why I agreed to meet him later, so he wouldn't go ahead and write anything before I had the chance to talk to Adam. I never thought . . .'

'So your husband didn't know that you were visiting Paul Deacon?'

Ellen slowly lifted her head. 'I should have told him. I wish I had. But Adam's a decent man, respectable, and I knew he'd hate the idea of me going into a prison. When I went to see Paul for the first time I didn't expect to go back. It was just a one-off, something I thought my father would want me to do, but then when I realized how few visitors he got I felt sorry for him and . . . I couldn't see the harm in going again.' She stopped, took a few deep breaths and gazed directly into his eyes. 'I don't suppose you approve of wives having secrets from their husbands.'

'I'm not a husband,' he said.

'But you're no stranger to secrets.'

Harry flinched at the remark, instantly reminded not only of what he was doing here but also of the evening he'd spent with Jess, the wine and the music, the laughs and the fumbled kisses in the back of a cab – while Valerie was waiting for him and Len was already lying dead on a cold grey pavement. None of it sat too easily with his conscience.

As if sensing his discomfort, she quickly continued, 'What I mean is that you must stumble across plenty of secrets in your line of work.'

'A few,' he agreed, relieved that she hadn't been referring to anything more personal. 'So have you been married for long?'

'Seven years. We met when I came over from Ireland.'

He glanced around the room but there were no wedding pictures on display. He would have liked to have asked why she'd got hitched to a man so much older than herself – he had read the marriage certificate – but it was too personal a question and anyway he would then have to explain how he knew about the age difference and that in turn would lead back to Len Curzon's somewhat disturbing scrutiny of her life. 'So what made you come over to London?'

She smiled again. 'Oh, the usual reasons: itchy feet, wanting to see somewhere else, to meet new people. You know what it's like when you're young; you can never wait to get away.'

Harry smiled back, understanding exactly what she meant. He had escaped from the suffocating claustrophobia of his own home when he was seventeen and it had felt like a major liberation. 'So what part of Ireland do you come from?'

'Cork originally,' she said, 'but we moved to Dublin when I was a baby and that's where I grew up. How about you? Have you always lived here?'

'More or less,' he said evasively. With his father now residing comfortably on the south coast there was no need for Harry to ever return to, or to even think about, the small northern town he had been raised in. Along with the accent, he had long since managed to consign that painful part of his existence to the dim and distant past.

But Ellen Shaw was unwilling to let him off so easily. 'More or less?' she repeated, her dark brows arching.

With anyone else, Harry would have clammed up. It's what he usually did. That era of his life was over – he *never* talked about it – but there was something about her, about her dark eyes and the lilting softness of her voice, which made him eager to confide.

'I grew up in the north,' he murmured, 'but I haven't been back in years.'

'Why not?'

Harry opened his mouth with every intention of explaining but then, like a warning, another loud clap of thunder shook the room and he had second thoughts. 'Oh, it doesn't matter. It's a long story.'

She paused, waiting a few seconds before she finally nodded. 'Maybe you'll tell it to me one day.'

'Maybe I will.' Like a shy teenage boy who had just been offered the vague chance of a date, Harry felt a thrill run through his body. Immediately, he tried to quash it. She was a married woman and he was . . . he wasn't quite sure what he was but certainly not in the position where he should be having any thoughts like these. God, he had to get back on track before he lost the plot completely.

The pause that had occurred was gradually growing into a silence. Harry tried to recall what else Jess had asked him to find out. She had specifically told him not to mention Grace Harper's name. *In case she realizes that we're on to her.* But Jess, he was sure, was barking up the wrong tree. Ellen was no more Grace Harper than he was. Still, unless he wanted major earache for the rest of the day, he'd better try and get some answers to her questions.

'Look, I hope you don't mind me asking,' he said, 'but have you ever heard of a man called Jimmy Keppell?'

Ellen hesitated, a shadow passing over her face. Her voice was more cautious when she spoke again. 'Of course I have. Paul shot his son.'

'Do you have any idea why?'

She looked at him, astounded. 'Why should I? We've never talked about things like that.'

'And you've never been curious?'

Ellen thought about it and frowned. 'I've always presumed that it was some kind of lovers' tiff.'

'*Is* Deacon gay?'

'I don't know.' She shrugged. 'It's hardly the kind of subject that comes up in general conversation. He was married but . . .' As if she'd already said too much, Ellen glanced down. She ran her hands nervously along the length of her thighs again. 'I suppose some men find it difficult to accept who they are. *What* they are. My father always thought that Paul was a little . . . ambiguous about what he wanted.'

'Ambiguous?'

Ellen sighed. 'He didn't spell it out. My father was a good Catholic man and the word "bisexual" never crossed his lips. He'd have rather drowned himself in the Liffey. It was only hints, you know, things he said occasionally.'

'Right,' Harry said. 'And do you have any idea what happened to Paul's wife?'

'Charlotte?' She gave another tiny shake of her head. 'She divorced him as soon as she could. She may still be living in London but I've no idea where.'

There was an even longer pause while Harry racked his brains for other questions he could ask.

Ellen glanced at the clock on the mantelpiece. 'I don't mean to be rude, Mr Lind, but unless there was anything else?'

'No,' Harry said, reluctantly getting to his feet. 'I don't think so. But thank you for your time. I appreciate it – and I'm sure my friend will as well.' Actually he wasn't sure if Jess would appreciate it; he had the feeling she wouldn't be too impressed with the outcome of this particular encounter but there wasn't much he could do about that.

116

'Well, I hope they find whoever did it.' She retrieved his coat from the radiator, now only slightly damp and passed it over to him.

'Thanks,' Harry said again. In the hallway, he took a card from his pocket and laid it on the small mahogany table. 'Just in case you think of anything else.'

Chapter Twenty-One

DI Frankie Holt looked like he'd swallowed a poisonous toad. His prominent Adam's apple leapt up and down in his throat. 'What the fuck's going on?'

Ray Stagg gazed at him with contempt. He hated the filth, always had and always would, and he hated the tame ones even more than the straight. Give them an inch and they'd take a mile. Give them a grand and they'd ask for ten. They always thought they were in control, always pulling the strings, until something like this happened and then they weren't so cocky any more. 'What are you asking me for? How should I know?'

'Keppell's your mate, isn't he? You introduced us. What's he playing at?'

Calling Jimmy Keppell a mate was like claiming you were buddies with a boa constrictor. Men like Keppell didn't have friends; they only had associates, people they were happy to crush at the first opportunity. Ray took another swig of whisky. He'd been drinking steadily since he'd heard about Tommo and didn't intend to stop until he ceased to be conscious. 'Why don't you ask him yourself? Your arrangement with him has nothing to do with me.'

'Like hell!' Holt retorted smartly. 'Do you really want Old Bill swarming all over the place? I don't need this shit on my patch.'

What the Inspector did or didn't need was of no interest to Ray. They had an arrangement – Holt tipped him off about forthcoming raids, any squealing illegals and whatever else that could affect the smooth running of his business empire – and in return Ray paid him regular and generous wads of cash. 'You're talking to the wrong man.'

'I can't keep covering for the likes of Keppell,' Holt said aggressively.

But Ray knew that it was bluster. Holt would do anything to save his own slimy skin, to prevent it all from coming down on top. He narrowed his eyes and glared at him. 'Who's asking you to?' Personally, he'd be more than happy to see that bastard Keppell hung, drawn and quartered for what he'd done to Tommo but that wasn't likely to happen in the short term. What made it worse was that Keppell had only done it to prove a point, to send a message to Ray about who was in control, to let him know that time was running out.

Holt could see that the conversation wasn't going quite as he'd intended. He'd wanted to exert his authority, to maybe put the squeeze on Stagg for an extra bung, but instead he was growing ever more anxious about what he'd got himself into. 'You were close to Lake; there are bound to be questions. This is a murder and that means it's MIT territory; it's not going to be easy to keep them off your back.'

'Or off yours.' Ray gave a thin hollow laugh. 'But I'm sure you'll find a way to sort it.'

'I thought there was a deal in place. I thought this wouldn't happen again, not after . . .'

He didn't need to complete the sentence. They both knew exactly what he meant. *Not after DI Holt had tipped off Jimmy Keppell about a raid on one of his crack factories and Keppell had left an explosive little surprise for the cops who had come bursting through the doors . . .*

'So write him a letter of complaint,' Ray said sourly. He was sick of talking to him, of even being in the same room. All the Inspector cared about was covering his own thoroughly bent and corrupt arse; he didn't give a damn about Tommo.

'There's no need for—'

'In fact, why don't you just piss off,' Ray said. 'Yeah, piss off and leave me alone.'

Holt hesitated for a moment but then, seeing the expression on Ray's face, quickly rose. He was better off out of here. There was no reasoning with Stagg when he was in this kind of mood.

Ray watched him walk out of the door. He snarled into his whisky, fighting against the urge to chase after him, to slam him hard against the wall and to shove his weasel teeth right down his filthy copper throat. But he still retained a modicum of sense. That would only provide a temporary outlet for his pain and frustration. What he needed was to organize something more permanent.

He took another drink and refilled his glass from the bottle. Where the hell was Al? He still couldn't understand how he'd found out about the charlie. Did the stupid sod have *any* idea of what he'd done? He thought about Tommo and thumped his clenched fist hard against the surface of the desk. This time Keppell had overstepped the mark and Ray was going to make sure he paid for it.

Chapter Twenty-Two

Harry slowly eased the car out into the traffic. It was hours since he'd had that final awkward conversation with Jess and the memory wasn't sitting too comfortably with him. But there was no reason for him to feel guilty, no reason at all. He had done what she had asked, gone through the motions, and it was hardly his fault if Ellen Shaw hadn't broken down and dramatically confessed to murder. And surely it wasn't his fault either that Jess's hunch, like Len Curzon's, had proved to be without foundation.

So why did he feel so bad?

It was to do with the expression on Jess's face when he had got up to leave, an accusing look that had made him feel like he was in the wrong, that he was turning his back on something he shouldn't. But that was just ridiculous. When push came to shove, this whole business had nothing to do with him; he had only been dragged into it by chance, through an ill-judged evening on the town fuelled by too much alcohol. There was a limit, surely, to how far any minor obligation could stretch.

His conscience, however, wouldn't stop nagging. Jess had no intention of abandoning her search for Len's killer and where that might ultimately lead her was anyone's guess. Working solo, she'd have no one to cover her back and that was hardly advisable if you were sniffing round the likes of Jimmy Keppell. Harry frowned as he gazed out through the windscreen. Perhaps he had been too hasty. In his desire to sever whatever tentative strings still bound him to Jess Vaughan, he had grabbed the first opportunity of escape.

Unwilling to dwell on it, he turned his mind to other things. He had spent most of the afternoon working through what remained of Denise's list of her husband's friends and associates. If any of them knew anything about Al's disappearance, they were doing a pretty good job of hiding it. Still, it hadn't been a complete waste of time. At least he could cross them off the list. Top detectives, he thought wryly, were renowned for their skilful use of the process of elimination.

So what did that leave him with? Not a whole lot more than when he'd got up this morning. Frustration was starting to niggle. What next? He pondered on the options for a minute or two. Eventually he came to a decision: when in doubt, it never did much harm to go back to the beginning and start again.

The traffic was heavy and it was a quarter to six when Harry pulled into the car park at Vista. The place was becoming depressingly familiar. He got out, locked the doors, and strolled through the entrance.

It was another hour or so before the club officially opened and the blonde was on reception again, possibly with the same piece of gum in her mouth. She looked up and scowled. 'Yeah?'

Harry strolled straight past her and headed for Ray Stagg's office.

'Hey!' she said, jumping to her feet. 'You can't just—'

But he was already there. He gave one fast knock and pushed open the door. Ray Stagg was sitting behind his desk. Well, not sitting perhaps so much as slumping. He was huddled over a tumbler of what appeared to be whisky and had the glazed semi-comatose expression of someone who'd been on the booze for most of the day.

'God,' Stagg said, raising his head. 'Not you, as well. What is this – a bloody cop convention?'

By which Harry presumed his visit had been preceded by some of his former colleagues. 'I'm not a cop,' he said, stepping inside and closing the door behind him. 'And, if you can still remember that far back, you employed me to find Al Webster.'

'Shit,' Stagg said, his lips twisting into a grin. 'So I did.' He knocked back another inch of his drink. 'And what have you come up with?'

'It's only been three days. I'm not a miracle worker.' Harry sat down. 'And it might have helped if you'd told me exactly why he'd disappeared.'

'Well, if I knew . . .'

'You know all right,' Harry said. 'Everyone does.' It was a shot in the dark but he had nothing to lose.

Ray Stagg stared at him, his eyebrows lifting. Abruptly he sat up straight and pushed back his shoulders. 'Really,' he said. 'How fascinating. Please feel free to share the news.'

Harry held his gaze and stared back. Stagg, surprisingly, had only the faintest slur to his voice. He was one of those men who even when thoroughly drunk could still – when he tried – give a passable impression of sobriety. His clothes were immaculate, his suit and shirt as pristine as if he'd just put them on. If Harry hadn't caught him unawares a few seconds ago, he could never have guessed at just how pissed he actually was.

'Al's done you over, hasn't he?'

Stagg feigned surprise. He even laughed. 'What?'

'Oh, come on, let's skip the bullshit. We both know it's true. How much did he take you for – a hundred grand, two? Or was it even more? Not to mention the effect on your reputation. And that . . . well, let's be honest, in your game that's kind of priceless, don't you think?'

'I don't have a clue what you're talking about.'

Harry paused for a moment and then slid the knife in. 'I'm sure that Tommy Lake would.'

At the mention of his name, Ray Stagg's face turned dangerously dark. His fingers tightened round the glass. 'This has *nothing* to do with what happened to Tommo.'

'Just a coincidence then,' Harry said.

Stagg glared at him. 'Call it what you like.'

123

Harry twisted the knife. 'And what would Jimmy Keppell call it?'

This time Stagg leapt to his feet, his eyes fiercely blazing. For a moment Harry wondered if he'd gone too far but then Stagg, thinking better of it, sank back into his seat. He gazed down at his drink for a while before slowly lifting his gaze. 'As from now you can consider our contract terminated.'

'You don't mean that.'

'You want it in writing?'

Harry shrugged, indifference painted across his face. 'As you like,' he said softly, 'but I was under the impression that you wanted Al Webster found.'

'I did,' Stagg said. 'I do. But let's be honest, Mr Lind, you haven't got a clue where he is.'

'Oh, I've got a few clues,' Harry replied, 'but they're not worth following up if you're not interested any more.'

'You're lying.'

'If you say so.'

Stagg hesitated, his pride battling with an even more urgent desire to wrap his hands round Al's treacherous throat. An uncomfortable silence filled the room. He took another drink, swallowed, and then slammed the glass down on the table. 'So why don't you just sod off and get on with it then?'

Harry knew how to quit when he was ahead. He quickly stood up. 'And you don't mind if I ask around the club?'

Stagg flapped a hand. 'Do what you like.'

At the door, Harry stopped and looked over his shoulder. 'I don't suppose you've ever heard of a man called Len Curzon?'

'Who?'

Harry shook his head. He wasn't even sure why he'd asked. 'It doesn't matter.'

Harry walked through to the main part of the club. The place looked different somehow, brighter, shinier, and with an even gaudier layer of glitz. The festive decorations had gone up and everything was covered in a dazzling mass of tinsel. It was busier too. There were more girls sitting around, drinking coffee and smoking cigarettes. He searched for the blonde with the long legs – there had to be some small reward for this thankless job – but sadly she was nowhere to be seen.

Methodically, he made his way between the tables, asking the same questions and getting the same predictable answers. Most of the girls knew Al but none of them could shed any light on his disappearance. It was all shrugs and frowns and Continental gestures. And they all denied, in various accents, having ever seen him on the Saturday night. Harry didn't believe a word of it. For the next fifteen minutes he optimistically scattered his business cards hoping that someone might be more willing to talk in private.

He was about to leave when he noticed his old pal Troy standing behind the bar. He looked about as friendly as the last time they'd met. Harry sauntered over and leaned against the counter.

'Is Agnes around?'

'Agnes?' Troy repeated.

'The blonde,' Harry said. 'What is she – Russian, Polish?'

Troy shrugged. He picked up a glass and started wiping it. 'I wouldn't know.'

'You wouldn't know what? What nationality she is or whether she's around?'

'Take your pick.'

'Thanks,' Harry said. 'I appreciate the help.' He turned to leave but the barman, after glancing furtively around the room, suddenly beckoned him back.

'You still looking for Al Webster?'

'You know I am.'

Troy leaned over the bar and lowered his voice. 'I might be able to help.'

Harry stared at him, suspiciously. 'Oh yeah?'

'What's it worth?'

'It depends on what I'm paying for.'

'Five minutes,' Troy murmured. 'I'll meet you in the car park. Round the side, near the fire exit.'

It was dark outside and cold. Harry rubbed his hands together and wondered if he'd been taken for a sucker; perhaps Troy just intended him to freeze to death. Should he leave? He had no great faith in the barman's ability to tell him anything useful but couldn't afford to pass over any possible leads either. He looked down at his watch and frowned. He'd been waiting ten minutes.

He wasn't coming.

Harry was heading back towards the Audi when he heard the click of a door and then the soft tread of approaching footsteps. He looked over his shoulder and squinted through the darkness. 'Hello?' There was no reply. The footsteps came closer. If it hadn't been for a passing car on the street, its headlamps providing a brief but timely wave of illumination, it would have been too late – Troy was only yards away and his arm was already raised. The slim solid shape of a baseball bat hovered above his head.

Shit! Harry caught a glimpse of the hatred in the other man's eyes before stepping smartly out of the way. But not quite smartly enough. The bat glanced off his shoulder and sent him spinning sideways. Troy wielded the weapon again and this time caught him hard across the right shin. Harry's knees buckled and he fell to the ground. Clutching at his leg, he groaned with pain while he tried to avoid the next blow. *Keep moving!* his brain was screaming. He had to think, and think fast, if he wasn't going to end up pulverized. The adrenalin was starting to pump, that old fight or flight instinct coming into play, and as flight clearly wasn't a feasible option . . . Harry rolled twice, focused his attention, and then lunged for Troy's ankles. He caught him off balance and brought him crashing to the ground. The bat slipped from his hand and skittered across the concrete.

Now, one on one, Harry stood a better chance. He might be injured but he was still stronger and more powerful than the kid. Or at least that was the theory. Troy didn't seem quite so convinced. Like a cornered wild animal he launched straight into another attack, hurling himself on top of Harry, lashing

126

out, thumping, kicking and clawing while a vile stream of abuse flooded out of his mouth. Harry raised his hands to protect himself from the worst of the blows. It was a frenzied assault but it couldn't be sustained. Harry held back, waited until he felt his opponent start to weaken, and then quickly jerked up his left leg and kneed him as hard as he could in the groin.

With a sharp intake of breath Troy tumbled back, his eyes wide with shock. Harry pushed him off and then twisted round to finish the job. He had just raised a fist, intending to slam it as hard as he could into Troy's jaw, when the door behind them opened again and a narrow stream of light fell across the concrete. He heard the sound of a pair of high heels clattering swiftly towards them.

'No!' a woman's voice cried out. 'Please!'

Harry turned to look.

Agnes gazed back, standing over him now, her scared eyes pleading. 'Please,' she said again. 'Please, you don't hurt him.'

Which Harry couldn't help but feel was rich bearing in mind the fact that *he* was actually the intended victim here. But then again, seeing as she'd asked so nicely and was wearing so little, it seemed churlish to ignore the request. He hesitated, sat back and then got slowly to his feet.

'Thank you,' she said. Reaching out a hand, she laid it lightly on his arm.

He tried not to stare at the contours of her body, so distinctly displayed through the flimsy fabric of her dress. This time, although the garment was of a similarly minuscule size, it was a different colour, a pale shade of mauve perhaps although he could have been wrong – his vision was a little bleary. There was no mistaking, however, the fear in her eyes.

'Are you okay?' she said. 'Your face . . .'

Now that she had mentioned it, Harry became aware of a harsh stinging sensation along his left cheek and forehead. His left eye wasn't feeling so great either. Swiping at them with the back of his hand, he glanced down and saw the smears of red. The little shit had drawn blood. Great! By tomorrow, he'd look

127

like he'd been in a goddamn cat fight. But that was the least of his problems. His right leg felt like it had been put through a crusher. He automatically reached for it but then as quickly pulled back. Drawing successfully on his reserves of male machismo, he said, 'I'm fine. It's not me you have to worry about.'

They both gazed down at Troy. He stirred on the ground, his hands still cradling his balls.

'Get up,' Agnes said to him.

Troy opened his eyes and peered vaguely towards her.

'Come on,' she urged. 'Now!'

There must have been something in her voice, perhaps simply its air of urgency, which propelled him into action. He slowly staggered into an upright position, his face looking grey. Small panting breaths were still escaping from his lips.

'Go inside,' she said. She glanced nervously at Harry as if he might try to prevent it but when he didn't she made a fast shooing motion with her hands. 'Go on! Go on!'

They watched as he stumbled towards the door. When he was safely inside, she turned towards Harry. 'Thank you,' she said again.

'Don't mention it.'

'He doesn't know what he's doing,' she said. 'He is . . . how you say – impulsive? He is young, very young.'

Harry snorted. 'Old enough to try and beat my brains to a pulp.'

'You survive,' she said. Her green eyes stared purposefully back at him. 'So will you ring police?'

'Why shouldn't I? I've just been attacked by a bat-wielding maniac.'

Agnes pulled a face. 'The cops will make trouble.'

'Unlike your friend.'

Her pink lips curled down at the corners. 'I know. Is very bad. But he's worried, afraid, yes? He thinks you try and make trouble for me.'

Harry leaned back against the bonnet of a nearby car and

rubbed at his shin, provoking a pain sharp enough to make him wince. 'And why should I do that?'

Her slender shoulders lifted in a shrug. 'You can have good guess. Some persons don't much care for foreigners.'

He looked at her. 'Are you here illegally?'

'No,' she said, 'not at all,' although a faint tremble in her voice told him that it might not be true. 'I have passport. You wish to see?'

'No, I don't wish to see. I'm not from immigration. It's got nothing to do with me.'

Agnes wrapped her arms around her chest and stared at him.

Harry could see she was shivering, although whether it was from the cold or from fear he couldn't really tell. Perhaps it was a combination of both. 'You should go inside,' he said, 'before you catch your death.'

'And wait for police to come?'

Harry shook his head. 'Did I say I was calling the police?'

It took a moment for his words to sink in. When they did she moved forward and flung her arms around his neck. He could feel her long fair hair brushing against his neck and smell the strong scent of her perfume. 'Thank you,' she murmured. 'Thank you so much.'

Enjoyable as her embrace was – it was a while since any woman had pressed her breasts quite so enthusiastically against him – Harry gently disentangled himself. 'It would be useful if you could find some way of keeping your friend's temper in check.'

'Yes,' she said. 'I promise.'

'And if you can help *me* sometime?'

'Help you?' she said, smiling. 'Of course. Very much.' Her eyes were sparkling now, filled with relief. She leaned over him again and kissed him full on the lips. Her mouth, incredibly soft, was sweet and moist. 'You know where I am. I'm always here. Whatever you want—'

'No!' Harry said, suddenly aware of the bargain she was trying to make. 'That's not what I meant.' He saw her face fall and paused, trying to think of a diplomatic way of explaining.

He couldn't claim he wasn't tempted – what red-blooded man wouldn't be? – but the persistent throbbing ache down the length of his shin was enough to distract him from any more lecherous feelings. 'It's not that I don't like you,' he said. 'I do. You're very . . .' He cleared his throat. 'Very attractive. But the only reason I'm here is because I'm looking for Al Webster. So if you know anything about him, about where he is . . .'

She smiled again. 'I wish but . . . I know nothing. I'm sorry.'

'Okay,' he said.

'But if I hear of him . . .'

'I'd be grateful,' Harry said. 'That would be good.'

'Good,' she repeated softly, the word sounding more like a sultry invitation than any form of agreement. Swivelling on her high heels, she gave him one last lingering look before walking away. 'Goodbye. I see you soon, I hope.'

Harry knew that he'd just been seduced into letting Troy off the hook but he had ceased to care. The kid was a loose cannon and someone else, hopefully sooner rather than later, would finish off the job for him. Harry's mind was preoccupied with watching her slim hips sashay seductively away from him.

After she'd gone, he limped cautiously towards the Audi, crawled inside and pulled the door shut. Could he drive? He turned the key in the ignition, put his foot down and yelped in agony. A vicious shooting pain ran the length of his right leg. He waited a few seconds and then tried again. 'Ah!'

The damage was worse than he thought. He needed help.

Harry reached for his phone and scrolled down through the menu. He tried the office first but only got the answering machine. For once Lorna had managed to get away before the clock struck seven. He tried Mac's mobile but that was turned off too. Hell! Under normal circumstances, he'd have rung Val but with everything that had happened recently his pride recoiled at the very thought of it. He could imagine what Jane Anderson would say when she heard: *That guy always comes running when he needs something.*

130

His finger kept on pressing, rolling through various friends and acquaintances – none of whom he'd been much in contact with recently – until he came to the end of the list. Jess Vaughan's number stared up at him. Could he? No. No way. He was better off calling a cab than getting in touch with her again. But no sooner had he made that decision than he realized it would mean leaving the car here overnight and that in turn would mean that Troy, if he got his second wind, might be overly tempted to use that cute little baseball bat again.

All things considered Jess seemed like the lesser of two evils.

Chapter Twenty-Three

The phone rang four times before she picked up. 'Hello?'

'Jess?' He felt a momentary doubt but it was too late now to change his mind. 'Hi, it's Harry. Where are you?'

'At home,' she said.

That was good. It would mean, if she agreed, that she could be here in less than fifteen minutes. 'Are you sober?'

She sounded incredulous. 'What are you,' she said, 'the flaming drink police?'

Harry raised his eyes towards the dark night sky. He might have known this wasn't going to be easy. 'Sorry, it's just that I need a favour. I'm stuck in Shoreditch, at Vista.' Before she could jump to any fanciful conclusions about what he'd been doing in a place renowned for its prostitutes and drugs, he quickly added: 'I've had some trouble, nothing serious but I can't drive. I was wondering if you could get a cab over here – I'll pay for it, naturally – and then drive me and the car back to Kentish Town.'

There was a short silence.

'Have you tried Yellow Pages? I think what you're looking for is a chauffeur.'

Harry pulled a face. After the way he'd walked away from her this morning, she had every right to tell him where to go. It was hardly as if she owed him any favours.

'Would it help if I begged?'

She gave a laugh, the kind that wasn't entirely sympathetic. There was another worrying silence. Eventually, she expelled a short exasperated breath. 'Where are you?'

He gave a sigh of relief. 'Thanks. In the car park, to the far left as you go in through the gates. Do you know how long you'll be?'

'Don't push your luck,' she said. 'I'll get there when I can.'

While he was waiting, Harry shifted carefully over to the passenger seat. He rolled up his trouser leg and examined the damage; there'd be a mighty bruise by tomorrow but he didn't think anything was broken. As regards the rest of his body, the damage was only superficial. There was an ache in his shoulder and his left eye, caught by what he liked to think of as a lucky punch, was starting to close. He peered in the mirror and wiped away the blood on his cheek.

It was another twenty minutes before the taxi rolled in through the entrance. He watched as she paid off the cabbie and then, as she turned, flashed his lights. Jess walked over to the car, got in and stared at his face.

'Jeez,' she said, screwing up her eyes. 'What happened to you?'

'A brief encounter with an irate barman.'

She grinned. 'What did you do, insult his cocktails?'

'Something like that.' Harry smiled thinly back.

'I take it you haven't called the cops.'

'It's not that serious. And anyway, I know how it works, remember? I've got better things to do than spend half the night down the nick giving a statement.' In fact, Agnes's plea hadn't been the only reason he wanted to avoid his former colleagues; he had no desire to explain what he was doing here or how he'd been stupid enough to be taken by surprise by some jumped-up little scrote.

Jess gave him a quick sideways glance. 'And here was me thinking that you always played by the rules.'

'Perhaps you don't know me as well as you thought.'

She put out her hand. 'You got the keys then?' He passed them over and she jiggled them between her fingers for a moment, gazing at the dashboard.

'You *can* drive, can't you?' Harry said anxiously.

'No, I just thought I'd come over and play dodgems with your bright shiny Audi.' She grinned again, put the key in the ignition and switched on the engine. 'There's no need to look so worried. I'm only savouring the delights of being behind the wheel again. My motor spent so much time in the garage I had to scrap it six months ago.'

'And you haven't got another because . . .?'

Jess groaned out her reply. 'Because junior reporters get paid a pittance in wages and I figured it was cheaper to use public transport than to fork out for yet another useless heap of junk that I could barely afford to keep on the road. Besides, the parking outside the flats is abysmal.'

'Right,' he said, bending down to rub his shin.

She pulled the car out and headed towards the exit. 'Are you sure you wouldn't like me to take you to hospital?'

'No thanks.'

Jess glanced down towards his leg. 'It's not broken, is it?'

'No.' He snatched his hand away, the abruptness of the action increasing the ache in his shoulder. As he leaned back, he noticed Agnes standing in the doorway to the club. Smiling, she took a step forward, raised a hand and waved at him.

He smiled back.

'Who's your friend?' Jess said.

'Her name's Agnes – she's a hostess here.'

Jess lifted her brows. The woman was a stunning blonde with the face of an angel and a figure to die for. Dressed in something so short and flimsy that it barely existed, she must have been close to every heterosexual man's dream. 'Really?' she said. 'And are you on first name terms with all the girls at Vista?'

Harry sighed, deliberately ignoring the implication. 'You need to turn right here.'

'It's one way,' she said. 'Where else would I go?'

She joined the traffic and took another right on to Great Eastern Street, then wound down the window and lit a cigarette. 'You don't mind, do you?' She glanced down towards his leg which he was surreptitiously rubbing again. 'Maybe you should get that checked out by a doctor.'

'I don't need it checked out,' Harry said. 'If there's one advantage to having a leg full of steel, it's that it takes more than a jerk with a baseball bat to make a dent in it.'

'A baseball bat,' she said. 'That must have been painful.'

'I wasn't expecting it,' he said.

Jess heard the defensiveness in his voice. Sensing his discomfort, she was wickedly tempted to take advantage. 'Who would be?' Had the fight been something to do with the beautiful Agnes? She wouldn't be surprised; it would hardly be the first time two men had made fools of themselves over a woman. She opened her mouth, about to pursue the subject, when her conscience got the better of her. She suddenly remembered what Len had told her, about how those two poor cops had been blown to oblivion and how Harry Lind had been lucky enough, if lucky was the word, to have walked in just behind them.

'So how's the case going?' she said instead. 'No sign of Mr Webster yet?'

Harry frowned at her. 'How did you know—'

'You told me. The other night, when we went up West together. I believe it was around the third bottle of wine.' Her mouth crept into a smile again. 'You sure that bat didn't catch you over the head?'

Had he told her? Harry couldn't recall but then he had been three sheets to the wind. And it didn't really matter. Al's disappearance was hardly the secret of the century. 'I doubt he's even in the country.'

'Except he didn't take his passport,' Jess said. She smiled as she saw the expression on his face. 'Yes, you mentioned that too. I have an amazing capacity to absorb and retain information even when I'm well and truly pissed.'

'Quite a talent.'

'Thank you,' she said. 'So what were you doing at Vista?'

'Wasting my time. But I'm pretty good at that.'

'Join the club,' she said.

135

Harry nodded, and gave her a sideways glance. 'And just in case you were wondering, I was there on business. I had to see Ray Stagg again.'

'Of course,' Jess said. 'And how was the delightful Mr Stagg?'

'Unhappy, drunk and not much in the mood for conversation.'

'You don't think he had anything to do with . . .' Jess glanced towards his leg again.

'No,' he said. 'Why should he?'

'You tell me. First his brother-in-law goes missing, then his old mate Tommy Lake gets murdered and now one of his barmen is running riot with a baseball bat. *I* wouldn't like to be too closely connected to him at the moment.'

Harry shrugged, turned his face away and stared out of the window.

They were approaching Kentish Town before he spoke again and then it was only to give directions. Jess let him guide her through the back streets. After she'd found a space and parked, he got out, held on to the door for a few seconds, and then limped slowly towards the house.

Jess remained standing by the car. She stood back, not quite sure what she was supposed to do next. 'Here,' she said, holding out his keys.

He glanced over his shoulder. 'You're coming inside, aren't you? At least let me make you a coffee for your trouble.'

Jess hesitated.

'Please,' he said. 'And I can call you a cab to get home.'

She could have called one herself – she had her mobile with her – but that would mean standing around in the cold until it finally arrived. And anyhow, she was curious enough to want to see where he lived.

'Okay,' she said.

His flat was on the ground floor of an old terraced house. Jess followed him inside and looked around. It was bigger and far tidier than her own flat but devoid of anything in the way of character. Too neat and tidy perhaps. The living room was painted pure white and everything was in its place – the leather sofa, the matching leather chairs, the glass-topped coffee table, the upright contemporary lamps. It had a stark, almost sterile air to it. The only personal touch was a photograph on the mantelpiece. Jess stared at, examining the image of Harry and a beautiful female companion. She was one of those tall cool blondes, an elegant Grace Kelly type.

'What does your girlfriend do?' she asked.

'Valerie's a cop.'

Jess nodded. 'I bet the bad boys don't put up too much resistance when *she* tries to arrest them.'

Harry gave a thin smile.

'So how come you didn't ring her?' she asked. 'Couldn't she have picked you up?'

'She's away for a few days.' Hoping to change the subject as quickly as he could, he reached into his pocket for his wallet and pulled out a tenner. 'Hey, I still owe you for that cab.'

'Forget it,' she said. 'I'll claim it off expenses.'

But he hobbled across the room and pushed the note into her hand. 'Please. I insist. I wouldn't like you to be accused of defrauding the *Hackney Herald*.'

'God forbid,' she said.

'Sit down. I'll put the kettle on.'

'You sit down,' she said. 'I think you're more in need than me.'

Jess could see the kitchen from where she was standing. Without further discussion she walked on through. This room, thankfully, wasn't quite so impeccable. There were dishes in the sink and toast crumbs scattered over the counter. There was even an empty pizza box lying on the table. She had a suspicion that in the absence of the lovely Valerie, Harry was reverting to sloppier ways.

She switched on the kettle and plucked a jar of instant coffee from one of the cupboards. 'Milk and sugar?' she called out.

'Just milk.'

While she was waiting for the kettle to boil, she stepped back into the doorway. 'Are you sure you don't need a doctor?'

137

'Yes,' he said.

'That eye looks sore.'

Harry automatically lifted a hand to it and flinched. 'Skilled as they are, I don't think doctors can do much for a black eye.'

'What about the leg?' she said.

'What about my drink?' he said.

Jess knew when to take a hint. Smiling, she retreated to the kitchen. A couple of minutes later she emerged with two steaming mugs of coffee.

'Thanks,' he said. 'And thanks for coming out too. I owe you one.'

Jess curled up in one of the comfy leather armchairs. An idea had dawned on her. 'Now, it's funny you should mention that . . .'

Harry peered over the rim of his mug. A low groan slid from his mouth. 'Why do I get the feeling that I'm about to regret it?'

'I don't know,' she said. 'Because you have a naturally suspicious mind?' She took a sip of the coffee. It wasn't the best she'd ever tasted but at least it was hot. 'It's just that I was wondering . . . I mean, seeing as you're probably not going to be able to drive for a day or two, if I could maybe borrow your car tomorrow.'

'Do *what*?'

'I wouldn't ask,' she said, 'only I need to go to Maidstone prison and it's going to take me all day if I have to mess around with buses and trains.'

'Maidstone prison,' he repeated.

'I got a visiting order from someone today.' She gave him a wide smile. 'We reporters live rich and varied lives.'

'Is this to do with Ellen Shaw?'

Jess shook her head. 'Not specifically. BJ – he's the guy I'm going to visit – saw Len a couple of weeks ago. They talked about something and I just want to find out what it was.'

'And he couldn't tell you over the phone?'

'He didn't seem too keen on the idea.'

Harry thought about it. He wasn't too keen on *this* idea either. There was no reason, other than his inbuilt prejudices about women drivers in general, why he shouldn't lend her the car – it would only be sitting out on the street – but he still had his reservations.

'Don't worry,' she said. 'I'll take good care of it. I promise. And I'll have it back by six at the latest.'

'It's not that,' he said. 'Look, I don't mean to sound patronizing but have you really thought this through? Do you actually know anything about this guy?'

Jess laughed. 'Well, thanks for the concern but it's only BJ. He might have spent his entire life getting into trouble but he's harmless enough.'

'That's not what I meant.'

'So what did you mean?'

Harry's brow furrowed while he tried to figure out a diplomatic way of saying it. 'You don't think that maybe, with the shock of Len's death and everything, you might not be . . . the thing is . . .' He paused, hearing himself start to stumble, and took a deep breath. 'Only you are still grieving and sometimes—'

'Oh *please*,' she interrupted. 'Save me the psychoanalysis. You think I've lost the plot, right? You think I'm seeing murder and mayhem, secrets and lies, a whole conspiracy where it doesn't exist.'

As it happened she wasn't too far off the mark. Harry shook his head. 'I didn't say that.'

'You didn't have to. It's written all over your face.'

'Look, I've a right to be concerned if—'

'A *right*?' she repeated, her voice incredulous.

'Sorry,' Harry said, quickly raising his hands. 'Not a right, okay. That wasn't the word I should have used. I'm just worried about you, about where all this could be leading. It's not always easy to think straight when . . .' He stopped abruptly, realizing he was only making things worse.

But instead of getting angry, she suddenly threw back her head and laughed. 'God, you really know how to put your foot in it, don't you?'

'It would appear so,' he said.

She leaned forward and sighed. 'Well, I'm touched by your concern but believe me I'm not going into this with my eyes closed. And you could be right, I may well be chasing after imaginary ghosts, but it's something that I have to do. You understand that, don't you?'

Harry could appreciate her need to find out the truth, was even impressed by it, but he also felt obliged to point out the downside. 'But do *you* understand that Jimmy Keppell is not going to be happy if you start digging around and raking up the past? Don't forget that it was his son who was murdered.'

'I haven't forgotten,' she said. 'And I'm not a complete idiot. I'm going to tread carefully.'

Harry wasn't convinced that her idea of treading carefully was quite the same as his but he nodded anyway. 'Okay,' he said. 'You can borrow the car if you want.'

Her face lit up. 'Thank you.'

'On one condition.'

Jess stared at him, her bright smile gradually fading.

Harry had a feeling that he might live to regret what he was about to say but still went ahead with it. 'I want to come with you.'

'For God's sake, I'm only going to Maidstone nick. I don't need a bodyguard.'

'And I'm not offering to be one. In case you hadn't noticed, I'm barely capable of walking.'

'So why bother?'

Harry shrugged. He was sure that the longer she spent alone the more she would come to believe her own wild suspicions and that was only going to lead her into trouble. Perhaps, if he stuck by her for a while, he might be able to introduce some reason into her thinking. 'Why not? I'm going to be at a loose end tomorrow. And there's not much else I can do looking like this; a black-eyed private investigator doesn't inspire much confidence.'

She frowned at him.

'That's the deal,' he said. 'Take it or leave it.'

Jess hesitated for a moment before standing up and picking his car keys off the table. 'Okay,' she said. 'If that's what you want, I'll pick you up at twelve.'

'Don't be late,' he said.

Harry limped to the bathroom and stared at his face in the mirror. It wasn't a pretty sight. His left eye, half closed, was swollen and bruised. A year ago this couldn't have happened. A year ago he'd have been faster on his feet, quicker to react, and no upstart little shit like Troy could have taken him so completely by surprise. Swearing softly, he leaned his head against the coolness of the glass.

Back in the living room, he poured himself a drink and thought about calling Val. He even went so far as to pick up the phone but after listening to the dial tone for a few seconds changed his mind and carefully replaced the receiver. The last thing he wanted was for her to come back because he'd been hurt again. There was a limit to the amount of sympathy any man could take.

Raising the glass to his mouth, he knocked back its contents in one. What to do next? He didn't have a clue. All he did know was that he wasn't going to do it sober.

Chapter Twenty-Four

Jess sat in the visiting room, impatiently tapping her fingers on the table while she waited for Big Jay Barrington. Harry was waiting outside in the car. He'd hardly spoken a word on the way down and she knew enough about hangovers to recognize a blinder when she saw one. Still, it was hardly surprising after what he'd been through yesterday. In the hope that she might be able to ignite some small spark of interest in the Grace Harper case, she had left all the files on the back seat, a heap of paperwork for him to peruse while she was otherwise engaged. Whether he could actually focus on it was another question altogether.

BJ eventually strode through the door, a mountain of a man dressed in jeans and the regulation blue and white striped shirt. His dark brown eyes scanned the room twice, not even stopping as they swept over her, and she had to stand up to get his attention. Clearly she wasn't quite as memorable as he was.

'Hey,' he said, walking over to greet her.

Jess shook his hand, an action she instantly regretted as his mammoth paw inadvertently crushed her own much smaller fingers. 'Hi,' she murmured. 'Good to see you again.'

'No problem,' he said, sinking down into the chair. 'I still can't believe it. Mr C gone like that. An accident, huh?'

'A mugging,' she said, not willing to reveal too much. 'That's what the cops think.'

BJ slowly shook his head. 'Shit, man, that's grievous. The streets just ain't safe to walk any more.'

Jess suppressed a smile at the expression of outrage. That his

142

own antisocial activities might have contributed in some way to this parlous state of affairs didn't seem to have crossed his mind. 'Let me get you a drink,' she said. 'Would you like anything else?'

He asked for a Coke, some crisps and a Mars bar. Jess joined the queue at the counter and while she waited to be served wondered how best to proceed with the tricky subject of what BJ and Len had actually discussed. Was it better to admit that Len had told her nothing – she could be running the risk of BJ clamming up on her – or should she take the sneakier route of pretending to know more than she actually did?

The queue shifted forward and she got her money ready. The one thing she didn't want to think about began pushing its way into the forefront of her mind: not so long ago Len would have been standing here too, probably ordering the very same items and . . . No, she mustn't go there. That awful lump was crawling into her throat again. Instead, she tried to concentrate on what Len would do if he was in her shoes. *Whatever it takes*, she could almost hear him saying.

Jess returned to the table, put down the tray and shot a smile at him. 'Look, I never got the chance to talk in-depth with Len before . . . So I'm a bit vague, you know, about some of the details.'

'Okay,' he said, tearing the wrapper off his Mars bar. 'But he told you about Deacon, right?'

'Oh sure,' she lied, her heart beginning to thump.

BJ bit into the chocolate and began chewing. 'So what is it with that guy?' he said, his mouth still full. 'What's the angle?'

Jess tried to keep her voice casual. 'Len was researching an article about . . . er . . . politicians and crime.'

'Bloody long article, then,' BJ said, grinning.

She laughed. 'You're not wrong there.'

'And he told you about our deal, right?'

'Yeah.'

'So what do you reckon?'

Jess reckoned she had to be damn careful or she'd be exposed for the fraud she actually was. Were they talking money here? They had to be. What other kind of deal could Len have made with him? It wasn't strictly ethical, paying convicted felons for information, but now was hardly the time to start developing scruples. 'It's no problem.'

BJ seemed pleased, his mouth expanding into its wide gappy smile. 'So I'll be working with you?'

'If you're happy with that.'

'And you're experienced in this kind of thing, yeah?' He paused. 'I don't want to sound funny or nothing, and no offence meant, but I don't want to be working with a fuckin' amateur.'

'Strictly professional,' she said. 'I *am* a reporter.'

'Yeah, but how many *books* you written, lady?'

Jess stared at him, baffled. 'What?'

BJ folded his arms on the table, a wariness creeping across his face. 'Thought you said you and Len had talked?'

'We did,' she said, her mind frantically racing while she tried to suss out exactly what was going on. She was lost. Where on earth had the subject of books come from?

Fortunately, BJ didn't have the sense to keep his mouth shut. 'I ain't telling my life story to just anyone,' he said.

Jess gave a sigh of relief. So that was it! Len must have promised him a book deal in return for his cooperation. Or had he? Somehow she sensed that even Len wouldn't have been so rash as to actually promise anything. More likely it was a carrot he had dangled in front of an ambitious BJ's nose.

'Of course not,' she said. 'Who would? You're right to be cautious and I respect you for that. It's a matter of trust, isn't it?' She threw him one of her more generous smiles and then lied through her teeth. 'But you don't have to worry. I worked with Len on his last three books and I've been the ghost writer for a number of other best-selling biographies too.' Off the top of her head she reeled off the names of several infamous villains, only one of whom she had ever met and that was at some tedious book launch where the drunken wretch had spilled a glass of red wine down the front of her shirt.

BJ's eyes widened. 'No kidding,' he said. 'So what's Davey Pullman really like?'

Jess shook her head. 'First rule of the trade, BJ – never discuss your subjects with other people. Confidentiality, from start to finish, is what it's all about. Obviously you don't spend months talking with a man without learning a secret or two but you have to know when to keep your lips firmly zipped. I mean, there are things I could tell you about Davey but . . . Well, you understand where I'm coming from, don't you?'

BJ looked impressed. 'For sure,' he said. 'You can't go talking behind no man's back. That wouldn't be right.'

'It wouldn't,' she agreed. Jess sat back and sipped on her coffee. This was easier than taking sweets from a baby. BJ was proving so simple to manipulate that she felt almost guilty.

He looked across the table. 'So are we on? Is the deal still in place?'

And then Jess took her gamble. 'There's only one thing,' she said. 'You and Len hadn't exactly *made* a deal, had you?'

BJ's face fell and he shifted uncomfortably in his seat. 'But he was keen, man. He *was*. He was well up for it.'

'Really?' Jess said, frowning. 'Only I got the impression that it was rather dependent on the information you might be able to provide.'

'About Deacon?' he said.

Her heart skipped a beat. 'So you do have something?'

'I'm working on it.'

Jess frowned at him. How often had she heard *that* before? Thinking of Len, she was tempted to lose her temper but had the sense to keep calm. 'That's not good enough.'

'Give me a couple of days,' he said.

'I can't wait around forever.'

'You won't need to.'

It was shortly after three when Jess escaped from the blank magnolia walls of the visiting room. She pulled up the collar of her coat as she walked down the street to where Harry was waiting in the car. She got in and sat down beside him.

'Good visit?' he said, glancing up from his newspaper.

'Delightful,' she said. 'It's always a joy to spend time in one of Her Majesty's Prisons.'

'I can imagine.'

Jess settled in and fastened her seatbelt. 'So what have you been doing?' Glancing over her shoulder she saw the files still sitting on the back seat. There wasn't much sign of them having being disturbed. 'Not working *too* hard, I hope.'

'Just catching up on world events.' He put the paper down as she pulled out from the kerb. 'Doesn't it bother you,' he said, 'going into jails?'

'You say that as if I make a habit of it.'

'Sorry,' he said, frowning at the imposing grey stone wall that ran around the prison's perimeter. 'It's just that these places make the hairs on the back of my neck stand on end.'

'Probably your guilty conscience.'

Harry grinned. 'You could be right. So how did it go?'

'Not bad,' she said, 'although I can't actually work out if BJ's got anything useful to offer or if he's just stringing me along. He's desperate to see his name in print. Apparently Len discussed a possible book deal with him in return for information.'

'I didn't realize BJ was such a big name in the criminal world.'

'He isn't. Still, you can't blame a guy for trying.' Jess gave a wry smile. 'The only thing I did learn for certain was that this was where Len saw Ellen Shaw for the first time. He must have followed her back to Camden.'

'Which you'd pretty well guessed already.'

'I wonder if he recognized her straight away or—'

'*Thought* he recognized her,' Harry said. 'There's not a shred of evidence to suggest that Ellen Shaw is anyone other than who she claims to be.'

'So what happened to Grace Harper then?'

Harry gave another of his weary sighs. 'Sadly, she probably met the same fate as Theresa Neal.'

Jess glanced at him, surprised. So he *had* been looking

through the files. Theresa, a ten-year-old, had disappeared a few days before Grace Harper. It had been another three years before her remains were found buried on Hampstead Heath. 'You think the two cases are connected?'

'Don't you?' Harry said. 'They went missing around the same time. They lived within half a mile of each other. I'd say that was a pretty good connection.'

'Okay,' Jess said. 'But it still doesn't add up. Two murders so close together suggest the start of a killing spree, something frenzied and out of control. So why didn't it go on? Why did it suddenly stop?'

'There could be all sorts of reasons,' Harry said. 'Perhaps he realized he was under suspicion and took off. He might have gone abroad. Or perhaps he was killed in an accident. He could even have topped himself.'

Jess snorted.

'And something else,' Harry persisted, trying to provide the voice of reason. 'If Ellen Shaw *is* Grace Harper then why should she bother to pretend otherwise? What's she got to gain by it?'

That was a question still weighing heavily on Jess's mind. 'How should I know? She was only eight when she disappeared. Anything could have happened.'

'Then perhaps you could also consider the possibility that Ellen Shaw is exactly who she says she is.'

'You're only saying that because you fancy her.'

Harry, caught unawares by the comment, turned his flushing face towards the window. 'Now you really are clutching at straws.'

'We'll see,' she said softly.

They had just reached the motorway and Jess put her foot down, eager to get home. A long night's work awaited her. She would take those files apart, page by page, until she found what she was searching for. If it was the last thing she did, she was going to make Harry Lind eat his words.

Chapter Twenty-Five

They had just emerged from the Blackwall Tunnel when Harry's phone started ringing. He felt a spark of hope – it could be Valerie – but as he lifted the mobile off the dashboard saw that the number was unrecognized. Should he bother answering? He was tempted to let it go to voicemail but then thought better of it.

'Hello?'

There was silence from the other end.

'Hello?' Harry repeated. Again there was nothing. Pulling a face, he gazed out at the car in front, a car Jess was getting dangerously close to. He was about to hang up and offer some heartfelt advice on the wisdom of keeping a sensible distance – his bumper didn't need any further damage – when he heard the thin sound of breathing. 'Who is this?'

'Is Agnes,' a small voice finally whispered.

'Agnes?' he repeated, surprised.

A small strangled sob was the only response.

Instantly the call had his full attention. 'What's wrong?' he said. 'Are you okay?'

'You must come. *Please*. I must talk with you.'

'Are you in trouble? Is this about Al?'

The anxiety in his tone alerted Jess who turned to look at him. 'Watch out!' he almost yelled as the car in front braked and she came perilously close to smashing into it.

'For God's sake,' Jess snapped back. 'I'm miles away! You could get a bleeding juggernaut between us.'

Harry glared at her before returning his attention to Agnes.

'Sorry,' he said into the phone. 'I'm sorry about that. Where are you?'

'The club,' she said. Her voice had an air of urgency to it now. 'You come soon, yes?'

'Don't worry. I'll be there.' He glanced at his watch, thinking of the Friday rush hour traffic. 'But it's probably going to take about half an hour. Agnes, can you tell me what's—'

'Hold on,' she said.

He waited, hearing another noise like a door being opened. Then the muffled sound of footsteps, of voices. 'Agnes?'

Abruptly the line went dead.

'Shit,' he murmured. Quickly he tried to call her back but her phone was already turned off. 'Shit,' he said again.

Jess kept her eyes on the road as she spoke. 'Problem?'

'Look, can we head for Shoreditch, for Vista? I think Agnes is in trouble.'

'Are you sure?'

He turned to stare at her. 'What do you mean, am I sure?'

Jess was still seething from the way he had barked at her earlier. Her driving might not be up to his exacting standards but at least she didn't jump through hoops every time some slutty blonde hostess batted her eyelashes. 'Are you sure you're not being set up? What if that barman's waiting for you again?'

'Yeah, right,' Harry snarled. 'Or what if this girl's in serious trouble and actually needs my help?'

Jess wasn't convinced but she still shut her mouth. If Harry Lind wanted to play the knight in shining armour then who was she to interfere?

It was another twenty-five minutes before they pulled in to the forecourt of Vista. The day had slipped into darkness and a cold sleety rain was falling. Jess parked close to the entrance where there was extra light coming from the street.

'You're getting to be a regular,' she said. 'Perhaps they'll give you a discount.'

Harry paused as if preparing to deliver a few well-chosen words, but then clearly decided that it wasn't worth the effort.

Instead, still clutching his phone, he got out and leaned over to slam the door. 'I shouldn't be too long.'

But Jess had no intention of staying there unaccompanied. She knew what had happened to Harry when he'd been loitering alone in the car park. Even with the doors locked, she wouldn't feel safe. Not that she had any intention of telling him that. 'I'm coming with you,' she said. 'I've never been inside before. It could be an education.'

'Not much of one. They're not even open yet.'

'That's okay. I've got a vivid imagination.'

For a moment he looked as if he was going to object but she was already out of the car and shrugging into her coat. If they started debating the issue now it would only waste more time. 'Don't worry,' she said. 'I won't interfere.'

'No,' he said firmly. 'You won't.'

They walked together towards the entrance with its blue neon sign. Jess wrapped her scarf tighter round her neck, buried her hands in her pockets and smiled. It had just occurred to her that she was possibly about to become the most overdressed female to ever step across the threshold. She sniffed as the cold wet air made her face turn pink. Now her nose had started to run too. Great! Was there no end to her glamour? She stopped to get a tissue from her bag, blew her nose and then as she looked around for a bin her attention was caught by a flash of white on the far side of the car park. What was it? Just a carrier bag, perhaps, that had drifted in from the street. Except there seemed to be some kind of shadow attached to it.

Harry, who had strolled on and was almost at the door, turned and said impatiently, 'Come on. What are you doing?'

'Hang on a sec,' she said.

She heard a sigh escape from Harry's lips but, never able to deny her innate curiosity, began to head towards the mystery object. As she peered through the darkness, it gradually took on a more recognizable shape. An uneasy feeling was starting to blossom in the pit of her stomach. It looked like . . . Her mind, however, refused to believe it and she continued to

150

advance until she was only yards away. From this distance she was no longer able to delude herself. This was no figment of her imagination. Her eyes widened with fear and her legs began to shake. There was blood everywhere. She could see it. She could smell it. Oh God! She was staring at a corpse.

'Harry,' she croaked, the air rushing from her lungs.

But she must have spoken too softly for him to hear. Or perhaps she hadn't spoken at all. Maybe she had opened her mouth and only fear had tumbled out. Her pulse was racing, her heart pounding against her ribs.

Jess swallowed hard and tried again. 'Harry!'

This time she must have yelled because she heard his footsteps clatter noisily across the forecourt. Seconds later he was standing next to her. She listened to his shock, to the sudden intake of breath and then the long exhalation.

'Fuck!'

Harry quickly took her arm and pulled her back. Gazing down he absorbed the beaten face of a man, the pulpy mash of the nose and mouth, the broken jaw. From the twisted way the body was lying, it looked as if both of his legs had been broken too. There were numerous stab marks on his arms and chest but the final denouement had probably come with a wound to the heart. The whole of his white shirt, apart from a section at the right shoulder, was drenched in blood.

'Stay here,' he said to Jess.

Harry knelt down beside the body but didn't touch; he knew better than to interfere with a crime scene. He let his eyes roam over the shattered flesh and bones, the image gradually imprinting itself on to his mind. What was he looking for? He wasn't sure. Just some tiny clue perhaps, something that could make a difference.

'Do you know him?' Jess whispered. Her mouth was dry and she could barely speak.

'It's *him*.'

She shook her head, not understanding.

'The barman,' he said softly, getting up to stand with her again. 'The guy who attacked me. It's Troy.'

'God.' Jess wanted to stop staring at the corpse but couldn't. It was as if she couldn't drag her gaze away; the harder she tried, the more impossible it became. Her stomach was churning. She had never seen a dead body before – not even one that had died peacefully – and this one had been despatched to whatever higher authority it had gone to with the maximum of violence.

Harry put his arm around her shoulder and forcibly turned her around. 'There's nothing we can do.'

Jess's stomach, however, had other ideas. Shaking free of his hold, she staggered a few feet and dramatically threw up against the wall. The smell rose up to assail her and for the next ten seconds she continued to heave, a disgusting empty retching that made her whole body shake. Leaning her forehead against the chipped red brick, she felt hot tears running down her cheeks.

Harry looked on with sympathy but knew better than to go to her. Death, even for the witnesses, was a lonely affair. There was nothing he could say or do. He'd seen more bodies than he cared to remember but had never grown immune to the horror. Although nausea was tugging at his own guts too, he clenched his fists and fought against it. Instead, he got out his phone and raised it to his ear. He had to make the call.

Harry provided the facts as quickly and succinctly as he could. *His name was Harry Lind. He was in the car park of the Vista nightclub. There had been a murder. They had to get here as soon as they could.*

As he put the phone back in his pocket, Jess stumbled from the wall. He grabbed her arms and propelled her away. 'Come on,' he said. 'The police will be here soon.'

She didn't say anything. Her face was pale and drawn.

'It's okay,' he murmured. 'You'll be okay.'

While they were waiting in the car, Harry suddenly remembered Agnes. What had happened to *her*? He felt an urge to run inside the club and search but knew that he couldn't. He couldn't leave Jess and he couldn't leave the body either.

Jess slumped over the wheel and her pale brown hair fell around her face. 'Sorry,' she mumbled.

'What are *you* sorry for?'

She glanced at him. 'At least I didn't throw up over your shoes.'

'For which I'm truly grateful.'

As the squad cars arrived, with their blue lights flashing, Harry sighed. The full implications of what this would mean were just beginning to sink in. Vista fell under the authority of his old station – the station Val still worked at – and if she was on duty then she'd probably be first on the scene and . . . Harry saw the bright red Citroën pull in through the gates and dropped his head into his hands.

'Not to worry,' Jess said, forcing a smile as she opened the door. 'At least we've both got alibis.'

But that, as Harry was anticipating, could prove to be a double-edged sword.

Chapter Twenty-Six

It was fifteen minutes since the police had arrived and Valerie was still wearing that *How could you do this to me?* expression. They were sitting in the foyer of the club while the SOCO team sniffed around the body in the car park. He could tell that she hadn't quite worked out what she was most annoyed about yet – his connection to a corpse, his embarrassing presence at a seedy nightclub or that his companion was a young curvy journalist from the *Hackney Herald*. True, she had looked suitably concerned on first seeing the state of his face but whatever sympathy those injuries had evoked had long since dissolved. 'So you're telling me you had a fight with the victim last night?'

'About six o'clock,' he said. 'And it wasn't so much a fight as . . . well, more of an unprovoked attack. He came at me with a baseball bat.'

'And why should he do that?'

Harry shrugged. 'I was working on a case, asking questions about Al Webster. I told you about him – Stagg's brother-in-law. Troy seemed to take exception.'

'And you decided not to report this because . . .?'

'I couldn't see the point.'

Valerie's eyebrows shot up. 'You couldn't see the point?' she repeated archly. 'He attacks you with a baseball bat, almost breaks your leg, and you're happy to just let it go?'

'Not happy, exactly,' Harry said, 'but I couldn't see what it would achieve – apart from a few wasted hours down the nick.'

'You didn't consider that the next person to be assaulted might not be quite as lucky as you?'

As it happened, he wasn't feeling especially lucky. Finding a corpse wasn't one of his favourite pastimes and being grilled by Valerie didn't rate too highly either. 'Well, we don't need to worry on that score.'

She scowled at him. 'For God's sake, Harry, this is hardly the time to be—'

But at that moment the double doors leading to the main part of the club swung open and DI Holt strutted through. Harry glanced up. 'Any news on Agnes?'

The Inspector gave him a long hard look, almost as antagonistic as Val's, before finally deciding to answer the question. 'She's not here. No one's seen her for an hour or so.'

'She's in trouble,' Harry said. 'You've got to find her.'

Holt didn't appear overly impressed by the demand but then the disappearance of a foreign nightclub hostess probably came pretty low on his list of priorities. Ignoring Harry's plea he turned his attention to Valerie and, with an abrupt tilt of his head, gestured towards the front door. 'Can I have a word?'

While they talked out of earshot, Harry pondered on the fate of Troy. The kid had picked the wrong person to have a fight with this time. And Agnes must have realized it. Why else would she have called? His brow creased into a frown. Unless . . . but the idea that Jess might have been right, that someone *had* been trying to set him up, wasn't an option that he wanted to dwell on. However, it was an uncomfortable fact that if she hadn't noticed the body, he'd have gone on inside, been seen by the staff and – being in the right place at the wrong time – possibly ended up in the frame for murder. Not that it would have stuck, not with Jess as his alibi . . . but then Agnes couldn't have known that he'd arrive with a companion.

Valerie came back but didn't sit down again.

Harry smiled up at her. 'So has Holt got me down as his number one suspect?

'Very funny,' she said. 'Come on, I'll take you to the station. You'll need to get a statement sorted before you go home.'

He stood up. 'What's happening with Jess?'

'She won't be far behind.'

'And the car?'

'I'll get someone to bring it over. Have you got the keys?'

'Ah,' Harry said as he reached into his pockets. 'No, er . . . actually I think Jess must have them.' He watched Val's eyes narrow as if giving your car keys to another woman was tantamount to adultery. 'I was having problems driving,' he muttered. 'My leg . . .'

'Right,' she said, in that thoroughly disbelieving tone of hers. Then, as if the effort of having to relay this piece of information to one of her officers was an unnecessary strain on her already overstretched patience, she sighed and said, 'You'd better wait here.'

It was a few minutes before she returned, during which uneasy period Harry was able to ponder on how things were bound to get worse. On a personal front at least. At some point soon it was going to come out that he'd spent the entire day with Jessica Vaughan.

Harry could gauge the level of Val's temper from the force she used to slam the car door shut. Alone at last, she no longer needed to maintain any semblance of professionalism. She used the weapon of silence for the time it took to join the evening traffic and then turned her face to glare at him. 'How the hell did you get involved in all this?'

'You know how,' he said. 'I've already told you. I've been doing some digging, trying to get a lead on Al Webster. I got a call to come here and—'

'But why should this . . . this Agnes girl, call *you*? If she was in trouble or if she saw that Troy was in trouble, why not dial 999?'

'How should I know?' Harry said. 'I left her a card – I left cards with lots of the staff. Maybe she doesn't trust the police. Maybe they make her nervous. Maybe she's not even here legally.' He lifted his shoulders and shrugged, feeling a dull ache run the length of his spine. 'I wish I knew but I don't. I really don't.'

Val gripped the wheel a little too tightly as they pulled up at the lights. 'And so what about your little friend?' she said. 'What's her connection to all this?'

Harry had been wondering how long it would take to get around to Jess. And he suddenly understood why so many people lied when they were put under pressure. He was sorely tempted to do the same himself. Guilt was one of those curious things that could be conjured out of nowhere, pulled out of the ether to be dangled in your face like some vital piece of evidence. 'What do you mean – connection?'

'I was just wondering why your little friend was there with you tonight.'

Harry shook his head. 'Do you have to keep calling her that?'

'What?' she said.

'My *little friend*,' he said. 'You make her sound like a pony.'

Valerie drew in her breath and frowned. 'So what would you like me to call her?'

'By her name, perhaps.' Harry was aware that he was digging one almighty hole for himself but was growing too tired and frustrated to care. 'She's called Jess Vaughan and she's a reporter on the *Hackney Herald*. But you know that already. And unless Frankie Holt has lost his legendary skill in witness interrogation you should know why she was with me too.'

But instead of giving the expected nod Val hesitated, pausing long enough to make him suspect that Jess might not have been especially forthcoming. Shifting the car forward as the lights turned to green, she kept her eyes firmly on the road. 'Go on.'

Harry could have shut his mouth but was smart enough to realize that the more he tried to hide, the worse it would look when the truth finally came out. 'Look,' he said. 'She was a friend of Len Curzon's, okay? The guy who was stabbed in Camden. She's been having a rough time recently and . . .'

'And you thought you'd comfort her?'

'Don't be ridiculous,' Harry snapped. 'It's nothing like that.'

'So what is it like?' she said.

157

Now that was harder to explain. Harry fiddled with his seat-belt while he tried to come up with an answer that wouldn't condemn him to a lifetime of sleeping in the spare room. 'She's been working on a story – something Curzon left unfinished – and asked for my advice. That's why I went to Maidstone with her, so we'd have the chance to talk on the way.'

Her head snapped round again, her eyes widening. 'You went to *Maidstone* with her?'

Harry winced as he heard her accusing tone step up a pitch and instantly regretted the admission. She made him feel as though he'd just confessed to a dirty weekend in Paris. 'Maidstone jail,' he added quickly, hoping that the unromantic nature of the location might go some way towards appeasing her. 'She had to see an inmate there. I couldn't drive the car myself and it was only going to be stuck outside the flat and so I thought she may as well . . .' His explanation petered out into a shrug.

'My,' she said, 'that was very generous of you.'

Harry sighed in despair. 'There's nothing going on,' he said. And then immediately wished that he hadn't. The more he denied it, the guiltier he sounded. Valerie wasn't usually the jealous or possessive sort, confidence was her middle name, but with the way he'd been acting recently it was perhaps no great surprise that her suspicions had been raised. No one likes to be made a fool of.

Val pulled into the station, found a space and then switched off the engine. There was a short brittle silence.

'So what next?' Harry said.

'You know what next. It's the usual routine. We go inside, you give a statement and—'

'I meant us,' he said. 'What happens about *us*? Don't you think we need to talk?'

Val got out of the car and carefully straightened her skirt. She gave a small dismissive wave of her hand. 'This is hardly the time to be thinking about *that*.'

Chapter Twenty-Seven

Being under suspicion was an interesting, if somewhat disconcerting, experience. Jess had been aware of the phone calls being made, of her identity being checked, and of the cautious way she was being treated by the officers. Innocent until proven guilty? It hadn't felt like that. Still, it would all have been a good deal worse if she'd been alone when she stumbled on the body.

DI Holt had given her the third degree but she'd stuck to her guns, accurately relaying the facts and refusing to be intimidated. He had made her go over the story again and again as if intent on catching her out. The same questions, disguised by different words, had been repeatedly fired at her. Had she been a more vulnerable or easily influenced person, Holt's relentless technique might have worn her down, made her question her own memory, but Jess had come upon the likes of the Inspector before. He was a third-rate bully of limited intelligence, a man with more power than personality.

It seemed like an eternity since she had first arrived and now that she was free to go she tapped her foot impatiently while she waited for the cab. She had been offered a lift home but had turned it down; she had spent enough time in the company of coppers. She wondered what had happened to the Audi but wasn't about to ask.

Longing for a breath of fresh air – she had spent too many hours trapped first in Maidstone jail and now here in the police station – Jess would have stepped outside but the rain was tipping down and there was no shelter outside the building.

159

Standing by the door, she glanced over towards the counter to see DS Valerie Middleton giving her the evil eye. Holt might be a bully but Harry's girlfriend was a far more formidable prospect. At the moment she was looking Jess up and down in that way women do when they're subtly assessing the opposition. What did she think had been going on? Then, with a sinking heart, Jess suddenly recalled a certain evening not so long ago, a drunken fumble in the back of a cab, a kiss . . .

She quickly pulled herself together. Looking guilty wasn't going to help and Valerie couldn't even know about it unless . . . but no, she didn't believe for a second that Harry had actually told her. Even he wasn't that stupid!

Jess smiled thinly back while she wondered how a woman quite so beautifully designed could possibly possess any of the more usual female insecurities. Tall and slender, the Sergeant was dressed in a simple navy suit that was the epitome of practicality and yet still managed to draw attention to every curve of her immaculate figure. Her skin was the colour of pale honey, her cheekbones defined, her eyes a soft shade of hazel. Even her long fair hair was twisted back into a perfect glossy plait.

Jess made a mental note to renew her membership of the local gym. Her own body, which in a dim light could just about pass for voluptuous, was hovering on the brink of something less appealing. It wouldn't be long before she was staring the horror of plumpness straight in the face.

The Sergeant seemed in two minds as to whether she was going to approach or not. Jess sincerely hoped *not*. She'd already been at the receiving end of too many uncomfortable questions. All she wanted to do now was get home, have a long hot bath and try to put the miseries of the day behind her.

Jess gave a sigh of relief as the taxi drew up outside the gates. At last! Braving the elements, she rushed out through the doors and dashed across the forecourt. She jumped into the passenger seat and barked out her address.

The cabbie threw his fag out of the window and grinned at her. 'Had a grilling?' he said.

Annoyed by the presumption – did she really look that dodgy? – Jess glared back at him. 'Just a hard day, okay? And if you want a tip don't even think about taking the scenic route home.'

Harry raised his eyes to the ceiling and tried to keep his cool. How many times had they been through this? Holt knew he had nothing to do with it; he was just taking advantage of a God-sent opportunity to wind him up. 'So what are you suggesting? That I got in a fight and then went back for revenge the very next day?'

'It's been known,' Holt said smugly.

'And has it also been known for anyone to take a local journalist along to witness the event?'

'Well, perhaps if you could explain exactly what she was doing there with you . . .'

Harry shook his head and smiled. It was becoming increasingly obvious that Jess had told Holt the bare minimum and he wasn't prepared to fill in the gaps. Why should he? Her business was hers and it had nothing to do with what had happened to Troy. 'It was pure chance,' he said. 'We'd had a business meeting and she was with me when Agnes called. I asked if she could drive me to Vista and she did.'

'In your car?'

'Why not?' Harry said. 'Is that a crime? I can't drive at the moment and last time I checked there was nothing illegal about any qualified person driving a fully insured vehicle.'

Holt's nostrils flared, his mouth simultaneously turning down at the corners. 'How can we be sure that there even was a call?'

'Come on,' Harry said. 'Let's not even go there. I'm sure you've already checked my phone.'

Holt hesitated but, unsurprisingly, wasn't willing to make any hasty admissions. 'The CCTV wasn't working so we've only got Ms Vaughan's word that the two of you actually arrived at the murder scene when you say you did.'

161

'And mine,' Harry said. But *his* word clearly cut no ice with the Inspector. 'Why on earth should she lie for me?'

'Why indeed?' Holt sneered.

Harry wondered what Valerie had said to him. This was starting to feel more like an interrogation of his personal life than a murder inquiry. Leaning forward, Harry stared Holt straight in the eye. 'So what do you want me to say, Frankie? That I was bearing a grudge, got there half an hour earlier, beat the victim to a pulp, found somewhere to change my clothes and have a shower and then deliberately went back to report the discovery of a body? Just how stupid do you think I am?'

Holt, hearing the anger in his voice, shifted back an inch or two. 'There's no need to take that attitude.'

'I'm not the one with attitude.'

The two men glared at each other across the table. Holt was the first to look away. Aware that he had maybe crossed that invisible line between genuine inquiry and personal dislike, he quickly changed the subject. 'So tell me about Ray Stagg.'

'I'm sure you know as much as I do.'

'Except you're working for him, aren't you?'

'No,' Harry said. 'His sister is my client.'

'But Ray Stagg's still writing out the cheques.'

'I get paid by David Mackenzie,' Harry said. 'And I'm sure you're aware of who Mac is. He was a cop too, a good cop. Would you like to cast aspersions on *his* character as well as mine?'

Holt glared at him. 'So, can you give me a description of Agnes Bondar?'

Harry sighed. What was he playing at now? Unless he was completely incompetent he should have got that information from the staff at Vista. 'Are you even looking for her?'

'You haven't answered my question.'

'About five foot six,' he said resignedly. 'Slim. Blonde hair, green eyes.'

'And you've known her for how long?'

'I don't know her at all,' Harry said. 'I've only met her a couple of times. I've already told you. I was working on a case, searching for a missing person. We talked briefly at Vista, I left her my card and she rang me late this afternoon. She said she needed help, I went to the club and—'

'Right,' Holt said slyly.

Harry's patience, such as it was, was rapidly wearing thin. 'How much longer is this going to go on? You must have talked to forensics. You must know the time scale by now and unless you believe I'm the dumbest killer you ever came across then you haven't got one good reason to keep me here.'

'No one said you were a suspect.'

Harry felt like he was being treated as one. 'Fine,' he said, getting to his feet. 'So am I free to go now?'

Holt nodded and gathered up his papers 'Don't leave the country. We may need to talk to you again.'

Harry stalked out of the room, walked back along the corridor and approached the duty officer at the desk. It was only ten months since he'd been working here but a lot of the faces, including this one, were unfamiliar.

'Could I speak to Sergeant Middleton please? Tell her it's Harry.'

The woman he had addressed smiled nicely and picked up the phone. 'Just a moment.' She punched in a number and then had a brief conversation during which her cheeks turned faintly pink.

He knew what was coming.

'I'm sorry, sir,' she said, replacing the receiver. 'Only it seems she's . . . er, off duty now. I think she may have gone home.'

Harry nodded. 'Thank you.' He knew Val wouldn't be off duty – she was in the middle of a murder inquiry – but, even if that hadn't been the case, home was the very last place she'd have gone.

Chapter Twenty-Eight

After the events of the previous day, Jess had decided that the only way forward was to stay focused, to try and push the image of Troy's battered body to the back of her mind and to get on with the job in hand. Her leave wasn't going to last forever and if she didn't make some progress soon the trail was likely to go cold.

For Len's sake, she couldn't allow that to happen.

Sipping on her coffee, she stared down at the three brown folders on the table. Where to start? Deacon was perhaps best left alone until she saw what BJ came up with – if he came up with anything. Her hopes weren't too high on that score. She flipped open the slim Ellen Shaw file but then as quickly closed it again. If she wanted to find out the truth she had to go back to the beginning and that meant going all the way back to when Grace Harper had gone missing.

Jess lit a cigarette and began to peruse the thick pile of press articles. Coming so close on the heels of the other missing child, Grace's disappearance had initially sparked fears of a serial killer. The senior investigating officer had been a superintendent called Fielding. If he was still alive, he'd be retired by now. She'd have to try and track him down but the chances of being able to do that on a Saturday were slight. Jess made a note to chase it up on Monday morning and then returned her attention to the clippings.

Grace had disappeared on a Wednesday, on a hot summer's afternoon in early August. It was the school holidays and after lunch she had left through the back door and run along the alley to play with friends at a neighbour's house. At six o'clock, when she still hadn't come home, Sharon had gone round to pick her up. But Grace, she discovered, had never arrived. The other kids hadn't seen her. No one had seen her. Sharon raised the alarm and the police were called. By then her daughter had been missing for over five hours.

There wasn't much detail on Grace herself. Other than her age and physical appearance, there were only the usual emotive contributions from the Harpers' neighbours and friends – that she had always been a 'happy child', that she was intelligent, that she wouldn't just wander off on her own. Jess couldn't help noticing that, even at this early stage, they were all presuming the worst. Little Grace Harper, it seemed, had been dead and buried before the investigation had even begun.

She found herself staring down at pictures of the missing girl. A thin shiver ran through her. She took a drag on her cigarette and tapped the trembling grey residue into the ashtray. What was she doing? Perhaps everyone else was right and she was wrong. Perhaps even Harry Lind, although she hated to admit it, was seeing things more clearly than she was. With nothing to prove otherwise, there was every chance that poor Grace Harper *was* dead.

In which case Len had made one almighty mistake.

And if she wasn't careful, she might be compounding it.

Was that possible? Jess rapped her fingertips against the table and groaned. Now wasn't the time to start having those doubts again. Len Curzon might have been a hopeless drunk but even at his worst he'd been able to string a few coherent thoughts together. And he couldn't have been legless for the entire ten days he'd sat outside Ellen Shaw's flat.

'No,' she said firmly.

Pulling the file closer, she started reading again. There must be something in here. Eventually she found a short interview with an aunt, a woman called Joan Sewell. She was the sister of Grace's father and was vehemently protesting his innocence. From her comments it was clear that the finger of suspicion was pointing straight at Michael Harper. That was hardly surprising. In cases of this kind members of the family were usually the first to be investigated and, from what Jess could recall, Michael had had a history of violence.

She flipped back through the pages of her notebook and nodded. Harper had served two jail sentences for GBH, been fined for numerous minor incidents and been generally renowned for the ferocity of his temper. However, he had never been accused of any form of domestic violence and also had a rock solid alibi for the afternoon in question. He'd been at work at the time Grace had disappeared with enough witnesses to theoretically silence the worst of his accusers. Still, that never stopped the tongues from wagging.

Michael Harper had died over eighteen years ago and so whatever he knew – if he knew anything at all – had gone to the grave with him. His sister, however, could be very much alive and kicking. The local article Jess had been reading gave Joan Sewell's address as Peak Street. That wasn't too far away. Was it possible that, twenty years on, she could still be living there?

Jess grabbed the local phone book and ran through the listings. She found a handful of Sewells but only one registered in Peak Street. It was number thirty-four. Her eyes widened with surprise. Could it really be that simple? Well, sometimes it was but before she got too excited it was worth reminding herself that finding the address was the easy bit; getting Joan Sewell to talk could prove to be a far bigger hurdle. Should she call first? Maybe not. That would only give the woman an opportunity to slam the phone down. Face to face, Jess would have the chance to at least try and persuade her.

Jess changed out of her jeans and put on a pair of smart grey woollen trousers and a black jumper. She looked in the mirror, applied a smudge of lipstick and smoothed down her hair. This might be a waste of time but anything was better than sitting around in the flat.

It was one of those deceptively bright mornings where the sun was shining but the temperature was icy. The freezing air hit her as she walked out of the door. Jess tucked her chin into her scarf, pushed her hands deep into her pockets and set off briskly down the street. After twenty yards she crossed the road and took the shortcut through Victoria Park.

Fifteen minutes later she was standing alongside a terrace of small yellow brick houses in Peak Street. Some of the properties were bordering on the ramshackle but number thirty-four was neat and tidy, its windows gleaming and the net curtains white as snow.

She rang the bell and waited.

The woman who answered the door was in her late fifties. She was tall and angular with a thin face and narrow lips. Her hair was iron grey and cut unflatteringly short.

'Mrs Joan Sewell?' Jess asked.

The woman nodded, drying her hands on an apron.

So she had found her! Jess had to stop herself from smiling too broadly. 'My name's Jessica Vaughan. I'm sorry to disturb you but I was wondering if we could talk. I'm looking into the case of Grace Harper.'

At the mention of Grace, a light instantly sprang into Mrs Sewell's eyes. She took a step forward. 'Is there some news?' she said. 'Have you found her?'

By which Jess knew that she was asking if the body had been discovered. She could hear the emotion in her voice, a combination of dread and hope, dread that her worst fears had been confirmed, hope that Grace might finally be put to rest. 'I'm sorry,' she replied softly. 'I'm not from the police. I'm a reporter and I'm investigating several—'

But the word 'reporter' was enough to set off alarm bells. As if Jess had deliberately misled her, Mrs Sewell's eyes grew cold. 'Clear off!' she said. She flapped her hands in an effort to shoo her away. 'Can't you vultures leave anyone in peace?'

Her experience of the press had clearly not been a positive one. Already she had turned her back and Jess knew she only had seconds to persuade her. Once that door was closed it would never be opened again. 'I just wanted to say that I don't believe Michael had anything to do with it.'

Mrs Sewell stopped abruptly and looked over her shoulder.

'He was treated very badly,' Jess said quickly. 'And I was thinking, hoping, that maybe you could help me put the record straight.'

'What do you mean?' Her voice remained suspicious but was not entirely hostile.

Jess glanced deliberately towards the houses to the left and right as if the neighbours already had their noses pressed against the glass. 'Perhaps if we could talk inside?'

Mrs Sewell hesitated. Eventually, she nodded. 'I suppose I could give you five minutes.'

'Thank you.'

Jess followed her in. There was a tiny hallway with a mat on which she dutifully wiped her muddy feet before advancing into the living room. Everything, as she'd already anticipated, was scrupulously clean and tidy, all the surfaces gleaming and not a speck of dust in sight.

'Let me take your coat.'

Jess relinquished it reluctantly. It wasn't that much warmer inside than out. There was no central heating and the hissing gas fire was turned down low.

'Please, take a seat,' Mrs Sewell said. Then, as if she'd decided that a touch more hospitality might be in order, she produced the semblance of a smile. 'And I suppose you'll be wanting a cup of tea?'

After a morning spent swilling endless mugs of coffee, another drink was the last thing Jess wanted but she decided not to take the risk of offending her. 'Thank you,' she said, sinking down on to the sofa. 'That would be lovely.'

While her hostess marched purposefully through to the kitchen, Jess took a moment to look around. All the furniture was old but still serviceable, the dark green sofa with its matching chair, a couple of side tables, a mahogany glass-fronted cabinet filled with assorted pieces of china. The wallpaper was a faded pattern of pale pink rosebuds. But it was the mantelpiece that really drew her attention: ranged across its surface were the framed family photographs, amongst them a picture of a small girl dressed in white. Her hair was fair, her eyes wide and dark. Jess was in no doubt as to her identity. She stared at the child and the child, somewhat disturbingly, appeared to stare straight back.

'Hello, Grace,' she murmured.

And then Jess felt a sudden rush of guilt. Could any good really come from resurrecting the past, from opening old wounds and churning up emotions? Perhaps the truth, whatever it was, was best left buried.

But it was too late to back out now. Joan Sewell was returning with the tea. Her hands were shaking a little although it wasn't possible to tell if it was from a temporary anxiety or some more permanent ailment.

'Thanks,' Jess said, as a cup was placed on the table beside her. 'This is very kind of you.'

Joan Sewell sat down in the chair and then immediately leaned forward, her long fingers clasped together and a look of expectation on her face. 'So you want to know about Michael?'

Jess felt that guilt nibbling at her conscience again. She did want to know about him – and a lot more too – but didn't want to gain the information under wholly false pretences. Sometimes, as a reporter, you had to tell a few white lies but there was a difference between that and downright deception. She knew what this woman wanted – exoneration for her brother – but wasn't prepared to raise her hopes too much. Honesty, albeit in a slightly watered-down version, could sometimes be the best option.

'Look, Mrs Sewell, before we go on, there's something I have to tell you. I've only just begun to investigate this case and I can't put my hand on my heart and swear that anything will come of it or that I'll ever be able to clear Michael's name. Making rash promises like that just wouldn't be right. All I can say is that, having looked closely at the available evidence, I can see how unfairly he was treated and how harshly he was judged.' She paused to take a breath and to see if there was any response. When none was forthcoming, she quickly continued, 'And so that's why I'm here, why I've come to see you today. There are still too many unanswered questions and I want to find out the truth. I'm hoping you can help me do that.'

Joan, having listened carefully, frowned and took a sip of her tea while she mulled over the proposition. For the next ten seconds, she gazed intently down at her sensible brown brogues. Eventually, she lifted her head and nodded. Even this small glimmer of hope was apparently better than nothing. 'He was a good man,' she said.

Jess, recalling Michael Harper's criminal record, could have begged to differ but now was hardly the time to start quibbling over the odd spot of GBH. 'I'm sure he was.'

'And they made his life hell,' Joan said, 'the police, the neighbours, the papers. Even when they *knew* that he couldn't have done it, even when it had been proved, they wouldn't leave him alone.' Her narrow shoulders shuddered and her face flushed red. 'Michael never heard the end of it. It was unbearable. He'd lost his daughter, lost his lovely little girl, and they still wouldn't stop hounding him. They accused him of all sorts of terrible things.'

'It must have been vile.'

Joan's hands battled with each other, the fingers twisting and turning. 'It killed him,' she said. Her voice was strained now, tight and bitter. As if too many long-hidden feelings were slowly rising to the surface, she was struggling to keep her emotions in check. 'He tried to carry on, he tried his best but . . .'

'I'm sorry,' Jess said softly.

But the sentiment, even if it was heard, was not acknowledged. Joan Sewell had her mind on other things. 'And *her*. She was the worst of them all. If it hadn't been for her . . . That *bitch* was the one who put all those ideas into their heads.'

Jess started at the accusation. 'Bitch' was the last word she'd have expected to escape from this woman's prim and proper mouth but she could tell, from the exaggerated way in which it was spoken, that it had come straight from the soul. Jess could only take an educated guess at who she was referring to and her heart began to beat a little faster. 'Do you mean Grace's mother?'

Joan's lips twisted into a grimace. 'Our Michael never raised a hand to her – although God, she gave him reason enough – and he'd have sooner died than touch a hair on the head of that little one. Devoted to her, he was.' She stopped, as if suddenly aware that her mouth might be running away from her. She took a moment, her thin chest rising and falling, to gather her thoughts together. When she spoke again her tone was more moderate. 'Still, I'm sure she's got a different story to tell. I suppose you've already talked to her.'

Jess had a split second to consider what to do. Would it be more useful to say that she had or she hadn't? She went with her instincts. 'No. I thought it was more important to see you first.'

It was the right decision. Joan Sewell was obviously flattered. Perhaps it was the first time she had ever been given priority. She smiled, stood up and walked over to the mantelpiece. 'This is Michael,' she said, taking down a picture and briefly touching the face before passing it over. 'You only have to look at him to know that he couldn't do anything like *that*.'

Jess gazed down at the photograph. Michael Harper had been tall and broad, a thickset muscular man. She could see the kinks in his nose where it had been broken more than once. He had his hands on his hips and was staring straight into the camera. She wasn't sure what to say – No, *he doesn't look like a child killer* hardly seemed appropriate – and so she simply nodded.

Perhaps mistaking her silence for a form of scepticism, Joan began to argue his case again. 'Oh, he had a temper all right. I'll not deny that. He drank too much and was always in trouble. He was in prison too but that doesn't make him a wife beater or—'

'Of course not,' Jess said. She passed the photograph back, eager to pursue the subject of Sharon Harper.

The portrait was returned to its rightful place and Joan sat down again.

171

'So it wasn't a happy marriage?' Jess asked tentatively.

'No one could be happy married to a woman like that.'

'Really?' Jess said, hoping to prompt further revelations.

But Joan only sniffed and wrinkled her nose as if the bad smell of Sharon Harper might still be lingering in a corner of the room.

Taking a sip of her tea, Jess waited a few seconds. This was an avenue that needed exploring but she didn't want to appear too keen. Coming across as a scandal-mongering member of the press wasn't going to help. Joan Sewell was likely to clam up for good. Instead, Jess cleared her throat and said, conversationally, 'I suppose Sharon must have been quite young when they first got together?'

'Got herself in the family way, didn't she?' Joan sneered. 'She was only sixteen.'

Jess couldn't help thinking that it took two to tango – she hadn't got pregnant on her own – but sensibly refrained from sharing the reflection. Michael had been about ten years older, old enough surely to have mastered the basic art of contraception.

'He did the decent thing of course,' Joan continued. 'Other men, you wouldn't have seen them for dust but he stood by her. He did his best to make it work – for the sake of the baby.' Her hands jumped and started their restless dancing again. 'He loved that little girl. He'd have done anything for her.'

Jess left a respectful pause before asking, 'And Sharon? Was she close to Grace too?'

Joan made a loud snorting noise. 'Her? She was too busy running around with her fancy men to spend time with her own child. That poor little mite was lucky to have a hot meal on the table more than once a week.'

Jess felt her eyebrows shoot up. Now *that* was interesting. 'You mean she had boyfriends?'

'She worked in a nightclub.' As if the very nature of this occupation was proof positive of Sharon Harper's slatternly character, Joan shook her head reproachfully. 'What kind of mother has a job like that? Mixing with all sorts she was, out until all hours.'

'I see,' Jess said, trying to convey by the tone of her voice a similar level of disapproval. 'And was there anyone in particular she . . . er, ran around with?' Noticing Joan purse her lips at what had perhaps been interpreted as a rather prurient inquiry, Jess immediately sought to clarify the question. 'I'm only asking because it all sheds light on what Sharon was really like, what her true personality was and what Michael had to put up with. I mean, I think it's essential that people understand that.'

'When it came to that woman, he had the patience of a saint,' Joan said.

Jess was beginning to wish she'd been born with the same attribute. It seemed like every time she got close to prising open what could possibly be a can of worms, the lid was firmly slammed shut again. It was all so frustrating. Did she dare follow up on the subject of Sharon's boyfriends or should she wait and approach it later from a different angle? As it happened, she didn't need to make the decision. Joan Sewell was unable to resist another opportunity to put the knife in.

'Anything with a few quid in its pocket would do. She wasn't fussy. Money-mad, she was, always wanting new things, new clothes, shoes, holidays abroad. Michael worked his fingers to the bone but nothing was ever good enough. She'd rather be out gallivanting than at home taking care of her daughter.'

'And did he know that she was . . .?'

Joan scowled and flapped a hand. 'Oh, he knew all right but he always made excuses for her. He'd have put up with anything so long as she didn't leave him, so long as she didn't take Grace away.'

Jess smiled sympathetically. This was a very different picture to the one the press had painted twenty years ago, that of a devoted and doting young mother, but she wasn't sure if Joan Sewell's testimony could be entirely trusted either. There was too much anger colouring her opinions, too much bitterness. 'But what I still don't understand,' she said, leaning forward,

173

'is why Sharon should suggest that Michael had ill-treated her. Why would she do that?'

Joan expelled an audible sigh as if the answer was beyond the obvious. 'Well, it suited her, didn't it? She had to find some way of justifying herself, of explaining why she spent so little time at home. She didn't want the papers getting hold of any gossip and by suggesting that Michael had . . . had abused her, provided the perfect excuse for her behaviour. No one was going to blame her then, were they?' Her eyes brightened with what could have been rage, spite or simply justified resentment. 'She was only concerned about herself. Sharon loved playing the victim; she always had to be the centre of attention.'

Jess nodded, wondering at the same time whether it could really be true. Even if Sharon Harper had been unfaithful, even if she had been a less-than-perfect wife and mother, these were still harsh judgements. The disappearance of a child had to be devastating to any parent and it was hard to imagine anyone actually trying to take advantage of the situation. These thoughts, however, she kept to herself. It was best to move on. 'Tell me about Grace,' she said. 'Was she happy, do you think?'

'Happy enough,' Joan said. 'Considering.'

Sensing a return to the subject of Sharon's possibly endless inadequacies, Jess tried to move the conversation on. 'Did she come round often? Did you see much of her?'

'Not as much as I'd have liked. Sharon didn't like her visiting me.'

'And why was that?'

Joan pushed back her shoulders and lifted her chin. Sitting ramrod straight, she recited the words as though she was giving evidence in court. 'She was worried about what Grace might tell me.'

'And did she tell you anything?'

'She didn't need to,' Joan said. 'I could see it in her face.'

It was the kind of comment that made great tabloid copy but didn't go far towards providing any actual proof. 'So Grace *wasn't* happy.'

'I didn't say that,' Joan snapped. 'Michael took good care of her. She loved her dad. She loved coming round here too until . . .'

Jess put her cup down carefully on the table. 'Until?'

There was a long pause while Joan looked directly at her. A shadow passed across her lined face and the fingers of her trembling hands clenched together. Her gaze flickered and then dropped down towards the floor. 'Until she went missing,' she said.

Convinced she'd been about to say something else, Jess frowned. There was a clue being dangled right in front of her but she couldn't figure out how to reach for it, never mind pull it in. The woman wasn't being honest but she couldn't risk a confrontation. Jess had to keep her on side. 'It must have been awful. I can't imagine how you coped.'

Joan kept her eyes fixed firmly on the floor.

Jess persisted. 'I know this is a difficult question but do you have *any* idea of what might have happened that day?'

Finally, Joan looked up again but only to shake her head. 'If her mother had taken more care, Grace would still be alive.'

Realizing that she'd reached the end of the line, that Joan Sewell had said as much as she was going to, Jess got to her feet. There was no point outstaying her welcome. 'Well, thank you very much for your time. I really appreciate it. And thank you for the tea.' She took a card from her wallet and placed it on the table. 'This is my number. If you think of anything else I should know, please just give me a ring.'

Glancing over towards the mantelpiece, she gazed for a moment on the picture of Grace before returning to Joan Sewell. She had spent over twenty years waiting for news of her niece and Jess felt sorry for her, pity for her dreadful grief, but couldn't quite bring herself to like the woman. She pulled on her coat and headed for the door. She'd be glad to get away; it was a house full of bitterness and ghosts.

Out in the fresh air again, Jess breathed deeply and trotted towards the park. She needed to get home, to write everything down while it was still fresh in her mind. It was a shame she couldn't have taken notes or even taped the conversation but she had sensed that Joan would not talk freely if her words were being recorded.

Ten minutes later, while she was crossing the grass, she paused to turn her phone back on and almost instantly it started ringing. A sigh escaped as she read the caller ID; it was her editor, Toby Marsh. What did *he* want? Reluctantly, she picked up. 'Hi.'

'Please tell me it isn't true,' he said sharply.

She flinched as she heard the anger in his voice. For a second, irrationally, she thought it had something to do with Joan Sewell. Had she called up the paper already and made a complaint? 'What?'

'That you were present at a murder scene last night and didn't even call it in?'

'Oh,' she said, momentarily relieved before the full implication of what he was saying began to sink in. Her heart took another dive. 'How did you hear about that?'

'Never mind how I heard about it. Why the hell didn't you ring me?'

'I'm on leave,' she mumbled defensively.

His exasperated breath hissed down the line. 'You're a bloody reporter, Jess – you're never on leave. What's the matter with you?'

She felt her hackles rise. He might well be justified in his complaint but she wasn't in the mood for his bullying reproaches. 'Okay,' she said, 'let me put it another way: I've just lost a close colleague, a friend, and I'm still trying to deal with it. That's why I asked for time off, time to try and get my head together. Now yesterday, by some weird freak of fate, I accidentally stumbled on a corpse and I'm sorry if it disappoints you but the very last thing on my mind after seeing that body, after throwing up and then spending hours down the nick, was how good a story it was likely to make. And maybe that makes me a lousy reporter, I don't know, but I'd rather believe that it just makes me a fairly normal human being.'

There was a silence from the other end of the line. Jess dug the heel of her boot into the wet grass, still angry but also worried that she'd just put her job on the line. Having a go at your boss wasn't the best career move in the world. She waited for him to come back with some caustic retort but her bargaining power was stronger than she'd anticipated.

'Well, okay,' he said, his tone coming about as close to apologetic as it ever could. 'I can understand that. I'm sorry if you felt I was criticizing you. It's been a difficult time for all of us.'

'Yeah,' she said. 'It has.'

'But I hope you can see it from my point of view. I have a reporter right on the spot, right in the middle of it and . . .' He gave a small ingratiating laugh. 'Anyway, let's not go over all that again. It's not too late. If you come into the office now, we can still—'

'I can't,' Jess said.

'I'm sorry?'

'I mean I can't talk right now. Can I call you back?'

'When?'

'Soon,' she said. 'Half an hour.' Jess hung up before she said something else she'd regret. Shoving the phone back into her bag, she grabbed a cigarette and lit it. She wished she had the guts to tell him what to do with his point of view but insulting her editor wasn't going to pay the rent. Still, at least she could have the pleasure of making him sweat for the next thirty minutes.

Chapter Twenty-Nine

There was a sharp ring on the doorbell. Carefully, Harry got to his feet and limped towards the hall. Since the attack, the muscles in his leg had felt stiff and painful and his progress was slow. He was barely halfway across the room when another three rings, loud and impatient, cut through the air.

'For God's sake,' he muttered.

As soon as he answered the door he wished that he hadn't. Jane Anderson was standing on the other side. She had a large holdall in one hand and a mobile phone pressed up against her ear in the other. 'I've got to go. See you later,' she said into the phone before presenting Harry with the merest glimmer of a smile.

'I hope you don't mind,' she said, in the tone of voice that suggested she didn't really care whether he minded or not, 'but I've just come to pick up a few things for Val.'

Harry stared at her. 'You've *what*?'

'Don't worry, I won't be long.' With the determination of a bailiff she moved forward to gain entrance to the flat.

It was his instinct to bar her way and for a moment he did exactly that. 'Hang on,' he said. 'If Valerie wants her things, why doesn't she call round herself to get them?'

'Because she's busy. She's working today.'

'And she couldn't pick up the phone because . . .?'

'It's only a few clothes. What's the big deal? You can hardly expect her to live out of a suitcase.' Jane shook her head. 'I told her you'd be like this. Why do you always have to make everything so difficult?'

178

'Me?' Harry spluttered, glaring back at her. 'I'm not the one who hasn't even got the decency to call.'

She raised her eyes to the heavens. 'There's no need to make a drama out of it. Look, just go ahead and ring her if you like. I'm sure she'll be overjoyed at the interruption. And hey, don't mind me; I'm perfectly happy to stand out here in the cold and wait.'

Harry was tempted to slam the door in her face but suspected that was exactly what she wanted. It would give her the perfect excuse to bad-mouth him later. Refusing her entrance to the flat would hardly improve his relations with Val either. Reluctantly he stood back to let her in. 'You'll have to be quick,' he said. 'I'm on my way out.'

'Of course you are,' she said, her cynical gaze taking in his dishevelled state. Barefoot, unshaven and dressed in a pair of tatty jeans and an old T-shirt, he looked about as far from going out as any self-respecting man could be.

As they walked through the living room he saw her eyes greedily alight on the used mugs, plates and newspapers that were scattered around. She was probably taking note of the dust count too. He made an instant resolution not to let her anywhere near the bomb site that used to be the kitchen.

Fortunately the bedroom was in a reasonable state. Apart from yesterday's shirt thrown over a chair, the unmade bed and a stray black sock lying on the floor there wasn't too much to criticize. He waved her in. 'Help yourself.'

She gave him another of her thin worthless smiles before dumping the holdall on the crumpled duvet and going straight to the wardrobe. While she efficiently stripped the clothes from their hangers, Harry watched from the door. With her willowy figure, full mouth and wide blue eyes, he knew a lot of men found Jane Anderson attractive. There was no accounting for taste. Personally, he'd rather chew off his own fingers than spend a minute more than he had to in her company.

Harry put his hands in his pockets and continued to scrutinize her as she moved briskly to the chest of drawers and began emptying the bras, knickers and tights into the holdall.

Although he liked confident women, he had always found Jane aggressive rather than assertive. Today, with her determined expression and her long black hair tumbling down her back, she reminded him of one of those avenging Furies that the Ancient Greeks wrote about. He could see why she terrified anyone who crossed her.

As she was making no attempt to talk – and seemed quite happy to continue that way – Harry perversely tried to start up a conversation.

'So how's work going?' he asked.

She looked up and frowned. 'Fine. How's yours?'

'Fine.'

It was several years now since she'd stopped defending scumbag villains – too many of whom she had managed to get off – and moved into the field of employment law. From all accounts, and he could well believe it, she was equally good at this. Dealing with cases of discrimination, be it racial, religious or gender-based, was her speciality. Jane could sniff out a hint of bigotry from twenty paces and employers up and down the country quaked at the mention of her name. It was all very admirable, very worthy, but there was something about her holier-than-thou attitude that brought out the worst in him. He always felt the urge to express views he didn't feel, to come out with comments so politically incorrect that even his own father, a man widely renowned for his bigoted views, would flinch at their utterance.

'Val told me you'd been in a fight,' she said, pausing to stare at his face. As if he'd been involved in a drunken scrap, a result of some vile and unnecessary male machismo, her nose wrinkled with disgust. 'That's quite a black eye.'

'You should see the other guy,' Harry retorted, annoyed by her presumptions. '*He's* lying in the morgue.'

Jane's eyes darkened and her mouth fell open. 'Charming.'

Every inch of her body, much to Harry's satisfaction, screamed utter disgust. He grinned. His enjoyment, however, was short-lived. Picking up the bag, she pushed past him and headed for the bathroom. He watched as she almost emptied

180

out the cabinet, removing all the bottles and tubes that Val considered essential to the everyday maintenance of her face and body. *Just how long was she planning on staying away for?* It was a question he wanted to ask but couldn't.

Finally, Jane zipped up the holdall, turned and nodded. 'All done.' As if she wasn't just talking about the packing, there was a hint of gloating triumph in her voice.

Harry gladly escorted her towards the exit. On the short journey back across the living room, however, he had time to think that he had maybe played this all wrong. A little more remorse and a lot less pride might have been more useful in healing the ever-growing rift between him and Val. He thought about trying to say something meaningful or even, God forbid, vaguely apologetic but couldn't find the necessary words. Grovelling to the likes of Jane Anderson just wasn't in his repertoire.

Opening the door, Harry stood aside to let her leave. She shifted the heavy holdall on to her shoulder and turned to look at him. Their eyes locked in a moment of pure animosity.

'See you around,' she said.

'I'm sure.'

Her mouth curled up into a smile. There was something about that smile, about its self-satisfied smugness, that set his teeth on edge. Did she know something that he didn't? What had Val told her? Harry was temped to spit out a few words he'd regret, and a few words he probably wouldn't, but was distracted by Mac's unexpected arrival.

Striding up the drive with a brown paper bag in his hand, Mac suffered a temporary setback as he came face to face with the other visitor. He stopped dead in his tracks. 'Oh,' he said, his brows lifting. 'Ms Anderson.'

'Mr Mackenzie,' she replied. 'How nice to see you again.'

'Likewise.'

The two men watched as she strolled off down the street and climbed into a black BMW convertible. They were still

181

standing on the doorstep when the car swept smoothly past a few seconds later.

'We're in the wrong job,' Mac said enviously. 'How much do those damn things cost?'

'Don't even think about it.' Harry turned and stepped back inside the flat. 'Come on in.'

Mac followed, closing the door behind him. They went on through to the living room. 'So, I take it the delightful Ms Anderson wasn't here for tea and buns. Should I be worried?'

'Not unless you're planning on sexually harassing me in the workplace.'

'Tempting as that offer is, it's not on my list of priorities.'

Harry grinned. 'Well, that's one bit of good news.' His face quickly fell again. 'Actually, she was here to pick up some of Val's things. We appear to be having a break.'

Frowning, Mac sat down on the sofa. 'Sorry, mate. I didn't realize.'

'You know me. If I can screw up a relationship, I will. It's a natural talent.'

'You've not done too badly for the last five years.'

Harry shrugged. 'Anyway, enough of my troubles. What brings you round here on a Saturday?'

Mac lifted up the brown paper bag. 'Fresh bagels, cream cheese and salmon. I reckoned that after last night you might be in need of some comfort food. Never let it be said that I don't take care of my staff.'

'Thanks. I've got coffee on. Just give me a minute.' In the kitchen he quickly swept two cardboard pizza cartons and a heap of empty foil trays into the bin and then stared dolefully at the pile of washing-up sitting in the sink. Shaking his head, he filled two mugs from the percolator, added a splash of milk and returned to the living room.

'Ta,' Mac said. His gaze settled on Harry's face. 'That must have been quite some argument.'

Harry sat down and automatically lifted a hand to his eye. 'It looks worse than it is. And that, unfortunately, is more than can be said for Troy Jeffries.'

'Yeah, I'm surprised Holt hasn't got you on remand already.'

'It wasn't for the lack of trying.'

'I can imagine.' Mac bit down into a bagel and chewed, his large jaws working steadily. 'They pulled Stagg in as well but couldn't hold him. He wasn't even at the club yesterday.'

'Convenient,' Harry said.

'Perhaps. Although if you are going to murder members of staff, it's probably wiser not to do it in your own car park.'

There was some sense to that although Harry was loath to admit it.

'Anyway,' Mac continued, 'he's been pissed as a newt since Tommo died. Apparently the cops had to scrape him off the floor of his multi-million pound mansion.'

'That wouldn't have stopped him from picking up a phone and getting someone else to do his dirty work.'

'You think?'

'I don't know,' Harry said. 'No, probably not. You're right; even Ray Stagg wouldn't be stupid enough to shit on his own doorstep.' He scowled. 'I still can't work out if this has anything to do with Webster's disappearance. It could be totally unrelated. Maybe I should go back to Vista and start asking a few more questions.'

'Or maybe you should take a few days off. In fact, take a week. I insist. It'll give you time to get yourself sorted.'

Harry stared at him, bemused. 'I'm in the middle of a case, Mac. I can't just—'

'Not any more. I got a call from Stagg this morning. Our services, it appears, are no longer required.'

'What?'

'And before you ask, he didn't give a reason.'

Harry swore softly under his breath. This was bad news; if Stagg was pulling out then he'd either found Al or knew for certain that he was already dead. 'But what about Agnes? She's still missing. I can't just—'

'She's not your responsibility.'

Harry put down what remained of his bagel. He'd suddenly

183

lost his appetite. 'But it was me she called. She must have seen something. She may even have witnessed what happened.'

'All the more reason to leave it to the cops.' Mac glanced at his watch and lumbered slowly to his feet. 'Sorry, but I've got to get going. Try and look on the bright side; at least you're not working for Stagg any more. That has to be a bonus.'

'Yeah,' Harry said. 'But just promise me that as well as billing him for every goddamn minute I spent on this case, you add on substantial extras for injuries sustained.'

Mac hesitated, the briefest of pauses before his mouth broke into a smile. 'You bet.' As he strode into the hall, he decided to impart some fatherly wisdom. 'And you should really try and sort things out with Val. You two are good together. Leave it too long and it only gets harder.'

'Can I really be hearing this?' Harry laughed as he opened the front door. 'Mr David Mackenzie giving me relationship advice? As I recall, you've been divorced three times.'

'Exactly!' Mac said. He slapped Harry on the arm. 'And that's why I know what I'm talking about. You'd be wise not to make the same mistakes as I did.'

'I'll bear it in mind.'

'You do that,' Mac said, heading down the drive. Without looking back, he raised a hand and waved. 'And while you're off work, go to the doctor and get that leg checked out. You're no use to me if you can't bloody walk.'

Harry grinned and closed the door. His smile only faded as he limped back through to the living room and slumped down on the sofa. For a while he didn't move, not quite sure what to do next. His head was spinning with questions: What was Stagg playing at? Did he know where Al was? Where had Agnes gone? How was he going to resolve the situation with Valerie? How could he kill Jane Anderson without anyone finding out? And last, but not least, now that he was temporarily unemployed, what the hell was he going to do for the next week?

After a long study of the carpet, he raised his eyes and glowered at the mess around him. He needed to tidy up. His chances of winning back Val's affections would hardly be improved by having turned the flat into a carbon copy of the local tip.

It was almost an hour later when he heard the distinctive rattle of the letterbox. Going out into the hall, duster in hand, he saw his car keys lying on the floor. He bent down to pick them up and then pulled open the door. Nobody was there. His Audi, however, was parked outside. Stumbling barefoot to the gate, he stared left and right along the street but it was empty in both directions. If it had been Val, she'd made a speedy getaway.

He stood for a while feeling the icy cold seep into the soles of his feet. Slowly, he made his way back to the flat. No one, it seemed, was too keen to hang around today.

Chapter Thirty

Maddie Green flicked her long brown hair over her shoulder, giggled and passed the joint back to Zane. It was warm and smoggy in his bedroom and the purple walls were gently throbbing to the sound of trance. The steady beat had an almost hypnotic effect on her; she felt it deep inside her body as strong and relentless as her very own heartbeat.

'What are you thinking, babe?' he asked. They were sitting on the floor, at right angles to each other, and he nudged her foot with his. 'Tell me.'

Maddie was thinking about two weeks ago, about how sick she'd been the first time she'd smoked this stuff, but had no intention of admitting to that. Instead she giggled again and grinned at him. 'How bloody *bad* you are,' she said.

He laughed, taking a deep toke on the joint before flicking the ash in the saucer. He always liked it when she said things like that. 'You have no idea.'

But of course she did. Zane Keppell was bad through and through and that was why she loved him. He was tall and blond with dark blue eyes and muscles in his arms. He stole cars and set fire to them. He shoplifted. He thieved credit cards, phones, wallets and anything else that wasn't nailed down. He drank and smoked; he even dealt dope to his mates. Zane was the perfect embodiment of everything her mother despised.

Maddie smiled widely at him again. He put out his hand and for a second their fingers touched, skin against skin, and she drew in her breath. Lifting the damp end of the joint against her carefully glossed lips she was careful not to inhale too much. She was one of those girls, she liked to think, who learned from their mistakes.

Zane reached to his side and pulled out a shoebox from under the bed. He carefully placed his clingfilmed lump of dope, along with a packet of Rizlas, beneath an untidy heap of flyers, cards and photographs.

'Who's that?' Maddie asked, leaning forward. There was a picture of a young fair man lying on the top of the pile.

'That's my uncle,' he said.

'Show me.'

He passed her the photograph and then shuffled round so that his shoulder was leaning against hers. 'He was called Tony. You think I look like him?'

'Yeah,' she said, sensing that was what he wanted to hear. 'A bit.' In fact, he had softer features than Zane; Tony was more pretty than handsome with wide dark-lashed eyes and a soft pink mouth. There was something almost girlish about him.

'He died when I was three,' Zane said. 'He was only fifteen.'

'What happened?'

'This rich guy – he was well known, an MP – invited Tony to his flat and then he shot him.'

Maddie's eyes widened. 'What?' She wasn't sure whether to believe it or not. Zane wasn't a liar, exactly, but he did have a habit of embellishing the truth. Not that she cared too much – she was prone to a little drama herself. 'You're kidding?'

'No, I swear,' Zane said. 'He did. It was in all the papers and everything. You can check it out. The guy was called Deacon; he's still in jail.'

'But why did he—'

'Queer bastard, wasn't he?' Zane said. 'A fucking bender. He got obsessed and wouldn't leave him alone. When Tony wasn't having any of it, the shithead finished him off.' Zane quickly lifted a hand, formed a two-finger imaginary gun and made a shooting gesture with appropriate sound effects. 'Killed him,

187

didn't he, right there in his fancy penthouse flat. Shot him straight through the chest.'

'God,' Maddie said.

'Bloody queers. They're all perverts. I'd cut their fucking bollocks off and feed them to the pigs.'

Maddie murmured a faint ambiguous sound that she hoped would pass for agreement. It always made her uncomfortable when Zane expressed his less-than-liberal views on anyone who wasn't straight, white or Church of England. Living in London, this gave him plenty of scope to vent his bile on a regular basis. She knew in her heart that she ought to protest but was too eager for his approval to risk falling out with him. On this occasion she was able to justify her silence by telling herself that he was simply upset about his uncle.

Reaching over his thigh, she took another picture from the box. This one was of Tony standing with a girl in a back yard. She studied it for a while. The girl was pretty. She was wearing a short navy dress and Tony had his arm around her. They were both smiling. Maddie flipped it over and found some writing on the back. She read it and then looked at the photo again.

'Was she his girlfriend?'

'I guess,' Zane said. The joint was finished and he stubbed it out in the ashtray. He was still sitting close to her and she could feel his warm breath on her neck. 'Angie says that it was all Grandpa's fault.'

Maddie thought it was cool that he called his mother by her Christian name. She could never imagine doing that with hers. 'Why's that?'

'She says that if he hadn't been shagging that cheap little slut it would never have happened.'

Maddie frowned at him. The dope had turned her thoughts fuzzy and she couldn't make the connection between this remark and the story that had gone before. She had the feeling that she'd lost the drift, that maybe other things had been said that she'd already forgotten. 'Right,' she mumbled, worried that he might take offence at her lack of concentration.

But Zane already had his mind on other things. As if the mention of shagging had reminded him of what he *should* be doing, he took hold of her shoulder, leaned forward and kissed her. For a while she enjoyed the sensation of his lips against hers, of his gently probing tongue. She could feel the thrill run through her body. Her breathing grew faster and his grew more urgent too. Then his hands, as they always did, began to roam. They travelled the length of her spine, around her hips and up towards her chest. As his palm cupped her right breast and squeezed, she quickly pulled away.

'What's wrong?'

Maddie heard the peevish irritation in his voice – he didn't like not getting what he wanted – but she wasn't prepared to let him go any further. 'Nothing,' she said.

'What is it?' His tone had become gentle again, almost wheedling. He gazed into her eyes and stroked her hair. 'Come on, babe. You know I'll be careful.'

She was tempted, as ever, to give in to him and had to call on all her willpower to resist. Maddie might not know much about boys but she knew not to give away too much too soon. Girls who did that got themselves a reputation. Scrambling to her feet, she looked down on him, touched the crown of his head and smiled. 'Sorry, I'm running late. I've got to go.'

He gazed sulkily back up. 'You fancy meeting up tonight?'

Maddie did fancy it but knew it was impossible. Gullible as her mother might be, she couldn't afford to push her luck. Saturday afternoons spent with her girlfriends were fine but late-night absences were out of the question. Unless strict arrangements had been made, her mother expected her home by six and if she wasn't there all hell would be let loose.

'I'll call you,' she said.

'We're going up West,' he said. 'It'll be a laugh.'

'Yeah,' she said, pulling on her coat and heading for the door. 'I'll let you know.' She couldn't get into a discussion about it; she only had ten minutes to get to the station and didn't want to miss her train. Later, she would think up some excuse as to why she couldn't make it. It wasn't as if she could tell him the truth. Zane was fifteen and thought that she was fifteen too. If he ever saw her without make-up, she'd be doomed; it wouldn't take a genius to work out how old she really was and a thirteen-year-old girlfriend wouldn't do much for his street cred. However, she had no intention of allowing that to happen.

So long as she was careful, her secret should be safe.

Chapter Thirty-One

By Monday the bruising around Harry's eye had subsided and he looked more like he was in need of a good night's sleep than the recipient of a punch in the face. His leg was improving too although he wasn't yet sure if he could trust it with a brake pedal.

He stared out of the window at the scrap of back garden. An empty crisp packet blew aimlessly in the wind, occasionally catching on the twiggy branches of the few shrubs that were planted there. He didn't enjoy having time on his hands. What was he going to do with himself? It crossed his mind to go and visit his father; it had been over six months since he'd last seen him. He could get a cab to the station, catch a train down to the coast and be with him by lunchtime. Why not?

But already he could imagine the conversations they would have, his father's familiar look of disapproval and the way he would poke suspiciously at any plate of restaurant food that was placed in front of him. And Harry's recent injuries, although fading, would only increase the tension between them. Inevitably, they would return to that well-worn debate about why he should want to waste his life 'snooping into other people's business' when a perfectly good desk job had been on offer from the police. No matter how often Harry said that the very thought of it made his blood run cold, he wouldn't understand. There would be inquiries about Valerie too – questions he would need to deflect – and he really wasn't in the mood.

Harry leaned his forehead against the cool glass. It would be better to leave it, surely, until his face had healed. After all, there was no point in worrying him unnecessarily. It was a cheap excuse but one that he readily embraced. Once the decision was made he felt guilty but relieved. Henry Lind, he reflected, was not an unkind man, just a disappointed one. The problem was that Harry seemed to be the cause of most of his disappointments.

His mobile rang and he left the window to go and answer it.

'Yes,' he said.

'They let you out then?' Jess said.

'No, I'm serving fifteen long ones in Parkhurst and trying to look on the bright side.'

Jess expelled one of her loose breathy laughs. 'Hey, you're adaptable; I'm sure you'll survive. You just need to make some friends. I'm sure there must be lots of nice boys in there.'

'What a comforting thought.' He grinned and sat down on the sofa. 'So what can I do for you?'

'I hate to disturb your busy life but I need to check something out.'

Harry's smile wavered. She sounded worryingly upbeat and pleased with herself. 'Okay,' he said. 'Or maybe not. Do I really want to hear this?'

'Of course you do,' she said, 'unless you're the kind of man who has an aversion to the truth.'

'In my experience the truth isn't always an uplifting experience.'

'Just answer me one simple question and I'll leave you in peace. Did Ellen Shaw tell you that her father died last year?'

'Why?'

'It doesn't matter why,' she said. 'Did she or didn't she?'

Harry shrugged. He'd been hoping that she might have come to terms with Curzon's death and ditched the conspiracy

192

theories by now. 'I don't know. Perhaps. She might have mentioned that—'

Jess swiftly interrupted. 'Oh, come on! There's no *perhaps* about it. She told you that she'd gone to visit Paul Deacon because he was a friend of her father's. She told you that her father died last year.'

'I suppose,' he grudgingly admitted.

'Right,' she said.

'And that means?' Harry said.

She paused only long enough to inhale a small victorious breath before spilling it gently down the line. 'That means, my friend, that Ellen Shaw is an out-and-out liar. She lied to the police and she lied to you.'

Harry laughed. It came out sounding less cynical than he'd intended. 'And how, exactly, do you come to that conclusion?'

'You don't want to know,' she said.

But Harry always wanted to know, especially when his own judgement was being put on the line. He wasn't happy about the idea that Ellen Shaw might have deceived him. He was even less happy that Jess might be about to prove it. 'So where's the evidence?'

'I've got the proof sitting right here in my hands.'

'What kind of proof?'

'Rock solid,' she said. 'There's no disputing it.'

He could hear the confidence in her voice but, unwilling to fold without a semblance of a fight, he resorted to basic tactics. 'Which, seeing as you're on the end of a phone, doesn't actually mean that much.'

'You want to see?' she said. 'I'll show you if you want.'

Harry knew that he shouldn't rise to the challenge; if past experience was anything to go by, a meeting with Jess Vaughan was bound to end in grief. The whole Grace Harper business was a tragedy best left alone. Jess was pursuing a legacy that could only ever end in tears. He quickly made a decision. 'No' was what he needed to say and he needed to say it firmly. He didn't want to have anything more to do with it. Pressing the phone closer to his ear, he cleared his throat.

'Just tell me when and where,' Jess taunted.

'I'm at home,' he said. 'Come on round.'

The bell rang half an hour later. Jess waltzed through the door, dressed in a black leather jacket, blue jeans and black polo neck. Her eyes were bright. 'You won't believe this,' she said. She stopped suddenly and glanced over her shoulder. 'Hey, you're looking a bit better.'

He raised his brows. 'Why do I get the feeling that it isn't going to last?'

'Don't be like that,' she said. 'The quest for the truth is a good and noble one.'

'You've been reading those mind-improving books again.'

Smiling, she went through to the living room and took an envelope from her bag. She pulled out a piece of paper and passed it over. 'Here. Look at this.'

Harry unfolded the sheet and stared down. It was a photocopy of a cutting from the *Irish Times*, a short article about a Dublin car crash with two fatalities. 'And?' he asked after he had read it through a couple of times. He recognized the names of the victims but still couldn't understand what all the fuss was about.

'You see the names?' she said.

'William and Rose Corby. Ellen's parents, I presume. But so what?'

'Read the *date*,' she urged impatiently.

His eyes lifted to the top of the page and finally the penny dropped. 'Twelve years ago.'

'Exactly!' Jess said triumphantly. 'And she told you that her father died last year. Why should she lie about something like that?'

It was a good question. Harry frowned down at the cutting, considered some possible answers and then gave a shrug. 'You shouldn't jump to conclusions. There could be a perfectly logical explanation.'

'Yeah,' Jess said. 'There is. And it's that Ellen Shaw's a grade one liar.'

'Not necessarily.'

Jess took off her jacket and threw it over the back of the sofa. She sat down and gave him one of her exasperated looks. 'And how do you work that one out, Mr Detective?'

'Maybe when she talked to me, she wasn't referring to her real father. Maybe, after her parents died, she was adopted or fostered by somebody else.'

'What?' Jess said. 'No way! That doesn't make any sense. She would have been fifteen when they died in that crash so even if someone else did take her in she'd hardly start calling him Dad. No, there's only one rational explanation and that is that she was deliberately trying to put you off the scent.'

'The scent?' he said. 'I'm not a goddamn bloodhound.'

She grinned at him. 'Obviously not.'

Harry frowned and lowered himself into one of the chairs. Unable to refute her logic, he tried a different tack. 'Okay,' he said, 'so maybe she lied. She's not the first and she won't be the last, especially when there's a murder inquiry going on. That still doesn't mean that Ellen Shaw is Grace Harper.'

'No,' Jess agreed, 'but it does mean that she *could* be. Maybe it's a simple case of identity fraud. Grace could have been using Ellen's name for years; birth certificates are easy to come by. In fact, the real Ellen Shaw could be out there somewhere, completely unaware of what's been going on.'

It all sounded pretty far-fetched to Harry. 'What about National Insurance numbers?' he said. 'If what you're suggesting is true, it should have been spotted by now.'

Jess groaned. 'Oh, do you always have to be so negative! It's just an idea, a theory – let's not get bogged down by all the boring detail.'

He snorted. 'Spoken like a true journalist.'

Jess pulled a face. 'At least I'm trying to solve this mystery.'

'If there even *is* a mystery.' Harry leaned back and put his hands behind his head. 'So Ellen wasn't completely honest, fine, but that doesn't mean she isn't who she claims to be. It's a mighty leap from one small lie to what you're suggesting. And the reason for the lie could be quite straightforward – perhaps there is something more intimate going on between her and Paul Deacon, a relationship that she's trying to keep secret from her husband.'

'What, some kind of dangerous liaison?' Jess scoffed. 'Sweet nothings whispered across a prison table, promises of a beautiful future together?'

'It's a less preposterous theory than yours,' he snapped back.

'Well,' she said smugly, 'I might be tempted to agree with you if it wasn't for the fact that Paul Deacon had this press cutting in his cell and he only received it recently. Don't you think that's a little odd? If William Corby was such a great friend, why should he suddenly need a reminder of how he died all those years ago?'

Harry narrowed his eyes and stared at her. 'And are we talking about this *exact* press cutting,' he asked, holding it up, 'or another copy of it?'

'Does it really matter?' Then, seeing the expression on his face, she sighed and raised her hands. 'Okay, there's no need to look like that. So maybe I didn't obtain it by entirely righteous means. BJ *acquired* it for me. You know, the guy in Maidstone that I went to see on Friday.'

'Stole it, you mean.'

Jess could hardly dispute that but she lifted her chin and tried to brazen it out. 'I didn't ask him to,' she said. 'I didn't even know it existed. Anyway, there's no need to look so outraged; it's a press cutting, not a private letter or classified information. I could have found it myself if I'd spent the next three years trawling through the back issues of the *Irish Times*.'

'That's not the point,' Harry said. 'Once you start believing that the end justifies the means, then—'

'Yes, I know. It's the thin edge of the wedge. I get your point and it's a very worthy one. But don't tell you've never once broken the rules, never once crossed that strictly moral line of yours?'

Harry hesitated.

Jess laughed. 'There you go! Look, you don't mind if I make a drink, do you? I'm in desperate need of a coffee.'

He followed her through, leaned against the table and watched as she switched on the kettle and then quickly gathered mugs, coffee, milk and a spoon. Everything she did was imbued with a raw nervous energy. Harry felt a surge of admiration: he envied her single-minded determination and passion. He wasn't convinced that she was right but at least she had the courage of her convictions.

Jess glanced over at him. 'So how's your case going?'

'There is no case. As of Saturday, the services of Mackenzie's are no longer required by Mr Stagg.'

'Bummer,' she said. 'You can't be too pleased about that.'

'It happens.'

'Very philosophical.' She dumped a heaped teaspoon of coffee into both of the mugs and poured in the boiling water. 'I'm not sure if I could drop a case that easily. I mean, someone comes to you with a problem, employs you to investigate, you get halfway down the road and then . . .' She put the kettle back, picked up the spoon and began to stir the coffee. 'I'd feel kind of cheated.'

Harry couldn't deny it. 'There's nothing I can do,' he said. 'The client's terminated the contract. On top of which, Mac's laid me off for the week.'

She nodded, sympathetically. 'And there's still no news on Agnes?'

'Nothing.'

Jess continued to stir. 'You must want to know where she is, what happened to her. Now that, for me, would be the cause of endless sleepless nights.'

Harry skirted round the table and took the spoon from her fingers. 'I take it you're trying to make a point here.'

'Actually, I was thinking we could help each other.'

Harry heard a warning bell go off in his head. 'By which, presumably, you mean that I could help you.'

'It's not a one-way street. I was thinking more along the lines of mutual benefit. You can't drive but I'm sure you want to go places. I'd be willing to play chauffeuse.'

'And in return?'

Jess paused and took a sip from her mug. 'Seeing as you've got some free time, you could always pay another visit to Ellen.'

'And say what?'

'You could ask her why she lied to you. You could ask why she was *really* visiting Paul Deacon.'

Harry didn't feel a complete aversion to the idea. The prospect of seeing Ellen Shaw again had its attractions. However, he wasn't prepared to appear too keen. 'And how, exactly, would I get her to answer those questions?'

'Guile, wit, charm.' Jess gave a quick shrug. 'You're a private eye, aren't you? I'm sure you'll think of something.'

Harry pulled out a chair, sat down and leaned his elbows on the table. Getting involved with Jess Vaughan again was probably not the smartest move in the world but the proposed arrangement did have its advantages. 'Well, all right,' he said eventually, as if she had twisted his arm, 'but only on the condition that we split the time between your case and mine.'

She sat down opposite and smiled. 'And that would be the case you're not working on any more.'

'As opposed to your completely imaginary one.'

'We'll see,' she said smugly.

As if dealing with a particularly stubborn child, Harry gave a slow shake of his head. 'Okay,' he said, 'so let's get started. Tell me your thoughts on the Deacon situation.'

Jess cupped her chin in the palm of her hand and took a second to deliberate. 'Right, now my number one premise is that it's unlikely that Deacon and William Corby ever knew each other. Paul Deacon was a right-wing politician. William Corby

198

was an Irish Catholic train driver. I can't see them having much in common.'

'That's a rather elitist view, isn't it?'

She frowned at the interruption. 'I prefer to think of it as a realistic one. I've done my research. Deacon was born in London, had a privileged upbringing, went to Harrow and then on to Cambridge University. He was stinking rich and very ambitious. He also had a pretty fancy lifestyle, expensive flat in London, big pile in the country, exotic holidays abroad; when he wasn't in the House, he spent most of his time mingling with the glitterati. According to that press cutting, Corby worked on the railway for his entire life. So when and how exactly did they forge this unique and enduring friendship of theirs?'

'Who knows?' Harry said. 'I agree that it's unlikely but it's not impossible. You can't just dismiss it out of hand.'

'I'm not. I'm only going on the laws of probability. And if you factor in the oddness of Ellen Shaw lying about the date her parents died—'

'Then we're simply back to the idea that she had another reason for visiting Paul Deacon. Maybe romance, maybe business, maybe anything she didn't want her husband to know about. I don't see how it gets you any closer to making a direct link between her and Grace Harper.'

'Instinct,' she said.

'Which is hardly what you'd call a well-reasoned argument.'

Jess pulled a face. 'It doesn't mean I'm wrong either.'

That, in Harry's view, was a typically female response but he desisted from sharing the thought. 'So, putting Deacon aside for the moment, what else have you got?'

'There's the Theresa Neal murder,' she said. 'Everyone presumes that because *she* was murdered Grace had to be a victim too but . . .' She stopped and shook her head. 'I don't know. Actually, I was going to ask if you knew the guy who worked on those cases. He was a superintendent called Alan Fielding.'

'It was twenty years ago,' Harry said indignantly. 'Just how old do you think I am?'

Jess raised her eyebrows. 'Probably best if I don't answer that. So how would I go about tracking Fielding down?'

'I could make some calls,' Harry said. 'If I felt that the person asking for such a favour was being suitably respectful.'

She smiled. 'Consider me thoroughly chastened and full of respect.'

'Bearing that in mind, I might just be prepared to help. Although if he is still alive, he'll certainly be retired.'

'And what are the chances, if Mr Fielding *is* still breathing, of his actually agreeing to talk to me?'

Harry found himself frowning. 'Hard to say for sure. They're both unsolved cases and that's a sore point with most coppers. No one likes to be reminded of their failures. But then again, if there's the chance of some new leads, some new information . . . Personally, I'd want to know but that doesn't hold true for everyone.'

'If you could try, I'd appreciate it.'

He nodded. Ever since he'd missed the dinner last Monday, he'd been meaning to ring Scott Hall and apologize. Now he had two good reasons to make that call. Scott had worked in Hackney for years; if anyone knew what had happened to Fielding then he would. 'And is there anything else I should know about?'

She hesitated, fiddled with her hands and then glanced down at her coffee.

'Jess?'

She slowly looked up. 'Er . . . well, I did go and see Joan Sewell on Saturday. She was Grace's aunt.'

'You did *what*?' Harry's mouth dropped open.

Instantly, she was on the defensive. 'Don't worry. I was careful, I swear. You may find this hard to believe but I can actually do subtle and sympathetic. I didn't mention a word about the possibility of Grace still being alive. I wouldn't even think about going there with what I've got. All I told her was

200

that I was looking into some past cases, going through the evidence etc. She was perfectly happy to talk to me.'

'Happy?' he said.

'You know what I mean. Not happy, exactly, but okay with it. She could have thrown me out but she didn't. She *wanted* to talk.' Jess gave him one of her full-on antagonistic glares. 'And what's wrong with that? Some people are prepared to share their feelings, rather than bottling them all up.'

Harry suspected she was having a dig at him but wasn't prepared to rise to the bait. 'And she told you what?'

Jess provided a brief synopsis of her conversation with Joan Sewell, of how Michael Harper had been placed under suspicion, of how Sharon had allegedly been a less-than-ideal mother and wife. She let it all out in a few long sentences, took a deep breath and then sat back. 'It's not proof of anything and I'm not jumping to any of those hasty conclusions you detest so much but it does suggest that Grace might not have had the most perfect of parents.'

'But it doesn't really get you any further. All you're talking about here is rumour and gossip. How does it relate to Grace's disappearance?'

'I've no idea but it's a start. And once people begin to talk you never know where it might lead. If I keep digging around for long enough, something useful is bound to come up.' Jess tilted her head and gave him a small provocative smile. 'It's called investigating,' she said. 'You should try it sometime.'

Chapter Thirty-Two

Denise Webster jumped at the sound of the chimes. Every time the doorbell went she couldn't help wondering if it was the police. Al was dead. She was sure of it. Her stomach twisted as she walked along the hall.

She paused for a moment, trying to distinguish the shape behind the opaque glass. There only appeared to be one person standing there. For this kind of job, didn't they usually come in twos, one to break the bad news, the other to make the obligatory cup of tea? She allowed herself to relax slightly. Perhaps, on this occasion, she was safe.

It was a thought that evaporated the instant she opened the door.

Jimmy Keppell was standing right in front of her.

She stared at him, her eyes widening.

'Hello, sweetheart,' he said.

Denise, although she knew him by reputation, had only met him once before. It had been at one of Ray's parties and he had been charming enough then, the perfect gentleman, but she hadn't liked him. She had liked him even less since hearing the rumours about who was responsible for the dreadful murder of Tommy Lake. Her heart began to hammer. 'W-what do you want?'

He smiled. 'Mind if I come in for a minute?'

'Er . . .'

Before she had the chance to say anything more, he had pushed straight past, pulled her away from the door and slammed it shut. 'You and me,' he said, breathing heavily into her face. 'I think we need a little chat.'

'I don't . . . don't understand.'

'Don't you?' Grabbing hold of her arm, he dragged her through to the living room. 'Didn't Ray tell you to expect me?'

She struggled, tears coming to her eyes. 'Why should he—'

Keppell tightened his grip before pushing her roughly on to the sofa. He looked her up and down, his expression a combination of anger and contempt. 'Please don't make me hurt you, sweetheart.'

Denise stared up at him, terrified. What had she done? What did he want? None of this made any sense.

'Where's Al?' he said. 'Where is he?'

She shook her head. 'I don't know.'

Keppell leaned down, his thick arms stretching either side of her body. He pushed his face into hers again. His breath smelled old and sour. 'Wrong answer,' he whispered.

Denise's voice broke into a sob. 'I don't know,' she wailed. 'I swear I don't.'

He continued to hang over her, his cold inquiring eyes staring fixedly into hers, before abruptly standing upright again. 'Perhaps a drink will help jog your memory.'

She watched as he went over to the cabinet and examined the bottles.

'What would you like?' he said.

'Nothing,' she said.

'Oh, that's not very hospitable.' He turned to look at her again. 'I don't like drinking on my own. What are you having?'

Denise heard the underlying threat in the request. 'Vodka,' she said quickly. 'Vodka and tonic.'

'That's better,' Keppell said, smiling. 'There's no reason why we can't sort this out in an amicable fashion.'

He came back with a couple of drinks and placed them on the coffee table. When she made no move to pick up her glass, he picked it up himself and thrust it into her hand.

'Cheers!' he said.

'Cheers,' she echoed miserably. Her fingers were shaking as she raised it to her lips. She took a sip and shuddered. The vodka was neat.

Keppell laughed. 'Shame about what happened to Tommo. Friend of yours, was he?'

Denise took another gulp of vodka. She swallowed hard and nodded.

'There you go,' he said, his face becoming serious again. 'We have got one thing in common. We've both lost something that matters to us.'

Unsure of what else to do, she nodded again.

Keppell sat down beside her and stretched out his legs. 'I'm surprised Ray didn't mention it.'

'Ray?'

'Come on,' he said. 'Surely he's spilled his little secret by now.'

Denise stared down at her trembling knees. She was so scared she could barely think, never mind speak. 'No,' she finally mumbled.

'Shame,' he said softly. 'Only, Al's taken something that belonged to me and I want it back. And if you don't know where he is, if you can't tell me where to find him, then surely it's only fair that I take something of his in return.'

Denise glanced across at him. It took a moment for her to comprehend what he meant and when she did the understanding came with an accompanying jolt of horror. Instinctively, she shifted sideways but found herself trapped against the arm of the sofa.

Keppell quickly leaned over, took her chin in his left hand and jerked her frightened face towards him. 'Where's Al?'

'I don't know.'

'Last chance,' he snarled, his fingers digging hard into her cheeks.

'Please,' she cried. She tried to twist away but his grip held fast.

Suddenly his right hand shot up. He grabbed the gold hoop in her ear and with one violent tug wrenched it clear of the lobe. A fierce agonizing pain shot through her. As she opened her mouth to scream, his hand moved to stifle it. Clamping his palm across her lips he pushed back her head and spat into her face.

'Shut up, bitch!' he said. 'Shut the fuck up!'

Shivering, she could feel the blood running down her neck. The blood was warm but she felt cold, colder than she'd ever felt. The pain throbbed in her ear. Nausea rose from her stomach to her throat and she fought to keep it down.

Keppell slowly removed his hand. 'Tell me where he is.'

Denise shook her head. 'I can't. I don't know. I swear I don't.' The faint taste of vomit hovered in her mouth. She started to cry, a silent heaving kind of sobbing. *Why was this happening to her?* A stream of tears flooded down her cheeks.

Keppell grasped hold of her arm, then her legs, and in a couple of swift brutal jerks dragged her round so she was lying flat on her back on the sofa. Now she was trapped beneath him. His bearded face loomed over her, his lips pulled back over his teeth in a sneering grimace.

In a situation like this, she had always presumed that she would struggle, fight like a demon, but fear had completely paralysed her. She didn't dare move. She hardly dared breathe. Keppell was much older than her but much stronger too. She turned her head and saw the picture of her children on the mantelpiece. If she was to struggle, to try and get away then . . . The thought of Tommo drifted into her head. *Please God, help me.* She closed her eyes, a low groan of despair escaping from her lips.

Keppell forced her legs apart, his body bearing down. She could feel his weight on her. She could smell the stink of stale sweat, whisky and tobacco.

'*Please*,' she pleaded.

'What's the matter?' he taunted. 'Haven't you ever wanted to fuck a *real* man?'

She didn't answer. She couldn't.

'Look at me!' he demanded.

Her terrified eyes flickered open again.

205

Keppell was staring down, his gaze hard and cruel.

'Don't hurt me,' she begged.

He pressed harder against her. 'Where's Al? Where is he?'

All she could do was shake her head.

Then, just as she'd resigned herself to the nightmare that was bound to come, Keppell suddenly rolled off her, sat on the edge of the sofa and began to laugh. Standing up, he smoothed down his hair and straightened out the wrinkles in his jacket.

'Oh, don't worry, sweetheart,' he said mockingly. 'I'm not that fucking desperate. You might have been a looker once but personally I prefer my girls on the younger side.'

Denise lay very still, gazing up at him.

Leaning down, he whispered in her blood-soaked ear. 'Although I do have some friends who aren't quite as fussy. Next time you see Ray, be sure to give him my best.'

Chapter Thirty-Three

Harry stared at the thin black hand travelling around the clock face. Time appeared to slow as he watched it, to deliberately drag. It was ten past three and he was at a loose end again. Jess had taken the car and gone to see Scott Hall, a meeting that had been arranged almost as soon as it had been suggested.

It had been agreed that Harry would try and talk to Ellen Shaw tomorrow, but with nothing better to do he decided to bring the assignation forward. She only lived down the road, a twenty-minute walk at most, and even if she wasn't there the exercise would do him good.

He went into the bedroom, stripped off his jeans and T-shirt and changed into a white shirt and dark grey suit. He'd been aiming for reassuringly professional but had his doubts as he slipped the red tie under his collar and looked in the mirror. Was it all too formal? From what he'd seen of her flat, Ellen could hardly be described as conventional. But then the same couldn't be said of her husband. Perhaps she preferred her men dressed like ageing accountants . . . but then again, perhaps she didn't. Should he put his jeans back on? He instantly whipped off his tie, took off the suit and threw it on the bed.

For the next fifteen minutes, he raided the contents of his wardrobe, trying on clothes and as quickly discarding them. A heap of rejected garments soon lay scattered over the floor. He stared at the pile and sighed. In the end he settled on a pair of smart dark trousers, a crisp pale blue shirt and an expensive Armani jacket with a blue silk lining.

It was almost four by the time he reached Berry Square. In all his efforts to achieve the perfect look the one thing he'd forgotten was the weather. The heavens had opened when he was halfway down Rochester Road.

As he climbed the steps to number twelve, he bent to sniff his wet crumpled jacket. It had acquired the whiff of something that had been left in a cellar too long. Not a great smell, or a great look, for anyone who was hoping to make a favourable impression.

Harry was about to press the bell when he glanced over his shoulder and saw Ellen turn the corner. He had one of those déjà vu feelings. The same large black umbrella was raised over her head. Backtracking down the steps, he felt the breath catch in the back of his throat. The light was grey and grainy and her bright red coat stood out against the dimness of the afternoon.

Walking towards her, he tried to think of what it was he was going to say. Although he had the press cutting in his pocket, proof that she had lied to him, he had no intention of making any accusations. Unlike Jess, he was willing to give her an opportunity to explain.

Harry was only a few yards away when he became aware of the car crawling slowly along behind her. It was a vague kind of awareness, an everyday object in the periphery of his vision, but not anything he was taking much notice of. He was more concerned with how he was going to persuade her to talk to him again. It was only as the engine began to rev that he became aware of the driver's intention and by then it was almost too late. Suddenly the headlights were shining brightly, a foot was depressing hard on the accelerator and the car was heading straight for her.

'Ellen!'

Half-blinded, Harry lurched forward, grabbed hold of her shoulders and pushed her back against the wall. Her umbrella clattered to the ground. He felt her fright and surprise, heard the strangled gasp as she opened her mouth to scream – for that moment she must have thought that *he* was the one in the process of attacking her – and then there was nothing but the roar of the engine.

The car mounted the pavement and came so close they could have reached out and touched it. Only inches lay between themselves and the cold hard metal. He felt the harsh rush of air and then the splatter of water against his legs as the rear tyres kicked back a wave of rain from the puddles. Careering back on to the street, the driver smartly braked and squealed to a halt. For a few terrifying seconds Harry thought he was going to reverse and try again.

His pulse began to race, the adrenalin rushing through his veins. Did they have time to move? The nearest gateway was yards away and Ellen, rigid with shock, would probably need to be dragged there. He was about to do just that – they were far too exposed where they were standing – when the car suddenly flashed its lights and sped off into the distance.

As he slowly released his breath, Harry loosened his hold on her. 'Are you all right?'

She was staring straight ahead, still frozen to the spot.

'Come on,' he urged. He gave her arm a gentle shake. They needed to get off the street as soon as they could. Although it was unlikely that her crazy assailant would take a turn round the block and then come back for a second go, he wasn't prepared to take the risk.

As if emerging from a trance-like state, Ellen freed herself from his grasp and stumbled back. She gazed up at him, confused. 'What . . .?'

'We need to get inside,' Harry insisted.

But still she continued to stand and frown. In the dusk, her eyes looked almost black against the paleness of her face.

Harry tried to reassure her. 'It's me,' he said softly, not sure if she was still in shock or if she simply didn't recognize him. 'Harry Lind. We met last week. I came to see you about—'

'Yes,' she said, taking another step back. 'I know who you are.'

'We need to get inside,' he said again.

Ellen wound a loose strand of hair behind her ear and pushed her hands into her pockets. She glanced up and down the street before focusing her gaze on Harry again. Eventually, she gave a small acceptant sigh. 'Okay,' she said.

He bent down and picked up her umbrella.

They walked in silence towards the house and then turned up the path and climbed the steps. She scrabbled in her bag for her key but when she finally found it her hand was shaking so much that she couldn't get it in the lock.

'Here,' Harry said, taking the key from her. He unlocked the door and stood aside to let her in.

She paused before slipping inside and turning on the light. They both screwed up their eyes at the sudden brightness. Harry closed the door as she began to walk up the stairs. Following her, he found himself staring at her slim rain-splashed ankles. He thought about the car that had almost crushed them. He felt the need to say something positive.

'We should ring the police,' he said.

Ellen looked over her shoulder and frowned again. 'What for?'

Now it was Harry's turn to look bemused. 'Someone just tried to run you over.'

There was a short pause. 'What makes you so sure they were aiming for me?'

The question made him start. Until now, there had been no doubt in his mind that the driver had only had one victim in mind. Was he mistaken? He had been digging around in some fairly dubious stuff recently. But he quickly dismissed the idea. The car had definitely been heading for her.

'Did you get the registration?' she said.

He shook his head. 'No.' He hadn't had time to think about it. All he knew was that the vehicle had been large, a Range Rover perhaps, dark blue or black, and the windows had been tinted. He'd had his back turned as the car had swept past and even when it had stopped he'd been more concerned with what would happen next than with clocking the numbers on the plate.

210

'So why bother?' she said. 'There's nothing we can tell them.'

'Apart from the fact that some maniac just drove straight at us.'

'And then what? They can't do anything about it now. I've had enough of the police recently.'

Like the first time, she was climbing the stairs faster than he could. Having struggled to keep up, Harry took hold of the banister and finally swung himself on to the top floor landing. 'Oh, come on,' he said. 'You can't just let this go. What if the guy comes back? What if he tries again?'

Ellen stopped and turned to look at him. 'For all I know,' she said, 'you could have set this whole thing up.'

Harry laughed, astonished. 'And why on earth should I want to do that?'

'How should I know?' Unlocking the door to the flat – her hand was steadier now – she went inside, took off her coat and hung it on a peg. 'Maybe you want me to feel that I can trust you.'

'I can think of better ways of achieving that than a close encounter with a moving vehicle.'

She gave him a long hard look before her mouth eventually broke into a smile. 'Well, I guess that could be true.'

Harry closed the door, leaned the wet umbrella against the wall, and followed her through. He stood waiting while she glided from one lamp to another, bringing soft golden light into the room. She pulled the curtains across the windows, pausing only to glance briefly down at the street below. Then she turned to him again.

'Sit down,' she said. 'I don't know about you but I need a drink.'

Harry, aware of how wet his clothes were, perched on the edge of the red velvet sofa. He watched as she walked over to the old carved sideboard and poured out two stiff measures of brandy. She was wearing a navy blue dress that accentuated her slimness and wrapped around her throat was a red silky scarf. It was the very same colour as her lips. He tried not to stare too closely at those lips as she handed him the glass.

211

'Thank you.' He took a sip as she sat down beside him. The brandy was good. Harry cleared his throat, took a breath and then turned his head to look her again. 'So, would you like to tell me what's going on? And please don't say that you don't have a clue because you must have some idea of why that maniac would want to run you over.'

Ellen's dark eyes flashed but she kept her voice controlled. 'I don't,' she insisted softly. 'I swear. Unless my husband thinks it's a cheap and easy way to get rid of me.'

Harry wasn't sure if she was joking but felt a guilty surge of pleasure at the thought that all might not be rosy in the relationship between the Shaws. It wasn't a thought to be proud of and he instantly banished it to the back of his mind. He still couldn't work out why she had married someone so much older than herself. A father figure perhaps – which reminded him of the cutting he still had in his pocket. 'The truth usually comes out in the end,' he said. And then, wondering if that had sounded rather pompous, quickly added: 'I mean, if you do have any suspicions . . .'

'No,' she said shortly.

Harry could see that the subtle approach wasn't getting him anywhere and decided to be more straightforward. 'Why should I believe you?'

'Why shouldn't you?' She lifted the glass to her mouth. 'Do I look like the kind of person who tells lies?'

This gave him another opportunity to examine her face. It was the kind of face, he suspected, that no man would ever tire of looking at. 'Not willingly perhaps but we're all tempted, for one reason or another, to occasionally evade the truth.'

She suddenly laughed, exposing both rows of her small white teeth. '*Evade the truth*? That's a nice way of putting it, Mr Lind. You should have been in the diplomatic corps.'

He smiled back. 'So you're claiming that you've always been completely honest with me?'

'I'm not sure what you mean. After all, we barely know each other.' Ellen tilted her head. 'In fact, if we're talking honesty, perhaps *you'd* like to explain why you were so conveniently in the Square today.'

'I came to see you.'

'And that was because . . .?'

Harry took the by now rather crumpled piece of paper from his pocket and passed it over to her. 'I wanted to ask you about this.'

Ellen unfolded the cutting and gazed down. 'Ah,' she said, the corners of her mouth turning down. She glanced up at him again, her face a shade paler than it had been a moment before. 'Where did you get it?'

He shrugged. Now wasn't the time to get into an awkward conversation about the thieving habits of one of Jess Vaughan's associates. 'That doesn't matter. I'm just curious as to why you should have told me that your father died last year. You said that was the reason you went to visit Paul Deacon but if your parents passed away over twelve years ago . . .'

Leaning forward, Ellen put her glass and the cutting down on the table and dropped her face into her hands. Her sleek black hair fell like a screen across her cheeks, obscuring her expression. 'God, I should never have said that,' she murmured. 'I shouldn't. It's always the stupid lies that catch you out.'

Chapter Thirty-Four

Harry sat very still, remaining silent. Eventually, after a long tense minute, she looked up at him again. She wiped away the tears with the backs of her fingers.

'It's what I told the police. When you came along, I thought I'd better stick to the same story.' She hesitated and then stumbled on. 'But . . . but this has nothing to do with that poor man who was killed. That's *why* I lied, because I was scared that they'd think I had something to do with it. You do understand, don't you?'

Harry wanted to believe her but wasn't entirely sure that he did. 'I can help,' he said. 'But only if you're prepared to be honest with me.'

She shook her head despairingly. 'I can't.'

'You have to,' he said, 'unless you want to be looking over your shoulder every time you go out. Today wasn't an accident. We both know that. And next time you might not be so lucky.' He automatically thought of Len and dread ran through him. 'You can't do this on your own.'

Ellen suddenly got to her feet and walked briskly over to the window. She pulled back the curtain and peered down into the street again. 'I can't. I can't tell you.'

'So who else are you going to talk to?'

She hesitated and then gave a tiny shrug.

Harry sensed that she was weakening. 'And is keeping it a secret going to make it go away?'

She turned and shook her head again. 'You don't want to get involved.'

'I'm already involved,' he said. 'I could have been killed too. If you don't tell me then I'll just keep rooting around until I find out for myself. And I will . . . eventually. That's what I do.' He gave a wry smile. 'I'm very persistent.'

Ellen pondered on this for a while and then came back and sat down beside him. She placed her hands on her thighs and her fingers instantly curled into two loose fists. 'I don't want Adam to know,' she said.

'I'm not about to tell him.'

Her eyes narrowed as she looked over. 'It's not what you think,' she said. 'It's just that he's . . . he's a good man, decent, and I don't want him to worry. He doesn't deserve to be burdened with my problems. He'll get all worked up, upset and then . . .'

Harry, alert to the possibility of domestic violence, anxiously inquired, 'And then?'

'See?' she sighed. 'You're already jumping to conclusions – and you're wrong, completely wrong. Adam is a good man, a good husband; he hasn't got a bad bone in his body. But this isn't something I can share with him. It's too . . .' She stopped and lowered her head again, her hands clenching tighter. 'It's too complicated.'

Harry gave a nod. 'I understand.' In all honesty, he didn't understand a whole lot at the moment but hopefully that was about to change. Anticipating that he was going to learn a secret she was keeping from her husband provoked another of those rather shameful thrills. What was the matter with him? Harry Lind didn't do mad passion – or at least he hadn't since his distant teenage years. Love, yes – he loved Val, didn't he? – but this was something different, something entirely beyond his control. He wished he could understand why he felt so drawn to Ellen Shaw, why just sitting so close to her made his heart beat faster. A thin prickle of sweat had broken out on his forehead.

She leaned forward and picked up the press cutting. She held it for a second and then passed it back to him. 'You'd better keep this.'

He folded up the sheet of paper and put it back in his pocket.

'Look,' she said, 'if you'll just let me tell you, without any interruption, then I'd appreciate it. I can't stop and start. Is that okay? After, later, you can ask me what you like.'

Harry nodded again.

Ellen took a deep breath and began. She kept her face down, staring at the Persian rug as she talked. 'Well, as you've already gathered, my parents didn't die last year. I left Dublin straight after . . . after the accident. I couldn't stand to be in that house alone and I didn't intend to hang around and be taken into care. I was fifteen, old enough I thought to look after myself. I headed for London; I suppose it was just somewhere that I'd read about, a place where I could get lost in the crowd and start again. Of course when I arrived it wasn't quite the paradise I'd expected. I struggled at first but things got better. I looked older than I was and after a while I made friends, got a job and then one evening I was introduced to Tony.' She glanced up at him. 'Tony Keppell.'

Harry's jaw dropped open but he had the sense to bite his tongue. Now wasn't the time to interrupt.

'I suppose you've heard of them? The Keppells?' A tight strained laugh choked out of her throat. 'Of course you have. They're not exactly low-profile, are they? Tony and I became friends and then . . . we became closer. I liked him a lot. We were the same age and we understood each other. I'd lost my family and he felt isolated from his.' She stopped and took another breath. 'He was the youngest in the family,' she continued. 'Both his older brothers were part of the Firm, over six foot tall, strong, violent, busy getting respect and enjoying the power of lording it over the manor. Even his sister had a reputation. Tony was fifteen but they still treated him like he was a kid. He was smaller, more sensitive, kind of fragile. They used to tease him . . .' She paused again, her cheeks flushing pink. 'No, it was more than that; they used to *taunt* him and so he decided to . . .'

216

Harry could see the emotion in her face. He reached out his hand and placed it over hers. He thought that she might pull away but, as if she'd barely noticed, she only lifted her slim shoulders and shrugged.

'He'd met Paul Deacon before,' she continued, 'at some big charity gala – Jimmy Keppell always enjoyed playing the generous benefactor – and had heard the rumours. Everyone said that Deacon had a liking for young pretty men.'

Ellen stopped again and glanced at him. Sliding her hand away from his, she sat back and crossed her arms defensively across her chest. 'It all sounds so vile, so disgusting,' she said. 'And I suppose it was. But Tony was impulsive and he didn't think things through. He was determined to compromise Deacon and then blackmail him. He knew his weaknesses. Deacon was rich, married, in a position of power; he couldn't afford the scandal, especially of a relationship with an underage boy. I tried to talk him out of it but I couldn't. It was impossible. Once he'd made up his mind, he just wouldn't listen. He wanted the money so we could get away, start a new life on our own.'

Ellen shifted again, uncrossing her arms. 'And you pretty much know the rest,' she said softly. 'Tony made sure he was seen around with Deacon, in bars and restaurants. He wanted there to be plenty of witnesses. He made sure there were photos of them together too. Then, when he thought the time was right, he went round to Deacon's flat and—'

Her voice suddenly broke and she turned her face away. A single tear ran down her cheek. 'I should have stopped him,' she mumbled. 'I . . . I should have done something.'

Harry wanted to put his arm round her but fought against the impulse. She might see the gesture as unsuitable or predatory and the idea that she could think he was trying to take advantage was enough to make him hesitate. But that didn't mean he wasn't tempted. Quickly, he got to his feet and picked up her empty glass. 'What could you have done?' he said, walking over to the sideboard. 'You can't blame yourself for

217

what happened.' He poured another stiff brandy, carried it back and held it out to her. 'Here, drink this.'

She raised her face and struggled for a smile. 'Thank you.' She took a sip and then put it down. Pulling a tissue from her bag, she wiped at her eyes and gently blew her nose. 'So there you have it; the whole sordid story. It's not much to be proud of, is it?'

'It's not anything to feel that guilty about either,' he said. '*You* didn't go to the flat. *You* didn't try to blackmail Deacon.'

Ellen shook her head. 'No, it's not that simple. I was Tony's girlfriend. I knew exactly what was going on and I stood back and did nothing. That's just as bad.'

'I think you're being too hard on yourself. You were young. We can all look back with hindsight and wish we'd done this or done that. Ellen, you can't let it haunt you for the rest of your life. This wasn't *your* mistake.'

'You're very kind but they're just excuses, aren't they? We all have to take responsibility for our actions. I've spent years trying to hide from it, to pretend it never happened but . . .'

Harry didn't know what else to say to comfort her. Perhaps there was nothing that could be said. Instead he asked softly, 'Is that why you went to see Deacon?'

She stared down into her drink. 'I wanted to know what really happened that night. I had to know. I went to the trial but it was all so vague: Deacon was trying to cover up the relationship. Even then, when he was facing a life sentence, he wasn't going to admit that he was sleeping with a boy. He claimed they were just acquaintances. He said there had been a disagreement, a drunken row, then Tony had produced a gun – there'd been a struggle and it had gone off accidentally.'

'But you didn't believe him?'

Ellen glanced up at him again, her dark eyes full of confusion. 'I didn't know what to believe. I'd never seen Tony with a gun before but his father had plenty; that house was like an arsenal. It wouldn't have been hard for him to . . . he might have been scared that Deacon would turn on him. He might have taken it for protection.'

She paused. 'I'm not sure why I started thinking about it all again. It's been a long time and I thought I'd got over it – well, learned to deal with it at least. *Moving on*: isn't that what they call it?' Her smooth pale forehead wrinkled into a frown. 'I've always considered that a callous sort of phrase. I mean, you can't just leave the bad stuff behind, just shove it aside and pretend it never happened. It's always going to be there, casting its shadow. *You* know how that feels, don't you?'

As if she had hit a raw nerve, Harry started. He quickly reached for what remained of his brandy and knocked it back in one. Not for the first time, he wondered how Ellen Shaw was able to make him feel so utterly transparent. It was as though she could look straight into his soul and see all the dark and messy complications that were gathered there. 'I guess,' he mumbled into the glass.

'That's why you're so easy to talk to,' she said, 'because you do understand.'

Harry lifted his shoulders in a slight dismissive shrug. Was he being deliberately flattered? Perhaps. But he didn't really care. All he did care about was that he was sitting here beside her and that she was finally telling him everything. She was telling him things her husband didn't know, would possibly never know, and that filled him with a curious sense of awe and excitement.

Ellen reached out and for one nerve-tingling moment he thought that her intention was to touch him. Instead, she took the glass from between his fingers and carefully poured half the contents of her glass into his. 'I can't drink all this,' she said. 'You'll have to help me out.'

'I'll do my best.'

She held his gaze in a way that made his heart miss a beat. 'After all these years I suddenly realized that I had to see Paul Deacon. There were too many unanswered questions. So I wrote and told him who I was. I asked if I could visit. I was sure he'd refuse, that he probably wouldn't even write back, but he sent me a nice letter and a visiting order too. And I was so surprised, so *alarmed*, that I didn't do anything about it for another two months.'

'Alarmed?' Harry said.

'I think a part of me, the cowardly part, had been secretly hoping that he would ignore the letter or that he'd just send a blunt refusal. That way I could pretend I'd done my best to find out the truth without having to go through the actual process. It would have been his decision rather than mine.' She gave another of her thin sad laughs. 'But nothing's ever that easy, is it? I knew, as soon I received the visiting order, that I'd have to go and see him. It filled me with dread but I didn't have a choice.'

'It was a brave thing to do,' Harry said.

Her gaze wavered. 'Was it? I'm not so sure. I wonder now if it was simply selfish. I wasn't really doing it for Tony or for the "truth" – whatever that might mean – but just to appease my conscience.'

Harry knew all about guilt and conscience but now wasn't the time to dwell on his own enduring problems. 'That's not true.'

'Isn't it?' she said. Her hands tightened round the glass as she raised it to her lips. 'I wanted to believe that it was all Deacon's fault, that he'd murdered Tony in cold blood. I wanted it all to be black and white, to be completely straight-forward.'

'But?'

Ellen slumped over, putting the glass back on the table and burying her face in her hands. 'There was nothing cold about him. That was clear from the first time we met. His emotions were as strong as mine . . . and as confusing. He'd loved Tony, still loved him. He was trying to make as much sense of it all as I was.' She lifted her face and sighed. 'That's why I went back to see him again. And again. He was the only person I could talk to . . . about Tony, about the past.'

Harry was beginning to comprehend why this was some-thing she could never discuss with her husband. Long lost love wasn't the best subject for discussion over the breakfast table or at any place come to that. His initial jealousy had been towards Adam but now it was beginning to shift. Her deepest emotions were rooted in the past. He wasn't sure how to respond but knew there was one question that he had to ask: 'So who was in that car today?'

'I don't know who was in it,' she said. 'But I can guess who sent them.'

Harry hoped that she didn't mean who he thought she did. But his worst suspicions were immediately confirmed.

'Jimmy wants it left alone,' she said. 'He found out I was visiting Paul Deacon and thought . . . well, I'm not sure what he thought exactly – perhaps that I was planning on raking up the past. He doesn't want his son's name dragged through the mud again. I don't think he was trying to kill me today. It was just a warning, to stop stirring things up, to stay away from Deacon.'

An uneasy feeling was starting to spread through Harry's guts. 'So you're still in touch with Jimmy Keppell?'

'No,' she said. 'I wouldn't call it that. I hadn't spoken to him since the trial and then a couple of weeks ago, just after I'd been to Maidstone, he rang me – I have no idea how he got my number – and asked why I was visiting Deacon. I told him what I've told you, that I was just searching for some answers, but he wasn't happy. He told me to drop it, to stay away from him.'

'And did you tell him about Curzon? Did you tell him there had been a reporter asking questions?'

She could see where he was going and two pink spots instantly brightened her cheeks. 'God, no!' she said. 'I swear. I hadn't even met Len Curzon when I got the call. It was another week – no, more than a week before *he* came round.' She swallowed hard and a visible shiver ran through her. 'You don't think that . . .?'

Harry didn't answer the question directly. 'And you haven't heard from Keppell since?'

She shook her head.

'Did you talk to anyone about Len's visit?'

221

She gave another small shake of her head. 'No one. Well, only Adam and that was on the same afternoon as I was supposed to be meeting . . .' She paused, the memory of what had happened to Curzon causing her brows to furrow. 'And Adam wouldn't have mentioned it to anyone else. I mean, even if he'd wanted to, which he wouldn't, he didn't have the time. We were together from the moment I told him.'

'And what exactly did you tell him?' Harry said.

'Pretty much the same as I said to the police, that he was an old friend of my father's who had written to me out of the blue.'

'Okay,' Harry said. Worryingly, it was starting to look like Jess could be right: Curzon's death might have been deliberate. If Len had been watching Ellen, then maybe an anxious Jimmy Keppell had been too – and it wouldn't have taken him long to suss out that he had company. If he'd then spotted Ellen talking to Len, he may well have presumed that the two of them were working together, that she was selling her story to the press and . . . Harry quickly put a brake on his thoughts before he got too carried away. At the moment this was all just idle speculation. 'And you haven't been back to see Deacon since?'

'What, after *that* phone call?' She forced out a wavering smile. 'I'm not a complete fool.'

Harry smiled back. 'I never imagined that for a second.' He twisted the glass between his fingers, trying to clarify his thoughts. It was easier to look down, to stare into his glass, than to meet those large brown eyes of hers. 'But I still don't understand why Keppell should react like this. Especially when you've done as he asked. You've stayed away from Deacon. You haven't been back to visit him. So why should he suddenly decide to start threatening you?' He wasn't actually convinced that it had just been a threat – that car had come way too close for comfort – but didn't want to add to her fear. At the same time, he didn't want her to be too complacent about the situation either.

222

'No,' she said, puzzled. 'It doesn't make any sense, does it? Unless . . .'

He glanced up at her. 'Unless?'

'Perhaps he's still worried. I'm clearly not the only one who's been asking questions. If that reporter was on to it, then maybe others are too. Maybe Jimmy thinks I could still be persuaded to talk.'

Harry immediately thought of Jess. She had told him about her visit to Joan Sewell but that had nothing to do with this. In fact the whole Grace Harper theory was looking more ridiculous by the minute. It was a theory, however, that could be spilling over. He had no idea of who else Jess had been talking to, or what kind of hornets' nest she might have been stirring up, but perhaps it was having repercussions. 'But to talk about *what*? That's what I don't get. Nothing's changed since the trial; there's no new evidence, no new information, nothing that's going to change anything.'

'No,' she agreed, 'but Jimmy hasn't got over it, never has and never will, and he certainly doesn't want to see it splashed all over the papers again. It was hard enough for him the first time round.' Her lips drew into a slight sardonic smile. 'Big guys like Jimmy don't breed sons who sleep with men . . . and especially not for money.'

Or if they did, Harry thought, they certainly didn't want reminding of it. He was still thinking about what to say, about what to ask her next, when he saw her glance down at her watch.

'I'm sorry,' she said, 'but it won't be long before Adam gets back.'

Taking the hint, Harry stood up. She stood up too. As they walked from the room he felt like a secret lover being bundled out before the husband got home. It wasn't a bad feeling; on the contrary, it was oddly exciting, almost dangerously erotic. His gaze slid the length of her spine as she walked in front of him. 'Have you thought about talking to Adam?'

She stood by the door and looked up at him. Her wide eyes stared straight into his. 'Do you tell *your* wife everything?'

He had mentioned it before but he said it again. 'I'm not married.'

'No,' she said. 'But there is someone, isn't there?'

Harry shrugged. He wasn't sure if that was true any more. His relationship with Val was about as dire as it could be. She hadn't even spoken to him since Friday and that had only been because she'd had to. They seemed so apart now, so distant, that he wasn't sure if they could ever find their way back.

'It's okay.' Ellen touched him gently on the arm.

He felt his lungs expand, his breath draw in. 'We can't leave it like this,' he said. 'You're not safe. What if he tries again, what if he—'

'Don't worry. I can deal with Jimmy Keppell.'

Harry gazed down at her fragile frame and sighed. There were men ten times her size who must have uttered the very same words and were no longer around to say anything. 'You have to be careful.'

'I know that,' she said.

'You're not on your own.' Harry took out one of his cards and offered it to her. 'We could meet up again, talk about it.'

'I've already got your card,' she said.

He slowly returned it to his pocket. 'But will you use it?'

She didn't answer him directly. 'In case you're wondering,' she said. 'I was the one who sent the newspaper cutting to Paul Deacon. I thought it might be useful if anyone started asking questions about his connection to me.'

'Even though the dates didn't tally?'

Ellen gave a slight smile. 'I didn't think anyone would look into it that closely.'

There was a short silence as she opened the door and stood aside.

Harry hovered on the doorstep, knowing that he had to leave and desperately wishing that he didn't. He stared down at the stairs as he tried to think of something purposeful to say. He ran a few sentences through his head and as quickly dismissed them.

'Thank you,' she said softly.

As her fingers made contact with his arm, Harry felt that thrill run through his body again. 'Promise me you'll call.'

'My promises aren't worth much.'

Harry shook his head. 'Call me. I'll be waiting.'

Chapter Thirty-Five

Ray Stagg stood in his living room and gazed out over the floodlit garden. At the far end, he could see two of his men slowly patrolling the perimeter wall. The place was secure, built like a fortress – even the plate glass in the windows was bulletproof – but he wasn't taking any chances. Ever since Keppell had stopped taking his calls, he'd been preparing for the worst.

Turning, he picked up the ice-cold bottle of vodka and poured himself another stiff drink. There was no doubt about it: he was in the very deepest of shit. Keppell was out of control, on the rampage, behaving like a psycho. First there had been poor Tommo, then the barman and now the threats to Denise; it was only a matter of time before his own name jumped to the top of the list.

And the only way of preventing that was to do something about it – and fast.

He knocked back the vodka and refilled his glass. Jesus, as if life wasn't difficult enough. How had it come to this? The last thing he had ever wanted was to be at war with Jimmy Keppell!

He had thought about offering to pay the money back but knew that it would only be seen as a sign of weakness or, even worse, an admission of guilt. Anyway, this wasn't about the cash but about reputation and respect. Rumours were already spreading about how Keppell had been ripped off by a small-timer, by some no-hoper market trader with cabbage for brains. And the fact that that particular vegetable happened to be Ray's brother-in-law was reason enough for Keppell to extend his revenge to its logical conclusion.

So, if appeasement was out of the question, that only left one option: *he had to take him out.*

Ray smiled darkly down into his glass. From the moment he had heard about Tommo, heard what that bastard had done to him, he had known that he would never be happy until Keppell was six foot under and being eaten by the worms.

That, however, was easier said than done. Hiring someone could be risky; if Keppell got a whisper, he'd be dead meat before the deposit had even changed hands. Keppell was richer, more powerful and, most worryingly of all, reliably vicious in his retribution. Finding someone prepared to take on the job could be a problem.

He went back to the window and peered out towards the shadows bordering the edge of the garden. Ray didn't trust a soul, not even his own men; blind loyalty had disappeared years ago and the old principles were obsolete. Maybe he could hire someone from abroad? But you couldn't trust those foreigners either. He lit a cigarette and coughed up his disgust. It was a bad state of affairs when you couldn't even trust a goddamn assassin!

Which only left one other choice – he would have to do it himself. But how? Although he couldn't deny that pumping a chamber of bullets into Jimmy Keppell's chest would provide him with the ultimate of pleasures, it clearly had its downside too. He'd still be left with the tricky problem of dealing with the rest of the family. Revenge might be sweet but he didn't intend to spend the rest of his life looking over his shoulder. The Keppell dynasty was vast – Jimmy had two brothers and between them they had eight sons and even the sons had sons . . . and they were all in the family business.

Denise came into the room, looked at him and slumped down on the sofa. 'On your own, then?'

He glared back at her. After what Keppell had done, he'd had no choice but to move her and the kids into his house. She wasn't helping matters though, forever asking stupid questions. 'What does it look like?'

Denise curled her lip but didn't reply.

He knew what she thought: that this entire mess was his fault. And that was just beyond the pale. If it wasn't for her husband they wouldn't be in this situation in the first place. It was Al who was at the root of this nightmare; her own lying, cheating, no-good sod of a husband. He was the one who'd decided to take off with a vanload of shit that didn't belong to him. He was the one who'd committed the ultimate act of treachery, betraying everyone who'd ever stood by him. And where was he now? Where *did* thieving bastards hang out when they no longer had a home to go to?

'I don't suppose you've heard from him,' he said.

Denise stared down at the floor. 'You know I haven't.'

'Big surprise,' he said.

She slowly lifted her tearful blue eyes. 'It's not my fault,' she whined.

But as far as Ray was concerned, it was. She was the stupid cow who'd married him. And now he was left with the problem of sorting out the nightmare that her diabolical choice in men had created. He was feeling mad enough, drunk enough, to tell her about Agnes, about the slutty Russian blonde who Al had probably been shagging, but then thought better of it. A whining Denise was preferable to a hysterical one.

Had they been in it together: Al, Troy and Agnes? He'd known some unholy alliances in his time but they made an unlikely trio. He was sure, however, that Agnes was still alive – if Keppell had got hold of her, the body would have been found by now.

Al and Agnes must be holed up somewhere, probably in whatever shabby flat she was currently renting. The address she had given to the club was a false one. One of the other girls must know where she lived but none of them were talking; they were all too terrified by what had happened to Troy. He could have tried to beat it out of them but there were over thirty girls and bruises didn't do much for business.

228

Perhaps he'd been a little hasty as regards Harry Lind; the limping detective might still be useful. Holt had tipped him off about how Agnes had called Lind before she'd disappeared. Maybe she would call again. If she did, Ray wanted to be the first to hear about it.

One way or another, he was going to get Jimmy Keppell. And if he couldn't kill him with a bullet, he'd find another way to do it. Twenty years rotting in jail could be equally satisfying. With a bit of luck, Keppell would never see daylight again.

Chapter Thirty-Six

Harry got out of the shower, wrapped a towel around his waist and made a decision: one way or another he had to sort things out with Valerie. This state of limbo couldn't drag on forever. He tried her mobile phone but it went straight to voicemail. He then put a call through to the station and a woman informed him that DS Middleton had gone off shift. Would he like to leave a message? 'No thanks,' he said.

He dithered for a few minutes before reluctantly ringing Jane Anderson's number. 'It's Harry,' he said.

'I'm guessing it's not me you're after.'

'Is she there?' He pulled a face, preparing for one of those tedious lectures on how her best friend 'needed her space'. Surprisingly, it wasn't forthcoming.

'Sorry, she's not around. There's a birthday do for one of the lads. I think they've gone down The Fox.'

'Oh, right,' Harry said. 'Er . . . thanks.'

He hung up, still in a mild state of shock. It wasn't like Anderson to forgo an opportunity to put the knife in. Her actually being helpful was even more remarkable. In fact, it was probably a first. Perhaps the old witch was finally mellowing.

Harry quickly got dressed. He ordered a cab and was already standing on the doorstep when it arrived ten minutes later. On the journey there he began to worry. What if she took objection to his turning up uninvited? Val wasn't the sort to make a scene in public and could easily misinterpret the act as an underhand way of forcing her to talk to him.

The cab drew up outside the pub. Harry paid the driver and stepped out on to the pavement. He took a few determined strides forward but then hesitated again by the door. There was still time to change his mind. Even from outside, he could hear the rhythmic thud of the music, the sound of a party in full swing. He was growing dangerously close to bottling it – maybe this wasn't such a great idea – when a couple of guys came up behind and forced him to make a decision. He either had to move forward or stand aside.

Harry took a deep breath, pushed open the door and walked in. The second thing that struck him, after the volume of the music, was how crowded the place was; finding Val might take some time. It was a large pub, spread across three interconnecting rooms, and there appeared to be several parties going on simultaneously. He didn't recognize anyone in this particular section and, happy to delay the moment of reckoning, went over to the bar and ordered a double Scotch. He swallowed half of it before heading towards where he'd done most of his own drinking when he'd been working down the road.

After a while, the faces began to grow familiar. A few old colleagues smiled and asked how he was. 'Good,' he replied repeatedly, nodding over-vigorously and making the effort to smile back. As if in a hurry, he kept on walking and didn't stop to chat. 'Catch up later, yeah?' He sensed a slight uneasiness in their looks but it was nothing more than he'd expected. Coppers rarely knew what to say to people like him; he was a limping reminder of how it could all go so horribly wrong.

Harry gradually forged a path through the crowd, glancing right and left at all the tables. It was a couple more minutes before he finally saw her. She was sitting on one of the long leather sofas in a shadowy corner of the room. Her long hair was flowing around her shoulders and she was wearing a low-cut, dark blue silky top that he hadn't seen before. She looked beautiful, radiant, and her hazel eyes were shining.

231

He was about to approach when the full picture abruptly imprinted itself upon his brain. He stopped. Although she was sitting in a group of six, she was leaning especially close to one other person. And not just leaning . . . her hand was lightly placed on the thigh of the man beside her. Harry stared at him. It was Dean Chapman, the goddamn pathologist!

Harry's eyes widened and his stomach flipped over.

Lifting the glass to his mouth, he continued to watch. It was just a passing touch, it had to be, just some casual trivial touch . . . but the seconds ticked by and her hand still didn't move. *Come on,* he urged. He could feel the blood slowly draining from his face. This couldn't be happening. This was just a bad dream, wasn't it? Just another few seconds and she'd . . .

And then she did exactly what he'd been dreading most: laughing, she raised her wide pink mouth to Chapman's and kissed him on the lips.

On the bloody lips.

Harry froze. He felt angry, sick, disgusted; he wanted to go over there, to confront them, but his pride held him back. There was only so much humiliation a man could take. As their mouths split apart, he stepped smartly back and merged into the crowd.

Knocking back his drink, he headed for the exit. Shit! How stupid had he been? Why hadn't he realized? He was beginning to understand why Jane Anderson had been so keen to send him here; the bitch had *wanted* him to find out. Val was having an affair and she must have known all about it. It also accounted for some of the embarrassment he'd sensed as he'd walked through the pub. How long had this been going on for? Days, weeks, months?

Pushing his way through the crowd, he stumbled towards the doors. On the way out, he saw Frankie Holt leaning against the bar. The weasel looked at him and grinned. Did he know about it too? Harry felt angry enough to cross the room and take a swing but wisely resisted the temptation.

Out on the street, the cold evening air hit him with an icy blast. He pulled up the collar of his coat and began to walk.

He didn't know where he was going; he just had to get as far away as possible. The more distance he put between himself and Val, the less chance there was of him changing his mind and going back for one very public showdown.

As if he'd been repeatedly punched in the stomach, Harry's guts were aching. His head was spinning too, that image of the two of them going round and round, the moment when she had lifted her face to Chapman's and . . . *How could she?* Okay, so things hadn't been so great recently – they hardly qualified for Couple of the Year – but that was no excuse for . . . Deep in his pockets, his hands clenched into two tight fists. He growled down at the pavement. She could have had the decency to talk to him at least, to finish it properly instead of skulking around behind his back. It was the betrayal, perhaps, that hurt the most.

And why Chapman, for God's sake? Why had she chosen him? Harry couldn't grasp what any self-respecting female could see in a man who preferred the company of the dead to the living. At that thought, he gave a soft bitter laugh. Clearly, for all the time Dean Chapman spent in the presence of corpses, he was a still a more attractive option.

Harry was walking too quickly, forcing his right leg forward in a rapid jerky motion that was starting to cause him serious pain. Spotting a passing black cab, he raised his hand, flagged it down and crawled into the back seat.

'Kentish Town, please,' he instructed the driver.

As the cab made a U-turn, Harry leaned forward and rubbed his shin. The pain had become a dull relentless throb. Frowning, he thought about what he'd do when he got back – pack up what remained of her stuff, perhaps, stuff it into bin bags and chuck it on the doorstep. The thought of such revenge was only momentarily satisfying; it wouldn't change the fact that she would still be sitting in the bar with her new lover, her shoulder leaning too close against his, her hand still resting on his thigh . . .

He slammed his hand hard against the seat. Why should he spend the rest of the evening stressing over *her*? She wasn't exactly grieving over the end of their relationship so why should he? There were other, more important things, he could be doing.

He got out his phone, ran through the menu and found Jess's number.

Chapter Thirty-Seven

Harry was sitting at the bar, sipping on his second pint of Guinness, when Jess arrived.

'This had better be good,' she said. 'I've got somewhere to be and I'm already running late.' As if reminding herself of what she was missing, she glanced around the dreary interior of The Whistle.

Harry raised his eyes to the ceiling. 'Hey, no one twisted your arm. I didn't *make* you come.'

'As good as,' she said, taking off her long coat. Attired in a flimsy rose-coloured top, a black skirt and high-heeled leather boots, she was certainly dressed for somewhere a little more salubrious than this dingy back-street pub. 'You knew perfectly well that I wouldn't be able to resist.'

He grinned, looking her up and down. 'As it happens, you're not the first woman to have said that.'

Jess wrinkled her nose, her eyes darting towards his glass. 'Just how many of those have you had?'

'Only one,' he said, ignoring the earlier brandies and the two strong whiskies he'd already downed.

She didn't look convinced. 'Well, get me a red wine,' she said, 'and make it a large one. I have the feeling that I'm going to need it.'

As Harry caught the attention of the barman, she waltzed off towards the far side of the room and the trio of empty tables that were gathered round the fireplace. He smiled. By the time he'd finished divulging his news, he wouldn't be the only one feeling like a fool tonight.

While her drink was being poured, he glanced over his shoulder and saw her hesitate before finally choosing the table in the middle. And then it struck him . . . that was the very same table he'd been sitting at with Curzon the first time he'd met her. And this was also the very same pub that they'd been drinking in the evening Len had failed to turn up and . . .

Suddenly, he didn't feel quite so smug. Quickly paying for the wine, he picked up the drinks and went over to join her. 'I just realized,' he said. 'I'm sorry.'

She looked up at him, bemused.

'This was where we were last week when . . . before . . . before you heard about Len. I should have thought.' He put the glasses on the table and frowned. 'Look, if you'd rather go somewhere else . . .'

Jess shook her head. 'For God's sake,' she said, 'if I'm going to avoid every watering hole that Len ever frequented, there isn't a bar in London I'll be able to drink in. And where's that going to leave me?' Reaching out, she picked up her glass and smiled. 'But thanks for the thought. I appreciate it.'

Harry pulled up a chair and sat down beside her. 'Sorry,' he said again. 'It's not been the best of days.'

Jess's brows arched up. 'We've all been there at one time or another.' She paused, giving him the opportunity to share his woes if he so desired. When nothing was forthcoming she said, 'So, you've been to see Ellen Shaw. Are you going to tell me what you found out?'

Harry took a swig of his Guinness, followed by a deep breath, and then recited an only slightly edited version of his meeting. She listened carefully, absorbing each sentence and not interrupting – even when he told about the near-miss with the car – until he'd come to the end. By then over ten minutes had passed and her brows had shifted into two tight knots.

She stared down at her glass while she pondered on the

information. Slowly, she raised her eyes. 'So, do you really think Keppell was behind the wheel?'

'Not in person,' Harry said, 'but he may have been the one giving the orders.'

'Jimmy Keppell,' she murmured. 'Could he have known that Len was watching her?'

Harry shrugged. Jess had made the same connection that he had made himself a few hours ago. 'It's possible.'

'But I don't get it,' she said. 'If what she's told you is true, why should Keppell be so keen to shut her up? She isn't saying anything new, anything that could impact on *him*. This is all old history.'

'Old history that he doesn't want raking up again. His schoolboy son was sleeping with Deacon for money. The man has his reputation to consider.'

'No,' she said firmly. 'It's not enough. That was more or less implied at the trial. If he's so concerned about her talking to the press, he must be worried that she's going to tell them something else, something much more dangerous.'

'Like?'

'I don't know. Why didn't she give evidence back then? I mean, she didn't, did she? I haven't read anything about her in the court reports.'

'She was only fifteen. I doubt if the police were even aware of her existence.'

'But Jimmy Keppell was. Perhaps he persuaded her to stay out of it – paid her off or simply threatened her. Deacon was never going to admit to what had really been going on – the boy was underage, wasn't he? – but Keppell could have been worried that she'd crack in the witness box and spill out all the sordid details.' She frowned, not completely persuaded by her own reasoning. 'Or maybe she had other information he wanted her to keep quiet about. She must have heard all kinds of incriminating stuff from Tony.'

'I suppose,' Harry said.

'But why kill Len?'

'Hey,' Harry said, leaning forward over the table. 'We don't know for sure that he did. It was the first conclusion I jumped to but the more I think about it, the less likely it seems. Why *would* he? Len might have been the one poking around but what were the chances of his working alone? Half the staff on the *Herald* could have been aware of the story he was working on.'

'But they weren't,' she said.

'Yes, but Keppell couldn't have known that. Killing Len, and especially on Ellen Shaw's doorstep, would have been way too risky. He'd only be drawing attention to whatever it was he wanted to keep hidden.'

'He didn't seem too bothered about that today.'

Harry thought back to how the car had abruptly stopped, those few terrifying seconds when it seemed the driver might be about to reverse . . . and then the way he had just flashed his lights and taken off. 'I'm starting to think that she was right, that it was more of a warning, a way of showing her how vulnerable she is.'

Jess frowned again. 'Maybe Ellen Shaw hasn't told you everything.'

Harry was less than thrilled at the idea that yet another woman had been lying to him. 'Or maybe she has,' he argued.

They were both silent for a few seconds. 'Okay,' she said. 'But I still don't trust her. Do you really believe that tale about Deacon? Why should she wait all that time before going to see him?'

'I've told you why.'

'Huh,' she snorted. She waited for a moment but then, seeing the expression on his face, smartly changed the subject. 'Anyway, aren't you going to ask how *I* got on today?'

Harry had almost forgotten about her meeting with Scott Hall. 'Oh yeah,' he said. 'How was it?'

'Interesting,' she said. 'He was only a sergeant back then but, unlike Fielding, he had his doubts about the two cases being connected. He always suspected that the Theresa Neal murder was completely separate from the disappearance of Grace.'

'I see,' Harry said. 'Although I guess it's kind of academic now.'

'I don't follow.'

He wondered if she'd actually taken in anything he'd told her. 'Because it's pretty clear that Ellen Shaw *is* who she says she is. We know why she was avoiding Len, why she didn't want to talk to him, and it has nothing to do with some poor child who went missing over twenty years ago.'

'We don't know any such thing,' she vehemently protested. 'All we "know" is what she's decided to tell you. You might choose to believe her but that doesn't mean that I have to.'

'For God's sake, Jess,' he sighed. 'You have to let this go. Len was wrong. Why can't you accept it? There are people, relatives, out there who are going to get hurt if you keep digging up the past. It isn't fair on them.'

Her eyes flashed bright. 'And it isn't fair on Len that he's laid out in the bloody morgue.' She glared at him. 'Is this why you asked me here – just so you could say *I told you so?*'

'Of course not,' he retorted. 'And I'm not suggesting that you should give up searching for whoever killed him, not for a minute, only that it might be better if you don't get sidetracked by . . .' He stopped. An odd shivery sensation had suddenly erupted on the back of his neck. He had a flashback to sitting with an agitated Curzon who was trying to decide whether to talk to him or not. *You ever see a ghost, Harry?*

'What is it?' Jess said.

Harry glanced over his shoulder as if Curzon's drunken spirit might still be lurking in the pub. He rubbed the base of his neck. 'Nothing.'

'You should go easy on those,' Jess said, nodding towards his glass before rising to her feet and putting on her coat. 'Look, I've got to go. I'll call you tomorrow.'

Harry had been hoping that she might stick around but she clearly had better things to do. He watched her walk out of

239

the pub and then went to the bar to order another drink. His popularity with the female sex had apparently hit rock bottom. In the past few hours he'd been dumped by Valerie, bundled out of Ellen's flat in favour of her husband, and now even Jess Vaughan couldn't wait to be rid of him. Three in one day. Even for him, that had to be a record.

Chapter Thirty-Eight

Jess was on her second glass of champagne, holding the flute in one hand while she tried to fend off Toby's unwanted advances with the other. Persuading him to pull some strings, to secure an invitation to the book launch, had been the easy part; keeping his clammy palms off her backside was proving infinitely more difficult.

She finished her drink and smiled sweetly at him. 'Be a love and get me another, would you?'

As Toby obediently trotted off, Jess waited until he was out of sight and then swiftly dived into the crowd. The do was being held in one of the large reception rooms of a swanky Mayfair hotel. The place was packed and with a bit of luck he wouldn't find her again in a hurry. She refused to feel guilty about the abandonment. Okay, so she may have told a few white lies to get him to bring her here – that she was a huge fan of the photographer's work, that she could do with a night out to help take her mind off what had happened – but that did not give him the green light to spend the entire evening trying to get into her pants.

Anyway, she could hardly have told him the truth. That she was here to check out Charlotte Deacon, or Charlotte *Meyer* as she was now called, was hardly information that she wished to share. Jess had found the woman's details in the files that Len had left behind, proof that he hadn't spent all of his time sitting in the pub. Ms Meyer, having dumped Paul Deacon the minute he went down, had married again and was now the

241

successful director of a publishing house. It was the type of company that produced overpriced coffee table books for the idle rich to put on their overpriced coffee tables.

Hoping she'd achieved a safe enough distance from Toby's roaming hands, Jess stopped at a stand to have another flick through the big glossy hardback. There was no denying that the pictures were stunning but then so was the price. She winced. At eighty quid a copy, she wouldn't be rushing out to buy one.

Glancing up, she saw a waiter passing with a tray and managed to grab another drink. The room was full of faintly familiar faces, politicians, businessmen, broadcasters and journalists, as well as a host of B-list celebrities. She scanned the surrounding area for Charlotte, not sure if she would even recognize her. All she had to go on were the old press photos from twelve years ago. Then she had been a tall slim blonde – and twelve years younger.

Replacing the book, Jess wondered what she would do or say if she did finally get to meet her. Everything was so confused, so messy. The only thing of which she *was* certain was that the past was a web of lies and deceit. Could Jimmy Keppell have been responsible for Len's death? Was Ellen Shaw really who she said she was? Then she found herself thinking about Harry. What had been bugging *him* tonight? There had been something odd, weird, about the way he'd been behaving. Or had there? Her brow creased into a frown. She couldn't really claim to know him that well: a few drinks, a smooch in the back of a cab, a return trip to Maidstone and the mutual discovery of a corpse were hardly grounds for a profound understanding.

She was brought back to earth by a nudge to her shoulder. Jess turned to see Gerry Holland standing beside her. He was a reporter from one of the tabloids, a small round forty-something male with a mop of bright red hair.

'Well,' he said, grinning. 'What brings *you* here, sweetie? Don't tell me – the *Herald* is going upmarket?'

242

'You can talk,' she said. 'That rag you work for is hardly renowned for its love of the arts.'

'I only came for the champagne,' he said, lifting his glass.

Jess grinned back at him. 'And the chance of some gossip.' Holland, who could bitch for Britain, made his living from recycling rumour and hearsay. 'So, has anyone made a fool of themselves yet?'

'Early days,' he said. He nodded towards a young petite girl with arms like sticks and long dark hair. She was waving a glass around and already seemed well on the wrong side of sober. 'I've heard that little honey does a good floorshow after a bottle or too.'

'Who is she?'

'An actress – of a sort.'

'And what sort would that be exactly?'

'The *minor* sort,' Holland said snidely. 'She's got a bit part in one of the soaps but her boyfriend's a footballer, premier league, so she could be worth a line or two.'

Jess looked at her. She had a pretty face but was abysmally thin; her collar bone was jutting sharply through her flesh and her waist had the span of an adolescent's. 'The poor kid looks like she hasn't eaten in a month.'

'Probably hasn't,' he said.

Jess sighed and returned her attention to her own problems. 'Well, seeing as you've got nothing better to do at the moment you might just be able to help me. I was hoping to get a quote from one of the publishers – Charlotte . . . er, Meyer, is it? Some of the photos were taken in Hackney,' she lied, 'local interest and all that. You don't know where she is, do you?'

'I wouldn't bother,' he said dismissively. 'Just make something up.'

'That might be the way *you* do things,' she said, 'but at the *Herald* we aim for the bright shining clarity of the truth.'

'As if,' he sniggered, but had the grace to lift his head and give the impression of looking around. 'I saw her earlier. She's wearing a black dress.'

'Oh right,' Jess said. 'Well, that certainly narrows it down.'

Holland pursed his fleshy lips. 'For someone who's begging for help, you could at least make the effort to sound grateful.'

'Gratitude comes with results,' she parried. 'And I *never* beg for anything.'

He grinned again. 'You local hacks are way too tetchy.' He had another glance around the room and then, taking hold of her elbow, tilted his head towards the bar. 'She's over there, the tall one, the blonde with the handbag.'

Jess gazed over and saw her for the first time. She was impressed. Charlotte Meyer was in her early fifties but was still undeniably striking. Her eyes were clear blue, her hair sleek and shiny, her face elegantly sculptured. She looked a good ten years younger than she actually was although whether that was down to some fortunate DNA, a rigorously healthy lifestyle or the skilful intervention of a surgeon's knife was impossible to tell from a distance. Like a predatory male, Jess let her eyes roam down the length of her body. She had good legs too, long and shapely, ending in a pair of designer high heels.

'Well?' Holland said.

'Well what?'

'I thought you wanted to talk to her.'

'I do,' she said. 'I will . . . later. There's no hurry.' Whether she would actually approach her or not, she still had to decide. How exactly did you open a conversation about a woman's former husband and his conviction for murder? It wasn't a subject that rolled easily off the tongue. It was hardly a subject Charlotte would want to be reminded of either. No, it was better not to rush headlong into anything she might regret. This was going to take some thought.

In the meantime she might as well take advantage of being in the presence of one of the most indiscreet people in the country. When it came to premium bitching, there was no one to compare to Gerry Holland.

244

'I've just realized,' she said. 'Wasn't she married to that politician? What's his name, Paul . . . er . . .'

'Deacon,' he said.

'Yeah, that's it.' She nodded and then puckered her brows, pretending she couldn't recall much about him. 'Wasn't he involved in some kind of murder case? Or was that a different guy?'

Holland's mouth slid quickly into another of its wide greasy smirks. 'That was him all right. And he was heading straight for a place in the Cabinet before he shot his pretty little boyfriend straight through the chest.'

'No!' she said, acting astounded. She glanced over towards Charlotte Meyer again. 'That couldn't have made her too happy.'

Gerry gave a snort. 'She'd have bloody killed him if she'd had the opportunity.'

'I can imagine,' Jess said. 'Didn't she have any idea about what was going on?'

'Not a clue. She knew about the other women of course – Deacon wasn't the most monogamous of men – but he'd managed to hide his darker side. His liking for boys was his own dirty little secret.'

'Boys?' she repeated. 'So there was definitely more than one?'

'What do you think?' he said. 'A rich man like Deacon doesn't get to be forty-odd before deciding what he likes.'

'I suppose not,' she said.

Holland took a swig of his champagne and licked his lips. 'Don't get me wrong but it's not natural, is it? Gay, straight, I don't give a damn. Men, women, take your fancy – but fifteen-year-old schoolboys . . . well, what's all that about?'

Jess, thankfully, didn't need to think of an answer. To the left of them, the skinny dark-haired girl was kicking up a row. Hands were flying, voices had risen and a glass suddenly shattered on the floor. Gerry was off like a shot, eager for his next tabloid scoop.

She looked back towards the bar. Charlotte Meyer was heading for the Ladies.

Jess followed her.

The bathroom was almost as large as her flat but smelled ten times better. It was like entering a perfumery. Women were lined up under the stark lights of the mirrors, adjusting their hair and reapplying their lipstick. Jess saw her own reflection and flinched; her cheeks were flushed bright pink from the heat and her mascara had melted into two dark smudges under her eyes. She was still trying to repair the damage when Charlotte Meyer emerged from one of the cubicles.

Jess watched as she washed and dried her hands. For a moment she thought that she was going to walk straight out but then she laid her Gucci bag on the counter and took out her comb. As soon as the two girls between them had moved away, Jess shifted along until she was standing beside her.

'Hello,' Jess said, smiling. 'Congratulations on the book. It's very impressive.'

Charlotte glanced at her, a swift casual glance, before she nodded and said, 'Yes, thank you.'

Jess watched as the cool blue eyes made a quick practised survey of her face and clothes and knew that she'd been assessed, judged and dismissed within a matter of seconds. She was no one important. She wasn't worth wasting time on.

'And a good turnout,' Jess persisted. 'You must be pleased.'

This time Charlotte didn't bother to look at her or even properly open her mouth. 'Mm,' she said instead, leaning forward to focus her attention on the mirror.

Up to this point Jess had been feeling reasonably sympathetic – being married to a murderer couldn't be easy – but that emotion was rapidly draining away. Stuck-up bitch, she thought. She despised people, men or women, who couldn't make the effort to even pretend to be nice. And okay, Charlotte must have been making small talk all night, and it must have become disgustingly tiresome, but that was still no excuse for blatant incivility.

246

Jess was so annoyed that the words came out before she had time to think about the consequences. 'I hear your ex is writing a book too. It seems he has a little more to say about Tony Keppell – and the blackmail.'

Charlotte's face turned a satisfying shade of white. 'What?' she snapped. Her neck twisted round so fast she was in danger of breaking it.

Jess tried to keep her grin in check. At least she'd finally got her full attention. 'Oh, sorry,' she said disingenuously. 'Hadn't you heard?'

Charlotte's voice rose by a few harsh decibels. 'Heard? Heard from whom, exactly?'

Jess shrugged. Taking a tube of hand cream from her bag, she squeezed it, and began to slowly massage the cream into her fingers. 'You know, I can't remember. It's just something that's been doing the rounds, something on the grapevine.'

'Who are you?' Charlotte said. Her eyes had narrowed and her tone was viciously sharp.

Jess had been raised with the principle that honesty was always the best policy. Fortunately, it was a legacy that she'd managed to overcome. 'Rachel Evans,' she said brightly. 'I'm a freelance journalist.'

Charlotte glared at her.

Jess calmly put the cream back in her bag and turned away. 'It's probably just a rumour. I shouldn't worry about it.'

'Just a moment,' Charlotte demanded. Realizing that her waspish tone wasn't getting anywhere, she forced out a smile. 'Sorry,' she said. 'I was just a bit surprised, that's all. What are we talking about here?'

'Perhaps you should have a word with him about it.'

Charlotte didn't look too enamoured of the idea.

Jess walked towards the door. 'I have to go.'

'Hold on,' Charlotte said.

Jess didn't. She couldn't take the risk of being interrogated too closely. Quickly, she made her way through the crowd. At the exit she briefly glanced back. Charlotte was already at the bar, talking to a couple of bland grey-suited men. They looked suspiciously like lawyers. As their gaze swept the room, Jess slipped outside.

On the street, she headed for the tube. Did she regret what she'd done? Not at all. It was time to shake things up . . . and there was nothing like a bit of stirring if you wanted the truth to rise to the surface.

Chapter Thirty-Nine

It was late Tuesday morning and Harry was still waiting for Val to call. Surely someone must have told her that he'd been in The Fox last night, that he'd seen her with Chapman. Perhaps her silence was an indication of how little she cared. Perhaps she was even pleased that he'd been a witness; it saved her the trouble of relaying the good news herself.

Harry knew how easily he could play the injured party but was aware too that the breakdown of the relationship was not entirely down to her. And, if he was being brutally honest, his resentment was tinged with just a touch of relief. The past months had been a battleground – now, bar the compulsory shouting, it was virtually all over. Or was it? If he was so glad that it was finished, why did he feel so bad and why did his stomach keep churning? Why did he so desperately want to hear her voice again?

His phone began to ring and he quickly picked it up.

'Lind?' a male voice asked.

'Speaking,' Harry said.

'Ray Stagg. I need to see you.'

'What for?'

'What do you think?' Stagg said brusquely. 'You're supposed to be looking for a missing person, aren't you?'

Harry snorted down the line. 'As I recall, you've already fired me from that job.'

'Yeah, well,' he said dismissively. 'I was probably a bit hasty there, heat of the moment and all that. With what happened to Tommo and then . . . well, let's just say that my usual good judgement might have been impaired.'

'Right. So now you've changed your mind and I'm just expected to jump?'

'Don't be like that,' Stagg said. 'I've had some time to think about it, that's all. If you don't want the job, just say so. You're not the only private detective in town.'

'No,' Harry agreed. 'But I am the only one that Agnes rang.'

There was a short silence. 'You want the job or not?' Stagg snarled.

Harry was tempted to say 'not' but he'd only be cutting off his nose to spite his face. He needed to get back to work. He was worried about Agnes and his best hope for a lead must surely lie with the other girls at the club. Without Stagg's cooperation, however, it wouldn't be easy to talk to them. 'I'll have to run it past Mac.'

'Yeah, yeah,' Stagg said, as if this was a mere formality. 'Meet me tonight at Vista. Ten o'clock. Don't keep me waiting.'

Chapter Forty

Jess stared at the computer screen and nodded. She had finally got what she wanted: some good clear pictures of Ellen Shaw. Two hours she'd been sitting in the car, half freezing to death in Berry Square, but it had been worth the wait. She didn't care what Harry thought – the delightful Mrs Shaw, she was certain, was still hiding something.

After carefully choosing the photos she wanted, she pressed the button and printed them out. She was about to stand up and make herself a coffee when she had another thought. Slotting a CD into the computer, she saved all the pictures, along with her notes. It was never a good idea to keep all your information in one place; she'd drop the disk off at the office later.

Jess went to the kitchen and switched the kettle on. For the next few minutes, she tapped her fingers impatiently against the sink while she waited for the water to come to the boil. 'C'mon,' she murmured. Everything, from the case to the kettle, was moving too slowly. Was she making *any* progress? She was starting to feel like she was wading through sludge.

Back in the living room, she laid the photographs of Ellen across the table and compared them to the press pictures of the eight-year-old Grace Harper. She still couldn't say if Len had been right or wrong. There *were* similarities, especially around the eyes, but Ellen's hair was much darker and her mouth slightly different. Jess shrugged. The natural ageing process, a bottle of hair dye and a few shots of collagen could easily account for that.

Her mobile went off and she picked it up. 'Hi.'

'It's Scott,' the voice at the other end said. 'Scott Hall.'

'Hey,' Jess said. 'How are you?'

'Fine,' he said. 'Look, I remembered something after you'd gone. I wasn't able to check it out until this morning but I thought it might be useful.'

'Great,' she said. 'Fire away.'

'It's about Sharon Harper. I had this vague memory of . . . Well, it was getting on for a year ago and we got a call about a disturbance, a couple of women going at it hammer and tongs in the street. A real barney by all accounts and getting violent too. I didn't deal with it myself but I recognized the name.'

Jess's eyes lit up. So Sharon *was* still living locally. 'And it was her?'

'Yeah, it was her all right. Anyway, it didn't come to much; by the time the car got there, it was over and done with. Sharon had a few cuts and bruises but nothing too drastic and the other woman had done a bunk.'

'Do you know who she was?'

'No,' Scott said, 'and Sharon apparently refused to say.' He gave a soft laugh. 'If I was a betting man I'd put my money on an irate wife. She never was too fussy about the men she slept with.'

'Right,' Jess said. 'But no one got a description of her? Young, old, middle-aged?'

'Sorry,' he said. 'Sharon didn't want to press charges so . . .'

Jess frowned, disappointed. The first name that had sprung into her head was Joan Sewell – she certainly hated her sister-in-law enough – but somehow the idea of that prim restrained woman brawling in the street like an angry fishwife didn't quite ring true.

'However,' Scott continued, 'what I did manage to get is the address. I can't guarantee Sharon's still living there but the odds are pretty good.'

'Brilliant,' Jess said. 'Hang on a sec.' She reached across the

252

table and snatched up her notepad and a pen. 'Okay, I'm ready.'

'Burnley Avenue. Number sixty-one.'

'That's not far away,' she said, scribbling it down. 'Thanks. I appreciate it.'

'Are you going to talk to her?'

Fearing a Harry Lind-type lecture on her moral obligations when it came to digging up the past, she hesitated. 'Er . . . I'm not sure. Maybe. I haven't quite decided yet. Of course if I do, I'll be careful what I say. I know it's a sensitive subject.'

Scott Hall gave another of his soft laughs. 'Actually, I *was* going to suggest that you be careful – but more for your sake than hers. If Sharon gets even a hint that you might have ulterior motives . . . well, I'd make sure you're wearing your running shoes.'

Jess grinned. 'I'll bear that in mind.'

'Let me know how it goes,' he said.

'I will. And thanks again.'

Jess put down the phone and sat back in the chair. It was reassuring to know that she wasn't the only person in the world with doubts about the fate of little Grace Harper. She had been cautious about what she'd told Scott at their meeting, revealing only that she was doing some research on the case, but he'd said nothing to try and dissuade her. On the contrary, if today's phone call was anything to go by, he was actively encouraging her to go for it.

She was still pondering on her next move when the mobile rang again. This time it was Toby Marsh.

'What happened to you last night?' he said.

'Me?' she replied indignantly. 'More like what happened to you. You go off to get me a drink and an hour later I'm still waiting.'

'I couldn't find you.'

'Huh!' she said. 'The place wasn't *that* big. Are you sure you didn't stumble on some cute thirsty blonde and decide to give her my champagne instead?'

'I looked for you,' he insisted. 'I couldn't find you anywhere.'

'You should get your eyes checked out.' She waited a moment and sighed. 'Oh well,' she said forgivingly. 'No harm done, I suppose.'

There was a short silence.

'Toby?' she said.

'There's something else I have to talk to you about.'

He sounded serious. Jess pulled a face, hoping that he hadn't discovered what she was really doing with her leave. If he ever found out about those files she had taken . . .

'Yeah?' she mumbled.

'Er . . . it's about Len,' he said. 'I thought you'd want to know. Only it seems that the body's finally been released. His brother's arranged the funeral for next Monday; it's at the local crematorium, eleven thirty.'

It was the last thing she had been expecting. She sharply drew in her breath. *The body*, she repeated inwardly. *Len's* body.

She stared up at the ceiling. A few seconds passed.

'Hello? Jess? Are you still there?'

Feeling her hands beginning to shake, she tightened her grip on the phone. 'Does this mean the police have dropped the investigation?'

'No,' he said. 'I'm sure it doesn't. They just don't need his . . .' He stopped abruptly and gave a small embarrassed cough. 'I mean, I think they've completed everything they need to do, that's all. And it's for the best, isn't it? It's a good thing. At least he can be laid to rest now.'

Jess shook her head. How he was ever supposed to rest when his killer was still roaming free was beyond her. Still, that wasn't anything she expected Toby to understand. He was still convinced, like so many others, that Len's death hadn't been premeditated, that it was simply down to some crazed junkie, to some stupid random mugging that had happened to go wrong.

'Are you okay?' he said.

'Eleven thirty,' she said. 'That's fine. I'll be there.'

'Would you like me to call round, to pick you up? It's no trouble. I know that you and Len worked closely together, that you were friends.'

Jess closed her eyes. This was hard enough to deal with without Toby going all kind and considerate on her. 'Thanks,' she said, 'it's nice of you to offer but I'll be fine. Really, I will. I'll see you there. I'll see you on Monday.'

She put the phone down and buried her face in her hands. *Damn it!* Len's funeral was less than a week away and what had she achieved? Sod all! He'd left her his files, his suspicions and at least some of his accumulated wisdom and she was still pussyfooting around trying not to upset too many people.

Lifting her head, Jess wiped her eyes. She stared down at the address Scott had given her. If anyone held the key to the mysteries of the past it was Sharon Harper. There was nothing to stop her from going round: she had talked to Joan Sewell and got away with it – so why not take the next step?

Before she could change her mind, Jess leaned over, grabbed her brown leather boots and pulled them on. She picked up her bag and dashed out of the flat. She had just got into the car when her mobile started ringing again. Who was it now? Glancing down she saw that the caller was Harry. She was tempted to ignore him – he'd not been in the best of moods last night – but thought better of it. It was *his* silver grey Audi she was sitting in after all.

'Hey,' she said brightly.

'Are you sick?' he said.

Jess slid the key into the ignition. 'Why should I be sick?'

'Because you were out last night. Because it's getting on for midday and you're still not here. I thought we had a deal. I help you and you help me. It's not too complicated. So, weren't you supposed to play driver for me today?'

'Ah,' she said.

'What's going on?'

Jess fastened her seatbelt. 'Yes, you're right, you're absolutely right but I'm a bit tied up at the moment. I can be with you in . . . say a couple of hours?'

'Forget it,' he said brusquely.

Jess scowled at the windscreen. This was all she needed, Harry Lind having a sulk at her expense. 'Hey, I'm sorry, all right? I should have let you know. But if it's that important, I'll drop what I'm doing and come round straight away.'

'What I meant,' he said, 'is that there's no need to rush over. How about we make it this evening instead? I need a lift to Vista. About nine thirty. You think you could manage that?'

'Oh,' Jess said, relieved. 'Of course I can. Ray Stagg won't be too pleased though. I thought he fired you.'

'He missed me so much that I'm back on the pay roll.'

'Must be that fabulous wit and charm,' she said.

He ignored the comment. 'I need to see him. Then I have to talk to the girls, try and find out what they know about Agnes.'

'Well, good luck with that,' she said.

'Nine thirty,' he reminded her.

'Yeah, yeah,' she said. 'I heard you the first time. I'll be there.'

'Oh, and Jess,' he said, before he hung up, 'you will take care of the car, won't you?'

'I'll treat it like my own.'

He gave an exaggerated groan. 'Yeah, that's what I was worried about.'

Burnley Avenue should have been a short ten-minute drive away but the traffic was snarled up and moving at a snail's pace. Jess, stuck behind a bus, spent the time murmuring expletives and stressing over how she was going to get Sharon Harper to agree to speak to her. With Joan Sewell it had been relatively straightforward – Michael was always going to be her weak spot – but she didn't have the same leverage with Sharon.

It was twenty-five minutes before she finally arrived at her destination. She counted off the numbers on the front doors and after she reached forty-nine pulled into the first available parking space and switched off the engine. For a while she sat and gazed out through the windscreen. Burnley Avenue consisted of two rows of identikit dark brick semis, cleverly designed to blend in with the general grime of the area. The houses, box-like, bland and featureless, looked like they'd been built by a five-year-old with a set of Lego – although that was maybe an injustice to the creative flair of five-year-olds.

From where she was seated, Jess could see a couple of properties with their windows boarded up. One of them had a forlorn For Sale sign tilting sideways by the gate. It was December already but there was little sign here of any enthusiasm for the festive season. Not even a hint of tinsel. To her left the pavement was littered with fast food containers, fag ends and squashed tin cans. The road didn't appear to have been swept in the past year or so.

Jess dug in her bag, found her cigarettes and lit one. Winding down the window, she shivered in a blast of cold air. She peered towards number sixty-one. It didn't look any different to the rest of the houses. There was no obvious sign of life.

She still hadn't decided what to say.

A woman pushing a toddler in a pram strode past. A pair of teenagers came next, their blue jeans slung low and their faces buried in their hoods. Warily, she watched them in her rear-view mirror, aware of her probably unjustified prejudice but still unable to prevent a few niggling doubts. They turned left at the corner and the street was quiet again.

She finished her cigarette and threw it on the ground outside. She felt faintly guilty – it wasn't exactly improving an already shabby environment – but would have felt even worse if she'd stubbed it out in the perfectly pristine ashtray. Mr Lind had his standards.

'Time to go,' she muttered out loud. 'Move it, Vaughan! Shift!'

Quickly, before she could change her mind, she jumped out of the car but then stopped again, taking care to lock it. Across the road a dark blue Ford, minus its wheels, was jacked up on a heap of bricks. She felt a momentary qualm about abandoning Harry's pride and joy but what else could she do? She shouldn't be too long. She'd just have to cross her fingers and hope for the best.

Walking towards number sixty-one, Jess looked round again. Wasn't an avenue supposed to have trees? There wasn't a single one in sight. It was as if the local council had decided to ban anything with an inclination to turn green. Most of the front gardens, small mean squares, had been concreted over. Grey was the only enduring colour, from the sky to the ground.

Jess paused at the place where a gate had once stood, hesitated, then took a deep breath and strode up the path. She pressed the bell but couldn't hear any accompanying sound. She tried it again. Was it working? She took a step back and stared up at the house. It was in the same state as the neighbouring properties, the basic structure dilapidated, the brickwork crumbling, the exterior paintwork dull and flaking. It appeared, however, to have one exclusive feature: the front door had a wide crack running up the right-hand side as if someone had recently tried to kick it in.

Giving up on the bell, she rapped directly on the door instead. This time there was a definite movement from inside. After a further thirty seconds a teenage boy pulled open the door. He was pale and slight and looked about fourteen. His hair was a mousy brown. The wires of an iPod were trailing round his skinny shoulders.

'Yeah?' he said.

Jess smiled sweetly. 'Hi. Is Mrs Harper in?'

'Mam,' he shouted over his shoulder. 'Someone here to see you.'

'Who is it?' she yelled back.

The voice came from a room that wasn't too far away. The TV was blaring out, some midday chat show with accompanying waves of manic applause.

258

The boy looked at her again. 'Who are you?' he said, as if she might not have heard his mother's bellowing reply.

'Can I come in?'

'Can she come in?' he relayed back.

'Who is it?' his mother yelled again. Actually standing up and finding out for herself was clearly too much of an effort.

'My name's Jessica Vaughan,' she said, loud and firm enough for her voice to carry. 'I'd like to talk to your mother. It's important.'

The boy opened his mouth as if about to repeat it but then, smart enough to know that he was wasting his energy, immediately closed it again.

About twenty seconds passed before Sharon emerged. She was in her mid-forties and her hair was a bright artificial blonde. She was wearing a short red skirt, a black sleeveless T-shirt and a pair of sequinned flip-flops. Her legs were long, bare and ivory white. A cigarette hung between the fingers of her left hand. She looked Jess up and down with the kind of contempt she probably reserved for social workers. 'What do you want? If it's about our Darren,' she said, 'he's had the flu, that's why he's not been in school.'

Jess glanced towards the boy. 'He looks okay to me.'

'Yeah, well,' she said. 'He's getting over it.'

Discomfited, or perhaps merely bored by the exchange, Darren turned and scuttled up the stairs.

Jess remained standing on the doorstep. 'I'm not here about your son.'

'What then?'

'I'm a writer,' she said. 'I'm putting together a series of articles on unsolved cases and the impact they've had on the relatives involved.'

Sharon stared blankly back at her.

'I'd like to talk to you about Grace.'

At the mention of her daughter's name, Sharon's eyes narrowed and her mouth tightened into a thin straight line. 'What?'

'I'm sorry to call by uninvited.'

Sharon's brown eyes darkened. She glared at Jess. What she saw obviously didn't impress her too much. 'Fuck off!' she said. She reached for the door.

Jess was back in the same position she'd been in with Joan Sewell. She knew that she had to say something persuasive – and fast. She only had a few seconds. What sprang from her lips was a shot on the dark. 'That's okay,' she said, stepping back and raising her hands. 'That's fine. I understand. Joan said you wouldn't want to talk to me.'

Sharon stopped suddenly and scowled. 'You've been talking to Joan?'

'Oh yes,' Jess said. 'She's been very helpful.'

'What's that old bitch told you?'

Jess shrugged and did her habitual trick – the trick Len had taught her – of glancing to the left and right as if the neighbours might be watching. She lowered her voice. 'Perhaps if I could come inside . . .?'

Sharon hung on to the door, struggling to make a decision. She might not want to talk about Grace but she did want to find out what Joan had been saying. Curiosity finally won the day. She stood back and gestured with her head for Jess to follow.

'Suppose you'd better,' she said grudgingly.

Jess followed her inside, closing the door behind. *Don't blow it now, Vaughan. Tread carefully. Don't say anything stupid.*

The living room was to the right off the narrow hallway. It was about fifteen foot square and over-cluttered with furniture. It also looked like a tornado had blown through several months ago and no one had got round to clearing up the damage. The whole place stank of wet dog, stale cigarette smoke and booze, a gut-wrenching combination that made Jess glad she hadn't over-indulged the night before.

Sharon slumped down on a tattered beige sofa. She stubbed out her fag and immediately lit another. Guessing that if she waited for an invitation she'd be standing there forever, Jess shifted a pile of magazines to one side and lowered herself on to the edge of an easy chair.

The TV was still on, blaring out loudly. 'Would you mind?' Jess said, glancing towards the set. 'Just for a minute.'

Sharon shrugged, picked up the remote and put the TV on mute. For a few seconds she continued to gaze at the picture as if she might be missing something of vital importance.

'I realize how difficult this must be,' Jess began. 'As I mentioned, I've been looking into—'

'Just tell me what the stupid bitch said,' Sharon interrupted. 'Told you it was my fault, did she? What a rubbish mother I was?'

'I think she was more concerned with how Michael had been treated after—'

'*Him*?' Sharon said incredulously. 'That waste of space! How *he* was treated? Don't make me laugh. He only got what he deserved. That bastard came home wrecked every night, shouting the odds, acting like a fucking animal. Pissed all his wages up the wall, didn't he? Treated us like dirt. Don't suppose she happened to mention any of that.' She stopped to draw breath, sucking bitterly on her cigarette. 'They should have locked him up and thrown away the key.'

'You never thought about . . . er, leaving him?'

'Leaving him?' Sharon repeated. She stared at Jess as if she was from a different planet. 'You don't leave men like Michael Harper, love. Not if you want to keep on breathing.'

There wasn't much Jess could say to that so she fell back on the failsafe response of sympathetic understanding. 'God, it must have been awful for you.'

As if violent husbands were simply an accepted part of life's trials and tribulations, Sharon lifted her shoulders in a bored shrug. Her gaze drifted towards the TV again. Before she lost her attention, Jess quickly returned to the subject of her sister-in-law.

'Mrs Sewell . . . Joan . . . seemed kind of resentful that you wouldn't let Grace spend time round there. She claimed you deliberately kept her away.'

Sharon didn't bother to dispute it. 'You bet I did. You think I'd want any kid of mine spending time with that flaming freak?'

'Well, I can see how she might be difficult.'

'Not *her*,' Sharon said, 'although she was bad enough. That mad son of hers.' She paused and grinned. 'She didn't tell you about him, did she?'

It was news to Jess. She shook her head.

Sharon leaned forward, slapped her hands on her knees and cackled. 'There! What have I been saying? That witch wouldn't know the truth if it came along and bit her on the arse.' Then, as if this was a cause for celebration, she jumped up and walked over to a table in the corner. Picking up a bottle of vodka, she poured out a hefty measure. She took a large swig, refilled the glass and turned to Jess. 'Fancy one?'

Jess didn't. All of the glasses, opaque with grime, looked like breeding grounds for fatal bacteria. 'Lovely,' she said. 'Thanks very much.'

Sharon passed her a drink and then sat down again. 'I wouldn't let our Grace within a hundred miles of that house, not on her own, not with that weirdo hanging about. There was no knowing what he might do.'

In the spirit of the moment, Jess raised the glass to her lips but didn't drink anything. 'Tell me about him.'

Sharon laughed again, a nasty mirthless sound. She raised a finger to the side of her head and made a twisting motion. 'Not right upstairs, was he? Should have been put away somewhere but Joan wasn't having any of it. Francis he was called, a right little spastic.'

Jess flinched at the word. It was a long time since she'd heard anybody use it and a frown creased up her forehead. 'Dangerous?' she said, hoping that Sharon hadn't noticed her reaction.

Sharon shrugged again. 'I wasn't taking no chances. I mean you can't, can you, not with your own. World's full of nonces and what do the cops do about it? Fuck all! In and out of nick in a couple of years, roaming the streets, free to do

262

whatever they want again. It's a bloody disgrace! If I had my way, I'd—'

Before she could embark on what could prove to be a lengthy discourse, Jess swiftly interrupted. 'So you think Francis was a . . . a nonce, then?'

'As good as.' Sharon reached for her cigarettes.

'Here,' Jess said, grabbing her own pack from her bag, and offering it over. 'Have one of these.'

'Oh,' Sharon said. 'Ta.'

After they had both lit up, Jess sat back and waited for her to continue. She didn't. Jess gave her another prompt. 'So what made you think he was . . .'

Sharon's mouth curled down at the corners. 'Had straying hands, didn't he? Couldn't stop himself. Always *touching* people, *staring* at them.' She gave a visible shudder. 'I'm telling you, it made my flesh creep. You think I'd let my daughter near him? No way! She'd have been safer in a pit of snakes.'

'So where is he now?' Jess asked. She hadn't seen any sign of him at the house. 'Does he still live with Joan?'

'Nah,' Sharon said. 'He kicked it years back, some kind of brain thing.' She drank some more of her vodka. 'A mercy, if you ask me. At least he went before . . . Well, God knows what he might have gone on to do. Those sort of people ain't normal. It's not safe to have them wandering around.'

'So how old was he when Grace . . . when she went missing?'

Sharon thought about it. 'Fourteen, fifteen? He was big for his age though, tall, well built. Stronger than he realized, if you know what I mean.'

Jess was pretty sure that she knew what she meant. 'You think he might have had something to do with what happened to Grace?'

'It crossed my mind, course it did. Joan gave him an alibi, said he was with her all day, but that meant fuck all. She'd have sworn her boy was innocent if she'd seen him kill with his own bare hands. The cops went along with every word she told them.'

'They must have checked the story out.'

'I'm not saying it was him. I'm not making any accusations. All I'm saying is that he wasn't all there.'

Jess looked more closely at her. Could she be Ellen's mother? She tried to visualize her with darker hair. There was no doubting that Sharon must have been pretty once but her face was ravaged now, her skin dull and grey; there were bags under her eyes and deep grooves running from the corners of her mouth. It was a lesson, if one was needed, of the damage that resulted from an excess of grief, booze and cigarettes. Jess glanced down at the fag in her own hand.

'What about Joan's husband? What was he like?'

Sharon shook her head. 'Never met him. He died before I got together with Michael.'

'What was his name?'

'Dunno,' she said. 'I can't remember.'

Jess snapped her next question out before she could think too much about it. 'You think the cops did the best job they could?'

Sharon looked into her glass. It was empty. She stared at it with an expression of abject disappointment. 'The cops were bleeding useless.' She stood up again, grabbed the vodka bottle, filled her glass, sat down and placed the bottle beside her feet. 'It's been twenty years,' she said, 'and they still don't have a clue who took her. *That's* how good they were.'

Jess nodded. They were both silent for a while. From upstairs came the deep bass thud of heavy rock. She raised her eyes towards the ceiling and then looked back around the room. There were a couple of photographs hung up on the wall, both portraits of boys. She recognized one as the lad who had answered the door. The other one was older, blonder. There was no picture of Grace.

'You've got two sons?' she asked.

'Yeah,' Sharon said. 'Darren and Jase.'

'Does their father live here?'

She gave a grunt. 'Get real. Not gonna make the same mistake twice, am I?'

Jess smiled back. She wanted to ask if she ever wondered if

264

Grace was still alive but couldn't; it was just too close to the bone. She was also tempted to ask if she'd ever heard of Ellen Shaw but knew that wouldn't be a good idea either.

'Joan said you used to work in a nightclub.'

Sharon nodded. 'The Starlight,' she said. 'Had to, didn't I? Someone had to pay the rent, put food on the table. If I'd left it to Michael we'd have starved to death.' She took another swig from her glass. 'I suppose she had a go about that too? Yeah, I bet she did. That bitch was born with a knife in her hand.'

'She mentioned it,' Jess said. She was still holding the untouched glass of vodka. If she could have found somewhere to dump its contents, a convenient pot plant for example, she would have – but there was nowhere. Feeling Sharon's eyes fixed on her she lifted the glass to her lips, took a gulp, hoped for the best and swallowed. With luck the alcohol would counteract anything too poisonous.

'She still thinks it's my fault,' Sharon said.

'No one could ever think that.'

'She does.'

'But what do *you* think?' Jess asked. 'Who do you think was responsible?'

Sharon shrank back against the sofa. 'Who took my little girl?' Her eyes grew liquid. 'I'll never know now, will I?'

Chapter Forty-One

The silence was starting to get on Harry's nerves. She hadn't said a word for the past ten minutes and was driving with a stern concentrated expression on her face.

'Have I done something to annoy you?'

Jess shot him a sideways glance. 'Oh, please,' she said. 'Do you really think that everything's about you?'

'It's crossed my mind,' he said, trying to lighten the atmosphere.

'Well, think again. Some of us have got *serious* problems.'

Harry lifted his brows. He wasn't exactly on cloud nine himself. Valerie hadn't called and he still hadn't worked out whether he wanted her to or not. His leg was giving him grief, his future at Mackenzie's was looking less than secure, and he was on his way to meet Ray Stagg again. 'Anything you want to share?'

'No,' she said.

'Are you sure?'

Jess scowled. A noise came from the back of her throat, a low irritated sound.

Harry shut his mouth. Perhaps he should have got a taxi instead; even the mindless babble from an over-chatty cabbie would have been preferable to this chilly atmosphere.

Then, as they stopped at the traffic lights, she turned to look at him again. 'If you must know, it's Len's funeral on Monday.'

'Ah,' Harry said. 'I'm sorry.' He paused. 'So they've released the body.'

She didn't reply.

'And you're feeling guilty about it.'

Her eyes flicked quickly towards him again. She tapped her fingers against the wheel. 'Why should I feel guilty?' she snapped.

'You shouldn't,' Harry said, 'but you do. It's human nature. You're convinced you should have found some answers by now but you haven't. That makes you feel bad – it always made me feel bad when I was working on unsolved cases – but it's even worse for you because he was a friend.'

The lights turned to green and Jess shifted the car forward. She kept her gaze focused on the road ahead. 'I went to see Sharon Harper today.'

Harry was shocked although he tried not to show it. 'And?'

'Don't worry,' she said sarcastically. 'I didn't tie her down and flash a bright light in her face. They taught us not to do that at journalist school – well, only as a final resort. I gave her the choice and she was okay about it. And if you're going to ask if I found out anything useful then I really don't know. It turns out that Joan Sewell had a son, Francis, a few years older than Grace, who she neglected to mention when I talked to her. He's dead now. Sharon claims that he had mental problems although she had a rather less subtle way of describing it.'

'Did she think he had something to do with Grace's death?'

'With her *disappearance*,' Jess corrected. 'No, she didn't say that exactly.'

'But she implied it?'

Jess audibly breathed in, releasing the air in a long frustrated sigh. 'Yes. But then she didn't seem too keen to exonerate her husband either. And before you mention it, I realize that she needs someone to blame and that anything she says might not be entirely reliable.'

Harry nodded.

'So you've got my story,' she said. 'What's been bugging you?'

'Me?'

267

'I get the impression that you might not be your normal happy self.'

'I'm flattered that you've noticed.'

'Don't be,' she said. 'You're not that hard to read.' She took a sharp left. The road was long and clear but she kept her speed down. 'Let me guess – woman trouble?'

Harry stared at her. He wondered, not for the first time, whether the female of the species didn't have an unfair advantage when it came to the complex world of relationships; they always seemed to know more than they should. 'That could be interpreted as a sexist comment.'

Jess gave a snort. 'Or just an insightful one.'

'So what would your advice be,' he said, trying to keep his voice light, 'if that *was* the case?'

'I'd need to know the details,' Jess said. Pulling into the car park at Vista, she got as close to the bright lights of the front entrance as she could. 'But I'm not sure if I want to. I'm only here to drive. That's my part of the bargain. Psychological insights come extra.'

Harry released his seatbelt and got out of the car.

She got out too.

'What are you doing?' he said.

'What do you think? I'm not staying here on my own. The last time I was at this place . . .'

They both glanced over towards the wall where Troy's body had been lying.

'Oh,' Harry said. 'Yeah, right. Sorry.'

'Anyway,' she said, 'those girls are never going to talk to you. They won't trust a man. What you need is a woman's touch.'

'I thought you were only here to do the driving.'

'Call it a complimentary extra,' she said, 'seeing as I may have been a little remiss in skipping our appointment this morning.'

Harry smiled. It was probably as close to an apology as he would ever get.

There was a uniformed bruiser on the door, almost as wide as he was tall. He didn't look happy, perhaps because he'd drawn the short straw and was stuck outside on what was not an especially pleasant evening. There was no rain as yet but any icy wind was blowing across the forecourt. He watched, his thick arms folded over his chest, as Harry and Jess approached.

'I'm here to see Mr Stagg,' Harry said. 'I'm expected. The name's Lind.'

Practising his intimidation technique, the big guy stared hard at him. Then, when Harry didn't crumble, he bent his head and muttered into his walkie-talkie. 'Geezer to see the boss. Says he's expected.'

While they were waiting, the three of them stood in an uneasy silence. Harry wished he'd put his overcoat on; he could feel the wind slicing through the thin fabric of his suit and biting into his bones. Jess was more sensibly dressed in a woollen jacket and scarf. Gritting his teeth, he fought against the impulse to stamp his feet; tough guys didn't feel the cold.

Eventually the box crackled into life again. 'Tell him to wait in the foyer.'

The big guy seemed disappointed. He'd clearly been hoping for a spot of action – anything to relieve the boredom. Stepping aside, he opened the door and gave a jerk of his head. 'Okay,' he said.

Harry followed Jess inside, a pleasant shiver rolling through his body as he felt the welcome burst of warmth. At least Stagg didn't stint on the heating. Another guy, equally large, was standing just inside. Mutely, he waved them towards the leather sofa.

Harry sat down. If Stagg was being his usual punctual self, they could be here for a while. He could hear music coming through the walls, a dull grinding beat, the sound of male voices and a smattering of applause.

Jess shrugged out of her coat. Underneath she was wearing dark trousers and a tight cream shirt with the top three buttons undone.

Harry's eyes widened as he noticed the amount of cleavage on view. 'What's with the outfit? You're not here for a job interview.'

She grinned back at him. 'You want the girls to talk, don't you? I'm just doing my best to fit in.'

Surprisingly, Stagg emerged almost instantly from his office and strode over to them. It was hard to tell whether he was sober or not. He was wearing a fawn silk suit, beautifully cut, a white shirt and striped tie. Harry's own suit hadn't come cheap but it looked shabby in comparison.

Stagg nodded at Harry and glanced at Jess. 'Who's the broad?' he said as if she wasn't able to speak for herself.

'The *broad*'s called Jessica Vaughan,' she said, 'and she's helping Mr Lind with this investigation.'

'Since when?'

'Since now,' Harry snapped, irked by his attitude. 'You got a problem with that?'

Stagg gave a smirk, his eyes sliding down towards where Harry's gaze had been focused only a short time before. 'You need a girl to hold your hand, you go ahead – but she can wait out here while we talk.'

'I don't think so,' Harry said. 'And as I'm only going to repeat exactly what you tell me, you may as well save me the bother.'

Ray Stagg's jaw tightened, a muscle twitching at the side of his mouth. He wasn't the kind of man who was used to being challenged. For a moment he looked like he was going to argue the point but then had a change of heart. 'Whatever.'

They stood up and followed him into his office. Harry gave Jess a glance as they walked through the door. If she was the slightest bit perturbed by the multiple examples of female nudity on the walls she didn't show it.

Stagg took his seat and flapped a hand towards the chairs on the other side of his desk. Other than an empty in-tray, a white telephone, a bottle of Scotch and a half-full glass, there was nothing on the desk's surface. It was as ridiculously wide and as free of clutter as the last time Harry had been there.

Harry and Jess sat down.

Leaning forward, Stagg addressed his question solely to Harry. 'I take it you haven't heard from her?'

'No,' Harry said. 'Have you heard from Al?'

'You really think that bastard's going to get in touch with me?'

'You mean, after what he did?'

Stagg's eyes narrowed but he didn't rise to the bait.

'Oh, come on,' Harry said. 'This is about more than a husband going AWOL. Al's up to his neck in it. People have died. And Agnes . . . well, wherever she is, she's in a heap of trouble too. These aren't coincidences. You know it and so do I.'

Ray Stagg remained silent.

'I'm working in the dark,' Harry persisted. 'And that's not a place I like to be. Either you tell me what's really going on or you can sort it on your own.'

Stagg pursed his lips, giving it some thought. 'Then I'll take on someone else. There's plenty more where you came from.'

'You do that,' Harry said, 'and I'll be sure to let them know if Agnes gets in touch.'

There was a short stand-off as the two men glared at each other.

Eventually, if grudgingly, Stagg gave some ground. 'Okay, what if I was to say that Al *might* have taken off with some goods that didn't belong to him. Would that make a difference?'

'And could some of those goods have belonged to a certain white-haired gentleman who is not renowned for his forgiving nature?'

'It's possible,' Stagg conceded.

Harry smiled. 'And would it be safe to assume that some of those goods weren't entirely legal and that said gentleman isn't going to rest until he gets his property back?'

'Under the circumstances, that would seem to be a logical assumption.'

'Right,' Harry said. It was pretty much as he'd thought but there were still a few loose ends. 'So do you think they were all in this together – Al, Troy and Agnes?'

'Fuck knows,' Stagg said. 'Maybe. It's starting to look that way.'

Harry frowned. 'Only it doesn't make sense. I mean, if they were, why didn't they all take off at the same time? They must have understood the risks. Why would Troy and Agnes come back to work? Once they'd got what they wanted, there was no point in hanging around.'

'I suppose not,' Stagg agreed.

'So?'

'So *what*?' Stagg said. He raised his hands. 'You think I've got the answers? I don't. That's what I'm paying you for, isn't it?'

Harry stared at him. 'I'm also assuming that Tommo was involved in this, that he—'

At the mention of his friend's name Stagg's face twisted and he quickly looked down. 'He was doing me a favour, that's all. A one-off, nothing else. He didn't deserve . . . that filthy bastard shouldn't have . . .' He stopped abruptly, too experienced to let his mouth run away with him.

Harry couldn't pretend that he savoured the idea of being caught in the crossfire between Ray Stagg and Jimmy Keppell, no sane man would, but he was in too deep to back out now. There was Agnes to consider and Ellen Shaw too. He'd been doing a lot of thinking about Ellen today. He'd tried to ring her but had only got her answering machine. He hadn't left a message. If what she'd told him was the truth, then Keppell was making *her* life a misery too.

'What's the matter?' Stagg said, glancing up again. 'You scared?'

'Yeah – but not enough to walk away.'

'Good,' Stagg said, 'on both counts. You'd have to be a bloody fool to underestimate him. And I don't like working with fools.'

'You and me both,' Harry said.

There was another silence.

Jess shifted in her chair and crossed her legs. She looked at Stagg. 'Do you think Agnes is still alive?'

His cold blue eyes slowly swivelled towards her. While his gaze hovered somewhere lower than her chin, his mouth crawled into a smile. He left a short pause for effect. When he finally spoke, his voice was blatantly mocking. 'Are you a *good* detective, sweetheart?'

'The very best,' she said, smiling widely back. 'For example, and this is only a small one, I can sniff out a dead barman at fifty paces.'

'What?'

'She found Troy's body,' Harry said. 'Don't you read the papers?'

Stagg clearly did. His face went pale. Rising swiftly to his feet, he glared at Harry. 'She's a reporter. She's *that* reporter. You've brought a fucking journalist here?'

'Don't worry,' Harry said. 'She won't repeat anything she hears tonight.'

'And you expect me to believe that?'

Jess shrugged. 'Believe what you like – but it happens to be true.'

'You can trust her,' Harry said. 'You have my word.'

His word didn't seem to mean too much. Stagg leaned forward with his two fists balanced on the desk. He looked from one to the other, finally concentrating his attention on Harry. 'Are you taking the piss?' he hissed. 'Give me one good reason why I shouldn't—'

'Because you need me,' Harry said. 'I'm your last resort. That's why I'm here. Of course if you're not happy you could always give Jimmy a bell, see how *he's* feeling about things.'

Stagg seemed to suddenly deflate. He slowly sank back into his chair. His gaze swung back to Jess. 'Jessica Vaughan,' he said, his tone mildly threatening. 'I'll remember that name.'

'That's why I gave it to you,' she said, unperturbed. 'I'm the kind of girl who likes to be remembered.'

273

Ray took another swig of his Scotch. He played with his glass, rolling it between his fingers, before glancing up and eventually flashing a smile. It was a big smile showing all his bright white teeth. His mood had suddenly changed. He lifted a hand and smoothed back his sleek fair hair. 'You know, I've always liked a woman with balls.'

'I aim to please.'

'I like women who do that too.'

Jess gave him a long appraising look. 'Now, why doesn't that surprise me?'

Harry leaned forward and put his hands on the desk. He'd had enough of their banter. 'If we could get back to business?'

'Sure,' Stagg said, his sleazy gaze continuing to slide over Jess's curves.

'An address for Troy Jeffries would be useful.'

Ray Stagg got up and walked over to a tall filing cabinet in the corner of the room. He rummaged inside for a while, pulled out a sheet of paper, read the details and then replaced it in its file. Sitting back at his desk, he opened a drawer and took out a notepad. He wrote out the address, ripped off the sheet and passed it over to Harry. 'And don't bother asking me for the girl's. I gave it to the cops but it turns out she doesn't live there.'

'I'd like it anyway,' Harry said. 'If it's not too much trouble.'

Stagg raised his eyes to the ceiling but reluctantly got to his feet again. He went through the same procedure as before. 'Here,' he said, pushing the second sheet of notepaper across the desk.

'Thanks,' Harry said. He looked at the two addresses. The one for Troy was in Tottenham, the other in Stoke Newington. He folded them up and put them in his pocket. 'So what do you know about Agnes?'

'Like what?'

Harry frowned at him. 'Like who her friends were, who we should be talking to?'

'I've no idea,' Stagg said.

'She's your employee – or at least she was.'

274

'Yeah,' Stagg said, 'my *employee*, nothing else. There's a room out the back, a place for the staff to go on their breaks. You can talk to them there, ask them what you like.'

Ray Stagg stood up again and they followed him out of his office, through the foyer and into the dimly lit main part of the club. As they walked in Harry was surprised by how busy it was. For a Tuesday night, it was more crowded than he'd expected, over half the tables occupied by smart-suited city slickers, another quarter by what appeared to be a rowdy birthday party. The music was loud, the atmosphere charged.

Jess leaned against Harry's shoulder, whispering up into his ear. 'What's with the size of that desk?'

He smiled. 'I think it could be a classic example of male insecurity.'

'What, some kind of compensation?' She glanced at Stagg. 'Yeah, you could have a point.'

'I've never felt the need for a large desk,' Harry said.

She grinned back at him. 'No need to brag.'

There was a platform directly in front of them. A slim top-less girl, her body oiled and glistening, was gyrating around a pole. Her long fair hair was swinging round her waist. Her hips were slight, her shapely breasts of a size that couldn't be ignored. Harry paused to admire her natural rhythm.

Jess nudged her elbow into his ribs. 'Stop leering,' she said.

'I'm not leering. I'm detecting.'

'36D,' she said. 'What else do you need to detect?'

Ray Stagg had walked on ahead. He was already standing with the door held open to a room beside the bar.

Jess grabbed Harry's arm and pushed him forward. 'You start with the boys. I'll take the girls.'

Chapter Forty-Two

It was over an hour before they got together again. Harry hadn't learnt much, other than that the girls slipped on their robes before they came back in and that no one wanted to talk to him. The other barmen, the guys who had worked with Troy, had developed a collective form of amnesia. After four days, none of them could remember him too well. They couldn't remember much about Al either.

'Not sure how useful that was,' he said to Jess as they got back in the car. 'How about you?'

'I've left a pile of your cards but they're all pretty scared. They don't want to end up like Troy. Makes you wonder why they're still working here.'

'Because they don't have a choice,' Harry said. 'I bet most of them are illegals – and Stagg's probably responsible for bringing them in. They won't be staying out of love or loyalty. There'll be debts to be paid.'

They were out on the main road before Jess spoke again. 'Agnes was from the Ukraine. I met another girl, Irina, who was from there too. She didn't say much, none of them did, but she did mention that Troy Jeffries was pretty keen on Agnes.'

Harry nodded. That didn't come as any great surprise. He'd seen the way Troy had reacted the first time he'd talked to her and on his next visit he'd only had to mention her name . . . At the memory of the baseball bat, a sympathetic twinge of pain ran the length of his leg. 'Were they an item?'

'No, Agnes wasn't interested. Had her sights set on higher things apparently.'

That didn't surprise Harry either – not with that face and body. A girl like her could go a long way. 'Was there any bad feeling?'

'I don't think so,' Jess said. 'Irina claimed they were friendly enough. Still, you don't ever know what's going on inside another person's head.' She paused. 'Something else that might be useful, though: Troy used to do a bit of dealing. Nothing big-time, just some dope and a bit of coke.'

Harry's face jerked round. He stared at her. 'How did you manage to find that out?'

'Girl talk,' she said smugly. 'I'd explain it to you but we're sworn to secrecy.'

'Doesn't that give you an unfair advantage?'

'Only for most of the time,' she said.

Harry looked back towards the road. She'd done better than he had although he wasn't about to admit it. 'The drugs connection could be an interesting one. I don't suppose she mentioned who his supplier was?'

Jess shook her head. 'No,' she said, 'and she didn't tell me who killed him either.'

'So much for girl power.'

'So much for male detection,' she quipped back. 'Let's face it, the only useful things you learned tonight were some vital statistics and how lucky you are to have *me* asking the questions.'

He was still thinking of a way of effectively disputing either of those points when Jess glanced up into the rear-view mirror. 'For God's sake! What's that moron playing at?'

Harry glanced over his shoulder at the vehicle behind. It was moving quickly and was almost on top of them. The head-lamps were dazzling, bright white, and he screwed up his eyes. Suddenly it smashed straight into their rear, bumping them so hard that they hurtled to the left and shot up on to the pavement.

They were both thrown forward, their bodies making a dull double thump as they rebounded back.

'Shit!' Jess yelled, twisting the wheel to avoid an oncoming lamppost and struggling to keep the Audi under control. The tyres screeched as the car careered along the pavement for another twenty yards. Fortunately, there was no one walking along it. She quickly swerved back on to the street. Her mouth was open and her face was white.

The car behind accelerated and came for them again. This time the contact was even harder, the crunch of grinding metal disgustingly loud. The Audi lurched forward but stayed on the road.

'Go left!' Harry shouted. 'Left!'

Jess missed the turning and went straight on.

'Left!' Harry shouted even louder. He grabbed for the wheel.

Jess slapped his hand away. 'For fuck's sake!'

Harry looked over his shoulder. The car was still on their tail. 'Get off this street!'

Her voice was tight and scared. 'What do you think I'm try-ing to do?'

The car was pulling out and drawing alongside. It was big-ger, faster and more powerful than the Audi. Harry had just enough time to notice the dark tinted windows before it veered into them again. There was another vile scraping sound as the two cars came into contact. The Audi rocked. For a while, as if conjoined, the two vehicles hurtled down the street together.

Harry caught his breath. If they didn't do something soon they'd be run off the road and crushed against the wall. They'd end up as sandwich meat.

'Jess!'

Finally, with a harsh squeal of the brakes, she swerved left. Putting her foot down, she sped down a narrow road between two rows of tightly parked cars. It was a fortunate choice in that it was strictly single file. There was no room for another sideways attack.

The dark car followed but then halfway down the street abruptly stopped. Harry had just enough time to see it stop, flash its lights twice, a deliberate double blink, before they hurtled round another corner.

'You can slow down,' he said.

She didn't.

'Slow down!' he demanded. 'It's over.'

Jess checked her mirror. She wasn't taking any chances. 'They can still catch us.'

'They're not going to,' Harry said. 'They don't want to.'

In case his opinion proved to be unduly optimistic, Jess continued on for another five hundred yards. Then, with her rear-view mirror still clear, she gradually slowed and pulled in to the side of the road.

'God,' she murmured, leaning over the wheel. As if she'd been running, her breath was coming in short fast pants. 'What the hell was that? *Who* the hell was that?'

Harry leaned back in his seat. His heart was still pumping. 'Someone sending out a warning.'

'You call that a warning?' She glared at him. 'Some bastard just tried to kill us.'

He shook his head. 'If they'd wanted to kill us, they would have. They didn't have to stop. I think it might have been the same car that was at Ellen's yesterday.'

Jess gave a start. 'Keppell,' she said softly. She thought about it a moment and shivered. Then she reached into her bag, pulled out a pack of cigarettes and lit one with a shaky hand. Her voice was small and tight. 'So who was the warning for – you or me?'

'Hard to say,' Harry shrugged. 'Either of us. Both, maybe. I've been searching for Al, asking questions, talking to Stagg – he might think I'm getting too close to something. On the other hand, you've been digging around in the Paul Deacon case.'

They sat in silence for a while. There was a Chinese takeaway across the street. People came and went with nothing more to worry about than their rumbling stomachs.

Jess was the first to speak again. 'Shouldn't we call the cops?'

'Yeah,' Harry said, 'but not right now. Let's head back to your place and call them from there.'

'And tell them what?'

'The truth,' Harry said.

'And what would that be exactly?'

They looked at each other. They both had their reasons for not wanting too say too much to the police.

'That we'd been out for a meal, that some drunk smashed into us on the way back?' Harry suggested.

Jess nodded. 'I can live with that. You want to get out, take a look at the damage before we go?'

'I'd rather not.'

Chapter Forty-Three

The police had come and gone without asking too many questions and for this Harry was thankful. He'd had no desire to lie outright to them – at heart he was still a copper himself – but in the event it hadn't been necessary. Their story of a drunken driver had been accepted at face value, the details logged and a crime number provided. Now they were waiting for Snakey Harris to arrive. It was just after midnight.

Jess put another mug of coffee in front of him, pulled up a chair and sat down across the table. 'Snakey?'

'It's the tattoos. He looks like a walking advert for the Reptile House.'

'Ah,' she said. 'And he doesn't mind doing call-outs at this time of night?'

'I did him a favour once. Anyway, he's not too far from here – he's got a garage round the back of Dalston – and he tends to keeps late hours.'

'What kind of favour?' Jess said.

Harry looked at her and smiled. 'What do they do to you reporters – genetically modify your brains so you can't stop asking questions?'

She tilted her head to one side, studying him. 'I was just curious. And now that you're growing all evasive, I'm getting even more interested.'

'I wasn't being evasive. I was making a perfectly valid point.'

'Okay,' she said. 'Point taken. So what favour did you do for him?'

Harry could see that he wouldn't get any rest until he told her. Or at least told her something. The detail of Snakey's unfortunate foray into the world of stolen cars was probably best forgotten. 'Let's just say that he got himself in a bit of trouble. He was mixing with people that he shouldn't have and they took advantage. It was a few years back. He's not a bad bloke and I helped him out.'

'And now, in return, he helps you out.'

The smile faded from Harry's lips. Perhaps he was being unduly touchy but there was an edge to her tone that suggested a hint of impropriety about the arrangement. 'He doesn't do it for free, if that's what you're implying. I pay him for the work he does.'

Jess quickly raised her hands. 'Hey, I wasn't casting aspersions. I know you're a man of thoroughly upstanding principles.'

Harry frowned. She was the only person he knew who could make the words 'thoroughly upstanding principles' sound like their very opposite. As it happened he *did* always pay Snakey although it was also true that the charges for his car's yearly service and any repairs that were required came to rather less than any other garage he had ever used. This job, however, would go through the insurance company – giving Snakey plenty of scope to push up the bill and enhance his profit margins.

Jess laughed. 'You ever consider that you might occasionally be a little . . . over-sensitive about things?'

Harry realized that he was being teased but wasn't really in the mood for it. 'I thought women liked sensitive.'

'Sometimes,' she said.

'But not always.'

'It's not always appropriate.'

Harry was saved from having to make a response by the dull flat sound of the intercom buzzer. He crossed the room and answered it. 'Hello?'

'It's me.'

'I'll be right there.'

'Is that him?' Jess asked.

Harry nodded, went out into the main hallway and opened the front door. Snakey Harris was standing on the top step. He was a lean tallish man in his late forties with thinning salt and pepper hair and a long narrow face. In need of a shave, his cheeks had a dark purplish tinge to them.

'Thanks for coming out,' Harry said. 'I appreciate it.'

Snakey lifted his shoulders in a slow graceful shrug, smiled and walked back down the steps. 'That's all right, Mr Lind.'

Harry followed. He had long since given up asking Snakey to call him by his Christian name; it was something that he clearly didn't feel comfortable with.

The Audi was parked twenty feet away under a street lamp. Snakey carefully circled the car, running his fingers along the damage and making a deep tutting sound in the back of his throat. 'Had a spot of bother, then?'

Harry, standing back, stared at the smashed rear end. There was some serious damage to the side panels too. He presumed it was a rhetorical question. 'Can you sort it?'

'Sure.'

'How long?' Harry asked.

'About a week,' Snakey said. He nodded across the street. 'I've got you something until it's fixed.'

Harry followed his gaze. A white Vauxhall was parked behind Snakey's tow truck. Grimy and battered, it looked on the verge of falling apart. 'Impressive,' he said. 'Nought to sixty in less than an hour?'

'You said you didn't want anything too flash.'

'And you've certainly provided that.'

Snakey threw the keys at him. 'It runs. What more do you want?'

'I'll take your word for it.'

'So what happened?' Snakey asked. He was roaming around the Audi again, his fingers delving into all the dents and grooves. 'This was more than an accident, right?'

'Some drunk,' Harry said.

Snakey peered at him, his brown eyes bright with suspicion. 'A very determined drunk,' he said. 'You in trouble, Mr Lind?'

'No more than usual.'

As if that told him all he needed to know, Snakey gave a resigned shake of his head.

'How's the girlfriend?' Harry asking, changing the subject. 'Lisa, is it?'

'Linda,' Snakey said. 'She's good.'

Harry had only met her once and that was several months ago. Linda was a striking brunette, an investment banker who worked in the City. She was the latest in a long line of classy women that Snakey had dated over the years. For some reason, and it was a reason Harry had never been able to fathom, Snakey always had attractive female company. It wasn't as if he was especially handsome, witty or charming – and he certainly wasn't rich. Perhaps it was something to do with those tattoos. Most of them were covered up this evening but the blue-green asp coiled around his right wrist was still clearly visible. The head of the viper lay on the back of his hand between his thumb and index finger.

Harry stared at it. Maybe, if he split up permanently with Val, he'd get himself one too. She detested tattoos. She hated snakes even more.

'I'll get the truck,' Snakey said.

Ten minutes later the Audi was hitched up and ready to go. Harry took a piece of paper from his pocket and thrust it through the window of the cab. On it was written the registration number of a white Ford transit van. 'Give me a call if you ever see this on your travels, will you?'

Snakey looked down at the number. He opened his mouth and then closed it again. Some questions just weren't worth asking. Instead he glanced over his shoulder, nodded towards the car and said, 'I'll give you a bell when she's ready.'

'Thanks,' Harry said.

He gave a wave as Snakey drove off and then took out his phone and called a taxi. Time to go home.

Jess opened the front door as he approached the steps again. 'Everything okay?'

'Yeah.'

Harry stared after the tow truck until it turned the corner and disappeared from view. Then he followed her inside. He walked on through to the living room. 'Could I ask you something?' He paused. 'Do you think Snakey's attractive?'

Jess laughed. 'Hard to tell from a distance. Why, are you trying to fix me up?'

'No. Just curious.'

'Well,' she replied, 'six months ago I'd have probably said yes. He looks a little old but every woman with a car needs a good mechanic.'

'Right,' Harry said. Perhaps that was the secret to Snakey's success. 'And who said romance was dead.'

She gave a shrug. 'No harm in being practical.'

Harry took the keys from his pocket and passed them over. 'Here, these aren't much use to me at the moment. They're for the white Vauxhall across the road.'

'Really?' she said, smiling widely. 'Great.' Her smile disappeared as she went to the window and looked out. There was a small intake of disappointed breath. '*That?*'

'No point having a motor that's going to get you noticed.'

'No danger there,' Jess murmured softly. She gazed out at its rusty battered frame. 'Are you sure it even goes?'

'According to Snakey.' He reached out as if to take the keys back. 'Although if you don't think it's suitable . . .'

She quickly moved a sideways step away from him. 'Hey, did I say that? I'm sure it's just dandy.'

'Let's hope so.'

'And thanks,' she said, suddenly remembering her manners. 'Having a car does make it easier to get around. The wonders of public transport begin to pall after a while.'

'I can imagine.' Harry shifted from one foot to another. He had the feeling that the advice he was about to utter wouldn't be too well received. 'Er . . .' he began cautiously. 'I was just wondering if . . . well, bearing in mind what happened tonight,

285

whether it might not be a bad idea if you kept your head down for a day or two.'

Jess was still staring through the window, trying to come to terms perhaps with the dilapidated wreck she'd be driving around in for the next few days. She swung her face sharply towards him, her eyes narrowing a fraction. 'I see,' she said, her voice distinctly tight. 'And is that what *you* are going to be doing?'

Harry tried to sound convincing. 'Sure. I thought I'd go into the office and catch up on some paperwork.'

'Yeah,' she almost jeered, 'and I'm a bloody supermodel! Come off it. The first thing you'll be doing tomorrow is checking out those addresses Ray Stagg gave you.'

Harry couldn't deny it. Fortunately, he didn't need to. His cab, with perfect timing, was drawing up outside the flats. 'That's for me,' he said. 'Got to go.'

Jess walked into the communal hallway ahead of him. She opened the main front door and stood aside.

Harry strolled down the steps and then turned to look back up at her. He knew she was old enough, and smart enough, to take care of herself but he still felt responsible. She had no real idea of what she was doing, of the world she could be entering. Men like Jimmy Keppell were no respecters of age or gender. 'At least do me one favour,' he said. 'Don't answer the door to anyone you don't know.'

'Are you telling me to be careful?'

'No,' he said. 'I'm just asking you nicely.'

She stared down at him. Her mouth gradually curled up at the corners. 'I'll pick you up at ten,' she said.

Harry looked down at his watch. 'I won't hold my breath.'

'Make it eleven then,' she said.

Chapter Forty-Four

Friday was always a busy night at Vista. Ray Stagg knew he should be there but for now he had more important things to do. He glared at the security screen, watching the car that was idling at the entrance to the house. He lifted the glass to his mouth and took another drink. He glanced at his watch; it was almost seven thirty. He deliberately made the driver wait, tapping out the seconds with his fingers before finally pressing the button that unlocked the electronic gates.

The car, an old green Rover, rolled up the drive. It came to a stop and a moment later Frankie Holt stepped out.

Ray stopped to light a cigarette before going to meet him. Scowling, he took a few deep drags and let the smoke hiss out through his lips. Lord, he hated the filth and Holt was dirtier than most. Bent cops were useful, sometimes even essential, but they still made his flesh creep. It was the pretence as much as anything. All that hypocritical crap made his guts turn over. Good or bad, take your pick, but you couldn't have it both ways. He was careful, however, to wipe the worst of the distaste from his face before opening the door.

Frankie Holt nodded at him.

Ray stared blankly back. He didn't make an effort to be pleasant – there was no point arousing suspicion – and simply jerked his head to invite him in.

Holt, expecting nothing more, silently followed him inside.

Ray led him along the length of the hall, through a rarely used drawing room and then into the den. It was slightly larger than its name suggested, a windowless soundproof space

287

towards the rear of the house. The walls were cream, the carpet a beige deep pile and the brown leather sofa was large and comfortable. There were shelves covered with DVDs. There was a widescreen TV, an expensive music system and a bar full of booze. Porn magazines were scattered across a glass-topped coffee table. Enclosed within these four walls was everything a man needed to get away from the stresses of life. He watched as Holt's eyes roamed greedily around.

'I need to know what's happening,' Ray said brusquely. 'Why aren't you calling me?'

Frankie sank down on the sofa. 'It's not easy,' he said. 'It's not safe, either. Not while all this shit's going down.'

Ray poured a couple of neat whiskies, making Holt's especially large. 'Don't fuck me about, Frankie. I don't like it. I don't like it one little fucking bit.'

Holt grabbed the drink that was offered and instantly swallowed half of its contents. He leaned forward, cradling the glass in his hands. 'You think it's easy trying to keep a lid on it all? I'm a copper, for God's sake.'

Ray felt his usual revulsion as he heard the familiar self-pitying whine in Holt's voice. 'Please don't start on that again. We've all got our problems.'

'Keppell's out of control. I can't keep covering his tracks.'

'Isn't that what he pays you to do?' Ray said.

There was a short silence while Holt knocked back the rest of his drink and then wiped his mouth with the back of his hand. 'Yeah, well, Tommo was one thing but . . .'

Ray flinched at the casual dismissal of his friend's murder as a 'thing'. His chest tightened. His fingers automatically curled into two tight fists. Quickly, before it was noticed, he unclenched them again. It took an effort to keep his response sounding neutral. 'But what?'

'Now we're investigating the murder of your bloody barman too.'

Ray was still on his feet. He took the glass from the Inspector's hand, went across the room and refilled it. He gazed for a second at the pure amber liquid. The bottle of malt was a good one and wasted on the unrefined palate of a primitive like Holt. Still, there were times when sacrifices had to be made.

'From what I've heard,' Ray said cautiously, 'and it's only a rumour, Troy Jeffries might have been dealing. He was only a kid, probably didn't know what he was getting into. Perhaps he got out of his depth, tried to turn someone over and—'

'Someone?' Holt interjected. 'I saw the body. It had Keppell's calling card all over it.'

Ray picked up the bottle and the glass and carried them across the room. He placed them on the coffee table, within easy reach of his guest, and then settled down into the adjacent leather armchair. As if Holt had provided a particularly insightful response he took a deep breath before gradually releasing a well-rehearsed but thoroughly convincing sigh. 'You could be right.'

The room was warm, the central heating turned up high and a film of sweat – perhaps only partly down to the heat – was breaking out on Holt's forehead. 'So what's he playing at?'

'Fuck knows,' Ray said. And that was the honest truth. That Keppell was angry at being ripped off by a small-timer like Al was understandable but his response was rapidly becoming disproportionate to the crime. Killing Tommo should have been enough to prove his point, to let his enemies know that he couldn't be messed with, but it hadn't stopped there. The murder of Troy Jeffries was like some macabre icing on the cake.

Frankie Holt leaned forward and poured himself another whisky. He was still clearly anxious – his hand was trembling – but his eyes were starting to glaze. Ray studied his face carefully. Another few minutes, he thought, and the idiot's mouth would begin to run away with him. That was when he'd have the bastard. All he needed was for Holt to condemn himself without damning Ray's own ass to a lifetime in the slammer too.

'Keppell's always been trouble,' Ray said softly.

'I never trusted him,' Holt said. 'Not since . . .'

Ray Stagg glanced slyly towards the row of DVDs. The camera, a tiny piece of hi-tech genius, was invisible. No one could ever suspect that it was there.

Maddie Green looked in the full-length mirror, made a few last-minute adjustments to her make-up and then stood back to view the results. A pair of wide black-lined eyes returned her gaze. She tilted her head to one side. Not bad. She definitely looked a good few years older than she was. Her long brown hair, shining and freshly straightened, hung down to her waist. The foundation had smoothed out the imperfections in her teenage skin and the blusher, applied exactly as the magazines instructed, was discreetly highlighting her cheekbones. Her mouth was painted a deep provocative red.

She pursed her lips and stared hard at her reflection. Gradually, her gaze dropped down to the clothes she was wearing, skinny blue jeans and a simple scoop-necked red designer T-shirt with the slogan *Scandalous* scrawled across the front. It was scooped a little too low perhaps but the push-up bra gave her small developing cleavage the extra boost it needed.

Maddie turned sideways to the mirror and swivelled her slim hips. The borrowed high-heeled slingbacks made her legs look a few inches longer. Her mouth crept into a smile. Her mother would kill her if she saw her now . . . but of course she wouldn't see her – she was still at the office and wouldn't be home for another hour at least. By then Maddie would be well on her way to Chingford and her uptight mother would be none the wiser. This was one party that she couldn't afford to miss. It was Zane's sixteenth birthday and come hell or high water she was going to be there.

Chapter Forty-Five

Harry ordered a drink, a Scotch on the rocks, and then returned his attention to the evening paper. He wasn't really reading it, just scanning through the headlines while he waited for Jess to arrive. They'd arranged to meet at eight and it was barely seven thirty. Three days had passed since the car had almost run them off the road and nothing untoward had happened since. In fact, nothing much had happened at all.

Al Webster and Agnes were both still missing.

Val hadn't called.

Ellen Shaw hadn't been in touch either.

As promised, Jess had turned up on Wednesday morning and driven him over to Stoke Newington. The Vauxhall, cleansed of all its superficial dirt (she must have put it through the carwash), had been looking marginally better. Although it wasn't going to win any beauty contests – no amount of soap and water could disguise its fundamental flaws – the engine was running smoothly enough.

The address for Agnes, as Stagg had predicted, proved to be a dead end. The people living there, a Polish family, claimed to have been in residence for over a year and there seemed no reason to doubt their word. They had never heard of Agnes Bondar or received any mail for her. A local and time-consuming house-to-house hadn't yielded any useful information either. If anyone had recognized her description, they weren't willing to admit it. Harry wasn't surprised. This was London after all; people had a tendency to keep their eyes averted and their mouths shut.

They'd had no more success at Troy Jeffries' place. His flat-mate, a shy ruddy-cheeked nineteen-year-old called David Stanforth, had invited them in but had nothing to add to what Harry already knew. The boy, clearly horrified by what had happened, had answered the questions with a dull dazed expression on his face.

'We'd only been sharing for a couple of months. I didn't know him that well. I think he worked at some nightclub.'

And that was about the extent of his knowledge. David hadn't met any of Troy's friends, had never heard of an Agnes, and if he had realized that his flatmate was dealing then he certainly wasn't prepared to admit to it.

When he'd asked if they could look in Troy's room, David had waved a willing hand towards one of the doors, only informing them after they'd stepped inside the spare empty bedroom that Troy's parents had already been to pick up all his things.

Harry remembered thinking, another dead end, and then feeling an instant stab of guilt, not just for the unintended pun but for the awful coldness of the response. Whatever Troy Jeffries had been – and from his experience it couldn't be described as anything particularly pleasant – he was still someone's son.

It was after six when Jess had dropped him off and they had finally parted company. Harry hadn't seen her since. The car had been hers for the Thursday, free to do with as she wished. She'd had it all day today as well. Was she taking advantage? Perhaps. But he didn't much care. She'd had the courtesy, at least, to call and ask if he wanted to be driven anywhere.

Harry wasn't exactly sure why he'd suggested meeting for dinner. Ostensibly it was to catch up, to exchange news on their respective cases, but he suspected it was more to do with the rather bleak prospect of dining alone on a Friday night. Valerie, he was sure, would have company. At this very moment she was probably sitting in a fancy West End restaurant with an over-starched white napkin in her lap. He could imagine the kind of place Chapman would take her to, somewhere showy and expensive, and felt a spurt of anger at the thought of the two of them together.

The waitress arrived with his drink. Harry forced a smile and thanked her. Reaching for his glass, he wondered if he was becoming just a little too reliant on the comfort of alcohol. A brief image came to him of the empty bottles piling up in his recycling bin. It was only a temporary measure, he reassured himself, just a way of getting through these difficult times. Then, attempting to bury any further thoughts of Val's treacherous dinner date, he took a generous gulp of the Scotch and resumed his superficial reading of the paper.

Several minutes later, aware of a presence lurking to the right of his shoulder, he looked up again. It was Jess.

'You're early,' he said.

She threw her jacket over the back of the chair and sat down. 'Not as early as you.'

There wasn't much he could say to that and so he turned to get the waitress's attention instead. The girl arrived promptly and Jess ordered a Miller Lite. Harry flirted with the idea of refreshing his Scotch but decided against it.

Jess gazed around the room. 'I've never been here before.'

Harry had chosen the location, a small informal restaurant in the back streets of Camden, specifically as a place that couldn't possibly give the wrong impression. It served decent food at reasonable prices but could hardly be described as romantic. The light was too bright, the furniture too basic and the clientele too casual. He didn't actually suspect Jess of harbouring any secret yearnings but didn't want her to think that he might be either.

The waitress returned quickly with the beer and a glass, took out her notepad and asked if they'd like to order yet. Jess glanced down at the table. 'Is there a menu?'

'It's on the board behind the counter,' Harry said. 'The Special's good. That's what I'm having.' The dish of the day, chicken stew with dumplings, was not especially kind on the waistline but was almost as comforting as the Scotch.

'Okay,' she said, without bothering to read the rest of the list. 'That sounds fine.'

'Two Specials,' the girl said. 'And any more drinks?'

Harry, seeing that his glass was now almost empty, had a change of heart and ordered another Scotch. He wasn't driving so where was the harm? He had the feeling that Jess might have thrown him an inquiring glance – he deliberately didn't meet her gaze – but that might just have been his imagination.

After the waitress had left, Jess poured out her beer and took a sip. Then she made a longer more leisurely scrutiny of the room. Harry watched as her eyes slowly travelled over the bare cream walls, the formica-topped tables and the rather worn blue lino. Really, it was more of a licensed café than a restaurant. As if she guessed at his reason for inviting her here, a flicker of amusement passed across her face. Eventually, she looked at him again. 'So how's it going?'

He gave a wry smile. 'Much as it was the last time I saw you.'

'That good, huh?'

'I've spent the past couple of days in the office. No news of Agnes, nothing on Al.' He lifted his shoulders and shrugged. 'All quiet on the Western Front.' What he didn't mention, and had no intention of mentioning, were the three hours he'd spent in Berry Square yesterday. He'd walked round in the afternoon hoping to see Ellen again but she hadn't been in. He should have left straight away but hadn't. Instead, like a pathetic stalker, he'd hung around, patrolling the perimeter until the cold and a growing sense of hopelessness had finally driven him home.

'So really,' she said, 'when you called and talked about catching up, what you actually meant was catching up on *my* news.'

He smiled. 'By which I take it that you do have some news.'

'I might,' she said. Lifting the glass to her lips, she drank some more beer. 'I had another chat with Scott Hall today.' She paused and looked around, even taking the precaution of glancing over her shoulder. All the surrounding tables were occupied but no one was taking any notice of them. Still she lowered her voice. 'He remembers The Starlight – you know, the club where Sharon Harper told me that she used to work? It was in Soho. It doesn't exist any more but turns out that it was owned by . . . guess who?'

Harry shook his head.

Jess leaned across the table. 'Jimmy Keppell!' she whispered triumphantly. 'Don't you think that's a bit of a coincidence?'

Harry didn't. From his experience what most people called coincidence could usually be explained by the numerous laws of chance and probability. 'But Keppell owned a lot of clubs in his time; through the years there must have been thousands of girls passing through them. If Sharon was moving in that circle, their paths were likely to cross at some point. It's a tentative connection at best.'

Undeterred, Jess smiled back at him. 'I think it's pretty interesting.'

The food arrived, two large steaming bowls along with hefty chunks of bread on a side plate. The restaurant was over three-quarters full now with a pleasant background hum of conversation. For the next few minutes they dug into the stew.

'This is good,' Jess said.

'You say that as if you're surprised.'

She glanced up at him. 'Okay, I'll come clean. It did cross my mind when I first walked in that this could be some kind of subtle punishment for allowing your car to be trashed the other night. I mean, I know you're not supposed to judge a book by its cover but at first sight this place doesn't look that enticing.'

Harry put his fork down and laughed. 'It's nice to know you've got such a high opinion of me. And, incredible as it may seem, I don't *entirely* blame you for what happened. Granted, had I been behind the wheel, my reactions would have been a little faster but it's hardly your fault that you're burdened with the unfortunate DNA of the careful female driver.'

Jess gave a snort. 'Yeah, right. I only took my time because I was concerned about your panic threshold. You looked kind of pale when that car smashed into the back of us.'

'I do have that tendency when faced with imminent death,' Harry grinned. 'So did Scott have anything more to add?'

Jess nodded while she chewed. 'Yes, he was very helpful. He's been going through his old files, looking at the original case again. Joan Sewell's husband, Freddie, was something of a rabble-rouser by all accounts. He was a printer, big on the trade union front, but it was all a long time ago; he died before Grace was even born. Their son, Francis, was in trouble a few times too. He was cautioned over several incidents, mainly to do with "inappropriate behaviour", but he was never charged with anything.'

'Inappropriate?' Harry asked.

Jess lifted her shoulders. 'Seems that some local parents thought he was over-friendly with their kids. They didn't like him hanging around. His mental age at fifteen was about the same as their seven- or eight-year-olds but physically he was much bigger and stronger.'

Harry thought about it. 'So how does any of this tally with your theory about Sharon and Jimmy Keppell?'

'It doesn't,' she said. 'It's just another avenue.'

Harry finished off his stew and then drank down the rest of his Scotch. He glanced over his shoulder and caught the eye of the waitress. She came straight over. 'Same again,' he said, handing her his glass. He looked at Jess. 'Would you like another beer?'

She shook her head. 'Just a coffee, thanks.'

After the waitress had left, there was a lull in the conversation. Pushing his empty bowl aside, Harry gazed out through the window. There was a house opposite, its windows decorated with tiny flashing lantern lights. He stared out for a while, watching them flick on and off.

'So have you got any plans for Christmas?' Jess said.

'Not really.' It didn't seem likely that he'd be spending it with Val this year – or with Val's parents. He turned back towards her. 'How about you? You got family?'

'You could say that,' she murmured, raising her eyes to the ceiling. 'My parents are divorced but they've both married again – my mother three times, my father twice. They're rather fond of the institution of marriage, just not so good at sticking to those old wedding vows.'

'Hope springs eternal.'

'Something like that. Mum's set up home in California, soaking up the sun with hubbie number four. My dad's in the Shetlands, living on a self-sufficient happy-clappy farm where they all play guitar and think they're Joni Mitchell.'

Harry laughed. 'What, even the guys?'

Jess grinned at him. 'Hey, there's no discrimination on the happy hippy farm.'

'You got brothers or sisters?'

Jess's smile got wider. 'You're not going to believe me when I tell you this.' She left a short dramatic pause before holding up the backs of her hands, folding the thumb inside the left one. 'Nine,' she declared with an amused widening of her eyes. 'Six half-sisters and three half-brothers plus a varied selection of step-siblings – and please don't ask me who belongs to whom. I lost the drift years ago.'

'Wow,' Harry said. 'That's some collection. You close to them all?'

She shook her head. 'Not really. I mean we get on okay but we live in different places, even different countries for the most part. I don't see much of them.'

The Scotch and the coffee arrived. Harry swirled his glass, listening to the chink of the ice cubes, while he thought about what she'd just told him. He couldn't imagine what it would be like to have such an extended family.

'And you?' she said.

'Only child.'

'Lucky you.'

Harry's phone started to ring. 'Sorry,' he said, reaching into his pocket. He glanced at the screen; it was a number unknown. 'Hello.'

There was no response. He could hear the faint sound of music in the background.

'Hello?' He held the phone closer to his ear. Now he could hear breathing too, a series of rapid shallow breaths, as if the caller had been running or was scared or . . . His first thought was of the missing Ukrainian girl. 'Agnes? Is that you?'

Jess, who had been staring out of the window, immediately turned to look at him again.

'It's me,' a distant tiny voice quavered.

Harry recognized the voice as young and female but that was about the limit of it. 'Agnes?' he said again.

There was a series of gulps from the other end of the line as if whoever was there was trying not to cry.

'It's okay,' Harry said. 'Take your time. I'm still here.'

'It's me,' the girl eventually murmured again. 'It's Maddie.'

Harry tried to keep the surprise out of his voice. He wasn't even aware that Maddie Green had his number but then remembered that time she had made him call her mobile in the office. 'What's the matter, sweetheart?' he said gently.

'I'm at Zane's. There's a party. I don't . . . I . . .'

'What's happened? Can you tell me what's wrong?'

There was another gulp and then a sniffle. 'I don't feel well. I've been sick and—'

'What's the address?' Harry said quickly. He could hear the beeps going, an indication that her battery was running low. They could be cut off at any second.

'I'm in Chingford,' she said.

'Do you know the name of the street?'

'Er . . .' There was a long pause while she thought about it. 'Maddie?'

'R-Rexley . . . Rexley Drive,' she finally managed to stammer out.

'Okay. You stay there. Don't wander off. I'll be with you soon.'

298

Harry was standing up even as he put the phone away. From his wallet he pulled out a few notes to pay the bill.

'Problem?' Jess said, getting to her feet too.

Harry nodded. 'So much for a quiet Friday night. I don't suppose you fancy a drive out to Chingford?'

Chapter Forty-Six

Harry hadn't got the number of the house but, in the event, it didn't matter. The place was easy enough to find, the loud reverberating music providing a good enough clue for even the most dim-witted of detectives. He was surprised the neighbours weren't complaining, but then again, complaining about anything the Keppells did tended to have unpleasant repercussions.

Jess swung the car through the gateway and headed up the short gravel drive. The house was detached, a modern two-storey whitewashed building with a large obtrusive satellite dish attached to the front. Despite the cold there were a few kids standing around outside, swigging beer from cans and smoking cigarettes.

Harry got out and approached them. 'I'm looking for Maddie Green. Have any of you seen her?'

Perhaps suspecting he was a disgruntled father out to spoil his daughter's fun, they stared suspiciously back at him. 'Nah,' one of them said eventually. 'Don't know her.'

'About this tall,' Harry said, indicating with his hand, 'slim, long brown hair, grey eyes.' He paused, realizing that the description could probably apply to any number of females. 'She's a friend of Zane's.'

'Everyone here's a friend of Zane's,' the same boy replied. He was tall and blond and the victim of some over-prissy hair-styling. He had his arm around an exceptionally pretty girl in a short white dress and was clearly trying to impress her. 'This is his fucking party, man.'

The rest of the group gave a collective snigger.

Harry glared at them, his patience beginning to wear thin. He didn't have time for this. It was almost half an hour since Maddie had called and she hadn't been sounding too good then.

Jess, sensing his frustration, quickly stepped in. 'So where would we find Zane?' she said calmly.

The boy gave her a crude assessing look as if toying with the idea of another smart-arse comment but then, thinking better of it, simply gestured with his head towards the house. 'Where do you think?'

'Well, thanks for your help,' Harry said tartly. Walking past, he stepped through the open front door and gazed around. The place was heaving, a crush of teenage bodies overflowing from the rooms and filling up the hall. They were all, he noticed, in their mid-to-late teens, a good few years older than Maddie. The music, this close, was almost deafening. He could feel his ears start to ring.

Jess said something but he couldn't hear.

He screwed up his eyes and frowned at her. 'What?'

'I'll take upstairs,' she repeated loudly, 'if you want to check down here.'

'Okay,' he nodded, but then as soon as she started to move away he took hold of her arm. 'Hang on,' he said. Something had just occurred to him that, if he hadn't drunk quite so much Scotch, might have struck him earlier. He turned back towards the door.

'What are you doing?' Jess said.

He didn't answer. Instead, hovering in the porch, he stood and stared at the group they had just been talking to. He watched them for a few seconds, listening to their laughter, before stepping out on to the drive again.

'Zane!' he suddenly called out.

Instantly the blond boy turned his head. It was a reaction so immediate, so instinctive, that there was no doubt as to who he was. Harry sprinted towards him.

The boy, not letting anything as outdated as chivalry stand in the way of self-protection, swiftly pulled his girlfriend in front of him. Sheltered by her body, his arms around her, he raised his face and laughed.

'Where is she?' Harry snarled. 'Where's Maddie?'

'Who?'

Harry wanted to grab a handful of those over-coiffured locks, lift the cocky shit up off the ground and punch the truth out of him. Unfortunately the girl was standing between them. 'Tell me where she is!'

'No idea,' Zane said.

Harry took another step forward and stared down into his face. Bullying teenagers wasn't his favoured pastime but he was prepared to make an exception for this piece of slime. 'Well then, *find* her,' he demanded. 'This is your house. It shouldn't be too hard.'

'Find her yourself,' he sneered.

Jess gently touched Harry's arm. 'Come on,' she murmured. 'This isn't helping.'

Zane grinned up at him. 'You should listen to the little lady.'

Harry stared back at him for a few long hard seconds and then took out his phone. He pressed a few buttons and held it to his ear. 'Hello,' he said. 'Yes, put me through to the police, please.'

'Hey,' the girl said smartly. 'There's no need for that.' She pointed towards a path that ran round to the back of the house. 'She was in the garden. I think she's still there.'

Zane glared down at her. 'Shut your mouth!'

Pulling away from him, the girl glowered. 'What's the big deal, hotshot? Would you rather have the cops crawling all over the place?'

Harry didn't wait to hear the end of the argument. He quickly headed off along the path with Jess following behind. The garden was shadowy with a wide tree-lined lawn but there was a thin light escaping from the open back door. He saw her straight away. Slumped on the wet grass, close to the wall, she had her head down between her knees. The first thing Harry noticed was the jagged rip running up the side of her T-shirt and his stomach turned over. *Christ!*

He knelt down beside her and gently touched her shoulder. She was shivering. 'Maddie?'

She stirred but didn't look up. Her face was still shielded by the curtain of long brown hair. She stank of vomit and booze and there was also the faint but distinctive whiff of cannabis.

'It's Harry,' he said. 'Are you all right? Maddie, will you look at me.'

Eventually, she raised her head. A pair of tearful grey eyes blinked back at him. Her make-up was smeared and her nose was running. She was like a little frightened kid. But then, of course, that's exactly what she was – a child dressed up in adult clothing. Harry took off his jacket and placed it protectively around her shoulders. He tried to keep his tone calm and steady. 'Maddie, can you tell me what happened?'

Her lower lip trembled. She shook her head, a single tear rolling down her cheek.

He glanced up at Jess. 'I'd better call Lorna.'

'No!' Maddie wailed, suddenly finding her voice. 'Please don't ring Mum. Please don't tell her. She'll kill me. I'm not supposed to be here.'

'But—'

'Please,' she pleaded again. She grabbed hold of Harry's wrist as if to prevent him from getting out his phone. Her long red nails dug into his skin. 'I just . . . I . . . *She* was the one who started it all, that girl, that Cass.' The tears were starting to flow now, a steady stream running down her face. 'Zane invited me. *I'm* supposed to be his girlfriend and then she comes along and . . .'

Jess hunkered down on the ground beside them. Opening her bag, she got out a tissue and pushed it into Maddie's hand. 'Here,' she said briskly. 'Wipe your face with this, blow your nose and then tell us what happened.'

Harry glared at her – this was hardly a sympathetic approach – but surprisingly Maddie responded to the rather stern demand. Almost immediately she let go of his wrist, stopped crying and did what she was told.

303

Jess waited before placing her hands softly on Maddie's bare arms. She gazed into her eyes. 'We're worried about you,' she said. 'We just want to know that you haven't been hurt.'

'Hurt?' Maddie repeated dully.

'Your T-shirt's torn,' Jess said.

Maddie glanced down as if she hadn't realized. 'Oh.'

'How did it get ripped?'

'I don't know.'

'Are you sure that someone hasn't hurt you? Did Zane—'

'Jess!' Harry said, warningly. If she had been assaulted they needed to be careful. It was important they didn't put words into her mouth.

Maddie suddenly lurched forward, burying her face in Jess's shoulder. 'He wouldn't even talk to me,' she cried. 'He completely ignored me and *she* said I should go home. She said I wasn't wanted here.'

'It's okay,' Jess said to Harry. 'I think she's just had a bit too much to drink.'

The rain was starting to fall again, large steady drops that would shortly turn into a downpour.

'Let's get her into the car,' he said, 'before she freezes to death.'

Together they lifted her up and walked her slowly back round the path. She was shaky on her feet, stumbling, and it took a while for them to get her to the Vauxhall. The original group had disappeared from the front but a few party guests were gathered by the door. Harry didn't see Zane or the girl he'd been with.

He opened the passenger door but Jess shook her head. 'Better put her in the back,' she said, 'in case she throws up again. Little things like that tend to put me off my driving.'

After they'd manoeuvred her into the seat, Jess wound the window down a few inches. Harry dithered for a moment but then got in beside Maddie. He didn't want her sitting on her own if she felt sick.

304

'I'm going to get out of here,' Jess said, 'get away from the house. I'll find somewhere to park and we can talk there. You all right, Maddie?'

She gave a forlorn nod of her head. 'Yeah,' she mumbled.

Jess reversed down the drive and checked that the street was clear. She drove a few hundred yards, found a space, pulled in and switched the engine off. 'So,' she said, turning to look at the girl again. 'Where are you supposed to be tonight?'

'At my friend Layla's,' Maddie said quietly. 'On a sleepover. I often stay there. Mum doesn't expect me back until tomorrow.'

'Well, this is going to be a nice surprise for her,' Harry said.

Maddie's tearful eyes widened again. She buried her face in her hands as her voice rolled into a wail. 'Oh, please, don't take me home! She'll be mad, really mad. She'll never let me out again.'

Harry, unused to the histrionics of teenage girls, shifted uncomfortably in his seat. He glanced towards Jess, hoping for some moral support. He was disappointed.

'Maybe you shouldn't take her back like this,' Jess said. 'Look at the state of her.'

'So what do you suggest?' he snapped.

Maddie raised her head. 'Couldn't I stay with you and go back in the morning?'

'No!' Harry said instantly. It was completely out of the question, especially in the absence of Val. Being alone in his flat with a drunk, dishevelled teenage girl was the kind of mistake that led to wild accusations and stories in the tabloid press. Not to mention what Lorna would think if she ever found out. Damn it! He wished he'd called Lorna right at the start and then he wouldn't even need to be having this conversation.

'Tell you what,' Jess said. 'Let's go to my place. She can get cleaned up, have some coffee and then we'll take it from there.'

'She needs to go home,' Harry insisted.

'Sure,' Jess agreed, 'but another hour won't make much difference. Come on, her mother's going to freak if she sees her like this.'

Harry couldn't argue with that. Maddie looked and smelled like something dragged out of a gutter.

Maddie, sensing a temporary if not permanent reprieve, had the sense to keep her mouth shut. Her eyes flicked quickly between the two of them. Harry had the feeling that she was holding her breath.

'I don't like it,' he said.

Jess shrugged and started up the car again. 'You got a better idea?'

Chapter Forty-Seven

Harry was in the kitchen making a pot of fresh coffee. He was glad Jess had the real stuff; he needed more than a cup of instant to deal with this thorny problem. While he was watching it drip into the glass jug he poured himself a large brandy from the bottle in the cupboard; the Scotch was beginning to wear off, leaving a bad taste in his mouth.

'I'm going to leave the door ajar while you take a shower,' he heard Jess tell Maddie. 'Don't worry, no one can see you. I just want to make sure you're okay.'

A few seconds later she came into the kitchen and grinned. 'The joys of being young!'

Harry frowned at her. 'It's not funny,' he said.

She laughed. 'And it's not the end of the world either. Don't tell me you never did something you shouldn't when you were a kid.'

'That's not the point. I work with Lorna. It's a matter of trust. I should have rung her straight off. She'll go ballistic when she finds out about this.'

'She doesn't need to find out about it,' Jess said calmly. 'Maddie can stay here tonight and I'll run her back in the morning. By then she'll be clean *and* sober. Where's the harm?'

Harry could almost feel the harm gathering like large grey storm clouds all around him. If anything could have gone wrong recently it had – and now he was virtually inviting trouble into his life. 'You want me to lie to Lorna?'

'No one's asking you to lie. If she asks you if Maddie was at Zane's party tonight, if she calls you to go and pick her up, then obviously you'll have to come clean. But, all things considered, what are the chances of that?'

Harry took a drink and shook his head. 'That's not how it works and you know it. If this ever comes out, she'll never forgive me. I mean, what's it going to look like?'

'Oh, for God's sake,' Jess said. 'Lighten up, can't you?'

'No,' he said, annoyed. 'I can't. She's a thirteen-year-old girl and I found her drunk and sick at Jimmy Keppell's grandson's party. And she's probably been smoking dope. Jesus! And now, instead of taking her straight home, instead of ringing her mother, I'm being urged to collude in some ridiculous plot to pretend it never happened.'

'Hardly that,' Jess said. 'Perhaps you should think of it more as damage limitation.'

'And how exactly do you work that one out?'

Jess poured a small drink for herself. She looked down, swirling the brandy around the glass. 'Well, Maddie hasn't been hurt, apart from her pride – no girl relishes being dumped in public – and she's learned a useful lesson. She won't be going back *there* in a hurry. She's made a fool of herself and she knows it. So if you take her home now, how is it going to help?' She looked back up at him. 'Let's face it, there are going be ructions. You're only going to make things worse. It'll be knocking on midnight by the time we get to Kilburn and Lorna will probably be asleep. Do you really want to drag her out of bed and start explaining it all?'

Harry didn't. But he didn't like the alternative either. 'Better that than she finds out in some other way. What if she talks to Layla's parents?'

'I don't think she will. I just had a chat with Maddie and it seems these sleepovers are a fairly regular arrangement. She talked to her mother earlier, just before she got to the party. So far as Lorna is concerned, her daughter's safely tucked up by now. Do you really want to be the one to tell her something different?'

Harry didn't. He gazed down into his glass. There was sense to Jess's reasoning although he was reluctant to admit it. What was that saying – *What the eye doesn't see, the heart doesn't grieve over?* Lorna probably had enough problems without him adding to them. But he still didn't feel good about it.

Jess went out to check on Maddie. She came back and nodded. 'Still standing,' she said. Folding her arms, she looked at him. 'Look, it's your call, your decision. If you want me to drive her home then I will.'

'But you think it's the wrong thing to do.'

'I don't know,' she said. 'I'm just not sure what it's going to achieve – other than the obvious.'

Harry wasn't sure either. He put his empty glass beside the sink and poured strong coffee into two blue mugs. He thought about milk but then decided against it. Picking up one of the mugs, he walked through to the living room and sat down on the sofa. Jess followed him. She perched on the arm and sipped her coffee. Neither of them said anything. Eventually, they heard the sound of the shower cut off.

It was another few minutes before Maddie stepped tentatively into the silence of the room. She was wrapped in a white towelling dressing gown, its hem trailing on the carpet, and her pale cheeks finally had a bit of colour in them. She glanced at them both before sitting down at the table. 'Sorry,' she said softly.

Jess smiled at her. 'How are you feeling?'

She almost smiled back. 'Stupid.'

Jess went through to the kitchen and came back with a glass of water. 'Here, sip this slowly.'

'Are you going to tell my mum?' Maddie said. 'Are you going to make me go home?'

Jess looked at Harry. He looked back at her. Maddie nervously fiddled with the papers on the table. A set of photos slipped out of one of the files and she quickly tried to push them back inside. Then she stopped suddenly and stared. Her brow furrowed as she picked up one of the pictures with her fingertips. 'Why have you got this?'

Jess leaned over her shoulder. Maddie was holding one of

the close-up shots of Ellen Shaw that she had taken on Tuesday morning.

'Do you know her?' Jess said.

'She looks like . . .' Maddie peered a little closer at the print. 'Zane's uncle, the one who died, he had a girlfriend who looked just like her. He showed me a photo. She was kind of younger then but . . .'

'Tony Keppell,' Jess said.

Maddie nodded. 'Yeah. Why have you got a picture of her?'

Jess shrugged. 'Oh, no particular reason. It was just for a piece I was researching about the Deacon trial. I work for a local paper, the *Herald*. My files are always full of stuff.'

'So was Tony really killed?' Maddie said. 'I thought Zane might be making it up.' Her mouth twisted down at the corners. 'He lies about a lot of things.'

'Yeah,' Jess said. 'Teenage boys often do.'

Maddie continued to gaze at the photo. 'She's pretty, isn't she?'

Jess shot a sly glance towards Harry. 'Some people think so,' she said.

Harry pulled a face and turned away. Sometimes Jess irritated the hell out of him. In fact *sometimes* was rapidly becoming an understatement.

'Must have been awful, him dying like that.' Maddie gave a long dramatic sigh. 'Poor Grace.'

There was a sudden almost shocking silence, a weirdly surreal moment while the name seemed to hang suspended in the air. Then Jess's intake of breath was clearly audible. 'What?'

Harry jumped to his feet, felt his knee violently protest and quickly sat down again. He opened his mouth and closed it. His heart was starting to pound.

Maddie looked confused. Aware of their reactions, her eyes widened. As if afraid that she had said or done something that she shouldn't, she dropped the photograph and pushed it away from her.

'It's okay,' Jess said, gently squeezing her hand. She was trying as hard as she could to stay calm. It wasn't easy. A crazy mixture of dread and elation was flooding through her body. 'It's just . . . well, what makes you think this woman is called Grace?'

Still flustered, Maddie bit down on her lower lip and looked over towards Harry.

He forced a smile, trying to keep his voice in neutral. His attempt wasn't that successful. The words, as they emerged, sounded decidedly croaky. 'Don't worry,' he said. 'There's just been a bit of a mix-up. Was it Zane who told you? Did he tell you her name?'

Maddie shook her head. 'No.' Slowly she reached out and picked up the photograph again. She flipped it over. 'It was written on the back. It said *Tony and Grace*.'

'Are you sure?' Jess said. She needed to hear it again, to be certain she wasn't dreaming.

'Yeah,' Maddie said. 'Is it important?'

'Not really,' Jess said, at exactly the same moment as Harry said, 'Yes.' Their eyes met in an almost confrontational gaze before they swiftly looked away from each other.

Harry was the first to speak again. 'Sort of,' he said. 'Not that important but it's always good to get the facts straight. Did Zane tell you anything else about her?'

Maddie took a sip of her water. 'No.' She stared down at the photo again. 'Not really.' She paused. 'He mentioned something about his granddad.'

'About Jimmy?' Harry said.

'Yeah, except . . . well, it was more about what Angie said about him.'

'And what was that?'

Maddie took a moment to think about it. When she spoke, she was clearly quoting. 'That if he hadn't been shagging that cheap little slut it would never have happened.'

'What wouldn't have happened?' Harry said.

'I don't know. I was . . . I'm not sure. I wasn't really listening. I think he meant Tony getting killed.'

Harry's eyes met Jess's again. She held his gaze for a second

311

and then looked back at Maddie. 'Come on,' she said, standing up. 'I think it's time you were in bed.'

Harry would have paced if his leg had been up to it. Instead, he sat on the sofa, staring intently at his feet. His head was swimming. He was thinking about Ellen Shaw. He was thinking about what Maddie had said. He was thinking about Valerie too. Being deceived was becoming more than an occupational hazard – even the person closest to him was doing it.

Jess came back with two glasses of brandy. She pushed one into his hand. 'So,' she murmured.

Lifting his face, he looked at her. 'Is she all right?'

'She's fine.'

'Aren't you going to say *I told you so*?'

Jess stared straight back. There wasn't even a hint of a smile. 'Maybe I'll do the smug stuff later. Right now I need to try and get my head round this.'

Harry nodded. 'Can Ellen really be Grace Harper?'

'Len thought she was. Maddie seems to have confirmed it.'

'I don't understand. I just don't get it.'

She sat down beside him. 'You and me both.'

Harry took a swig from the glass. He suspected he'd already drunk too much but then how much was too much on a night like this? Maddie's revelation had shocked him back into a place too close to sobriety. 'I have to talk to her, to Ellen.'

'No,' Jess said. '*We* need to talk to her.'

'It might be better if I do it alone. She knows me.'

But Jess was adamant. 'No, I'm coming with you. You've seen her twice and she's lied to you twice.'

'Not entirely,' he said.

'Enough,' she said. She felt sorry for him but not half as sorry as she felt for Len. This was the break she'd been waiting for and there was no way she was going to let it slip through her fingers.

Harry looked at his watch. It was twenty past eleven. 'It's

too late to call now. I'll ring first thing tomorrow, see if I can get her to meet me.'

'*Us*,' Jess stressed.

'It might be better if I left that little detail out,' Harry said. 'I'll tell her I want to talk about Jimmy.'

'Don't mention the photograph.'

'I'm not an idiot,' Harry said. Although bearing in mind his recent track record that was maybe a matter of debate.

Chapter Forty-Eight

It was a crisp, bright sunny day. Standing in the middle of the piazza, Harry gazed up at the pale blue sky while he pondered on the wisdom of what he was doing. Jess wouldn't be happy when she found out; at best she would throw one almighty hissy fit – at worst she would cut out his heart and feed it to the pigs.

Since when had he turned into such a consummate liar? From the moment he'd got out of bed this morning, he'd barely spoken a word of truth. It had started with his call to Ellen. He'd had a story ready in case her husband answered: that he was ringing from the local police station, that it was only routine, just a few follow-up questions connected to the Len Curzon case. In the event he hadn't needed it. She had picked up the phone, listened to what he had to say about having some news on the car that had almost run them down, and suggested that they meet in Covent Garden.

Even before hanging up, he had known that he would not tell Jess. He had convinced himself that it was for the greater good, that Ellen was unlikely to talk if she was there, but it was only partly true. The bottom line was that he wanted to be alone when he saw her.

'It'll have to be tomorrow,' he'd said to Jess a few minutes later. 'She can't make it today.'

'Why not?' He had heard her frustration echo down the line. 'We need some answers. You should have insisted.'

'And what good would that have done? I'm trying to keep it casual. I don't want to scare her off.'

'I suppose,' she had muttered reluctantly.

'How's Maddie?' he'd asked, changing the subject. 'Did you get her home all right?'

'She's fine. Well, as fine as she's going to be after everything that happened. I took her back to Kilburn this morning.'

'Did Lorna see you?'

'Not unless she's got X-ray vision. I dropped her off round the corner.'

'Okay. Thanks. I'll call you later.'

Harry found himself wondering why he'd thanked her. After all, she was the one who'd persuaded him not to tell Lorna. It had been the wrong thing to do but now wasn't the time to start stressing over that particular mistake; it was just another regret on an ever-growing list.

He was still early. They weren't due to meet for another twenty minutes and so he meandered instead along the line of stalls, looking at the displays of jumpers and shoes and jewellery. Business was brisk. He stopped to examine a silver necklace, a delicate piece that Valerie would have liked. He thought about buying it for her for Christmas . . . until he suddenly remembered that in all probability there would be no exchange of presents this year. Quickly, he moved on.

Down the steps, on the lower level, a string quartet was playing. Harry leaned his elbows against the balcony railings, looked down and listened. The music was pleasant, even soothing, but not quite soothing enough to quell the bewildering statement that kept rolling through his head: *Ellen Shaw is Grace Harper.* He had tried all night to find an alternative explanation for what Maddie had seen but had come up with nothing. Well, not exactly nothing; for a while he had toyed with the notion that it could simply be a case of mistaken identity. She was only a kid and, on this occasion, not an entirely sober one. Could she have got it wrong? It was a hope he would have liked to hold on to but he knew it was pointless.

It was five to one as Harry made his way back to their meeting place. Situated on the west side of the piazza, St Paul's was a relatively small and yet somehow grand building designed, if he remembered rightly, by Inigo Jones. The Actors' Church – wasn't that what they called it? There were lots of theatres in the vicinity. To the fore of the four tall stone pillars, a fire-eater was spitting his flames towards the sky. A crowd had gathered. Harry scanned the watching faces but couldn't see her. Was it even worth waiting? Perhaps, as she had done with Len Curzon, she would simply fail to turn up. He had almost persuaded himself of it when he glanced to the left and saw her strolling across the square.

She was wearing a long cream raincoat. Her chin was up and her short black hair, sleek and shining, fell around her face. He felt a tightening in his chest as he stepped out from the crowd and went to greet her.

Her mouth broke into a smile. 'Hi. I'm not late am I?'

'No,' he said. He took another step forward. They were standing close, so close now that he could have leaned down and kissed her. It was an urge that he quickly suppressed. 'You're right on time. Thanks for coming.'

'Why shouldn't I?' she said.

Harry hesitated. 'I think we need to talk.'

'Well, that's why I'm here. You said you had something to tell me. You said . . .' She gazed up at him, her smile slowly fading. 'Oh God,' she said softly. 'You know, don't you?'

Chapter Forty-Nine

Ellen swayed a little on her feet. Harry took her arm and walked her quickly through a gate and into the confines of the small neat churchyard. There were wooden benches set along either side of a central path. She sat down, covered her eyes for a moment and then looked back towards the church. Her face, if it was possible, had turned even paler but there were two bright spots of pink on her cheeks.

'How?' she asked simply.

'There was a photograph,' Harry said. 'It must have been taken when you were . . . I don't know, fifteen or so. It was a picture of you and Tony. He'd written your name on the back.'

'That was careless.' She tried for a smile but didn't quite make it. Her lower lip was trembling.

'But it wasn't just that,' Harry said. 'Len Curzon was the one who originally recognized you.'

Ellen seemed genuinely surprised. 'Did he? He didn't mention it. I . . . I just thought he was after a story about Deacon.'

'I think he was at first but then—'

'He realized who I was.'

'Little Grace Harper,' Harry murmured.

He heard her catch her breath and then there was silence. A few minutes passed. He didn't push her. She would tell him when she was ready.

'It's odd,' she said eventually. She was staring straight ahead but her gaze seemed barely focused. 'It's as if I've always been waiting, that it was only ever a matter of time. You live with the constant fear of discovery, that one day someone will turn

317

in the street and . . . but now that it's happened, it's almost a relief.' She glanced at him, her dark eyes filled with emotion. 'Does that make any sense?'

Harry nodded. He understood the burden of secrets, how it felt to have to hold things in.

'I'm not sure how . . .' She stopped and cleared her throat. 'Who else knows about this?'

'Only Jess. She's the reporter I told you about, a friend of Len's.'

'She was the one who found the photo?'

'No,' Harry said. 'That was someone else but they don't understand the relevance. They don't know what it means.'

'But Jess does,' she said. Her hands twisted in her lap, her pearl-tipped fingers engaged in some private anxious battle. 'This is going to be quite a story for her, quite a coup.'

'I don't think that's her priority. She's more concerned with getting justice for Len.'

'Are you sure?' she said softly. 'Most journalists are only after headlines. I'm surprised she didn't insist on coming with you.'

Harry tried to hold her gaze but couldn't. Instinctively, he looked away.

Ellen immediately picked up on it. 'She doesn't know you're here, does she?'

'No,' he admitted. 'I wanted to talk to you first.'

'You're taking quite a risk,' she said.

'Am I?'

Ellen stared at him, her dark eyes searching his. 'You could be.' There was an edge to her voice now, something almost bitter. 'Don't tell me that it hasn't crossed your mind. After what happened to Len Curzon . . .'

Harry fought an impulse to look over his shoulder. What if he'd got it all wrong? What if she wasn't by herself, if someone else was with her? He thought of that dark car hurtling towards him. He thought of the sharp knife sliding swiftly into Curzon's chest. They were only yards from the crowds in Covent Garden but the churchyard was empty. All it would take was . . . He glanced towards the graves. Dead and buried, he thought, and a shiver ran through his bones.

She reached out and placed her hand on his arm. 'I didn't kill him,' she said. 'I swear I didn't. And I don't know who did.'

Harry took a deep breath and met her eyes. He had to make a decision and he made it instantly. 'I believe you,' he said. 'That's why I'm here. That's why I came alone.'

Her hand slid down his arm and wrapped around his hand. 'Thank you.'

It was another few minutes before she spoke again. Lowering her head, she gazed down at the path. 'What you need to understand is that I didn't grow up in an ordinary home. My father was an angry, frustrated man. He loved us but . . .' She paused, her fingers tightening around his. 'It was a confused kind of love.'

Harry remembered what Jess had told him about Michael Harper. 'He was violent?'

'Yes,' she said, 'among other things.'

He could imagine, although he didn't want to, what those other things might be. 'He hurt you.'

Ellen neither confirmed nor denied it. Her eyes stayed firmly fixed on the ground. 'My mother wanted to leave him. She wanted to get away but she knew what would happen. She'd been there before and . . .' As if the memory hit her with a sudden force, she flinched, her hand jumping inside Harry's. 'He was a big man,' she said, 'strong. He liked to have his own way.' Her voice began to choke. 'I'm sorry, I can't—'

'It's all right,' he said gently.

Ellen nodded. Her left hand rose to her face and covered her mouth. It was a while before she spoke again. 'It was getting worse,' she said. 'He was drinking more and . . . My mother was desperate. She knew *she* could never escape but there still might be a chance for me. That's when she started planning. In her mind, there was only one solution – she had to make me disappear.'

Harry could see where this was leading but couldn't quite take it in. It was all too bizarre, almost surreal. 'But there must have been other options.'

'Like what?' Ellen said. 'The police, a prosecution, a trial where we'd both have been forced to give evidence against him, to go over everything he'd done?' She shook her head. 'There was no guarantee he'd be convicted. And even if he was . . . well, it wouldn't be that long before he was out on the street again. She wasn't prepared to take the risk.'

'She could have left,' Harry said, 'got on a train, gone somewhere, *anywhere*.'

Ellen gave a sigh. 'Perhaps. But where could she go? It's not easy without money, without a home or a job to go to. She'd tried leaving before and . . .' A shiver ran through her. 'I think she was too scared to try again. The truth is you can't leave a man like Michael Harper. It's impossible. For him, we were possessions. He owned us. The only way she could be sure that he wouldn't come looking was if he thought I was dead.'

There was a long silence. Ellen sat very still. Occasionally, when Harry breathed in deeply, he could smell her perfume. The scent was very light. It seemed as delicate and fragile as she was. He wanted to say something useful, something comforting or reassuring, but no words came to him.

Ellen finally continued. 'She asked Jimmy to help her.'

'Jimmy Keppell?'

'They only lived a few streets away, him and his family. That's how I knew Tony. We grew up together. We went to the same school. My mother sometimes worked at one of Jimmy's clubs.'

The Starlight, Harry thought but didn't say it out loud. The pieces were slowly starting to slot together.

'He liked her,' Ellen said. She gave a thin smile. 'More than liked. That's how she persuaded him to help.'

'You mean they were . . .?'

She shook her head. 'God, no. Not then. She'd never have dared. My father would have . . .' She gave another quick shake of her head. 'But Jimmy always wanted the things he

320

couldn't have and my mother, at that time, was top of the list. She was very pretty, only twenty-five and despite everything she'd been through she still had this tremendous spirit. I can remember him coming round, the way he'd stare. I think he'd have been willing to do anything for her.'

Harry raised his brows. 'Anything?'

She turned her dark eyes towards him 'Almost anything.'

'Jimmy usually has fairly straightforward ways of dealing with problems.'

'These days, perhaps, but he wasn't quite so impulsive then. I'm sure he thought about it but his heart – such as it is – never ruled his head. He wasn't prepared to end up on a murder charge for any woman.'

'But he was prepared to help make a child disappear.'

Releasing his hand, Ellen suddenly stood up. 'It's cold,' she said. 'Can we go somewhere else? Do you mind?'

'Of course not.' As Harry got to his feet, he hoped she wasn't about to run out on him. He had to know what happened next. 'We could get a drink,' he suggested.

She nodded and started walking towards the gate. In less than a minute they had rejoined the crowd. The contrast between the peace of the churchyard and the noisy bustle of the piazza was extreme. They both hesitated for a moment, adjusting to the change of pace, before negotiating their way across the square. The pub was in the basement and Ellen halted again at the top of the steps. Gripping the railings, she gazed down.

'It looks busy,' she said.

Despite the chill in the air, the benches in the courtyard were full. The sound of voices, of laughter, drifted up to them. Most of the customers were surrounded by an assortment of gaudy carrier bags. Christmas shopping, Harry thought, and frowned. He tilted his head and tried to see through the open doors. 'There might be a table inside.'

'Do you think so?'

He was tempted to go down and take a look but then, picking up on the reluctance in her tone, immediately changed his mind. This was completely the wrong place to be: the atmosphere was too light-hearted, too festive. And it was all too public. It would be impossible for her to talk if she thought she might be overheard.

'No,' he said. 'Let's leave it. Come on, we'll find somewhere quieter.'

It was Saturday, however, and everywhere was bound to be busy. Afraid that he might never hear the end of her story, Harry racked his brains for an alternative. He couldn't take her to his flat – what if Val came back? – and they couldn't go to Berry Square. There was only one other option.

'What about the office?' he said. 'It's not too far from here. It should be empty.'

Ellen lifted her face but said nothing.

Harry couldn't decipher her expression – it seemed concerned, confused – and he instantly regretted saying that the office would be empty. *Oh no!* Did she suspect he was making some kind of indecent proposal? 'I didn't . . . I wasn't . . . I only meant that we wouldn't be disturbed.' *Christ*, he inwardly swore. That wasn't any better. What was the matter with him? It was barely ten minutes since she'd been revealing the abuse she had suffered as a child and already he was sounding like some pervert who couldn't wait to take advantage.

'Or maybe we could find another pub,' he said. 'Yeah, that might be better. I'm sure there must be—'

'It's all right,' she said, lightly touching his arm. 'I do trust you, you know. The office will be fine.'

Harry stared into her eyes. *Did* she trust him? He wanted her to but couldn't see how that was possible. They hardly knew each other and what she was about to tell him, what she'd already told him, would change her life forever.

Mac's office was only slightly more comfortable than the reception area but it was warm – or at least it would be once the heating kicked in – and there were two decent seats and a good supply of booze. He asked what she'd like to drink.

'Whatever you're having.'

Harry poured them both a stiff Scotch and soda and carried them over to the desk. She sat down in a swivel chair, lifted the glass and took a few sips before looking around. There wasn't much to view: the worn beige carpet, a cupboard, four metal filing cabinets and a calendar on the wall.

'Welcome to my world,' he said. 'Or rather the boss's world. We minions are usually consigned to the outer regions.'

'Won't he mind,' she said, 'about us using his office, drinking his Scotch?'

Harry sat in the chair opposite and shook his head. 'He's got more important concerns at the moment.'

She gave a thin smile and glanced at her watch.

He wondered where she was supposed to be, what she'd told her husband. Did Adam Shaw have any idea of who she really was? He couldn't imagine what it would be like to wake up one morning and find yourself married to a woman who had 'died' over twenty years ago.

Ellen's voice was low as she began to speak again. 'It was Jimmy who made most of the arrangements. He had this cousin, Rose. Her husband was an Irishman called William Corby. I'd met them a few times before and they seemed nice enough. The night my mother told me, we were sitting in the kitchen, just the two of us, and she gave me ice-cream, that Neapolitan stuff with the three different flavours. There were tinned peaches too.' She stopped, gave a hollow laugh and looked across at him. 'It's odd the things you remember, isn't it?'

Harry nodded.

Ellen lowered her eyes and gazed down at the desk. Tracing its old scars with the tips of her fingers, she seemed completely absorbed. 'She asked if I could keep a secret, a big secret, and of course I said Yes. Then she kissed me. She kissed me and said she knew that I would never let her down. She told me I'd be going to Ireland for a while, talked about it like it was

323

some kind of holiday. She couldn't come with me but promised we'd be together soon. In the meantime I had to listen very carefully, to do what I was told or . . . or my father would . . .' Pausing, Ellen lifted the glass to her mouth. Her hand was shaking. 'She said if I didn't keep the secret, if I didn't do exactly what I was told, I might never see her again.'

The silence that followed felt empty and immense. Harry wanted to fill it. He wished they were not separated by the solid stretch of desk, that he could reach out and touch her. But perhaps that was not what she wanted. Perhaps she needed the distance.

Quickly finishing the drink, Ellen held out the glass. 'Would you mind?'

He got up, poured another Scotch, weaker than the one before, and took it back to her.

'Thank you,' she said, raising it eagerly to her lips. She drank a third in one gulp, hesitated as if waiting for the alcohol to take effect, and then gave a long sigh. The tension in her shoulders eased a little.

'It all seemed to happen so fast. I know it was dark when we left the house. We went to a flat, some place of Jimmy's; I've no idea where it was. He drove us there in the car but then went away again. My mother cut and dyed my hair. I can remember . . . I looked in the mirror and didn't recognize myself. I was a different person. We both started laughing. It was like a game but serious too. I couldn't forget what she'd told me about not seeing her again. She made me keep repeating the same things over and over again: My name is Ellen Marie Corby and I'm seven years old. My birthday is the third of May.'

Ellen glanced at him, attempting a smile. 'I didn't like the seven bit much. What eight-year-old would? It's only now I can appreciate the advantage of being able to claim to be a year younger than I actually am.'

Harry smiled faintly.

'It's kind of blurry from then on,' she said. 'Jimmy came back with Rose and William and we got in the car again. My

324

mother wasn't with us. I don't recall any emotional farewells – perhaps I've blanked them out or maybe she didn't want to upset me. It was hours before he dropped us off; I must have slept for most of the journey. I've only got the vaguest memory of getting on a boat, an overnight ferry I suppose, and the next morning I was in Ireland. From that point on I ceased to be Grace Harper.'

Harry couldn't hold his tongue any longer. 'But why did the Corbys agree to it?'

'It *was* a risk, wasn't it? I'm sure Jimmy paid them but it was more than that. I believe they felt genuinely sorry for me. They knew what my father was like, what danger I was in. I suppose they wanted to protect me. And maybe . . .'

'Maybe?'

She frowned. 'I don't know. They'd lost their own daughter when she was just a baby. Rose couldn't have any more kids. Perhaps by giving me their child's name, her identity, they thought they could try and create something good out of bad. They thought they were doing the right thing.'

Harry knocked back the rest of his own drink. In the past he had always been clear on where the line lay between right or wrong. Now he was not so certain. 'And then?' he said.

'We went to a house in Dublin, something else that Jimmy must have fixed. We were strangers there. We didn't know a soul and no one knew us. So far as the neighbours were concerned we were just an ordinary family: Mum, Dad and little Ellen. There was no reason for anyone to connect me with the missing fair-haired girl in the papers.'

Harry could see how that would have worked. The best place to hide was in a city, in a crowd. And no one would be looking for a child who quite clearly wasn't being held against her will. The police wouldn't check the ferries for who had travelled the Tuesday night either – according to Sharon, Grace hadn't disappeared until the Wednesday afternoon.

'And from then on,' Ellen said, 'we just got on with it. I was never aware of the publicity, of all the madness that was going on. I didn't read the papers or see the news on TV; I guess they

325

were careful to shield me from all that. The weeks went by. I settled in, went to school and made new friends. I didn't hear from my mother but wasn't too worried – she had made me a promise and I firmly believed it. One day, I was sure, she would come to take me home. In the meantime . . . well, things weren't so bad. I was actually quite happy.'

Ellen twisted the glass between her slender fingers, half-closed her eyes and then opened them again. 'That must sound awful,' she said, glancing up at him. 'You know, even after all these years, it still makes me feel guilty to think it, never mind say it out loud.'

'It's not terrible,' he said. 'Perhaps, for once, you just felt safe.'

She stared at him for a long moment but then eventually nodded.

Harry looked down into his empty glass. More booze probably wouldn't help but then he didn't know what would. What was done was done and nothing could change it. Standing up, he retrieved the bottle of Scotch and the soda siphon and brought them both back to the desk.

Ellen watched as he topped up her drink and then poured himself a fresh one. 'The only thing that hurt was that *she* never got in touch, not even a phone call or a Christmas card. Rose would get upset if I asked about her. I could see the pain it caused and so after a while I just stopped asking.' Ellen twisted the glass in her hands again. 'I never stopped hoping though. I never forgot who my real mother was.'

Harry wondered how she'd done it, how it was possible to live such a lie for so long. 'Didn't you ever worry about being found out, when you were at school or—'

'No,' she said softly. 'I'd learned to keep my mouth shut. I was good at it, good at keeping secrets. And the longer it went on the easier it became. It was over a year, about eighteen months, when Rose . . . when she told me that . . .'

Harry heard her sharp intake of breath. He knew what was coming – or thought he did.

'She met me after school, walked me home and then . . . She told me that I had to be brave, to be strong. She told me that my parents . . . that they were dead.'

Harry started. *They?* It was true that Michael Harper had died then but Sharon had still been very much alive. 'What? Both of them?'

'Yes,' she said. Her dark eyes partly closed again. 'It was a long time before I found out the truth.'

Chapter Fifty

The room, although neither of them had spoken for a while, was not entirely silent. Harry could hear the muffled sound of the traffic and the faint ticking of the radiators. He was experiencing the same ambiguous feeling he had often known as a cop, a confusing seesaw between the desire to find out the truth and the worrying responsibility of actually hearing it.

Seeing Ellen stand up, he panicked for a second, thinking she was leaving. Instead she simply took off her raincoat and placed it neatly over the back of the chair. Underneath she was wearing a pair of black trousers and a black cardigan with small pearl buttons. He wondered what had made her choose to dress all in black today. Mourning clothes, he thought and then rapidly dismissed the notion as fanciful.

She sat back down and picked up her glass. 'I'd better tell you the rest,' she said, 'before I drink too much of this.'

Harry waited but she didn't continue. He let a few more seconds pass by and then gently prompted, 'So later, after they . . . after the accident . . . What made you decide to come back to London?'

'Where else would I go? I still saw it as home and there wasn't anything left for me there. It felt like the only thing to do. What you have to realize is that I didn't have a clue as to how "missing" I actually was. I wasn't aware that I'd been at the centre of a major crime investigation. If I'd known, it would have been different – I would never have dared to come back – but I thought all the secrets were over and done with, that there was nothing to hide from any more.' She gave a slow, despairing shake of her head. 'Just how wrong could I be?'

Harry didn't even attempt a reply.

'When I left,' she said, 'all I took with me were a bag of clothes and Rose's address book. That's how I knew where to find Jimmy. He'd moved out to Chingford and that's where I went a few days after I arrived. I hoped he might help with finding somewhere to stay.'

'That must have been quite a surprise for him.'

Ellen raised her eyes to the ceiling and gave a dry brittle laugh. 'He'd have probably had a heart attack if he *had* opened the door to me.'

A smile hovered briefly on Harry's lips. Any life-threatening shock to Jimmy Keppell could hardly be viewed as a bad thing. 'But it can't have been completely unexpected. He must have heard. He must have wondered if you'd—'

'No. That's the point: he didn't know. There was no one left to tell him. He and Rose weren't in regular contact – I suppose it would have been too risky – and I hadn't seen him since the night I'd left London. I didn't even think of him again until after the funeral, until I saw his name in her address book.'

Harry nodded. 'So you went round and . . .'

Her brow furrowed as she thought back to that afternoon. 'Tony was the only one at the house. I knew him straight away. He didn't recognize me though, not at first. I presumed it was just because I looked different to the girl he'd gone to school with all those years ago. I didn't know I was supposed to be . . .' She paused, concentrating on the desk again. When she looked up, her eyes were bright with tears. 'God, the poor guy thought I was dead!'

It was another hour before Harry had heard the end of the story. By then the light was starting to fade, the blue sky dimming to a pale silvery grey. The level in the Scotch bottle had dipped considerably too. Having eaten no lunch, he could feel the effect of the alcohol but instead of dulling his senses it appeared to be heightening them. He was overly aware of every movement she made, every nuance in her speech, every tiny detail of her face and clothes.

There was plenty to think about, too much perhaps, but what remained foremost in his mind was what she'd told him about her reunion with her mother. It was that particular encounter that struck the deepest chord. The meeting had not gone well. Sharon, exhibiting more fear than joy, had not welcomed her daughter with open arms.

For reasons of his own, Harry couldn't resist returning to the subject. 'You must have felt betrayed,' he said, 'that first time you saw her after all those years.'

Ellen scowled at the words. 'Why should I?' she said defensively. 'She was just confused, afraid. She'd lied to her husband, lied to the police, lied to almost everyone. It was a shock to see me again. After she'd let me go, after she'd made that ultimate sacrifice, I was suddenly there and . . .' Getting quickly to her feet, she went over to the window and stared determinedly down at the street. With her back still turned she hugged her arms around her. 'It didn't . . . *doesn't* mean she doesn't love me. It's more complicated than that. I don't expect you to understand.'

'More than you think,' Harry said. As he went to stand beside her, he could see her body trembling, her slim shoulders shaking with emotion. He laid his hand lightly on her arm and the shameful pain of his own past spilled out before he could prevent it. 'My mother left when I was five. She walked out and I haven't seen her since.'

Roughly, Ellen twisted away from his touch. 'It's not the same,' she snapped angrily. '*My* mother didn't desert me. It was the very opposite. She did everything in her power to try and save me.'

Harry flinched at the retort, his face starting to burn red. Why had he told her? It had been a mistake and he instantly regretted it.

330

But then, unexpectedly, she reached out for his hand and grasped it tightly. Her voice was filled with remorse. 'I'm sorry. I'm so sorry. I should never have said that.'

'Why not?' he said bitterly. 'It's the truth, isn't it?'

'The truth,' she echoed. She gazed at him and slowly lowered her face. Leaning in, she laid her forehead against his chest. 'Who knows what the goddamn truth is.'

They stayed that way, as finely posed as two characters in a tableau, until Harry gently disengaged his hand and put his arms around her. Immediately she seemed to melt against him, to fold into his embrace. It felt as natural as if they had always been together. And when she lifted her face again he instinctively knew what he would do next. He understood that he shouldn't, that it was stupid, reckless, wrong . . . but already his mouth was closing over hers.

He was aware, as their lips came together, of a mutual intake of breath. He felt her tongue search out his and for a while all he could take in was the softness of her mouth, its searching urgency and need. Moving a hand to the small of her back, he pulled her even closer. She made a soft moaning sound. He was shocked by the intensity of his desire. At that moment, with every nerve end ablaze, he believed that he had never wanted any woman more.

It was only as their lips briefly separated, as he bent to kiss her throat, that he felt a moment's hesitation. He wasn't sure what caused it, just the tiniest of voices perhaps, a warning whisper in his ear: *What are you doing?* And suddenly he found himself thinking about what she'd been through, about the amount of Scotch they'd drunk, about Valerie, about Adam . . .

As if his doubts had simultaneously leaked through to her, she abruptly pulled away. Without looking at him, she turned, walked over to the chair and picked up her raincoat. 'I'm sorry. I have to go.'

He wasn't sure if she was sorry about the kiss or about the fact she had to leave. 'What will you do now?' he said.

331

She buttoned up her coat, smoothed down her hair and gave a weary sigh. Eventually she raised her large dark eyes to him. 'It's over, isn't it? It's all going to come out. I'll have to talk to Adam and . . .'

As her voice choked up, Harry took a step toward her. She quickly lifted a hand, her palm out, her fingers splayed. 'Don't,' she said. 'Please don't.'

'I'll speak to Jess,' Harry said. He knew he wouldn't be able to persuade her to keep the lid on a story as big as this one but perhaps there was something else he could do. 'I'm sure she'll give you time, you know, some breathing space while you talk to Adam.'

Ellen nodded as she headed for the door. 'Thank you.'

'I'll come down with you.'

'No,' she said softly. 'I need . . . I think I need to be on my own.'

She walked out, leaving the door ajar behind her. She passed through the reception area and into the corridor beyond. Harry heard the old lift rattle up, heard the doors slide open and then close again.

As soon as she was gone, he felt the urge to run after her, to prevent her from leaving, but he didn't. Instead he turned back towards the window. He still couldn't accept what he felt for her; it was all too intense, too complicated. He wasn't good at love. He was even worse at showing it.

It was a while before she appeared again. Harry followed her progress as she walked along the street. As he stood there, he felt odd, dislocated, as if he was just waking from a dream. He placed his palms flat against the cool glass. He watched as she paused at the kerb, waiting for a gap in the long stream of traffic. She glanced left and right. What was she thinking? Was she thinking of him? Regretting his lack of action, he willed her to turn and look up.

She didn't.

'I'm here,' he whispered.

But it was all too late. Sensing her intention, a cry rose in his throat. Before he could do anything more than slam his hands impotently against the window, she had stepped straight into the road – and then there was only the screech of brakes, the awful stomach-churning thud and the slow-motion acrobatic twist of her body.

Chapter Fifty-One

Harry anxiously paced the hospital corridor. It was over fifteen minutes since the ambulance had brought her in and there still wasn't any news. Horrific images were revolving in his head: the dreadful arc of her back as the car had hit her, the slow fall towards the ground, the terrible picture of her lying like a rag doll in the gutter.

It was his fault.

If only he'd stopped her from leaving. Why hadn't he? He wanted to slam his fist against the wall. He was a fool, a bloody stupid fool! He should have realized just how imposs-ible it was for her.

As Harry turned to retrace his steps, he saw Jess appear at the other end of the corridor. He didn't know why he'd called her and could not recall exactly what he'd said; all he did remember was that his call had been disjointed and rambling, an urgent plea for help.

She rushed forward, placing a hand sympathetically on his arm. 'Hey, how is she?'

'I don't know. No one's told me anything. She was barely conscious when they brought her in. She's been taken for scans, X-rays, all that stuff.'

'Has anyone contacted Adam?'

'I think so. I gave them the number.'

'Why don't we sit down,' Jess suggested. She peered into the busy waiting room. There were a few free seats but they were crammed so close to the rest that it would be impossible to have a private conversation. 'Over here,' she said, leading him instead to a row of ten blue plastic chairs lined up in the corridor. They had probably been put there to deal with the usual evening overflow; Saturday night was always frantic in A&E.

Harry slumped down and put his head in his hands. He took a few deep breaths before he lifted his face to look at her again. 'She did it deliberately.'

'You can't be sure of that,' Jess said.

Harry groaned out his reply. 'I was watching from the window. She *saw* that car; she knew it was coming.' He squeezed his eyes shut and then opened them again. 'Oh God,' he murmured despairingly. 'What if she's dead?'

'This isn't your fault,' Jess insisted. 'It was all going to come out eventually. You can't blame yourself.'

'Of course I can,' he snapped back. 'I let her go. I let her leave on her own after—'

A white-coated man holding a clip file was approaching. Harry gazed up expectantly but he strolled on past.

'I should have realized what state she was in,' he continued. 'I should never have met her alone; I should never have talked to her in the first place.'

Jess raised her brows but had the sensitivity to keep her mouth shut. Now wasn't the time to get on to that particular subject. She sent up a silent prayer that Ellen Shaw – or should that be Grace Harper? – would survive; if she didn't Harry would have it on his conscience for the rest of his days.

Glancing down the corridor to reception, Jess recognized a tall man standing at the desk and gave Harry a nudge. 'That's him,' she whispered. 'That's Adam Shaw.'

Harry looked over, frowning. Personally, he wouldn't have recognized him from Len's grainy photos; he seemed older, greyer, but that was maybe down to the shock. 'Are you sure?'

'Absolutely,' she said.

They both continued to stare as a doctor, a brisk-looking woman in her early forties, arrived to speak to him. They weren't close enough to eavesdrop on the conversation. Instead Harry tried to gauge the prognosis from Adam's reaction but his face, blank and unresponsive, gave nothing away. Harry felt his heart begin to pump. It was bad news. It had to be. The two of them were talking for over five minutes before the doctor eventually pointed down the corridor towards them.

'Oh God,' Harry murmured, lowering his face into his hands again.

As Adam Shaw approached, Jess was the one to stand up and greet him. 'Hello,' she said, stepping forward. 'How is she?'

Behind her, Harry slowly got to his feet. Assailed by hopelessness, he could hardly bear to look at the man. *Please don't say it; please don't say she's dead.*

But Adam, after a short hesitation, suddenly smiled. His voice was breaking as he gave them the news. 'She . . . she's going to be okay. A broken wrist, three fractured ribs and a lot of bruising but no internal injuries. They say she's been lucky. They're going to keep her in overnight but she should be able to come home tomorrow.'

'That's wonderful,' Jess said.

The relief that ran through Harry's body was sublime. For a second he could hardly breathe.

'I just wanted to thank you,' Adam said, turning towards him. 'I understand you came here in the ambulance with her.'

Harry nodded, smiling blankly back. He still wasn't thinking straight. As he stared into the soft grateful eyes of the man in front of him, his mouth slowly opened and closed. What could he say? How was he going to explain what he'd been doing there?

Jess came to the rescue again. 'We were standing right beside her when it happened,' she said. 'It was such a shock, terrible. And it didn't seem right for her to be alone. That's why my husband went in the ambulance. I followed behind in the car.'

'Thank you,' he said. 'Thank you both so much.'

'We're just glad she's all right,' Jess said. 'Please don't let us keep you. I'm sure you must want to go and see her.'

'Yes, of course.' He put out his hand and took first Jess's and then Harry's. 'Thank you so much,' he repeated before walking away down the corridor.

Harry, still feeling the pressure of the man's handshake, gradually released a long low sigh of guilty relief.

Jess looked at him. 'You owe me,' she said.

'I know.'

'And you can begin by telling me the whole damn story.'

They were almost at Kentish Town by the time Harry had finished relating the events of the afternoon. Jess screwed up her eyes. It had started to snow again, a swirling blanket of white, and she was trying to keep at least some of her focus on the slippery road ahead.

'That is one tangled web.'

'I shouldn't have lied to you,' he said. 'But I honestly didn't think she'd talk if you came with me.'

'That's okay,' Jess said. 'I understand.'

'Do you?' he said gratefully.

'Of course I bloody don't!' she snapped. 'I thought I could trust you but I quite clearly can't. What is it with you and that woman?'

Harry averted his face and stared out through the window.

Jess tapped her fingers impatiently on the wheel as they waited at yet another set of traffic lights. She glanced over at him. He looked tired and drawn and miserable. 'I'm sorry,' she said. 'It's just the frustration talking. I know today hasn't exactly been a ball for you.'

'No, you're right to be angry,' he said. 'I went behind your back and I shouldn't. It was wrong.'

'Well, it's done now,' Jess said. She could never hold a grudge for long, especially towards people she liked. And for some obscure reason she did quite like Harry Lind. 'Let's forget it. Just promise me something – no more secrets, right?'

Harry nodded. 'It's a deal.'

She edged the car forward as the lights changed to green. Her mind was still processing everything he had told her.

'Okay,' she said. 'I've got a couple of questions. Why didn't Sharon go to Grace after Michael Harper died? I mean, her daughter wasn't in danger any more. Why was Grace told that Sharon was dead too?'

'Because Grace couldn't just be resurrected, could she?' Harry said. 'Sharon had done some major lying to the police and if they found out about it . . . Even bearing in mind the circumstances, she'd still be in deep trouble. No, the only way she could have been with Grace permanently was to leave London, leave her family and friends and take on a new identity too. Reading between the lines, I suspect Sharon wasn't prepared to make that sacrifice.'

'Delightful,' Jess said. She scowled, remembering her own conversation with Sharon Harper. 'And how did she explain *that* to Grace when she finally turned up on her doorstep?'

'She claimed she'd done it so that Grace could have a better life. By the time Michael died she was settled with the Corbys in Ireland and seemed happy enough but if she was always going to be waiting for her mother to appear . . .'

'Oh, very altruistic,' Jess snorted. 'And a good way of making sure that she didn't take it into her head to come looking for her when she was old enough.'

'That could be true,' Harry said softly, 'but maybe it's not that black and white. The Corbys could have put a lot of pressure on Sharon. If she'd begun going over for regular visits Grace would never have really accepted them as her parents and there was a far greater chance of the secret slipping out. And let's face it, if it had, Sharon wouldn't have been the only one facing major trouble from the Law. At the moment we can't be sure what her real motivation was. Only *she* knows that. Perhaps we shouldn't be too quick to judge.'

'I guess,' Jess said reluctantly. She was starting to wish that it was all more black and white. These shades of grey only muddied the waters. 'So what does Grace think?'

Harry shrugged. 'She wants to believe that her mother did it for the right reasons.' He sighed. 'Although I don't suppose it helped smooth things over when she discovered that Sharon had started an entirely new family in her absence; she had two small sons by the time they met again.'

Jess could barely imagine what Grace must have felt; the sense of betrayal must have been devastating. 'And does she still see Sharon?'

'Rarely.'

'That's not surprising.'

Jess drove in silence for a while, trying to figure out how all this could be connected to Len's death. Would Grace have been prepared to kill to stop the truth coming out? She couldn't see why. It was Grace, after all, who was the victim in this unholy mess. Sharon and Jimmy Keppell were better candidates. They both had more to lose.

'Len was murdered because of this,' she said angrily. 'I'm sure of it. Do you think it was Keppell?'

'He'd be more than capable,' Harry said, 'but why would he take such a risk?'

'Because if it all came out he could be charged with . . . I don't know, conspiracy to pervert the course of justice, wasting police time?'

'He could,' Harry agreed, 'but only if Sharon and Grace were prepared to give evidence against him. And what were the chances of that? With the Corbys gone, there's no way of proving he was ever involved.'

'Perhaps he did it to protect Sharon.'

'Perhaps.'

'Or maybe Sharon killed Len,' she said.

Harry lifted his hands and dropped them wearily back on to his knees. 'Could she actually have been that desperate? If she knew the story was about to blow she'd have been better off going to the police, coming clean and claiming mitigating circumstances – after all, Grace *was* being abused – than facing a murder charge.'

Jess was unwilling to sacrifice all her theories without at least the semblance of a fight. 'Yes, but people don't always do rational things. She might have acted on the spur of the moment.'

Harry lifted his brows but said nothing more.

They fell into silence again.

Without much recollection of actually getting there, Jess found herself in the street where Harry lived. She pulled into the nearest empty space, a short distance from his flat, but kept the engine idling.

'So what happens now?' Harry said tentatively. 'This is one hell of a story but if you take it to the cops, to the paper, then—'

'I know,' Jess interrupted. She gave him a long hard look. 'I do understand the concept of moral responsibility. And although it may surprise you to hear it, I've even got a conscience. I'm not some heartless hack who'll do anything for a headline.' She paused. 'I need time to think it through. It's Len's funeral on Monday. I won't make any decision until after that.'

Harry gave a small grim smile, nodded and then got out of the car. 'Thank you.'

'Just one last thing,' she said, before he closed the door. 'Do you swear you've told me *everything* that happened today?'

He hesitated, thinking of that final kiss.

'Harry?'

'Yes,' he said, leaning down to look her straight in the eye. 'Absolutely everything.'

Harry remained standing on the pavement as she drove away. He waited until the car disappeared around the corner. He felt exhausted, drained of every emotion other than relief. Ellen was still alive; that was all that really mattered.

Pushing his cold hands deep into his pockets, he began to trudge through the snow towards the flat. It was only as he approached the gate that he felt a weird prickle on the back of his neck. *Someone was watching him!* Twisting around, he surveyed the street but there was no one in sight. He gazed along the pavement, at the windows of the houses opposite and at all the parked cars. No one. Perhaps he was just imagining it. It had been a long and stressful day. Touching the back of his neck, Harry frowned. He walked up the drive, unlocked the door, closed it behind him and quickly pulled the bolts across.

Chapter Fifty-Two

By Monday morning the snow was ankle deep and still falling. Harry traipsed down the road to the corner shop. He had rung the hospital and discovered that Ellen had been discharged; now he was fighting the temptation to call her at home. Not a good idea, he knew, as Adam would probably answer the phone.

By the time he got back with milk and a paper, Valerie's red Citroën was parked outside the flat. He felt his heart sink. In his present frame of mind, an argument was the last thing he needed. Was she here to pick up more of her things? If so it might be wiser if he just left her to it and walked around the block for half an hour.

Had it not been for the weather he might have done exactly that but the prospect of slowly freezing to death was, on balance, marginally less desirable than the inevitable row.

'Hey,' she said, coming out of the kitchen to greet him. She was wearing a dark red sweater, faded jeans and boots. Her long fair hair was tied back in a ponytail.

Harry took off his coat and smiled thinly.

'No need to look so pleased to see me,' she joked. Then, sensing the darkness of his mood, she gave a small apologetic nod of her head. 'No reason why you should be, I suppose. I should have called first. I'm sorry.'

'It's still your home,' Harry said, a little churlishly. 'You don't need to make an appointment.'

She hesitated as if unsure how to respond. Then she settled for the most placatory option. 'I was just making coffee. Would you like one?'

He passed her the pint of milk. 'Here, you'll need this.'

Val went back to the kitchen and Harry followed her. On the way, he glanced briefly round the living room, checking for empty cases or holdalls. There were none in sight. He sat down at the table while she sorted out the coffee.

'How have you been?' he said.

'Oh, so-so.' She put a mug in front of him, pulled out a chair and sat down opposite. 'You?'

Harry shrugged. 'Busy,' he said.

Her smile, which had been fairly feeble to start with, faded away completely. She had been hoping, perhaps, for some small indication that he might have missed her. When it wasn't forthcoming she took a sip of hot coffee and then gently cleared her throat. 'How's the case going?'

'It isn't,' he said shortly. 'You found out who killed Tommy Lake yet?'

She sighed. 'I think we all know who did that. The problem is proving it. Sometimes I wonder if Holt even wants to. He's so deliberately obstructive, it drives me crazy.'

'He's not a great one for cooperation – or for female detectives.'

'No,' she agreed. 'And you haven't got any leads on Al Webster?'

'Not a whisper,' he said.

There was an awkward silence. Harry felt confused and unsettled by her presence. He knew they were tiptoeing around each other, both staying on neutral ground, neither of them comfortable with starting *that* conversation. He had more than one reason for not wanting to get involved in a lengthy discussion: apart from the fact that he wasn't prepared for it, that he was still unsure of what he actually wanted, it was also Len Curzon's funeral at eleven thirty. He had to be there. He had to find out what decision, if any, Jess had made.

Eventually, when the silence had gone on for too long, she lifted her soft hazel eyes and looked at him. 'What are we going to do, Harry?'

'Do?' he repeated disingenuously.

'I know you must be mad at me,' she said. 'Maybe I shouldn't have walked out like that. And I shouldn't have refused to take your calls. It's just . . . you didn't really leave me with too many choices. What was I meant to think when you promised me a meal, a chance to talk, an evening when we were supposed to try and sort things out, and then didn't even bother to turn up?' Her lower lip trembled. 'You really let me down. You didn't even ring to make one of your usual lousy excuses.'

Harry heard the dreadful hurt in her voice and winced. He imagined how she must have felt, sitting here and waiting for him. He noticed the dark shadows under her eyes and the sadness in her face. All the old feelings for her came rushing back. She was right; he *had* treated her badly. He'd been treating her badly for months and she hadn't deserved any of it. But then, just as he was about to apologize, he suddenly remembered what had happened in the meantime. With startling clarity the image of her and Chapman flashed into his head. His guilt instantly flipped into anger and resentment. He stared at her, astounded. How dare she act like the injured party?

'You've got a nerve to talk about being let down!'

She frowned at him, her eyes widening with surprise. 'What?'

'Don't act all innocent. I saw you in The Fox last week. I saw you with Dean Chapman.'

It took a few seconds for the full implication of what he was saying to sink in. 'Oh God,' she said, lowering her face into her hands.

'I saw it all,' Harry said. He could feel the rage, the humiliation growing inside him. 'I saw you attached to his lips like some bloody limpet.'

'Why didn't you . . .'

344

'What? Let you know I was there?' Harry sat back and glared. 'I didn't want to spoil a lovely moment.'

'It's not what you think,' she said. Her eyes, looking up at him again, were brimming with tears. 'It really wasn't.'

Harry could barely stand to look at her.

She groaned. 'Yes, okay, I did kiss him but . . .'

'But it didn't mean anything, right?'

Valerie's eyes flashed bright. 'No, it didn't – at least not in the sense that you're suggesting. You want to know why I did it?' She didn't wait for an answer. 'I was tired and fed up and . . . and feeling insecure with everything that was going on between us. And yes, I'm sure it sounds pathetic – perhaps it is – but I was flattered that someone else was actually interested. If you think that's a shitty excuse, then you're right. But it was a kiss, nothing more. I didn't sleep with him, not that night, not any night.'

'Yeah, right,' he said, provocatively.

'We're not having an affair,' she said. 'I've never been unfaithful to you.'

'If you say so.'

They stared at each other across the table.

Val was the first to look away. 'It was a moment of weakness, of stupid drunken weakness,' she said. 'I'm sorry that you saw it and I'm sorry if it hurt you.'

'And you think that's good enough?' he said.

She shook her head. 'I'm not sure what would ever be good enough for you.'

'And what's that supposed to mean?'

Val looked straight into his eyes. Her shaking voice was filled with emotion. 'You've been pushing me away for months.'

'So it's all my fault,' he said. 'That's rich.'

She expelled her breath in a long frustrated sigh. 'Perhaps you should stop being quite so hypocritical. Are you telling me that you've never done anything you shouldn't in all the time we've been together?'

The reproach caught him off guard. Harry thought about

snogging Jess in the back of the taxi. He thought about leaning down to kiss Ellen, of the way he had wanted her . . . still wanted her. By the time he realized that Val's accusations were little more than a shot in the dark, his guilty hesitation had been enough to condemn him.

'Well, I guess I just got my answer,' she said. Stumbling to her feet, Val grabbed her coat and stormed out of the flat. She slammed the door so hard behind her that the whole building shook.

Chapter Fifty-Three

Jess was only half listening to the droning voice of the priest. He was reciting a rather drab eulogy, the content of which bore no relation to the man she had known. Had he ever actually met Len? Her gaze, after wandering around the chapel, alighted again on the cheap wooden coffin. A shiver ran through her.

The turnout was even smaller than she'd expected. There were only fifteen people in attendance: the mourners comprised four relatives, some friends and a smattering of colleagues from the *Herald*. Toby was sitting beside her in the second row. Hardly a grand send-off, she thought sadly.

As the tears in her eyes threatened to overflow, she pondered on Len's last big story. His recognition of Grace Harper had set off a chain of events that had come to a halt, temporarily, with her. Harry's revelations had given her plenty to think about. Armed with a bottle of vodka and too many cigarettes, she had spent all Sunday trying to decide what to do. She still had the dull blinding headache to prove it.

The decision as to whether she should reveal Ellen Shaw's true identity, however, had still not been resolved. She mentally listed the reasons why she shouldn't keep quiet: there was the simple matter of the truth, the fact that the police had been misled and the Theresa Neal inquiry jeopardized, but top of the list was Len's murder – she *had* to find out who was responsible for that. On the other hand, there was Ellen's clearly fragile state of mind. If Harry was right and she had deliberately walked out in front of that car, who could say what she might do next?

She was still trying to work out if there was any kind of compromise to be made, any means of bringing Len's killer to justice without destroying Ellen, when the small congregation embarked on a feeble rendition of 'Abide with Me'.

Jess stared down at the hymn book. She suspected that Len would never have let anything as minor as a qualm of conscience stand between him and a front page story. He was a hack through and through and a major scoop was everything. She glanced sideways at Toby. God, if he had any idea of what she was withholding, he would hang her out to dry!

A few minutes later the dark red curtains slid across the coffin, obscuring it from view. She closed her eyes, unwilling to witness the final moments.

What should I do, you old sod? she found herself silently asking.

'You need a bloody drink, girl,' she heard him replying and had to stifle a slightly hysterical and thoroughly inappropriate laugh.

Len's sister-in-law glanced over her shoulder and frowned. Jess took out a tissue and dabbed at her eyes. She had met Edith Curzon earlier, a thin pinched woman who having travelled all the way from Birmingham seemed to view Len's murder as rather more of an inconvenience than a tragedy.

After a few more bars of solemn music, the funeral was over. Everyone trooped silently out of the chapel. As she left, Jess noticed Harry sitting at the back. He must have come in after the service had started. She knew what he wanted and it wasn't to pass on his deepest condolences.

Jess wasn't in the mood for a discussion. Outside, she told Toby that she'd call him later and then, splitting off from the rest of the group, quickly walked away. She strode around the corner to the memorial garden and lit a cigarette. Here the snow was untouched, crisp and white. She had been hoping for some peace and quiet but it didn't take long for Harry to catch up with her.

'What do you want?' she sighed.

'I was just wondering if—'

Jess gave a short bitter laugh. 'Look, I know I said I'd make a decision after Len's funeral but I didn't expect you to take it quite so literally.'

'No,' he said, shuffling his feet. 'I'm sorry. I'm not here to pressure you.'

'Really?' she said. 'Only you're doing a pretty good impression of it.'

'I just thought you might like to talk things through.'

As it happened Jess would have liked to talk to someone, but it couldn't be him. He was far too close to Ellen, too emotionally involved. She couldn't trust him to be objective. 'I'll ring you when I've made a decision.'

Harry opened his mouth as if to ask when that might be but then had the sense to button it. Instead he gave a small nod of acknowledgement, raised his hand in a wave and went to walk away.

'Hang on a moment,' she said. 'Are you all right to drive now?'

Turning, he glanced down at his leg. 'I think so.'

Jess took the keys from her pocket and held them out. 'Here, you may as well take these. The car's parked by the chapel.'

'There's no hurry.'

'Please,' Jess said. 'I can't hold on to it forever.' It was a shame to lose the wheels but better that than feeling she was under any obligation. When she finally made her choice, it had to be for all the right reasons.

Harry reluctantly accepted the keys. He took a few steps and then stopped and glanced back. 'Are you sure you're all right?'

For a second she hesitated, tempted to give in to her need to talk about Len, about all the mess that was whirling around inside her head. What she wouldn't give for a shoulder to cry on! But that shoulder couldn't be Harry Lind's. 'I'm fine,' she said. 'I promise. I'll call you.'

Jess watched him walk along the path. There was still time to change her mind, to call him back, but she couldn't. She mustn't. She could not afford to be influenced by anyone else.

It was only a minute or two before she heard the tramp of footsteps behind her again. Presuming it was Harry, she whirled around in frustration. 'What is it now? What do you—'

As she saw who it was, the words dried in her throat. Her eyes widened in astonishment.

Charlotte Meyer was standing right in front of her.

Dressed in a long white coat and matching fur hat the woman had the appearance of a devilish Ice Queen. 'There's no need to look so surprised, dear,' she said, in that cool upper class voice of hers. 'You weren't that hard to find. A quick flick through the guest list and then all it came down to was a process of elimination. Your editor was very helpful when I asked him the name of that nice young journalist he'd brought along last week.' She gave a thin unpleasant smile. 'Oh, by the way, what name are you going by today – Rachel or Jessica?'

Jess took a nervous drag on her cigarette while she tried to figure out what to say next. It was never comfortable being caught out in a lie. Deciding that the only form of defence was attack, she slowly exhaled the smoke and said: 'This is hardly the best of times. As I'm sure you're aware, I've just been to a funeral.'

'I don't suppose there ever would be a good time,' Charlotte replied. 'We're all busy people, aren't we?' She paused, that thin smile hovering on her lips again. 'But I think you owe me an explanation.'

Jess, riled by her callousness, was tempted to claim that she didn't owe her anything. If she decided to leave, there was nothing Ms Meyer could do to stop her. But then again, the very reason she'd tried to stir things up in the first place was to make something happen. Now that it had, it would be foolish not to follow through. 'I doubt if I can tell you anything you don't already know.'

'That's hardly the point,' Charlotte said. 'It's what you're going to do with that information that interests me.'

'Do?' Jess said.

Charlotte frowned. 'Please don't play games with me, Jessica. I've already talked to Paul and I know he has no intention of writing a book.'

Jess shrugged, threw the cigarette on the ground and put her hands in her pockets. If she had to stare at that supercilious expression for a second longer, she was likely to say something she'd regret. 'Shall we walk?' Without waiting for a reply, she headed towards the old part of the cemetery and Charlotte had little choice but to fall in beside her.

Flanked by the tilting gravestones, they strolled side by side along the path. Their feet made a thin crunching sound in the snow. There were only the grey stone angels, their ice-filled hands clasped in prayer, to witness the conversation.

Charlotte was the first to speak again. 'Paul didn't tell you about the blackmail, so who did?'

'I'm not at liberty to reveal that,' Jess said, with just a hint of smugness. It was a phrase she had always wanted to use.

Charlotte gave a contemptuous snort. 'You don't need to. There's only one other person it could be. That bloody woman has a lot to answer for.'

Jess wasn't sure which bloody woman in particular she was referring to. Did she mean Ellen Shaw? She had been Tony Keppell's girlfriend but had not – at least so far as Jess was aware – played an active part in the blackmail. All she could do was try and provoke Charlotte into revealing a name. 'You don't think she has the right to tell her side of the story?'

'Right?' she scoffed. 'I don't think blackmailers should have any rights at all.'

'Maybe not,' Jess said.

'But that won't stop you from repeating every filthy lie she tells you!' Charlotte almost spat the words out. 'Your sort are all the same.'

'And what sort would that be?'

Charlotte shot her a look, her eyes bright with venom. 'Paul's still languishing in prison because of that tramp. Don't you think he's suffered enough?'

Jess raised her brows. What she really meant was that *she* had suffered enough. But, surprisingly, she did feel a twinge of pity. Charlotte Meyer was abrupt and arrogant and too used to getting her own way but she had also been embroiled in a scandal that must have come close to destroying her. For a woman of her social standing, the humiliation and disgrace could not have been easy to bear.

'Look,' Jess said, 'I do have some scruples. Why don't you talk to me, tell me your side of things? That way I get to see the whole picture.'

Charlotte gave an abrupt shake of her head. 'I'm not talking to the press,' she said, apparently oblivious to the irony of the statement.

'I wouldn't quote you. It can be completely off the record.'

'I'm not interested,' Charlotte said. She gave Jess a haughty glare. 'If you insist on going ahead with this, I'll have no choice but to consult my lawyers. I'll have them draw up an injunction.'

'Okay,' Jess said brightly. 'I'll look forward to hearing from them.' She was pretty certain that it was an empty threat; Charlotte wouldn't be here now if she'd already found a legal solution to the problem.

'Right,' she said, 'if that's how you feel then . . .' Charlotte faltered, her face beginning to crumple. Suddenly she looked her age. Even the immaculate make-up couldn't disguise the deep lines of worry etched across her forehead. When she spoke again, she sounded close to tears. 'Why is she doing this?'

Jess, sensing that the best response was silence, lifted her shoulders in the tiniest of shrugs.

352

Charlotte took a moment to compose herself. Taking a pristine white handkerchief from her bag, she blew her nose and stared off into the middle distance. 'I suppose she's claiming that Paul *offered* her the money. Well, that might have been true at the start – I mean, it was the only decent thing to do, wasn't it? – but later, it was pure extortion. Surely even you can see that.'

Jess tried not to take the latter words too personally. She had more important things to focus on – like who they were actually talking about. Surely Tony Keppell had been the one who was blackmailing Deacon? How had Ellen become the villain of the piece and what was all this 'later' business? She had to be careful what she said, very careful; if Charlotte suspected, even for a second, just how much in the dark she was then this conversation would be over.

Jess offered what she hoped was a suitably ambiguous statement. 'She strikes me as a rather sad person.'

'Sad?' Charlotte repeated incredulously. Her left arm rose and fell in a gesture of frustration. 'I suppose you would think that. Just because . . . Oh, I can see how it must look. And I can see how she'll get everyone's sympathy: the poor innocent girl seduced and then abandoned by her rich married lover, left to bring up a child alone, struggling to make ends meet. It's all good tabloid fodder, isn't it? Except, there was nothing innocent about that tart and Paul didn't abandon her. He might not have been able to provide exactly what she wanted but the financial settlement was more than generous.'

Even as Charlotte spoke, Jess was desperately trying to absorb the information she was receiving. Sparks were going off in her head. So it was Ellen he'd been sleeping with, not Tony! That put a different slant on things. Ellen (or should it be Grace? – she still wasn't sure what to call her) – must have met Paul Deacon after arriving in London, had an affair and fallen pregnant. She must have turned to Tony to help get the cash out of him.

'That can't have been easy for you to deal with,' Jess said.

Charlotte glanced at her and then slowly raised her eyes to the pale blue sky. Whatever reservations she might have felt about talking seemed to have melted away. 'I wasn't aware of it then,' she said. 'Paul was always very discreet about his extramarital affairs. He didn't tell me until . . . Well, you know what happened next.'

Jess assumed she meant the shooting of Tony Keppell. 'Yes.'

Charlotte shook her head. 'And that doesn't bother you? I mean what kind of woman, what kind of *mother*, could use the abduction of her daughter as a good excuse to extort another fifty thousand pounds?'

Jess's heart almost stopped. *What?* While her feet came to a halt, her brain went into overdrive. She had got it all so wrong! It wasn't Ellen who Deacon had had the affair with – it was Sharon Harper. 'So Paul was—' She smartly put a brake on the sentence, stopping herself from blurting out *Grace Harper's father*.

Charlotte, alert to the sudden pause, turned to look at her.

'So Paul was . . . was asked to pay again,' Jess finally managed to stammer out.

'Forced,' Charlotte said. 'The bitch threatened to go to the press, to reveal the true identity of Grace's father if he didn't pay up.'

Jess took a deep breath while she hastily rearranged her 'facts'. She had a weird half-elated, half-sick feeling in the pit of her stomach. So the truth was finally coming out. 'Why didn't he just go to the police? I mean, surely it had reached the point where—'

'Why do you think?' Charlotte said. 'He'd have been a prime suspect, wouldn't he? Members of the family always are. They might have thought . . . And how much time would they have wasted on him when they could have been searching for the real killer? It would only have muddied the waters.'

Muddied the waters? Jess could hardly believe what she was hearing. Anger rose up inside her. 'I don't suppose the publicity would have done much for his career either.'

'That wasn't why—'

354

'No,' Jess snapped out. 'I'm sure it never entered his head . . . or yours. You know, it's kind of hard to figure out which is worse – a mother who uses her child that way or a man who refuses to publicly acknowledge his own daughter even after she's gone missing.'

Charlotte Meyer visibly flinched. Jess couldn't tell if she'd hit a raw nerve or if the woman was genuinely offended. Either way she could see that the shutters had come down. Jess kicked herself. What had she done? It was stupid and completely unprofessional to have reacted so emotionally. Unless she quickly built some bridges she had no chance at all of hearing the end of the story.

'I'm sorry if that sounded harsh,' Jess said, adopting a more conciliatory tone. 'I can understand that you and Paul must have been under a lot of pressure.'

As if in two minds as to whether she should walk away, Charlotte looked back along the path. Then she switched her gaze to stare at Jess. Her blue eyes were cold and impenetrable.

'It can't have been an easy decision to make,' Jess persisted. Sensing that she wasn't making much headway, she suddenly thought of something Charlotte had mentioned earlier. 'It's all too easy to pass judgement and . . . and that's what Sharon is probably counting on. If she says that Paul *offered* her the second lot of money to keep quiet then that's a far cry from blackmail. She could, theoretically, claim that she accepted it because she needed the funds to help in the search for Grace.'

'But that's not true,' Charlotte said, a dark flush spreading across her cheeks. 'For God's sake, it wasn't like that at all. She wanted the money for herself. She's just a cheap little slut.'

Not that cheap, Jess thought, recalling the cash Sharon had managed to get from him. Back then, almost thirty years ago, fifty thousand could have bought a house with plenty left over. And then she'd managed to procure another fifty grand too. Sharon certainly knew how to take advantage of a situation. Jess wondered briefly if any of the money had gone to the

Corbys but then pushed the query to the back of her mind. She didn't have time to think about that now. She had to move things on, to find out what had happened next.

'And then Tony Keppell came back for more,' Jess said. 'That must have been quite a shock. What was it – about seven years after Grace had disappeared?'

Charlotte frowned down at the ground. 'I told Paul not to pay,' she said. 'I told him it was never going to end.'

'And so he —'

'No!' she said, glaring up at Jess. 'Paul would never even have considered that. He hated violence. He abhorred the very thought of it.'

'How did Tony Keppell know about Paul's daughter?'

'*She* told him of course. I mean, we both realized who was behind it all. Tony was only a boy; he was just the messenger. Sharon had been sleeping with that gangster father of his for years.'

Jess knew that on this occasion it hadn't been down to Sharon but she nodded as if in agreement. Charlotte clearly had no idea that Grace was still alive.

'Anyway,' Charlotte continued, 'we paid, we paid for months and months but Tony just kept on asking for more until . . .'

'One day he went too far?'

'I don't know.' Charlotte turned her face away. 'I wasn't there. They had a meeting in the flat. It turned into a row. Paul was at the end of his tether. But it was an accident – I'm sure it was – Tony pulled a gun and . . .'

Jess waited a moment. 'So why didn't he mention any of this in court? If the jury had known he was being blackmailed, being *threatened*, it could have put a whole different slant on the trial.'

'I don't see how. Whatever the reason, Paul still killed him, didn't he? Nothing could ever change that.'

There was a long silence. And yet it was not quite a silence. Even after they were spoken, Charlotte's words continued to hang in the chill midday air. Jess didn't quite believe in the starkness of her statement; it was based, she suspected, more on fear and guilt than anything else. Perhaps Paul had kept quiet to protect her. If the truth had come out, Charlotte would inevitably have been implicated too. They had not just turned their backs on a child who had gone missing but had actually paid for the privilege of doing so.

Jess gazed bleakly out across the long lines of graves as she tried to figure out if any of this had brought her closer to finding out who had killed Len. Ellen had certainly been economical with the truth. But then so had her mother. And so had just about everyone else who had been involved in this whole vile charade. Over the years, the lies had piled up, one on top of another, until . . .

'Well,' Charlotte said eventually, 'I take it that you're going to drop this ridiculous idea of publishing her story now you know what she's really like.'

Jess said nothing.

Taking her lack of response as a positive sign, Charlotte smiled. 'I knew you'd see sense in the end. It's been nice to meet you, Ms Vaughan.' She glanced down at her diamond-studded watch before extending a slender white-gloved hand. 'I'm so glad we understand each other.'

Jess didn't want to touch her. It felt wrong, almost disgusting, but as it also seemed the only way of getting rid of her she reluctantly reached out and shook her hand.

'Goodbye,' Charlotte said.

'Goodbye.'

After she'd gone, Jess wandered a few yards off the main path. The snow was deeper here, almost covering her ankles. She could feel the cold seeping through her boots. Sweeping a layer of ice away, she perched down on the edge of a grave. The once-grand but now crumbling mausoleum apparently housed a Mr Herbert John Jenkins and his family. She lit another cigarette, leaned over and pulled a few skinny weeds up by their roots.

'Well, Herbert,' she murmured. 'Who says the dead can't come back to haunt you?'

Chapter Fifty-Four

Harry wasn't sure why he'd waited. By now the battered Vauxhall was the only vehicle left in the car park; even the rather grand Bentley, driven by the Lady in White, had pulled away ten minutes ago. She had not given him a second glance.

He watched as Jess came into view, trudging along the path with her shoulders hunched, her hands deep in her pockets and her head down. He couldn't tell whether this stance was down to the cold or because she was deep in thought.

Jess was only a few yards from the car when she looked up and saw him. She frowned before coming forward and opening the passenger door.

'What are you still doing here?' she said.

Harry gestured out towards the falling snow. It was coming in ever-faster flurries now, sweeping down against the windscreen. 'Do you really want to walk home in this? Anyway, I thought we had a deal – as I understood it we're supposed to be working together.'

Jess gave a sigh and then climbed into the car.

Harry was surprised. It wasn't like her to just give in. He'd expected a lot more resistance, a show of indignation at the very least, a few choice words on the subject of listening to what people told you. But none of it was forthcoming. Instead she leaned back against the seat and briefly closed her eyes.

Watching her, a small seed of dread began to take root in his guts. He had the feeling that whatever was coming next was something that he might not want to hear.

'Do you know who that was, that woman I was talking to?' she said.

Harry shook his head.

'It was Deacon's ex, Charlotte Meyer.' Jess turned her face to look at him. Her grey eyes were soft, almost pitying. 'I hate to tell you this but I think Ellen may have skipped a few essential details when you had your little chat.'

Fifteen minutes later Harry was still sitting with his hands on the wheel, gazing out across the cemetery. His head was spinning. So Ellen was Paul Deacon's daughter. So she had conspired with Tony Keppell to blackmail her own father. So her father had killed her boyfriend. And Sharon had been up to her ears in all kinds of . . . God, it all just kept on going round and round! He couldn't think straight. He wished he could just stop thinking at all.

'How did Ellen find out about her real father?' he said.

Jess shrugged. 'Through Tony, I suppose; he must have heard Jimmy talking. Or maybe Sharon told her.'

Harry remembered standing in Berry Square when the dark car had come hurtling towards them, what Ellen had told him after they'd climbed those interminable steps to her flat. He remembered their next conversation in Covent Garden, the way she had looked at him, that final kiss before . . .

'She lied to me,' he said.

'She's been lying, one way or another, for most of her life.'

Harry couldn't argue with that. He was so confused, so frustrated, that if Jess hadn't been there he'd have willingly banged his head against the wheel. The truth, it seemed, was in a constant state of flux. A part of him wanted to go straight to Camden; he needed to see Ellen face to face, to stand in front of her and demand some answers, but at the same time he knew that it was a purely emotional response. 'So what do we do next?'

Before she had the chance to answer, Jess's phone started to ring. 'Sorry, I'll switch it off.' She took it out of her bag but then noticed the caller ID and immediately lifted the phone to her ear. 'Jess Vaughan.'

It was a short conversation. Jess did more listening than speaking but eventually said, 'Do you mean right now?' There was a short pause. 'No, that's fine. I'll be there.' She glanced at her watch. 'In about fifteen minutes.'

She ended the call and looked at Harry. 'That was Joan Sewell. She's at Sharon's house. They want to see me.'

'I thought those two hated each other.'

'With a vengeance,' she said. 'Do you want to drive or shall I?'

Chapter Fifty-Five

It was a while since Harry had last visited Burnley Avenue, back when he was on the Force, and it hadn't exactly come up in the world. He parked near Sharon's house. 'I suppose I'd better stay here,' he said reluctantly. He was eager to know what the two women wanted – it had to be connected to Ellen – but didn't want to step on Jess's toes.

'Yeah, I think so,' she said. She raised a hand to her face, bit on her nails for a moment and then changed her mind. 'No, perhaps you should come in; I could do with a witness if they're about to come clean – or someone to keep them apart if they start rowing. But don't tell them you're a private eye. I'll just introduce you as a colleague.'

'They might not be prepared to talk in front of me.'

Jess gave a shrug. 'Let's see.'

As they walked up the path, Harry noticed the split running down the side of the door. 'Is that a legacy from your previous visit?'

Jess grinned at him. 'You know what I'm like; kick the door down first, ask questions later.' She rapped on the rotten wood and then took a step back.

As if someone had been waiting on the other side, there was instant movement, first the sound of a bolt being drawn and then the turn of a key in the lock. The door opened a few inches, restrained by a thick metal chain. A pair of sharp inquiring eyes peered through the narrow gap.

'Hello, Joan. It's me, Jessica Vaughan.'

There was a short pause while the door was closed again and the chain removed. When the owner of the eyes was finally revealed, Harry saw a tall gaunt woman with iron grey hair. She looked at Jess and nodded. Her gaze transferred to him. 'Who are you?'

'This is Harry Lind,' Jess said. 'He's a colleague.'

Joan's brows shifted up. 'I thought you were coming on your own.'

'I didn't say that. We're working together. That's all right, isn't it?'

Joan Sewell hesitated. While she considered the options, she kept her arm protectively across the door. Eventually, as if sensing that Jess would not be moved on the matter, she nodded and stood aside.

Harry followed Jess into the hall. His nostrils quivered. The place stank of stale cigarette smoke and old cooking. He tried not to breathe too deeply. They went along a narrow hall, passing a closed door to the right before entering the kitchen.

'I was just brewing up,' Joan said. 'Sit down and make yourselves comfortable.'

There didn't seem much hope of that, Harry thought, as he viewed the four rickety chairs gathered round the table. While Joan fussed with the kettle and teapot, he made a quick survey of the room. It was a tip, every surface littered with used cups and plates and cardboard takeaway boxes. The lino floor was scuffed and so ingrained with dirt it was impossible to tell what the original colour had been. He caught Jess's eye but she quickly looked away.

'Where's Sharon?' Jess said.

'She's just nipped out. She won't be long.' Joan gave the tea a stir, put the lid on and brought the pot to the table. Three clean mugs were placed beside it, a sugar bowl and a carton of milk. 'We'll just give it a minute to draw.'

Outside in the yard a dog whined and scratched at the door.

'Should I let him in?' Harry said.

'Best not,' Joan said. 'He isn't good with strangers.'

362

Harry didn't pursue it. He felt sorry for the mutt – it was cold out there – but he didn't much welcome the prospect of being mauled either. Knowing his luck, the dog would go straight for his leg.

Joan Sewell sat down, her spine as straight as a ramrod, and placed her hands demurely in her lap. She was the very image of respectability. Wearing a brown tweed skirt, a matching jacket and cream jumper, she looked more suitably dressed for a meeting at the Women's Institute than a conversation in this squalid kitchen. A simple string of amber beads hung around her neck. It was the only jewellery she was wearing other than the worn gold band on her finger.

'How are you?' Jess said.

'Quite well, thank you. It's kind of you to ask. How was the funeral?'

Jess looked at her, surprised. 'How did you—'

Joan tilted her head towards a copy of the local rag, lying folded on the table. 'There was a notice in the paper, dear. I like to keep up with the local news. Was there a good turnout?'

'Not bad,' Jess lied. 'It was a nice enough service.'

'I remember him of course. I remember them all from . . . from when poor Grace went missing.' She gave a small weary sigh. 'Oh yes. It's been a long time but I never forget a face.'

Harry started. Hadn't Len Curzon said exactly the same thing? *I never forget a face.* He had a flashback to sitting in The Whistle, cynically raising his eyes to the ceiling as Len peered into his beer. He'd been such a fool! He should have listened to him. He should have taken the old soak more seriously.

Joan poured out the tea. 'Help yourself to milk and sugar.' She nodded at Jess as she passed her a mug. 'It's about time we all got together and had a little chat.'

'Yes,' said Jess. 'I suppose it is.'

Harry found Joan Sewell disconcerting. There was something not quite right; her eyes were too bright, her manner almost artificially composed. The whining dog was beginning to grate on his nerves too. And then he realized what else was

363

bugging him – if Sharon had just 'nipped out' then why were there only three mugs on the table?

'Where's Sharon gone?' he said abruptly.

As if he were being deliberately rude, Jess turned and glowered at him.

But Joan Sewell wasn't offended. She put the pot down, her thin mouth slowly widening. Her glittering eyes met his. 'Well, not to heaven, Mr Lind, that's for sure.'

There was a short bemused silence.

Harry's heart gave a jolt. He hoped she didn't mean what he thought she did. He could feel his throat start to dry. 'Where is she?'

Joan didn't reply. She just continued to smile, her gaze sliding slowly sideways.

Harry pushed back the chair, stood up and walked into the hall. 'Where are you going?' he heard Jess call out. He paused for just a second before pushing open the door to his left. He knew what he'd find but it still came as a shock.

The breath stormed out of his lungs. *Oh God!*

Sharon Harper was lying on the sofa. Stretched out on her back, she might have been asleep if it hadn't been for those glazed brown eyes staring blindly up. Harry rushed forward and knelt down beside her. Pushing aside her hair, he quickly searched for a pulse. He knew, even as he went through the motions, that it was a waste of time. She'd been dead for a while. She'd been shot through the chest.

From behind, he heard Jess's swift intake of breath, followed by what might have been a stifled scream.

He took out his phone and began to dial.

'What are you doing?' Joan said.

'Calling 999.'

'It's a bit late for that.' The words were cold but not as cold as the barrel of the gun that was pushing into his temple. 'Put it down,' Joan said. 'She doesn't require an ambulance and I don't wish to talk to the police right now.'

Harry did as he was told.

Joan kept the gun pressed hard against his head. She reached out a foot and kicked the phone across the room. 'We're going back to the kitchen,' she said. She looked across at Jess. 'You want to hear the rest of the story, don't you? You want to know the truth.'

Jess's face was white. She stood, her gaze flying between Joan and Sharon, her throat making fast gulping movements as if she was trying not to throw up.

Joan took a few steps back. 'Stand up,' she said to Harry.

He stared at the gun in her hand. It was a small Glock pistol. Where the hell had she got that? He stood up slowly.

'The kitchen,' she repeated.

Jess went first, stumbling as she left the room. Harry walked behind her. He wondered if he should take a chance; he was taller and stronger than Joan Sewell. If he swung around fast enough he could probably disarm her . . . But what if he got his timing wrong? She was smart enough to be keeping her distance. All it would take was one slight squeeze on the trigger and . . .

He had waited too long. The opportunity, had it ever been present, had now passed.

'Sit together on the far side of the table,' she ordered.

Joan pulled out the chair opposite. She kept the Glock pointed at Harry. It was beginning to shake a little. He suspected that was more down to the strain of holding it than to any real anxiety. She had murdered once and from the cold expression on her face would not hesitate to do so again.

Joan laid the gun down on the table but kept her finger on the trigger. The barrel was pointed straight at Harry's abdomen. 'Please don't do anything stupid,' she said. 'I might be old but I'm not incompetent.'

Harry nodded. The proof of that statement was lying in the room next door. His heart was still pumping. Had she lured Jess here to kill her too? No wonder she'd been less than pleased to see she hadn't come alone. And now she had two people to get rid of instead of one. What he needed was a plan

of action. Did he have one? No. In that case the only alternative was to play for time.

'We're not the only ones who know about Grace,' he said.
'If we don't report back to the office, people are going to come
looking for us.'

Joan ignored him. The threat, had it even registered on her
consciousness, appeared to have no impact. She directed what
she had to say at Jess. 'I guessed what you were up to on that
day you came to see me. I could have sent you packing but I
wanted to find out how much you knew.'

Jess stared back. Still almost paralysed with shock, she was
making a valiant attempt to pull herself together. 'I didn't
know anything.'

'No,' Joan said. 'But you had your suspicions. You thought
Grace might still be alive even if you didn't have the proof.'

'When did *you* find out?'

'About a year ago.'

'How?' Jess said.

For the first time Joan produced what could almost be
described as a genuine smile. 'I saw her coming out of the
cemetery. It was raining, pouring down; she had an umbrella
up and she walked straight past me. I only caught a glimpse
of her face but that's all it took. Apart from the hair, she
looked just like Sharon had at her age. Like two peas in a pod.'

'Why didn't you stop her?' Jess said. 'Why didn't you say
anything?'

'I was too . . . too shocked, too confused. I thought it was
her but . . . how could it be? It wasn't until I got to Michael's
grave, until I saw the flowers on it, that I was certain. I was
the only one who ever went there. By then it was too late.
She'd already gone.'

'And then?' Jess said.

'And then I came round to see Sharon.' Joan gave a small
high-pitched laugh. 'She told me I was mad, that I'd been seeing things. She told me I was crazy. She said that Grace was
dead. But I knew she was lying – it was in her eyes. I could
see the fear in her eyes.'

'You had a row,' Jess said. 'The police were called.'

Harry glanced at her. It was the first he'd heard about it.

'She'd lied to me,' Joan said. 'She'd let me go on grieving for all those years. What kind of a woman could pretend that her own child was dead? She let everyone think that Michael was responsible, that he might have . . . Do you have any idea how many times my brother was interviewed by the police? Do you know what it's like to have the finger of suspicion pointed at you, day in, day out, for months on end? She killed him. That bitch killed him with her lies!'

Harry was tempted to respond that if it hadn't been for Michael Harper Grace would never have had to be hidden in the first place, but wisely kept the comment to himself. He wondered why Ellen had left the flowers: A gesture of forgiveness perhaps?

'Sharon had to be punished. It's only right.'

'The Law could have punished her,' Harry said sharply. 'Why didn't you go to the police?'

Joan's eyes narrowed into slits. 'The police,' she repeated contemptuously. 'What would they have done?'

'They could have—'

Jess kicked her foot against his ankle. 'I can understand,' she said sympathetically. 'They made a lot of mistakes.' She threw Harry a warning glance as if to tell him to shut his mouth. 'They got it all wrong about Michael. They didn't have a clue, did they? I don't suppose they treated you or Francis too well either.'

'Francis didn't understand what was going on. He was only a boy but the police would have blamed him too if they could have got away with it.' While she spoke, Joan continued to glare at Harry, her thumb gently stroking the handle of the Glock. It was apparent that she hadn't exactly taken to him. She was toying, perhaps, with the idea of closing his mouth on a more permanent basis.

'How terrible,' Jess said. 'It must have been hard for him – hard for *all* of you.' Her voice sounded croaky. She paused, her eyes fixed on the gun, before clearing her throat. 'So what did you do next?'

Harry released his breath as Joan's attention finally returned to Jess. He slowly unclenched his buttocks. Just for a moment there his bowels had become worryingly loose.

'I waited. I was patient.' She gave another of her thin, slightly hysterical laughs. 'I'd already waited twenty years; a little longer wasn't going to make much difference. Sharon had to be in contact with her. Oh, I knew she'd keep her distance for a while – after seeing me, she'd have warned Grace off – but it was only a matter of time.'

'And eventually you saw them together?'

Joan nodded. 'About six weeks ago. They met in a café in Camden. I followed Grace back to Berry Square.'

'But you didn't approach her?'

'No.'

'Why not?' Jess said.

'I needed to think, to decide what to do. I didn't want to scare her off. I didn't want her to disappear again. Once I knew where she lived, there wasn't any hurry.'

Harry kept very still while he listened to the exchange between the two of them. Jess was doing a pretty good job of keeping Joan Sewell talking. He wasn't sure if this was a delaying tactic or if she had a different agenda; perhaps she was simply intent on hearing the rest of the story.

'Why do you think Sharon hid Grace away in the first place?' Jess said.

Joan's mouth twisted into an ugly grimace. 'It's obvious, isn't it? She hated Michael, wanted to hurt him, destroy him. She always was the vindictive sort. She took away the one thing, the only thing he ever really loved; she took away his baby girl and then tried to suggest that he might have killed her.'

Jesus, Harry thought, the woman was truly deranged. 'Couldn't she just have divorced him?'

Jess threw him another of her glowering looks.

But Joan's expression was more pitying than angry. She spoke as if she was in the company of a particularly slow individual. 'What you have to understand, Mr Lind, is that Sharon didn't want Grace – she'd never really wanted her – but she couldn't bear Michael to have her either. This way she could get rid of her child and her husband and still have the public's sympathy. It put her exactly where she wanted to be – right at the centre of everyone's attention.'

'I see,' Harry said cautiously.

Before he could say anything even slightly less cautious, Jess swiftly intervened again. 'So you've just been waiting?'

'And thinking,' Joan said.

'Have you been back to Berry Square?'

'Of course,' Joan said. 'I've been watching over her. Someone had to protect the poor girl. None of this is her fault.'

Harry glanced down at the table. It was light and flimsy and, if his right leg had been in better shape, he would have had the confidence to bring his knee up hard and fast and tip it over. He could still, possibly, use his left leg. However, it was also possible that if he got it wrong the gun would go off and, depending on the trajectory, send a bullet straight through his head.

'Did you see anyone else there?' Jess said.

Joan's face grew dark. Her voice grew harder too. 'If you're referring to your friend then yes, I saw him. Len Curzon was hanging around, all hours of the day and night. That filthy little hack just couldn't stay away. I knew what he was up to. He'd made Michael's life a misery and he was going to do the same to Grace. That's why I had to help her.'

'Help her?' Jess repeated hoarsely.

'What choice did I have? He knew who she was. He was going to ruin her life, splash her all over the papers again. I saw him talking to her that morning. I saw how scared she was.'

Jess leaned forward, her eyes blazing. 'It was you,' she said. 'You killed him!'

Joan didn't deny it. She didn't even bother to try.

Harry sensed the time for talk was over. Jess was enraged and Joan Sewell's fingers were starting to twitch. Resorting to the most basic of techniques, he glanced towards the kitchen door and widened his eyes.

As Joan instinctively turned her head, he forced his left knee up against the underside of the table and sent the whole lot, cups and all, flying towards her. The next few seconds were a frantic noisy blur. As she fell back the gun went off, shattering the kitchen window. Jess screamed. Harry felt blood on his face. Outside the dog went ballistic, clawing at the door.

Had he been hit? Had Jess? He didn't know. All he did know was that the gun was still in Joan's possession. Launching himself round the side of the overturned table, he scrabbled on his hands and knees, reaching for her hand. Bits of broken crockery cut into his palms. Joan struck out at him. Even crumpled on the floor, she wasn't giving up without a fight. Her legs were trapped but her arms were free. She tried to twist, to point the Glock towards his chest. He reached out and slammed her wrist against the floor. It took a moment, a seemingly eternal moment, to wrestle the gun from her.

Harry finally grabbed it and breathed freely again. Joan lay back and groaned. It was a long low despairing sound. Slowly he got to his feet and looked over at Jess. She was still sitting on the chair. Her face was white and her left hand was clutched to her right shoulder. Blood was leaking between her fingers.

He rushed over to her. 'Jess! Christ, you've been shot.'

'It's not too bad. It only winged me.'

'Let me help.'

Jess shook her head. 'I'm okay. I'm fine.' She managed a shaky grin. 'But if you've finished playing Action Man perhaps you could do something useful and call for an ambulance.'

Chapter Fifty-Six

It was three days since Harry had stared down the barrel of the Glock and wondered if his time was up. He was still unsure as to whether Joan Sewell had intended to kill them. Maybe she had simply chosen Jess as the person she was going to confess to. Personally, it wasn't a risk he'd been prepared to take but then again he wasn't the one who'd ended up with a bullet through his arm.

Thankfully, Jess was okay. It shouldn't take too long for the wound to heal although she'd be doing more dictating than typing over the next few weeks. At least she'd got her headline story, a scoop that should send her career into orbit. That made him feel slightly less guilty about it all.

Harry parked the car and walked slowly into the foyer. According to Val, Sewell had freely admitted her guilt. Bent on vengeance, she'd gone round to Sharon's house; it was time, Joan had claimed, for her to pay for what she'd done. She had been adamant, however, that the gun wasn't hers. It was Sharon, realizing her intent, who had suddenly produced the Glock. There had been a brief struggle and what Joan had lacked in strength she had made up for in sobriety. Sharon had been drunk and unsteady on her feet. The gun had gone off and . . . well, he knew the rest.

Harry switched his thoughts to Valerie. Things were no better on the relationship front. She had been less than impressed by his disarming of a double murderer (albeit one of almost pensionable age) or his discovery of yet another corpse. It probably hadn't helped that he'd been in the presence of Jessica Vaughan again.

Later, he'd had the pleasure of being interviewed by Frankie Holt and a new DCI called Ian Jenkins. Holt had been his usual charming self, determined to find some way of screwing him over. Harry couldn't work out why Frankie detested him so much. They had never been friends exactly but had worked together, in reasonable harmony, for the three years before Harry was caught in the crack-factory blast. From that point on, Holt's attitude had changed. Perhaps working on the premise that bad luck was contagious he had not even bothered to visit him in hospital.

Apart from the dubious accusation of withholding evidence, there wasn't much else Holt could hang on him. Even the 'withholding evidence' angle was tenuous. Okay, so he had discovered on Saturday afternoon that Grace Harper was still alive but bearing in mind the circumstances he could hardly be blamed for not rushing down the station.

'She walked straight out in front of a car. She wasn't in a fit state to talk to anyone. It seemed only fair to give her a few days.'

'Yeah,' Holt had replied, 'a few days to pack up her stuff and get the hell out of here.'

Harry could remember the sinking sensation in the pit of his stomach. His mouth had gone dry. 'She's gone?'

'Of course she's fucking gone,' Holt had sneered. 'What did you think she was going to do – sit around and wait for the cops to arrive?'

That Ellen Shaw was actually a victim rather than a perpetrator in this whole stinking mess was a concept that Frankie seemed unable to grasp. Just the fact that Ellen had been living under a false identity for the past twenty years was enough to make him want to bang her up and throw away the key.

Fortunately DCI Jenkins had a less judgemental attitude. They had taken a break and Jenkins had returned ten minutes later minus Frankie Holt but with a more sympathetic DC and a lukewarm plastic cup of coffee. The exchange had been a welcome one. Harry had gone on to answer most of their questions but, careful to try and protect Jess, had kept some of his answers deliberately vague. What *she* chose to reveal was up to her.

Harry went up in the lift, stepped out and waited for a moment in the corridor. Where had Ellen gone? It was a question he was unlikely to get an answer to. Wherever she was, she was with Adam. The Berry Square flat had been rented and the two of them had packed up their belongings and, according to the neighbours, left on the Sunday afternoon. The police had publicly expressed a wish to talk to her but with Sharon Harper dead and Joan Sewell safely locked up it was doubtful they would search that hard.

He pushed open the doors and went into the office.

Lorna glanced at him from behind the desk and then stood up, her blue eyes wide and accusing. 'Why didn't you tell me?'

Harry stopped dead in his tracks. Oh God, had she found out what had happened on Friday night? Had she heard about the drunken party at Zane Keppell's house? One of the details he had omitted during the interview was Maddie Green's identification of the photo of Grace. He could only hope that Jess had done the same. Having a gun thrust against your temple seemed suddenly inconsequential compared to what an angry mother could do to you.

'I'm sorry?' he muttered.

'You could have been killed!' she said. 'We were all worried sick when we heard. Why didn't you call?'

A sigh of relief escaped from Harry's lips. 'Oh, sorry. I was stuck down the station for hours. I did try and call Mac yesterday but—'

'You sit down,' Lorna said, fussing round, 'and I'll get you a coffee. Mac's out at a meeting but you can tell me all about it.'

It was Warren James who rescued him from yet another cross-examination. Strolling in, he must have noticed Harry's look of anguish. While Lorna's back was turned he gave him a wink and said, 'Hey, good to see you again. If you're not too busy could I have a quick word? It is kind of urgent. It's about the Westwood case.'

'Sure,' Harry said. 'Glad to help.'

'The paperwork's in the other office.'

Harry took the coffee from Lorna. 'Thanks,' he said to her. 'I've just got to deal with this and then I'll be back.'

'You should be taking it easy,' Lorna said.

'I will. I am. Don't worry. We'll catch up later, okay?'

Escaping to the corridor, Harry nodded at Warren. 'Thanks for that.'

'No problem,' Warren said. 'I know Lorna means well but she can be a bit . . . well . . .'

'Over-protective?'

'Yeah,' Warren laughed. 'I guess that's one way of putting it.'

They walked a short distance along the hall to what was spuriously referred to as the 'other office' but which was in reality no more than an oversized storage cupboard with only one small window near the ceiling. The carpet was grey, the walls a slightly grubby shade of white. A formica-topped desk, currently occupied by three computers, and a couple of swivel chairs took up most of the available room.

Harry sat down. 'You must go crazy working in here.'

'I've known worse,' Warren said. 'And at least there are no distractions. It's a good place to come if you want some peace and quiet.'

'So how *is* the Westwood case going?'

'It isn't,' Warren said. 'He'll get away with it. Half the time there's no one at the house. Mac hadn't got the manpower to keep the surveillance going.'

That wasn't good news. Harry glanced down at the desk. To his left there was a newspaper open at the jobs page. In the computer section a few of the vacancies had been circled with a red ballpoint pen. He reached out and pulled the paper towards him. 'What's with the job hunt? You planning on moving on?'

374

Warren looked uncomfortable. He frowned, sat back in his chair and shrugged. 'Just considering the options. I've got a kid to support. I've also got a millstone of a mortgage. I can't afford to hang about. Once the ship starts to sink, you either jump or you go down with it.'

'You think things are that bad?'

'Bad enough.'

Harry gave a groan. He really should have had that chat with Mac. As his gaze slid down the Situations Vacant column, he began to wonder what kind of future he might be facing. Not a very bright one judging from what was currently on offer.

'There's a rumour going round,' Warren said.

Harry glanced up.

'I'm not claiming that it's true,' Warren said. 'It's only what I've heard.'

'Go on.'

'People are saying Mac's got gambling debts – big ones.'

'You're kidding, right?' Harry's initial reaction was to laugh but then he grew more serious. Mac had always had a fondness for poker; it had got him into trouble on more than one occasion. 'Shit,' he murmured. 'And are people saying *who* he owes the money to?'

Warren pulled a face. 'You're not going to like it.'

'Tell me anyway.'

'Ray Stagg.'

Harry gave another groan. Suddenly it all made sense: why Mac had taken Stagg on as a client, why he'd given the case priority, why he'd been so keen for Harry to find Al. Doubtless, Stagg had been putting the pressure on. No wonder he'd looked so smug when Harry had first gone to see him. He jumped to his feet. 'I need to talk to him.'

'You'll be lucky. He hasn't been in since Friday.'

'Lorna said he was in a meeting.'

Warren raised his brows. 'Lorna says what she's told to say.'

'Sod it,' Harry said. 'I'll go over to his flat then.' If Mac had reverted to his former ways, he'd probably be drowning his sorrows in a bottle of whisky. He was about to leave when his phone started ringing.

It was Snakey Harris.

'Just wanted to check that the car was running smoothly, Mr Lind.'

Snakey had returned the Audi yesterday morning minus all its dents and looking good as new. 'Thanks. Yes. Like a dream.'

There was a short pause. 'And are you still searching for that white van?'

Harry's fingers tightened round the phone. He'd forgotten all about giving him the registration. 'Absolutely,' he said. 'You haven't found it, have you?'

'Masey Street,' Snakey said, trying not to sound too triumphant. 'Number nineteen. It's in the drive.'

'Are you sure?'

'Yeah,' Snakey said. 'I put the word out – on the quiet, mind – and asked a few people to keep their eyes peeled. Old Teddy Duxton spotted it last night. It's parked right in front of the house but there's a big hedge so you can't see it from the road.'

Quite what Teddy Duxton, an elderly small-time offender with a penchant for 'peeping', had been doing loitering behind a hedge in Stoke Newington was a question Harry preferred not to ask. At this precise moment he didn't give a damn. 'You're a star, Snakey. I owe you one.'

'My pleasure, Mr Lind.'

Harry hung up and put the phone back in his pocket.

'Good news?' Warren said.

'Could be. I hope so. I just got an address for where Al Webster could be hiding out.'

'You going there now?'

'You bet,' Harry said. He was halfway out of the door when he looked back and said, 'You want to come along?'

Warren grabbed his jacket off the back of the chair. 'I'm right behind you.'

A few minutes later they were down in the car park. As they

approached the Audi Harry felt that prickling sensation on the back of his neck again. He glanced around but there was no one there. What was wrong with him? He must be getting paranoid. Shaking his head, he unlocked the doors and climbed into the driver's seat.

Chapter Fifty-Seven

Masey Street was on the edge of Stoke Newington and Newington Green, just beyond the boundaries of where Harry and Jess had conducted their unofficial door-to-door inquiries after Agnes had disappeared. Number nineteen was a large detached house. Although once a sturdy and desirable property the building was now crumbling, its outer structure neglected, its interior divided into too many shabby flats and bedsits.

Harry peered through the snow-covered windscreen. Warren tapped his fingertips against his thigh. After having checked out that it actually was Al's van sitting in the drive, they'd been parked up for the past three hours, watching as the afternoon slowly faded into darkness. There had been no movement, in or out, since they'd arrived although a few lights had gone on in the house.

Harry had spent some of the time explaining the details of the case. For the rest of it, he'd had his mind on other things. He couldn't get Ellen out of his head. There were people you met, who you made a connection with, who were just too hard to let go of. Ellen Shaw was one of those people. She'd got under his skin and he couldn't stop thinking about her.

He looked at his watch. It was almost six o'clock. They could either sit tight and hope for a break – the kind of break where someone might decide to venture out for a pint of milk – or take matters into their own hands. Harry opted for the latter. He was too impatient, too frustrated, to wait any longer.

The only problem now was finding out which flat they were actually holed up in.

'Got any ideas?' Warren said.

'Only the one.'

Five minutes later Warren approached the house with the evening paper under his arm. He started pressing each of the bells in turn. There was no response to his first three attempts but after the fourth ring the door was answered by a tall skinny guy with wet hair and a towel around his shoulders.

'Yeah?'

'I'm here about the van.'

'What?'

Warren glanced over his shoulder. 'It is for sale, isn't it?'

'Dunno, mate.'

'It's in the paper,' Warren said, thrusting it under his nose. 'I rang earlier. I was told six o'clock.'

'I don't know anything about it.'

Warren added a peevish note to his tone. 'Shit, man. I've come all the way from Balham. Are you telling me I've had a wasted journey?'

'It's not *my* van,' the guy said defensively. 'Didn't you get a name?'

'I didn't catch it,' Warren said. 'It was a woman with an accent. This was the address she gave me.'

The guy frowned while he thought about it. 'Well, it's not Sarah, that's for sure, and it's not . . . I guess you could try the basement. There's a foreign girl living there.'

Warren looked at the bank of bells. 'Which one is that?'

'Not here,' the guy said, flapping a hand as if eager to get rid of him. 'Round the side and down the steps.'

'Right,' Warren said. Before he could make any further comment the door was swiftly closed in his face.

He went back to the car and passed on the good news.

'Okay,' Harry said. 'I've got an idea.'

Warren listened carefully to the plan. 'You sure about this?'

'Yeah, it's the only way. You take the motor and I'll see you later.'

After checking that there was no other exit, Harry walked back round to the side of the house and gazed down the flight of stone steps that led to the basement. There was a light on but the curtains were tightly closed. He moved quietly down the steps and stood for a while listening at the door. The TV was on, the evening news clearly audible.

Harry knocked gently.

No one answered.

He tried again, a little louder. This time there was definite movement from inside before the TV was abruptly turned off. But still no one came to the door. Harry leaned in close. 'Agnes? Are you there? It's Harry, Harry Lind.'

Silence.

'Agnes?'

Harry waited a moment before he quickly rapped his knuckles against the door again. 'Agnes? Come on. You either talk to me right now or you'll be spending the rest of the evening down the cop shop. I've got the phone in my hand. I'm going to give you ten seconds and then—'

The door finally opened a few inches. Agnes peered out, looking about as scared as anyone could look.

'It's all right,' Harry said. 'I'm alone. Can I come in?'

She thought about it and then, resigned to the fact she had no other option, opened the door fully and stood aside.

Inside, the flat's proportions were what estate agents would describe as 'compact'. The living room, incorporating a tiny kitchen area, was about twelve foot square and had the distinctive smell of damp. A half-open door to the right revealed a shower cubicle and toilet and a closed door to the left presumably led to the bedroom. There were a couple of lamps, a small table with two folding chairs and a scattering of house plants. But what really drew Harry's attention was a heap of blankets lying neatly folded on the old green sofa.

He turned to Agnes. 'You should have called me back,' he said. 'I wanted to help.'

'I wish to but . . . but am too afraid.'

'Because of what happened to Troy?'

At the mention of his name, Agnes slumped down on the sofa and covered her mouth with her hand. She looked like she was going to cry. 'What they do is very bad.'

Harry, recalling the state of Troy's battered body, nodded. 'Yes, very bad.' He picked up the blankets, placed them carefully on the floor and sat down beside her.

'You want to explain what happened?' he said gently. 'You want to tell me about it?'

Agnes hesitated, in two minds perhaps as to how much she should reveal, and then it all came tumbling out.

'Everyone talk about Al at Vista – he do something wrong, in big trouble. Troy, he look at me and guess. He think I know where Al is gone to. Every day he say: Where is he, where is he? He never stop.' She flung her hands out. 'I think he is my friend but then am not so sure. He say people very angry and they hurt me bad. Troy say he help but I think not. I hear him talk on phone. He wants the money off these men. He promise to tell where Al hides. And later I see the men come.'

'How many men?' Harry said.

'Four,' she said. She gave a shiver. 'All big, very strong.'

'Would you recognize them again?'

Agnes shook her head. 'Outside,' she said. 'In car park. I not see clear. I watch from window but is very dark.'

Harry had the feeling that she wouldn't identify them even if she was able to. She would be too terrified to act as a witness. 'And then?'

'They talk to Troy . . . I call you, yes, on phone? I very afraid. I think Troy tell them of me. I – I see them hit hard and Troy fall to ground. I do not know what to do so . . . so I go, leave fast. I stop taxi and come to flat.'

'And you've been here ever since?' Harry said.

381

Agnes gave a shrug before leaning forward and covering her face with her hands. Her voice was thin and shaky. 'Where else?'

Harry nodded. This explained why Troy had been less than welcoming on the few occasions that they'd met; he must have hoped that a painful encounter with a baseball bat would be enough to put him off his search for Al. With rumours of a generous reward on offer from Keppell, Troy wouldn't have wanted anyone else muscling in on the action. But then he had made a fatal mistake. Concerned perhaps that someone else might secure the money before he could, he had moved too soon, calling Jimmy and claiming that he knew more than he did. And Jimmy Keppell wouldn't have been in the mood for time-wasters. So when Troy hadn't been able to come up with the goods . . .

'If only I stay,' she murmured. 'If only . . .' She was crying now, her shoulders gently heaving.

'Troy made his own choices,' he said. 'If you'd stayed, you'd probably be dead too.'

The only thing Harry couldn't figure out was why she and Al hadn't done a runner. What were they doing still holed up in this dingy place? With a van full of drugs they could have been miles away by now – not just out of London but out of the country. It didn't make any sense. There was only one way of finding out the whole truth.

While Agnes still had her face in her hands, he stood up and softly crossed the room. Quickly he pushed open the bedroom door. 'Would you care to join us?'

There was a short pause before Al eventually accepted the invitation. He shambled out looking tired and dishevelled. Gone was the rosy-cheeked family man with the happy smile; he was in need of a shave and his eyes were bloodshot.

'You're a cop, right?' he said. He sounded almost relieved about it.

Harry shook his head. 'Private investigator. Your wife hired me.' It wasn't quite the truth but it would do for now.

Al sat down in a chair by the table, leaned forward and put his hands between his knees. He rocked gently back and forth for a few seconds. 'How is she?'

'Worried sick. Why did you do it, Al?'

Al's only response was a low pained moan.

'Is my fault,' Agnes whispered through her tears. 'Is all my fault.'

'It was your idea?' Harry said, turning towards her. He was still finding it hard to comprehend how these two had ever managed to strike up a conversation, never mind plan a drugs robbery. It must have been down to the money because whatever bound them now had nothing to do with sex; their relationship, judging from the blankets he had lifted from the sofa, was purely platonic.

'An accident,' she said.

That was one way of putting it. Harry raised his brows but Agnes didn't elaborate. He glanced towards Al who was staring determinedly down at the brown frayed carpet. 'Your brother-in-law isn't too happy with you either.'

Surprisingly, Al didn't seem too alarmed by this piece of information. 'He wouldn't give a toss if he never saw me again.'

'That could be true but he's still less than pleased that you waltzed off with his property.'

Al looked up, frowning. 'His . . .?' Then his forehead suddenly cleared. 'Oh, *that*. Christ, Ray always was a tightwad. It's hardly going to break the bank, is it?'

Now it was Harry's turn to look confused. 'What do you mean?'

Al shrugged. 'It's only a few lousy cases of vodka.'

Harry stared at him. Was Al being deliberately dense, playing some kind of game? No, he didn't have the brains for it. Which could only mean that . . .

Agnes wiped her eyes with the back of her hand. 'He come from nowhere. He step out in front, right in front of van.'

'Shit!' Harry murmured. The truth was finally dawning on him. The two of them didn't have a clue what was hidden in those cases. Al's disappearing trick had been down to something else entirely. 'Are we talking hit-and-run here?'

Al's intake of breath was followed by a long despairing sigh. His scared exhausted gaze met Harry's. 'He's dead,' he said softly. 'I killed him.'

Harry expelled a resounding sigh of his own. He remembered his phone call to Valerie, the day she'd told him about the gangland murder in Hackney; she had mentioned a hit-and-run then but he had not made the connection. There had been too many other things on his mind. He tried to keep his voice calm. 'Okay,' he said. 'You want to tell me about it?'

Al made a vague movement of his head that might have been a nod. He opened his mouth but no words came out. Then, as if trying to scrub the guilt from his skin, he began to rub at his face with his hands. He was a man on the edge, close to breaking point.

Harry decided to help him along. 'It was a Saturday evening. You'd spent the day on the market and then Ray called. You were to go to Tommy Lake's lock-up, collect some booze and take it to Vista. You got through the first part okay but somehow you never made it to the club. After you left Tommo—'

Al finally picked up on the narrative. 'I – I drove down through Dalston. Agnes was standing at the bus stop. I knew she must be on her way to work so I stopped and asked if she wanted a lift.' As if his offer could be all too easily misconstrued, a dark blush rose to his cheeks. His hands fluttered to his face again. 'I wasn't . . . I mean, I was just being friendly. There wasn't much point in her waiting around for a bus when we were both headed in the same direction.'

'Absolutely,' Harry said. 'I understand.'

Al swallowed hard before continuing. 'The traffic was pretty heavy, all jammed up, so I took a shortcut through the back streets. We were almost there when—'

'Is all because of me,' Agnes interrupted. 'I talk, show pictures on phone – you know, pictures of girls at club. We laugh and . . .'

Harry could see how that might have been a little distracting. 'And then?'

'He just appeared,' Al said. 'There were cars parked on either side of the street. It was dark. He came out of nowhere. He just walked out and . . .' He bit down hard on his knuckles. 'I didn't see him.'

'Did you stop?'

Al's head jerked up. 'Yes, I stopped. Of course I stopped. He was lying in the road. I got out of the van and went to look but . . . but he wasn't moving. He wasn't breathing. His eyes were open and there was blood coming from his mouth. I should have called an ambulance. I should have called the cops. I know I should, but—'

'You panicked,' Harry said.

'I could see he was dead. I didn't know what to do.'

Harry thought of everything that had happened since, of the two other deaths, of the two brutal murders that had stemmed from this single accidental killing. His stomach turned over.

Harry's gaze swung from Al to Agnes. 'And so you came back here.'

She nodded. 'I stay for while and then go to work. I get there late and Troy, he notice it. I say the buses bad but he not believe. This is why, later, he think I know about Al.'

Harry was still trying to slot the final pieces into place. 'So what about the vodka?'

Al looked bemused. He had just confessed to running a man over and Harry was stressing over some knocked-off bottles of booze. 'What?'

'The boxes you picked up from Tommo. Where are they now?'

'Where they've always been – in the back of the van.'

Harry laughed. It was a knee-jerk, slightly manic response. He couldn't help contemplating all the local junkies, the

385

dealers, the punks who must have walked past that hedge over the past few weeks completely oblivious to what was lying on the other side. And then he thought of something else. 'What about the bag? Denise said that you took an overnight bag from the wardrobe.'

Al frowned.

'A black Nike holdall,' Harry said.

'Oh yeah, that. The zip broke on mine so I grabbed that one instead. I had some CDs I needed to take to the stall.'

Harry raised his eyes to the ceiling. All it had taken was one false clue to convince him that Al was guilty of a premeditated crime. Had it not been for that single piece of 'evidence', he might not have jumped so readily to any of the more obvious conclusions. Al Webster had experienced a crisis all right but it hadn't been of the mid-life variety.

'So what was the plan?' Harry said. He glanced around the room. 'Or were you intending to hide out here forever?'

It was clear from Al's expression that nothing as solid as a plan had even begun to take form. From the moment of the accident panic must have replaced any logical thought. Harry turned his attention back to Agnes.

'Is that why you thought I was looking for him, because of the accident?'

She gave a nod. 'Troy say people unhappy with Al. I think they are friends, yes, of this poor man who died. I think they wish to hurt him.'

'And no one mentioned drugs to you?'

Agnes stared at him, puzzled. 'What is to do with drugs?'

Harry was about to start explaining when a slight noise, not much more than a scrape, came from outside. His ears pricked up. There was someone on the steps. He was halfway to his feet when the door suddenly burst open. An oversized goon, wielding a sawn-off, came hurtling into the room.

'Don't move!' he yelled. 'Nobody move!'

Harry, caught in the unfortunate position of being almost upright, was unable to curb the rest of the movement. As he

386

straightened up, the guy – hyped up on adrenalin or maybe something less natural – must have perceived him as a threat. Instead of shooting, however, he swung the gun smartly towards Harry's head, catching him hard across the jaw. His knees buckled and he crumpled to the floor.

Chapter Fifty-Eight

By the time Harry managed to look up again, everything was hazy. His brains were still rocking. He gently shook his head. It was a mistake. Even that careful movement had the effect of substantially increasing the pain in his jaw. One thing was clear however – he was staring straight down the barrel of a shotgun. The owner of the weapon, an ugly-looking bloke even in soft focus, was standing over him with a sneer on his face.

There was an eerie silence in the room, one of those ominous post-cataclysmic sort of silences, as if the whole world was holding its breath. Harry squinted. To his left he was faintly aware of Agnes curled up on the sofa. Opposite, Al was sitting rigidly, his hands on his knees, his eyes unblinking and his mouth wide open. He looked like one of those victims of Pompeii, caught in burning hot ash with their forms preserved forever.

All of these impressions were garnered in a matter of seconds. Harry found himself staring at the shotgun again. He wondered if he was about to die. Oddly, he didn't feel as bothered as he thought he should. Perhaps it was because this whole scenario seemed not just familiar – it wasn't that long since Joan Sewell had been waving a pistol at him – but almost inevitable, a natural finale to everything else that had gone on recently.

And then a familiar mocking voice cut through the silence. 'For heaven's sake, Rizzer, hasn't anyone ever told you that it's bad form to slug a man with a limp?'

The pug-faced goon gave a snigger before stepping aside.

388

'Hello, Harry,' Ray Stagg said.

Harry gazed up at him and groaned. 'I'd like to say it was a pleasure to see you again but—'

'Yeah,' Stagg said. 'It's mutual but thanks for leading us here. I'm very grateful.' He tilted his head towards Al. 'It's always good to catch up with family.'

Al's blank brown eyes didn't flicker. There was no response at all. His body remained perfectly still, his gaze fixed. It was hard to tell if he was even aware of Ray's presence.

'You've been following me,' Harry said.

Stagg grinned. 'Sweet of you to notice . . . but a bit late, don't you think? I heard you private dicks were supposed to have an instinct for that kind of thing.'

Harry rubbed at his jaw. It hurt when he spoke but at least he could still speak. 'It comes and goes.'

Stagg glanced at Agnes, sighed, and looked back at Harry. 'Well, this is nice,' he said. 'All of us here together. Quite a reunion.'

A small strangled sob escaped from her throat. Harry hoped she was too scared to move; he didn't fancy her chances if she tried to make a run for it.

'Okay,' Stagg said. 'Now, you know what I want. We can either—'

'It's in the van,' Harry said.

'What?'

'What you're after is in the back of the van.'

'Don't fuck me about,' Stagg said. Unable to accept that anything could be that simple, he glanced towards the goon who was obviously able and more than willing to blow Harry's brains out. 'I haven't got the time or the patience.'

'It's all there,' Harry said. 'You want me to show you?'

'You're lying.'

'Fine,' Harry said. 'Believe what you like.'

As if he'd been looking forward to beating the information out of him, Stagg seemed disappointed. His upper lip curled into a snarl. 'So where are the keys?'

Still in a state of shock and apparently struck deaf and dumb, Al continued to stare straight ahead. Harry looked at Agnes and nodded. She didn't say anything but a trembling hand eventually rose to point towards the shelf above the television.

Ray walked over and picked the keys up. He gave a laugh, threw them into the air and caught them again. He glared at Harry. 'This had better not be a wind-up.'

'It isn't.'

'So let's go take a look,' he said. 'Just you and me.' His cool blue eyes narrowed. 'And while we're gone my friend Rizzer here will make sure no one gets any stupid ideas.'

Harry got the message. He stumbled to his feet. The pain in his jaw had become a dull steady throb.

'Hold on,' Stagg said. 'Hold it right there and spread your arms.'

Harry did as he told, waiting while Stagg quickly patted him down. When he was sure that he wasn't carrying, Stagg stood back and grunted. 'Okay,' he said. 'You go first.'

Slowly Harry preceded him out of the door. The chill night air slapped against his face; if nothing else it had the useful effect of waking him up. He climbed the eight stone steps and then limped round to the front where the white van was parked. It was dark but not too dark to see. There were street-lamps beyond the hedge and a thin lemon glow escaped from the windows of the house.

'So what's the catch?' Stagg said.

'There isn't one,' Harry said. 'What you want is right here. It always has been. Al never intended to rip you off.'

'Like hell he didn't.'

'So why isn't he miles away by now? He's had the time and more. What's he doing cowering in some shabby London basement when he could be getting sunburn, peeling the skin off his nose and sipping cocktails in the Caribbean?'

Ray Stagg gave a derisory snort. 'Because he bottled it,' he said. 'Because he's a bloody moron.'

'No,' Harry said. 'He had an accident. He ran a guy over.'

390

Stagg didn't look convinced. He didn't look too interested either. They were standing by the back doors to the van. Ray pushed the keys into his hand. 'You open up.'

While he fiddled with the lock, Harry considered his options. He wasn't sure if Stagg was armed or not. Probably not. On a purely sartorial level he wouldn't want to spoil the elegant line of his expensive silk suit and on a more practical one it was doubtful that he'd take the chance of being caught in possession of a firearm. Ray left that kind of responsibility to his mindless minions. He could possibly take him out but if Rizzer got even a hint that something was wrong he was liable to start shooting.

Harry opened the doors and stood back. He watched as Stagg leaned over, grabbed one of the boxes and pulled it towards him. He removed a couple of vodka bottles and peered inside. Lifting out a bag, he stared at it and then quickly slashed it open with a penknife. He dipped a finger inside and licked it with his tongue. 'Well, fuck me.'

'It's like I told you,' Harry said.

Stagg grinned. 'I always suspected you might be an honest man.' He delivered the statement as if it was an insult.

'So what next?'

'What do you think?' Stagg said softly.

Harry hoped he hadn't misjudged the situation. For all his recent disappointments, he had no immediate desire to stop breathing. 'If you kill me, you're going to have to kill Al too . . . and somehow I don't think your sister is going to be too happy about that.'

'She'll get over it.'

'I doubt it.' Harry glanced back towards the flat. 'Al's her husband. He's also the father of her kids. You're going to have to murder three people – and for what?'

'Silence?' Ray suggested coldly. 'Money?' For a second his expression was deadly serious but then his eyes suddenly brightened and his mouth widened into that familiar slimy grin. He laughed. 'No need to shit yourself, Harry. I'm not going to knock anyone off – unless I have to.'

'Meaning?'

'I'm sure we can come to a mutually agreeable arrangement.'

'And what kind of an arrangement would that be?'

'A simple one. I take the gear and you forget you ever saw it. You walk away and you keep your mouth shut.'

'And why should I do that?'

'To help out a friend of yours.'

Harry frowned, feigning ignorance. 'And who would that be?'

'Ah, come on, we both know who we're talking about. Mac's up to his neck in it. That poor guy just never learns, does he? Show him a pack of cards and his brains float out the window. He owes me over eighty grand and the profits from that two-bit agency of his are hardly going to pay it off. So this is the deal – you stay quiet, I'll wipe the debt, Mac keeps his business and you keep your lousy job.'

Harry pretended to think about it. 'And what about Agnes?'

'What about her? She's hardly going to go running to the cops. Have you ever seen her passport?'

'And Al?'

'It's like you mentioned earlier – he's family.'

'And what about me?'

Stagg stared at him for a good few seconds before he started to laugh again. 'Oh, I get it,' he said. 'You want a little extra for your troubles.'

'And if I do?'

'Nothing wrong with that,' Stagg said. 'We all need to make a living. How much are we talking about – ten grand, twenty? I hope you're not going to get *too* greedy.'

Harry gazed up towards the sky. The clouds were low and grey. A few flakes of snow were starting to fall again. 'Before we get into the finer detail, I think there's something you should see.'

'I've seen as much as I need to.'

'Humour me,' Harry said. He backed along the hedge to the entrance of the drive and gestured across the road. The silver Audi was parked directly opposite. And behind the car, Warren was standing with his elbows leaning on the roof. He had a phone against his ear. 'You think I didn't know you were tailing me? My partner only drove around the block a few times so you'd think I was alone. He's got the cops on fast dial and he's just waiting for the nod.'

Stagg's face grew tight. It didn't take him long to come back with the anticipated retort. 'And Rizzer's waiting too.'

'Which is why you should tell him to lay off unless you want to spend the next twenty years in the slammer.'

Ray Stagg glared at him. 'So how much do you want?'

'It's not about money.'

'I need the gear back,' Stagg insisted. His face had turned pale. 'It doesn't belong to me.'

'Tell it to the judge,' Harry said. 'Only I think you'll find there's a bag of charlie in that van with your prints all over it.'

Stagg stared down at his Gucci shoes for a moment. Then he raised his eyes and smiled. 'Okay, so what if I offer you something that money can't buy?'

'And what would that be, exactly?'

'No,' Ray Stagg said. 'You're right. You're not the kind of guy to make a deal – not even if it means nailing the bastard who killed two of your colleagues and crippled you forever.'

Harry flinched. 'What?'

'You heard.'

'You're lying,' Harry said.

'I've got proof. I'll show you – but we wipe those prints first.'

'Forget it.' Harry had been waiting years to get the goods on Ray Stagg. He wasn't going to let him wriggle off the hook that easily.

'Think about it,' Stagg said. 'They're never going to make the charges stick. I'm not the one in possession of the gear – Al is. It's his van not mine. So, yeah, I looked in one of the boxes to check that the vodka wasn't damaged. What's wrong with that? I found a curious bag inside, a bag that shouldn't have been there, and I opened it. Imagine my shock when I discovered something that looked suspiciously like cocaine.' He gave another of his sharp sarcastic laughs. 'Any decent brief will have this whole *misunderstanding* sorted out in a matter of hours.'

Harry shook his head. 'Good effort, Stagg, but if you're that confident, why even bother to try and make a deal?'

He raised his shoulders in a leisurely shrug. 'Because it would still be an inconvenience, a tedious waste of time. I have better things to do with my evenings than spend them down the local nick.' He paused. 'And then, of course, there's the other small matter – those poor dead comrades of yours.'

Harry bristled but remained silent.

'Admit it,' Stagg said. 'Tell me there isn't a little niggling doubt. Tell me that it hasn't crossed your mind, even for a second, that I could just be speaking the truth. Are you really going to let this opportunity slip through your fingers?'

'Give me one good reason why I should believe you.'

Stagg thought about it. 'Okay,' he said. 'Haven't you ever wondered why you never managed to turn up one damn thing on your somewhat over-frequent raids on Vista?'

'Because someone was whispering in your ear.'

'Spot on. I just hate bent coppers, don't you?' Stagg reached into his jacket pocket, slowly enough not to cause any unnecessary alarm, and took out a pack of Gitanes. He hit the pack lightly against the back of his left hand until a cigarette jumped free. He lifted the pack and pulled the cigarette out with his lips. Then he lit it, inhaled deeply, and exhaled a long slow stream of pungent smoke. 'And have you ever considered that the very same person might also have been whispering in Jimmy Keppell's ear?'

'Keppell?' Harry repeated.

'Well, it was his factory you walked into,' Stagg said smugly. 'Or didn't you realize that?'

Harry hadn't realized that.

'And quite a lucrative one too – there's a lot of money, allegedly, to be made from crack cocaine – until some low-life made an anonymous call. There's no sense of loyalty today, is there?' Stagg paused again, savouring the moment. He took another drag on his cigarette. 'Fortunately for Keppell, he had a friend, a very good friend, who tipped him off and gave him the time he needed to plan a thoroughly unpleasant surprise for you all.'

Harry studied him closely. His pulse was starting to race. Stagg couldn't be trusted but what if he was telling the truth? He had a flashback to that dreadful bloody room, that room filled with dust and death and despair. A stew of anger was bubbling in his guts. 'You've got a name?'

Ray Stagg looked across the street at Warren. 'Not before you tell your guy to put his phone down.'

'And what about your guy?'

The two of them locked eyes. It was an impasse that could not be resolved unless one of them gave way.

'Why should you want to put Keppell in the frame?' Harry said.

Stagg pulled on his cigarette again. His eyes turned dark. 'I grew up with Tommy Lake.'

Harry studied him closely. Stagg was a sly one but he had a look, an edge to his voice, that made him wonder. It was the first time he had seen anything even approaching humanity in his face. He took a chance on his instincts and looked over at Warren. 'Ten minutes,' he called out. Warren nodded.

Stagg nodded too.

'Shouldn't you call Rizzer?' Harry said. 'He might be getting worried.'

'He won't get worried until I tell him to.'

'So let's talk,' Harry said.

'In the van.'

Harry shook his head. 'I don't think so.' He had no intention of passing beyond Warren's field of vision. 'We talk here or not at all.'

'Okay,' Stagg said. He reached back into his pocket and took out a tiny Dictaphone. 'This is just a taster. I have the whole thing, with visuals, on a nice clear tape.' He glanced up and down the street, then over his shoulder, before pressing the play button.

A voice floated tinnily into the evening air. Harry recognized it as Stagg's: *Keppell's always been trouble.* And then another voice, a voice that was familiar but which he couldn't quite place. *I never trusted him. Not since that goddamn mess at the factory. He was only supposed to get out of there, that was the deal, not blow the whole bloody building to pieces.*

It came to Harry suddenly, turning his blood to ice. 'Holt,' he murmured. 'Jesus Christ.'

Stagg switched off the machine. 'There's more, a whole lot more, chapter and verse in fact. Your mate tends to chatter on when he's had a few bevvies.'

Harry felt his heart thumping, a sickening rage-filled beat that thrashed against his chest. Sweat prickled on his forehead. For a moment he could barely breathe and then, unable to contain the ferocity of his anger, his hands balled into two tight fists. If there had been a wall beside him he would have taken out his frustration on the brickwork.

Stagg took a step back. 'Yeah,' he said softly. 'The world's full of traitors.'

'Holt,' Harry muttered again.

'This is how I see it,' Stagg said, speaking low and fast. 'You let me take the gear now and I give it back to Keppell. That way I get him off my back. In a few days' time I'll give you the tape. I presume you know someone you can trust with it . . . or are they all on the take down that nick?'

Harry snarled at him. 'Don't push it!'

Stagg raised his hands. 'Okay, okay.'

Harry tried to concentrate, to figure out where to go next. His throat was dry and he had to force the words out. 'Keppell won't be happy when he finds out what you've done.'

'No reason why he should find out,' Stagg said, 'not if we play this properly. I doubt the tape will be admissible in court. It's just a lever, a way of getting Holt to spill his guts – and he will. He'll give them dates, times, everything, the minute he thinks his own neck's on the line. He'll be more than willing to give evidence against Keppell.'

'And what if he incriminates you too?'

'He can try,' Stagg said, 'but he'll be wasting his breath. There's no proof I ever gave him a penny. Sure, we were friendly for a while; he used to come to the club and even dropped by my house for drinks occasionally, but when I discovered what he was really like . . .' That smarmy grin appeared again. 'I'm sure if you have a quiet word, they'll be persuaded to see it from my point of view. Let's face it, all I'm doing here is my civic duty – helping them catch a bent piece of filth and nail a cop-killer at the same time.'

Harry took a series of long deep breaths. In his head, that name kept descending like a jackhammer: *Holt, Holt, Holt.*

Stagg threw the cigarette butt down and ground it to a pulp with his heel. 'So what do you say, Harry? If we work together, they could both be history by Christmas.'

Harry knew what he was going to do, what he *had* to do. There was no other choice. He despised Ray Stagg but he loathed Holt and Keppell even more.

'Whatever it takes,' Harry said.

'It's a deal then,' Stagg said. He put out his hand.

Harry didn't take it. He couldn't. It would have been like shaking hands with the Devil.

Chapter Fifty-Nine

It was the day before Christmas Eve. The last week had been a long one and Harry had spent too much of it in small stuffy rooms with a series of stern-faced policemen. That he had once been a copper himself seemed to hold no sway with them. The questions had come thick and fast, an intensive interrogation that hadn't stopped until they'd finally got Ray Stagg's video in their hands.

Still, there had been some consolations, the arrest of Jimmy Keppell being the most satisfying. The gangster hadn't submitted without a fight which had added an extra charge of assault to the crime sheet. Holt was in custody too, doing exactly what Stagg had predicted he would: singing like a canary seemed the most suitable cliché. Even the drugs had been recovered although not in quite the quantity that might have been expected. Harry suspected that Ray had taken a more than generous commission for his trouble.

He stared out through the windscreen. By now he should have been on his way to the coast, heading down to see his father, but instead he was with Jess hurtling along the motorway en route to Maidstone jail. He still wasn't quite sure why.

It was three days since Jess had called and asked if he'd be prepared to visit Paul Deacon. 'He wants to see you.'

'Why should he want to do that?'

'I've no idea,' she'd replied. 'And you won't have either unless you make the effort to find out.'

'Do you think it's about Ellen?'

Jess had delivered one of her full-on sighs. 'No, I imagine he wants to discuss the current deficiencies in Britain's foreign policy.'

'There's no need to be sarcastic.'

'And there's no need to be obtuse. Do you want to come along or not?'

'Well, I'm kind of busy but . . .'

So now he was driving through the Blackwall Tunnel, caught in that dim confined space part way between darkness and daylight. He was making an effort to concentrate, to keep well back from the car in front. Recent events kept running through his head. Valerie had been his first port of call after talking to Ray Stagg. He could still see her face turning as pale and grey as his own must have been. Although the news wasn't anything she'd wanted to hear, she hadn't been slow to respond. She had set the wheels in motion and those wheels were still turning.

'I appreciate you coming to me first,' she'd said.

Whether that appreciation might ultimately extend to having a conversation about their own future remained to be seen. As things stood, it was kind of doubtful. How did he feel about that? He still wasn't sure.

Jess glanced at him. 'You liked her, didn't you?'

'Who?'

'Grace,' she said. 'Ellen.'

Harry really didn't want to go there. She still occupied too many of his thoughts. 'I felt sorry for her.'

Jess gave him a look. 'You got too involved. Maybe I did too.'

'Maybe you had better reason.'

She shrugged and then tactfully changed the subject. 'So what's happening with Al?'

'He's out on bail. The guy he ran over was stinking drunk; it's likely Al would still have hit him even if he had been paying attention. He might serve some prison time, or if he gets a smart lawyer – and I'm sure Stagg will oblige – he may escape with a fine.'

'You don't sound too happy about it.'

'If he hadn't done a runner, Tommy Lake and Troy Jeffries would still be alive.'

Jess thought about it. 'They'd still be alive if they hadn't got involved in the first place. No one forced Tommo to stash the drugs and no one made Troy pick up the phone and call Jimmy Keppell.'

Perhaps she had a point. 'I guess,' Harry said.

'And Agnes?'

'She's back working at Vista.'

Jess's eyes widened in surprise. 'Tell me you're kidding.'

'Where else would she go?' Harry said. 'She's not got that many choices. At least Al had the decency to keep her name out of it. He told the police he'd been sleeping in the van since the accident. She'll be okay – well, as okay as any girl working in a place like that. Stagg won't touch her. He knows the score; he knows that I'll be keeping an eye on her.'

Jess grinned. 'I bet you will.'

'It's not like that.' Harry pulled a face. 'I only meant—'

'Oh, lighten up,' she said, slapping him lightly on the arm. 'You don't need to take everything so seriously.'

'You're right,' Harry said. 'I mean here we are, two relatively young carefree people heading for a fun afternoon out at Maidstone jail. What's to moan about?'

She laughed. 'It could be worse.'

'Easy for you to say with all those bright shiny prospects looming ahead. Just how many job offers have you had since that article came out?'

'A few,' she replied coyly. 'But you're hardly in the dole queue either. I'm presuming that Mac *will* be able to salvage the business now he's got Ray Stagg off his back.'

'Yeah, it looks that way.'

'No need to sound so enthusiastic.'

They came out the other side of the tunnel, emerging into a bright white landscape. A few flakes of snow were still falling. He turned the windscreen wipers on.

'I'm trying my best.'

'Try a bit harder. You're good at what you do, Harry. Just because things don't always turn out exactly as you'd like doesn't mean you should give up.'

'I'm not,' he said. 'I've just got a lot on my mind.'

Jess nodded. 'Are you worried about meeting Deacon?'

'I never said I was worried.'

'You don't say a lot of things. Fortunately my skills as a major investigative journalist enable me to read between the lines.' She paused. 'Well, either that or you're completely transparent.'

Harry raised his brows. A few easy retorts rose to his lips but he swallowed them again. This wasn't the time. The truth was, for all her flippancy, she was right: he *was* anxious. He felt thoroughly uneasy about the visit. 'I just don't understand why he wants to see us.'

'He doesn't want to see *us*,' Jess said. 'He only wants to see you.'

'But I thought—'

'He only rang me because he couldn't contact you. He kept getting your answering service.'

Harry tried not to think about how often he'd had his phone turned off recently. Or, more to the point, how often he'd been too drunk to answer it. 'So you've only come along for the ride?'

'What, to hold your hand?' Jess laughed again. 'It's a sweet thought but no. I've got a delightful visit of my own to look forward to – with Mr BJ Barrington. And if you're feeling a touch apprehensive, just imagine what I'm going through. I'm in the joyous position of having to inform a ten-foot giant of a man that his dreams of being the subject of a number one bestseller aren't exactly going to come true.'

'And how are you going to do that?'

'Tactfully?' she suggested.

Chapter Sixty

Having gone through all the necessary procedures, Harry was seated in the visiting area. It was a long room painted in the usual shade of utilitarian magnolia. The tables were laid out in straight rows a couple of feet apart and a raised platform, occupied by three prison officers, dominated the end closest to the entrance. A few sad strands of tinsel, a nod to the festive season, were slung across the windows.

Harry was one of a mere handful of male visitors; most of the tables were occupied by women. Jess, who had gone in before him, was sitting a few yards in front. She looked over her shoulder and smiled. He smiled back before switching his gaze to the rear of the room. For the next ten minutes a steady trickle of inmates continued to come through the door.

Although he wasn't sure if he'd recognize him, he was in no doubt when Paul Deacon finally walked in. A tall upright man, he didn't look too different from the press photos taken over twelve years ago. Only his hair had changed: the black had turned to grey and was receding from his forehead.

Harry stood up and Deacon strolled over.

'Mr Lind?'

'Harry,' he said.

'Thank you for coming.'

They shook hands. 'I'm still not quite sure why—'

'Grace asked me to talk to you.'

Harry felt his heart jump. 'You've heard from her then?'

Deacon pulled out the chair and sat down. There was something overly precise and controlled about his movements.

'She sent me a letter.' He leaned forward and placed his elbows carefully on the table. 'And if you're about to ask if I know where she is now then ... no, there was no return address.'

'Did I ask?' Harry said.

Deacon gave a thin smile. 'You'd have got around to it.'

Harry couldn't deny that. He couldn't help wondering too if the letter had been posted from abroad. And then another thought occurred to him. 'Does she know about her mother? Does she—'

Paul Deacon nodded. 'She's heard. She knows that Sharon's dead – and how she died. I don't think she'll be returning for the funeral.' He paused, his forehead creasing into a series of ridges. 'There are, however, certain facts that she believes you should be made aware of. Personally, I think she's wrong but this is her decision and I have to respect it. I haven't exactly been the perfect father but this is the one thing that I *can* do for her.'

It occurred to Harry that he wasn't going to like what he was about to hear. His level of anxiety shifted up a few notches. It was clear that Deacon wasn't happy but bearing in mind his history of sweeping anything even faintly inconvenient under the carpet – including the existence of a daughter – that was hardly surprising.

As if reading his mind or perhaps just his expression, Deacon said, 'I don't suppose you have a very high opinion of me.'

'Does it matter what my opinion is?'

'No, but it is important, for Grace's sake, that you trust me enough to accept that what I tell you today is the absolute truth.'

Paul Deacon had the kind of smooth cynical face that was more than capable of deceit but at this moment there was a shadow of desperation hanging over it. Perhaps for the first time in his life he was actually trying to do the right thing. Against his better instincts, Harry found himself feeling almost sympathetic. He was in the presence of a man who had paid, and was still paying, for all the dreadful mistakes he had made.

'Okay,' Harry said. 'I'll bear it in mind.'

Deacon lowered his head and then looked up again. 'I met Sharon at a party. It was a long time ago. I was married and I loved my wife but . . . It was just a fling but then Sharon told me she was pregnant and as soon as I was sure that the child was mine I agreed to support her.'

'You agreed to pay her off,' Harry said. 'There's a difference between cash and support.'

'Yes,' he said.

'And your wife didn't know anything about it?'

'Not then.'

'Was Michael Harper aware that Grace wasn't his?'

Deacon shrugged. 'It wouldn't have been that hard to figure out. But he was in love with Sharon; he wanted to be with her. From what I understand, he didn't ask too many questions.'

'But he must have resented Grace. After all, she was another man's child.'

'No, I don't think so. For all his faults, Michael did his best to be a decent father.'

Harry stared at him in disbelief. *Decent?* How could anyone describe what Michael Harper had done as decent? Anger grew inside him, a fountain of rage that threatened to overflow. Gritting his teeth, he leaned forward across the table. Deacon was either completely in the dark – and surely that wasn't possible – or he didn't view what had occurred as in any way abnormal. 'Are you trying to tell me that—'

Deacon quickly raised a hand. 'You haven't heard the whole story,' he said sternly. 'Don't start passing judgement until you have.'

Harry glared at him for a few seconds longer and then sat back, still scowling.

'So,' Deacon continued, 'I didn't hear anything more until eight years later when Grace went missing. By then Sharon had become more seriously involved with that gangster, Jimmy

404

Keppell. He was the one who got in touch demanding further payment. It was blackmail, pure and simple.'

'I know all this,' Harry said impatiently. 'And you coughed up, right? You paid because you didn't want your name splashed all over the papers. You didn't want the world to know that you had a child by another woman, a child you had no contact with and who had now gone missing, and you especially didn't want the police to come around asking awkward questions.'

Deacon didn't even try to deny it. He gave another of his thin smiles. 'Just bear with me, please.'

Harry deliberately looked at his watch. He was beginning to suspect that the purpose of this visit was more to do with Deacon justifying his shabby behaviour than anything Ellen had specifically asked of him.

'When Grace came back to London,' Deacon said, 'after the Corbys died, it didn't take her long to find out the truth. She linked up with Tony Keppell and he filled her in on all the details. It was a shock for her, discovering that Michael wasn't her real father.' He paused, clearing his throat. 'Instead her father was a man who had turned his back on her twice over, who had preferred to pay hard cash than to ever publicly acknowledge her existence. She felt betrayed and rightly so. She wanted . . . I was going to say revenge but perhaps that's too strong a word. Perhaps it was simply some kind of justice.'

'And who could blame her?'

'Quite so,' Deacon agreed. 'And it didn't help matters that her mother was less than pleased to see her. Sharon tried to keep her at a distance; she was terrified that her new life, a life that had been constructed on a lie, was about to come crashing down about her ears.'

'But what she'd done in the past, she'd done to protect Ell . . . protect Grace. It might not have been the right thing but it was done with the best of intentions. Grace understood that; others would have too.'

'It's more complicated than that,' Deacon said.

405

Harry wasn't sure that it was. 'At least she had Tony,' he said.

'Hardly. He was just a means to an end, a way to get at me.'

Recalling what Ellen had said, Harry narrowed his eyes. 'That's not true.'

'Oh, I know what she told you: that they were close, that they were in love, but that wasn't the case – at least not on her side. Tony was weak and stupid, a disappointment to his family. He was easy to manipulate. Grace had him twisted round her little finger.'

'What's the deal here?' Harry snapped. 'You think you can excuse what you did by bad-mouthing her? You think I don't know about what you and Tony—'

'I think it might be better if you wait until I've finished.'

'And is that likely to be any time soon?'

There was a short antagonistic silence. Harry wished he hadn't come. He considered standing up and walking out. He didn't need to listen to this garbage.

Deacon was the first to speak again. 'I apologize,' he said softly, 'if I've upset or offended you. I wasn't intending to be critical of Grace, merely attempting to relay what she asked me to. These are as much her words as mine.'

Harry gave a growl. 'Oh yeah?'

'It makes no difference to me whether you believe it or not. You have the good fortune of being able to leave right now if you wish to do so.' Deacon steepled his fingers and stared calmly across the table. 'To be honest, if you did make such a choice it would be a relief. I'd have fulfilled my promise to Grace without having to tell you anything more than you already know.'

Harry could see why he'd become a politician. He'd probably been a damn good one too if good meant playing the kind of game that always got you exactly what you wanted. Much as he wanted to, he couldn't just walk away; he was going to have to see this through to the bitter end. 'Go on,' he said roughly. 'I'm still listening.'

Deacon gave a slight bow of his head. 'Tony approached me at a charity do. He was there with his father – Jimmy always gave very generously at charitable events, particularly the high-profile ones where the press were likely to be present – and he asked if he could have a quiet word. It didn't take him long to get to the point. I presumed he was working on behalf of Jimmy and Sharon – coming back for seconds, so to speak.'

'And you had no idea that Grace was still alive?'

Deacon shook his head. 'Of course not. That was the one thing he was never going to divulge. I'd already come to terms with the fact that she must be dead and my being the secret father of a "murdered" child gave Tony the kind of leverage he needed to screw me for every penny he could.'

'But it wasn't just to do with money,' Harry said. 'You developed a relationship with him.'

Deacon barked out a laugh. 'No! At least not in the sense you're referring to. I have my weaknesses – I'll willingly admit it – but boys, men, males of any age aren't one of them. The only relationship I ever had with Tony was a purely financial one.'

Harry stared at him. This was all a bit different from Ellen's account. 'But you still paid up?'

'Plenty of times.' Deacon ran a hand across his face. 'He asked for a thousand at first and then a few thousand more but then it soon became clear that it wasn't just money he was after – he demanded to be taken out to fancy restaurants, to clubs, to bars.'

'And you obliged?'

'I didn't have much choice.'

'And then he upped the stakes.'

'If you call putting a gun to my head upping the stakes then yes, he certainly did that. He came to the flat one night and demanded twenty grand. He also produced a set of photographs. They showed us together at various times and in various places. There was nothing especially compromising about them but in the wrong hands they could have been

407

misinterpreted.' Deacon paused. 'They'd decided to add an extra dimension to the blackmail.'

Harry noted the use of the word 'they'. His mouth curled down in disgust. He knew that Ellen had been involved but not in the way that Deacon seemed to be suggesting. 'Which was when you decided that enough was enough?'

'I thought he was just playing the big man. I didn't think the gun was loaded. God, I didn't even think that it was real.'

Harry shrugged. 'We all know what happened next. If you've brought me here to explain that you acted in self-defence then fine, I'm sure you weren't entirely to blame.'

'This is nothing to do with that,' Deacon said sharply. 'It's to do with Grace. It's to do with why she came to see me ten months ago.'

'It must been a shock – finding out that she was still alive after all these years.'

A shadow passed across Deacon's face again. 'That's between her and me. We talked it through. We came to terms. I never asked her to forgive me. How could she?'

'How indeed,' Harry said.

'And she didn't come to play Happy Families. There was something else on her mind. She couldn't deal with what had happened to Tony. She couldn't bear to feel responsible for another death.'

Harry started. A cold chill slipped down his spine. 'What do you mean – *another* death?'

Deacon lowered his eyes and slowly raised them again. 'Are you sure you want to hear this?'

Harry wasn't sure at all. His palms were starting to sweat. What he really needed was a double shot of whisky but a strong hit of caffeine would have to do. 'I should have asked before. Would you like a drink?'

'Tea would be fine,' Deacon said. 'Milk, no sugar.'

Harry stood up, slid between the two tables to his left and joined the short queue at the refreshment counter. He was glad of the escape, even if it was only temporary. There was a part of him that wanted to walk, to get out of that room as fast as his legs could carry him, but he knew that he couldn't. Whatever was coming could not be avoided. Deacon's words kept revolving in his head – *another* death, *another* death. What did he mean? He glanced across at Jess who was deep in conversation with BJ. She was waving her hands around and BJ was grinning back. The old Vaughan charm seemed to be doing the trick. The queue shifted forward too quickly. Harry bought the drinks and took them back to the table.

Chapter Sixty-One

Deacon picked up his cup. He stared at it, frowned and put it down again. Like a doctor preparing to break bad news, he carefully adjusted his expression. 'Grace didn't mean to hurt her.'

'Hurt her?' Harry repeated. 'I don't understand.'

'As you may recall,' Deacon said, 'she wasn't the only child who went missing that August.'

'Theresa Neal,' Harry muttered. 'But her disappearance had nothing to do with . . .' As he realized what Deacon was implying, he vehemently shook his head. 'You've got this all wrong.'

'No,' Deacon said firmly. 'I haven't. You're going to tell me that the two girls didn't know each other but they did. They went to different schools but didn't live that far apart. Occasionally their paths crossed. It was just a casual friendship but on the day in question Theresa was on her way back from the park. She took a shortcut through the alley, saw Grace in the yard and stopped. Sharon had company, Jimmy Keppell, and was – how shall I put it? – *entertaining* him. Grace had been told to stay outside.' He paused, perhaps to gather his thoughts or simply to wait for Harry's permission to continue.

'Go on,' Harry urged.

'After a while the girls got bored and went into the house. They were just doing what kids do, larking about. Keppell had left his jacket over the back of a chair. The chair got knocked over and a gun fell out of his pocket. Grace picked it up. She didn't know it was real. How could she? They ran around for

410

a while; it was just a toy, a game, cops and robbers. Then she pulled the trigger and . . .'

Harry stared at him. He could feel the blood draining from his face.

Deacon's eyes avoided his. His gaze dropped down to the table. 'She can't remember much after that – it was the shock, I suppose.'

The words choked out from the depths of Harry's throat. 'My God.'

'By the time Sharon got downstairs it was too late. She should have rung for an ambulance but Christ knows what went through that crazy head of hers. She couldn't have saved Theresa but she should still have made the call. No one could have blamed Grace. It was just an accident, a terrible accident. But instead Sharon decided to try and cover it up.'

'Her or Jimmy Keppell?' Harry hissed angrily. 'It was *his* bloody gun.'

'I don't suppose either of them were thinking straight – or overjoyed at the prospect of having to explain why a ten-year-old girl was lying dead on the kitchen floor.'

'So they decided to take matters into their own hands?'

Deacon nodded. 'They panicked. Keppell was in possession of an illegal firearm, a gun that had been used to kill a child. He was looking at jail time. Sharon may have been trying to protect Grace, or even Jimmy, but it was probably herself she was really taking care of. She was never the most altruistic of women. She must have seen the future flashing before her: what Michael would do, how the police would respond, how she'd be judged. And let's face it, she *would* have been judged. She'd have been well and truly crucified. Having sex with her gangster lover while her daughter played with his gun downstairs? It wouldn't have gone down too well in a courtroom. And the tabloids would have had a field day. You can imagine the headlines.'

'And so Keppell . . .'

'Yes, he took Theresa away. He buried her on Hampstead Heath.'

411

Harry thumped his fist down on the table. 'For fuck's sake!' One of the patrolling screws looked over his shoulder and stared at him. Harry glared back. Being on the wrong side of authority was becoming uncomfortably familiar these days. He leaned closer to Deacon, his voice tight and low. 'But why would he do that? Putting conscience aside – I'm sure the bastard doesn't have one – why would he take the risk? What if someone had seen Theresa? How the hell were they going to explain that?'

'They must have decided that the gamble was worth taking. She'd never been there before; there was nothing to really connect the two girls. And she'd used the alley, so unless one of the neighbours had been in their own back yard—'

'No one would have noticed her.'

'Quite.'

Harry was silent for a while, struggling with the immensity of what he'd just heard. It was too much to take in. He thought of all the lies Ellen had told him, of the lie she had lived for the past twenty years. Still, she had been honest about one thing at least – Keppell *had* been determined to keep her quiet. He remembered the black car mounting the pavement in Berry Square and shuddered. Harry understood now why he'd been so determined to prevent the truth from coming out.

'So Michael didn't . . . didn't abuse her?'

'No,' Deacon said. 'That was just a story. Michael had his faults but he tried his best to be a good father. And that was another major problem for Sharon and her boyfriend. They couldn't rely on Grace to keep quiet. What if she told him what had happened? They decided there was no choice but to make Grace disappear as well.'

Harry nodded. It was all making sense in a twisted, deranged, disgusting kind of way. Then he suddenly recalled what Joan had said to the police, about how it was Sharon who'd produced a gun. A terrible thought occurred to him. 'Was it a Glock?'

Deacon looked bemused. 'I'm sorry?'

'Keppell's gun,' Harry said quickly. 'Was it a small Glock pistol?'

'I've no idea. Does it matter?'

Harry knew it did. Maybe Sharon had kept the gun for all these years. It was possible. She might not have trusted Keppell to get rid of it. Or, more likely, she hadn't trusted Keppell full stop. She could have kept it for her own protection and if that was the case then she'd been shot by the same gun that killed Theresa Neal . . .

Harry felt sick to his stomach. He thought of all the suffering, all the pain and misery, that had ensued from one dreadful decision made over twenty years ago: Theresa Neal's parents had never known the circumstances of their daughter's death, Curzon had been silenced, Ellen had been forced to live a lie, Joan Sewell's grief had soured into bitterness and Michael Harper – innocent of the abuse he'd been accused of – had been hounded into an early grave. And the legacy didn't stop there; now Sharon's two sons had been left without a mother too.

Still dazed by what he had heard Harry hunched forward, his face twisted with shock and bewilderment. 'So what happens next? What am I supposed to do?'

Deacon shrugged. 'She asked me to tell you the truth.'

'And does she expect me to take that truth to the police?'

'That's up to you.'

Harry shook his head. He was not sure what good, if any, would come from revealing this particular horror.

'Take your time,' Deacon said. 'Think it over.' He got to his feet and nodded at one of the screws. Then he looked again at Harry. 'Thank you for coming.'

Harry, taken aback by this abrupt withdrawal, stood up too. 'Is that it?' His surprise was promptly superseded by a feeling of resentment. A huge responsibility had just been passed to him and the burden felt too great, too overwhelming.

Deacon gave a soft smile. 'She trusts you. She knows you'll do whatever's right.'

Outside the gate, Harry shoved his hands deep into his pockets and gazed along the grey stone wall encircling the jail. He thought of all the prisons that people built for themselves and for others. He thought of Ellen and an ache rolled through his chest.

Perhaps silence was the best way forward. Without her corroboration the truth could only ever be hearsay. Nothing could be proved. And Jimmy Keppell, the only other surviving witness, was already facing a life sentence – one way or another he would get his just reward. Yes, he should keep quiet. Or should he? There were the Neals to consider – surely they deserved to know exactly how and why their daughter had died. And then there was Michael Harper too. His reputation had been ruined. Perhaps, even in death, a man deserved some justice.

She knows you'll do whatever's right.

The snow drifted down and settled on his shoulders. Out of the corner of his eye, Harry thought he saw a flash of red. He quickly turned his head but there was no one there.

M
Kray   8/08